Secret

is revealed?

Acclaim for Lynne Graham, Jacqueline Baird and Day Leclaire

About Lynne Graham

"Lynne Graham's strong-willed,
hard-loving characters are the sensual stuff
dreams are made of."
—*Romantic Times*

About Jacqueline Baird

"Readers will enjoy Ms. Baird's engaging style."
—*Romantic Times*

About Day Leclaire

"Day Leclaire makes a potent magic…with
dynamic characters (and) riveting scenes."
—*Romantic Times*

Her Baby Secret

TEMPESTUOUS REUNION
by
Lynne Graham

THE VALENTINE CHILD
by
Jacqueline Baird

THE SECRET BABY
by
Day Leclaire

MILLS & BOON®

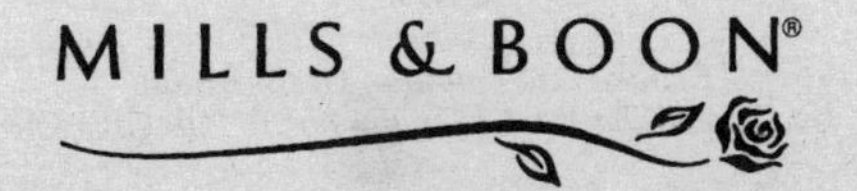

All the characters in this book have no existence outside the imagination of the author, and have no relation whatsoever to anyone bearing the same name or names. They are not even distantly inspired by any individual known or unknown to the author, and all the incidents are pure invention.

*Harlequin Mills & Boon Limited,
Eton House, 18-24 Paradise Road, Richmond, Surrey, TW9 1SR*

Tempestuous Reunion, The Valentine Child and *The Secret Baby* were first published in Great Britain by Mills & Boon Limited in separate, single volumes.

ISBN 0 263 81538 2

05-9906

*Printed and bound in Great Britain
by Caledonian Book Manufacturing Ltd, Glasgow*

Lynne Graham was born in Northern Ireland and has been a keen Mills & Boon® reader since her teens. She is very happily married with an understanding husband, who has learned to cook since she started to write! Her five children keep her on her toes. She has a very large old English sheepdog, which knocks everything over, and two cats. When time allows, she is a keen gardener. Lynne has been writing for Mills & Boon since 1987 and has now written over 25 books, which are loved by readers worldwide—she has had more than 10 million copies of her books in print.

TEMPESTUOUS REUNION

by

Lynne Graham

CHAPTER ONE

'MARRY you?' Luc echoed, his brilliant dark gaze rampant with incredulity as he abruptly cast aside the financial report he had been studying. 'Why would I want to marry you?'

Catherine's slender hand was shaking. Hurriedly she set down her coffee-cup, her courage sinking fast. 'I just wondered if you had ever thought of it.' Her restless fingers made a minute adjustment to the siting of the sugar bowl. She was afraid to meet his eyes. 'It was just an idea.'

'Whose idea?' he prompted softly. 'You are perfectly content as you are.'

She didn't want to think about what Luc had made of her. But certainly contentment had rarely featured in her responses. From the beginning she had loved him wildly, recklessly, and with that edge of desperation which prevented her from ever standing as his equal.

Over the past two years, she had swung between ecstasy and despair more times than he would ever have believed. Or cared to believe. This beautiful, luxurious apartment was her prison. Not his. She was a pretty songbird in a gilded cage for Luc's exclusive enjoyment. But it wasn't bars that kept her imprisoned, it was love.

She stole a nervous glance at him. His light intonation had been deceptive. Luc was silently seething. But not at her. His ire was directed at some imaginary scapegoat, who had dared to contaminate her with ideas, quite embarrassing ideas above her station.

'Catherine,' he pressed impatiently.

Under the table the fingernails of her other hand grooved sharp crescents into her damp palm. Skating on thin ice wasn't a habit of hers with Luc. 'It was my own idea and... I'd appreciate an answer,' she dared in an ironic lie, for she didn't really want that answer; she didn't want to hear it.

Had the Santini electronics empire crashed overnight, Luc could not have looked more grim than he did now, pierced by a thorn from a normally very well-trained source. 'You have neither the background nor the education that I would require in my wife. There, it is said,' he delivered with the decisive speed and the ruthlessness which had made his name as much feared as respected in the business world. 'Now you need wonder no longer.'

Every scrap of colour slowly drained from her cheeks. She recoiled from the brutal candour she had invited, ashamed to discover that she had, after all, nurtured a tiny, fragile hope that deep down inside he might feel differently. Her soft blue eyes flinched from his, her head bowing. 'No, I won't need to wonder,' she managed half under her breath.

Having devastated her, he relented infinitesimally. 'This isn't what I would term breakfast conversation,' he murmured with a teasing harshness that she easily translated into a rebuke for her presumption in daring to raise the subject. 'Why should you aspire to a relationship within which you would not be at ease... hmm? As a lover, I imagine, I am far less demanding than I would be as a husband.'

In the midst of what she deemed to be the most agonising dénouement of her life, an hysterical giggle feathered dangerously in her convulsed throat. A blunt, sun-browned finger languorously played over the knuckles showing white beneath the skin of her clenched hand. Even though she was conscious that Luc was using his customary methods of distraction, the electricity of a powerful sexual chemistry tautened her every sinew and the fleeting desire to laugh away the ashes of painful disillusionment vanished.

With a faint sigh, he shrugged back a pristine silk shirt cuff to consult the rapier-thin Cartier watch on his wrist and frowned.

'You'll be late for your meeting.' She said it for him as she stood up, for the very first time fiercely glad to see the approach of the departure which usually tore her apart.

Luc rose fluidly upright to regard her narrowly. 'You're jumpy this morning. Is there something wrong?'

The other matter, she registered in disbelief, was already forgotten, written off as some impulsive and foolishly feminine piece of nonsense. It wouldn't occur to Luc that she had deliberately saved that question until he was about to leave. She hadn't wanted to spoil the last few hours they would ever spend together.

'No... what could be wrong?' Turning aside, she reddened. But he had taught her the art of lies and evasions, could only blame himself when he realised what a monster he had created.

'I don't believe that. You didn't sleep last night.'

She froze into shocked stillness. He strolled back across the room to link confident arms round her small, slim figure, easing her round to face him. 'Perhaps it is your security that you are concerned about.'

The hard bones and musculature of the lean, superbly fit body against hers melted her with a languor she couldn't fight. And, arrogantly acquainted with that shivery weakness, Luc was satisfied and soothed. A long finger traced the tremulous fullness of her lower lip. 'Some day our paths will separate,' he forecast in a roughened undertone. 'But that day is still far from my mind.'

Dear God, did he know what he did to her when he said things like that? If he did, why should he care? In probably much the same fashion he cracked the whip over key executives to keep them on their toes. He was murmuring something smooth about stocks and shares that she refused to listen to. You can't buy love, Luc. You can't pay for it either. When are you going to find that out?

While his hunger for her remained undiminished, she understood that she was safe. She took no compliment from the desire she had once naïvely believed was based on emotion. For the several days a month which Luc allotted cool-headedly to the pursuit of light entertainment, she had every attention. But that Luc had not even guessed that the past weeks had been unadulterated hell for her proved the shallowness of the bond on his side. She had emerged from the soap-bubble fantasy she had started building against reality two years ago. He didn't love her. He hadn't suddenly woken up one day to realise that he couldn't live without her...and he never would.

'You'll be late,' she whispered tautly, disconcerted by the glitter of gold now burnishing the night-dark scrutiny skimming her upturned face. When Luc decided to leave, he didn't usually linger.

The supple fingers resting against her spine pressed her closer, his other hand lifting to wind with cool possessiveness into the curling golden hair tumbling down her back. *'Bella mia,'* he rhymed in husky Italian, bending his dark head to taste her moistly parted lips with the inherent sensuality and the tormenting expertise which all along had proved her downfall.

Stabbed by her guilty conscience, she dragged herself fearfully free before he could taste the strange, unresponsive chill that was spreading through her. 'I'm not feeling well,' she muttered in jerky excuse, terrified that she was giving herself away.

'Why didn't you tell me that sooner? You ought to lie down.' He swept her up easily in his arms, started to kiss her again, and then, with an almost imperceptible darkening of colour, abstained long enough to carry her into the bedroom and settle her down on the tossed bed.

He hovered, betraying a rare discomfiture. Scrutinising her wan cheeks and the pared-down fragility of her bone-structure, he expelled his breath in a sudden sound of derision. 'If this is another result of one of those asinine diets of yours, I'm likely to lose my temper. When are you going to get it through your head that I like you as you are? Do you want to make yourself ill? I don't have any patience with this foolishness, Catherine.'

'No,' she agreed, beyond seeing any humour in his misapprehension.

'See your doctor today,' he instructed. 'And if you don't, I'll know about it. I'll mention it to Stevens on my way out.'

At the reference to the security guard, supposedly there for her protection but more often than not, she suspected, there to police her every move, she curved her cheek into the pillow. She didn't like Stevens. His deadpan detachment and extreme formality intimidated her.

'How are you getting on with him, by the way?'

'I understood that I wasn't supposed to get on with your security men. Isn't that why you transferred Sam Halston?' she muttered, grateful for the change of subject, no matter how incendiary it might be.

'He was too busy flirting with you to be effective,' Luc parried with icy emphasis.

'That's not true. He was only being friendly,' she protested.

'He wasn't hired to be friendly. If you'd treated him like an employee he'd still be here,' Luc underlined with honeyed dismissal. 'And now I really have to leave. I'll call you from Milan.'

He made it sound as if he were dispensing a very special favour. In fact, he called her every day no matter where he was in the world. And now he was gone.

When that phone did ring tomorrow, it would ring and ring through empty rooms. For tortured minutes she just lay and stared at the space where he had been. Dark and dynamic, he was hell on wheels for a vulnerable woman. In their entire association she had never had an argument with Luc. By fair means or foul, Luc always got his own way. Her feeble attempts to assert herself had long since sunk without trace against the tide of an infinitely more forceful personality.

He was now reputedly one of the top ten richest men in the world. At twenty-nine that was a wildly impressive achievement. He had started out with nothing but formidable intelligence in the streets of New York's Little Italy. And he would keep on climbing. Luc was always number one and never more so than in his own self-image. Power was the greatest aphrodisiac known to humanity. What Luc wanted he reached out and took, and to hell with the damage he caused as long as the backlash did not affect his comfort. And, having fought for everything he had ever got, what came easy had no intrinsic value for him.

'The lone wolf,' *Time* magazine had dubbed him in a recent article, endeavouring to penetrate the mystique of a rogue among the more conventional herd of the hugely successful.

A shark was a killing machine, superbly efficient within its own restricted field. And wolves mated for life, not for leisure-time amusement. But Luc was indeed a land-based animal and far from cold-blooded. As such he was all the more dangerous to the unwary, the innocent and the over-confident.

Technical brilliance alone hadn't built his empire. It was the energy source of one man's drive combined with a volatile degree of unpredictability which kept competitors at bay in a cut-throat market. She could have told that journalist exactly what Luc Santini was like. And that was hard, cruelly hard with the cynicism, the self-interest and the ruthless ambition that was bred into his very bones. Only a fool got in Luc's path... only a very foolish woman could have given her heart into his keeping.

Her eyes squeezed shut on a shuddering spasm of anguish. It was over now. She would never see Luc again. No miracle had astounded her at the eleventh hour. Marriage was not, nor would it ever be, a possibility. Her small hand spread protectively over her no longer concave stomach. Luc had begun to lose her one hundred per cent loyalty and devotion from the very hour she suspected that she was carrying his child.

Instinct had warned her that the news would be greeted as a calculated betrayal and, no doubt, the conviction that she had somehow achieved the condition all on her own. Again and again she had put off telling him. In fear of discovery, she had learnt to be afraid of Luc. When he married a bride with a social pedigree, a bride bred to the lofty heights that were already his, he wouldn't want any skeletons in the cupboard. Ice-cold and sick with apprehensions that she had refused to face head on, she wiped clumsily at her swollen eyes and got up.

He would never know now and that was how it had to be. Thank God, she had persuaded Sam to show her how to work the alarm system. She would leave by the rear entrance. That would take care of Stevens. Would Luc miss her? A choked sob of pain escaped her. He would be outraged that she could leave him and he had not foreseen the event. But he wouldn't have any trouble replacing her. She was not so special and she wasn't beautiful. She never had grasped what it was about her which had drawn Luc. Unless it was the cold intuition of a predator scenting good doormat material downwind, she conceded shamefacedly.

How could she be sorry to leave this half-life behind? She had no friends. When discretion was demanded, friends were impossible. Luc had slowly but surely isolated her so that her entire existence revolved round him. Sometimes she was so lonely that she talked out loud to herself. Love was a fearsome emotion, she thought with a convulsive shudder. At eighteen she had been green as grass. Two years on, she didn't feel she was much brighter but she didn't build castles in the air any more.

'*Arrivederci*, Luc, *grazie tanto*,' she scrawled in lipstick across the mirror. A theatrical gesture, the ubiquitous note. He could do without the ego boost of five tear-stained pages telling him pointlessly that nobody was ever likely to love him as much as she did.

Luc, she had learnt by destructive degrees, didn't rate love any too highly. But he had not been above using her love as a weapon against her, twisting her emotions with cruel expertise until they had become the bars of her prison cell.

'What are you doing with my books?'

Catherine straightened from the cardboard box and clashed with stormy dark eyes. 'I'm packing them. Do you want to help?' she prompted hopefully. 'We could talk.'

Daniel kicked at a chair leg, his small body stiff and defensive. 'I don't want to talk about moving.'

'Ignoring it isn't going to stop it happening,' Catherine warned.

Daniel kicked moodily at the chair leg again, hands stuck in his pockets, miniature-tough style. Slowly Catherine counted to ten. Much more of this and she would scream until the little men in the white coats came to take her away. How much longer was her son going to treat her as the wickedest and worst mother in the world? With a determined smile, she said, 'Things aren't half as bad as you seem to think they are.'

Daniel looked at her dubiously. 'Have we got any money?'

Taken aback by the demand, Catherine coloured and shifted uncomfortably. 'What's that got to do with anything?'

'I heard John's mum telling Mrs Withers that we had no money 'cos if we had we would've bought this house and stayed here.'

Catherine could happily have strangled the woman for speaking so freely in Daniel's presence. He might be only four but he was precociously bright for his age. Daniel already understood far too much of what went on around him.

'It's not fair that someone can take our house off us and sell it to someone else when we want to live here forever!' he burst out without warning.

The pain she glimpsed in his over-bright eyes tore cruelly at her. Unfortunately there was little that she could do to assuage that pain. 'Greyfriars has never been ours,' she reminded him tautly. 'You know that, Daniel. It belonged to Harriet, and on her death she gave it to charity. Now the people who run that charity want to sell and use the money to——'

Daniel threw her a sudden seething glance. 'I don't care about those people starving in Africa! This is our house! Where are we going to live?'

'Drew has found us a flat in London,' she told him yet again.

'You can't keep a donkey in London!' Daniel launched at her fierily. 'Why can't we live with Peggy? She said we could.'

Catherine sighed. 'Peggy really doesn't have enough room for us.'

'I'll run away and you can live in London all on your own because I'm not going without Clover!' Daniel shouted at her in a tempestuous surge of fury and distress. 'It's all your fault. If I'd had a daddy, he could've bought us this house like everybody else's daddy does! I bet he could even have made Harriet well again... I hate you 'cos you can't do anything!'

With that bitter condemnation, Daniel hurtled out of the back door. He would take refuge in one of his hiding places in the garden. There he would sit, brooding and struggling to cope with harsh adult realities that entailed the loss of all he held dear. She touched the solicitor's letter on the table. She would be even more popular when he realised that their holiday on Peggy's family farm was no longer possible either.

Sometimes—such as now—Catherine had this engulfing sense of total inadequacy in Daniel's radius. Daniel was not quite like other children. At two he had taken apart a radio and put it back together again, repairing it in the process. At three he had taught himself German by listening to a language programme on television. But he was still too young to accept necessary sacrifices. Harriet's death had hit him hard, and now he was losing his home, a much-loved pet donkey, the friends he played with... in short, all the remaining security that had bounded his life to date. Was it any wonder that he was frightened? How could she reassure him when she too was afraid of the future?

The conviction that catastrophe was only waiting to pounce round the next blind corner had never really left Catherine. Harriet's sudden death had fulfilled her worst imaginings. With one savage blow, the tranquil and happy security of their lives had been shattered. And right now it felt as though she'd been cruelly catapulted back to where she had started out over four years ago...

Her life had been in a mess, heading downhill at a seemingly breakneck pace. She had had the promising future of a kamikaze pilot. And then Harriet had come along. Harriet, so undervalued by those who knew her best. Harriet...in his exasperation, Drew had once called her a 'charming mental deficient'. Yet Harriet had picked Catherine up, dusted her down and set her back on the rails again. In the process, Harriet had also become the closest thing to a mother that Catherine had ever known.

They had met on a train. That journey and that meeting had forever altered Catherine's future. While they had shared the same compartment, Harriet had tried repeatedly to strike up a conversation. When you were locked up tight and terrified of breaking down in public, you didn't want to talk. But Harriet's persistence had forced her out of her self-absorption, and before very long her over-taxed emotions had betrayed her and somehow she had ended up telling Harriet her life-story.

Afterwards she had been embarrassed, frankly eager to escape the older woman's company. They had left the train at the same station. Nothing poor Harriet had said about her 'having made the right decision' had penetrated. Like an addict, sick for a long-overdue fix, Catherine had been unbelievably desperate just to hear the sound of a man's voice on the phone. Throwing Harriet a guilty goodbye, she had raced off towards the phone-box she could see across the busy car park.

What would have happened had she made that call? That call that would have been a crowning and unforgivable mistake in a relationship which had been a disaster from start to finish?

She would never know now. In her mad haste to reach that phone, she had run in front of a car. It had taken total physical incapacitation to finally bring her to her senses. She had spent the following three months recovering from her injuries in hospital. Days had passed before she had been strong enough to recognise the soothing voice that drifted in and out of her haze of pain and disorientation. It had belonged to Harriet. Knowing that she had no family, Harriet had sat by her in Intensive Care, talking back the dark for her. If Harriet hadn't been there, Catherine didn't believe she would ever have emerged from the dark again.

Even before his premature birth, Daniel had had to fight for survival. Coming into the world, he had screeched for attention, tiny and weak but indomitably strong-willed. From his incubator he had charmed the entire medical staff by surmounting every set-back within record time. Catherine had begun to appreciate then that, with the genes her son carried to such an unmistakably marked degree, a ten-ton truck couldn't have deprived him of existence, never mind his careless mother's collision with a mere car.

'He's a splendid little fighter,' Harriet had proclaimed proudly, relishing the role of surrogate granny as only an intensely lonely woman could. Drew had been sincerely fond of his older sister but her eccentricities had infuriated him, and his sophisticated French wife, Annette, and their teenage children had had no time for Harriet at all. Greyfriars was situated on the outskirts of an Oxfordshire village, a dilapidated old house, surrounded by untamed acres of wilderness garden. Harriet and Drew had been born here and Harriet had vociferously withstood her brother's every attempt to refurbish the house for her. Surroundings had been supremely unimportant to Harriet. Lame ducks had been Harriet's speciality.

Catherine's shadowed gaze roamed over the homely kitchen. She had made the gingham curtains fluttering at the window, painted the battered cupboards a cheerful fire-engine red sold off cheap at the church fête. This was their home. In every sense of the word. How could she persuade Daniel that he would be as happy in a tiny city flat when she didn't believe it herself? But, dear God, that flat was their one and only option.

A light knock sounded on the back door. Without awaiting an answer, her friend Peggy Downes breezed in. A tall woman in her thirties with geometrically cut red hair, she dropped down on to the sagging settee by the range with the ease of a regular visitor. She stared in surprise at the cardboard box. 'Aren't you being a little premature with your packing? You've still got a fortnight to go.'

'We haven't.' Catherine passed over the solicitor's letter. 'It's just as well that Drew said we could use his apartment if we were stuck. We can't stay here until the end of the month and the flat won't be vacant before then.'

'Hell's teeth! They wouldn't give you that extra week?' Peggy exclaimed incredulously.

As Peggy's mobile features set into depressingly familiar lines of annoyance, Catherine turned back to the breakfast dishes, hoping that her friend wasn't about to climb back on her soap-box to decry the terms of Harriet's will and their imminent move to city life. In recent days, while exuding the best of good intentions, Peggy had been very trying and very impractical.

'We have no legal right to be here at all,' Catherine pointed out.

'But morally you have every right and I would've expected a charitable organisation to be more generous towards a single parent.' Peggy's ready temper was rising on Catherine's behalf. 'Mind you, I don't know why I'm blaming them. This whole mess is your precious Harriet's fault!'

'Peggy——'

'Sorry, but I believe in calling a spade a spade.' That was an unnecessary reminder to anyone acquainted with Peggy's caustic tongue. 'Honestly, Catherine... sometimes I think you must have been put on this earth purely to be exploited! You don't even seem to realise when people are using you! What thanks did you get for wasting four years of your life running after Harriet?'

'Harriet gave us a home when we had nowhere else to go. She had nothing to thank me for.'

'You kept this house, waited on her hand and foot and slaved over all her pet charity schemes,' Peggy condemned heatedly. 'And for all that you received board and lodging and first pick of the jumble-sale clothes! So much for charity's beginning at home!'

'Harriet was the kindest and most sincere person I've ever known,' Catherine parried tightly.

And crazy as a coot, Peggy wanted to shriek in frustration. Admittedly Harriet's many eccentricities had not appeared to grate on Catherine as they had on other, less tolerant souls. Catherine hadn't seemed to notice when Harriet talked out loud to herself and her conscience, or noisily emptied the entire contents of her purse into the church collection plate. Catherine hadn't batted an eyelash when Harriet brought dirty, smelly tramps home to tea and offered them the freedom of her home.

The trouble with Catherine was... It was a sentence Peggy often began and never managed to finish to her satisfaction. Catherine was the best friend she had ever had. She was also unfailingly kind, generous and unselfish, and that was quite an accolade from a female who thought of herself as a hardened cynic. How did you criticise someone for such sterling qualities? Unfortunately it was exactly those qualities which had put Catherine in her present predicament.

Catherine drifted along on another mental plane. Meeting those misty blue eyes in that arrestingly lovely face, Peggy was helplessly put in mind of a child cast adrift in a bewildering adult world. There was something so terrifyingly innocent about Catherine's penchant for seeing only the best in people and taking them on trust. There was something so horribly defenceless about her invariably optimistic view of the world.

She was a sucker for every sob-story that came her way and a wonderful listener. She didn't know how to say no when people asked for favours. This kitchen was rarely empty of callers, mothers in need of temporary childminders or someone to look after the cat or the dog or the dormouse while they were away. Catherine was very popular locally. If you were in a fix, she would always lend a hand. But how many returned those favours? Precious few, in Peggy's experience.

'At the very least, Harriet ought to have left you a share of her estate,' Peggy censured.

Catherine put the kettle on to boil. 'And how do you think Drew and his family would have felt about that?'

'Drew isn't short of money.'

'Huntingdon's is a small firm. He isn't a wealthy man.'

'He has a big house in Kent and an apartment in central London. If that isn't wealthy, what is?' Peggy demanded drily.

Catherine suppressed a groan. 'Business hasn't been too brisk for the firm recently. Drew has already had to sell some property he owned, and though he wouldn't admit it, he must have been disappointed by Harriet's will. As building land this place will fetch a small fortune. He could have done with a windfall.'

'And by the time the divorce comes through Annette will probably have stripped him of every remaining movable asset,' Peggy mused.

'She didn't want the divorce,' Catherine murmured.

Peggy pulled a face. 'What difference does that make? She had the affair. She was the guilty partner.'

Catherine made the tea, reflecting that it was no use looking to Peggy for tolerance on the subject of marital infidelity. Her friend was still raw from the break-up of her own marriage. But Peggy's husband had been a womaniser. Annette was scarcely a comparable case. Business worries and a pair of difficult teenagers had put the Huntingdon marriage under strain. Annette had had an affair and Drew had been devastated. Resisting her stricken pleas for a reconciliation, Drew had moved out and headed straight for his solicitor. Funny how people rarely reacted as you thought they would in a personal crisis. Catherine had believed he would forgive and forget. She had been wrong.

'I still hope they sort out their problems before it's too late,' she replied quietly.

'Why should he want to? He's only fifty... an attractive man, still in his prime...'

'I suppose he is,' Catherine allowed uncertainly. She was very fond of Harriet's brother, but she wasn't accustomed to thinking of him on those terms.

'A man who somehow can't find anything better to do than drive down here at weekends to play with Daniel,' Peggy commented with studied casualness.

Unconscious of her intent scrutiny, Catherine laughed. 'He's at a loose end without his family.'

Peggy cleared her throat. 'Has it ever occurred to you that Drew might have a more personal interest at stake here?'

Catherine surveyed her blankly.

'Oh, for goodness' sake!' Peggy groaned. 'Do I have to spell it out? His behaviour at the funeral raised more brows than mine. If you lifted anything heavier than a teacup, he was across the room like young Lochinvar! I think he's in love with you.'

'In love with me?' Catherine parroted, aghast. 'I've never heard anything so ridiculous!'

'I could be wrong.' Peggy sounded doubtful.

'Of course you're wrong!' Catherine told her with unusual vehemence, her cheeks hot with discomfiture.

'All right, calm down,' Peggy sighed. 'But I did have this little chat with him at the funeral. I asked him why he'd dug up another old lady for you to run after——'

'Mrs Anstey is his godmother!' Catherine gasped.

'And she'll see out another generation of downtrodden home-helps,' Peggy forecast grimly. 'When I ran you up to see the flat, that frozen face of hers was enough for me. I told Drew that.'

'Peggy, how could you? I only have to do her shopping and supply her with a main meal every evening. That isn't much in exchange for a flat at a peppercorn rent.'

'That's why I smell a big fat rat. However...' Peggy paused smugly for effect '...Drew told me that I didn't need to worry because he didn't expect you to be there for long. Now why do you think he said that?'

'Maybe he doesn't think I'll suit her.' Thank you, Peggy for giving me something else to worry about, she thought wearily.

Peggy was fingering the solicitor's letter, a crease suddenly forming between her brows. 'If you have to move this week, you can't possibly come up home with me, can you?' she gathered frustratedly. 'And I was absolutely depending on you, Catherine. My mother and you get on like a house on fire and it takes the heat off me.'

'The news isn't going to make me Daniel's favourite person either,' Catherine muttered.

Unexpectedly, Peggy grinned. 'Why don't I take him anyway?'

'On his own?'

'Why not? My parents adore him. He'll be spoilt to death. And by the time we come back you'll have the flat organised and looking more like home. I've felt so guilty about not being able to do anything to help out,' Peggy confided. 'This is perfect.'

'I couldn't possibly let you——'

'We're friends, aren't we? It would make the move less traumatic for him. Poor little beggar, he doesn't half take things to heart,' Peggy said persuasively. 'He won't be here when you hand Clover over to the animal sanctuary and he won't have to camp out *en route* in Drew's apartment either. I seem to recall he doesn't get on too well with that housekeeper.'

Daniel didn't get on too terribly well with anyone who crossed him, Catherine reflected ruefully. He especially didn't like being babied and being told that he was cute, which, regrettably for him, he was. All black curly hair and long eyelashes and huge dark eyes. He was extremely affectionate with her, but not with anyone else.

'You do trust me with him?' Peggy shot at her abruptly.

'Of course I do——'

'Well, then, it's settled,' Peggy decided with her usual impatience.

The comment that she had never been apart from Daniel before, even for a night, died on Catherine's lips. Daniel loved the farm. They had spent several weekends there with Peggy in recent years. At least this way he wouldn't miss out on his holiday.

Six days later, Daniel gave her an enthusiastic hug and raced into Peggy's car. Catherine hovered. 'If he's homesick, phone me,' she urged Peggy.

'We haven't got a home any more,' Daniel reminded her. 'Africa's getting it.'

Within minutes they were gone. Catherine retreated indoors to stare at a set of suitcases and a handful of boxes through a haze of tears. Not much to show for four years. The boxes were to go into Peggy's garage. A neighbour had promised to drop them off at Drew's apartment next week. She wiped at her overflowing eyes in vexation. Daniel was only going to be away for ten days, not six months!

Drew met her off the train and steered her out to his car. He was a broadly built man with pleasant features and a quiet air of self-command. 'We'll drop your cases off at the apartment first.'

'First?' she queried.

He smiled. 'I've booked a table at the Savoy for lunch.'

'Are you celebrating something?' Catherine had lunched with Drew a dozen times in Harriet's company, but he had always taken them to his club.

'The firm's on the brink of winning a very large contract,' he divulged, not without pride. 'Unofficially, it's in the bag. I'm flying to Germany this evening. The day after tomorrow we sign on the dotted line.'

Catherine grinned. 'That's marvellous news.'

'To be frank, it's come in the nick of time. Lately, Huntingdon's has been cruising too close to the wind. But that's not all we'll be celebrating,' he told her. 'What about your move to London?'

'When will you be back from Germany?' she asked as they left his apartment again.

'Within a couple of days, but I'll check into a hotel.'

Catherine frowned. 'Why?'

Faint colour mottled his cheeks. 'When you're in the middle of a divorce you can't be too careful, Catherine. Thank God, it'll all be over next month. No doubt you think I'm being over-cautious, but I don't want anyone pointing fingers at you or associating you with the divorce.'

Catherine was squirming with embarrassment. She had gratefully accepted his offer of a temporary roof without thought of the position she might be putting him in. 'I feel terrible, Drew. I never even thought——'

'Of course you didn't. Your mind doesn't work like that.' Drew squeezed her hand comfortingly. 'Once this court business is over, we won't need to consider clacking tongues.'

She found that remark more unsettling than reassuring, implying as it did a degree of intimacy that had never been a part of their friendship. Then she scolded herself and blamed Peggy for making her read double meanings where no doubt none existed. She had inevitably grown closer to Drew since he had separated from Annette. He had become a frequent visitor to his sister's home.

In the bar they received their menus. Catherine made an elaborate play of studying hers, although she did have great difficulty with words on a printed page. The difficulty was because she was dyslexic, but she was practised at concealing the handicap.

'Steak, I think.' Steak was safe. It was on every menu.

'You're a creature of habit,' Drew complained, but he smiled at her. He was the sort of man who liked things to stay the same. 'And to start?'

She played the same game with prawns.

'I might as well have ordered for you,' he teased.

Her wandering scrutiny glanced off the rear-view of a tall black-haired male passing through the foyer beyond the doorway. At accelerated speed her eyes swept back again in a double-take, only he was out of sight. Bemusedly she blinked and then told herself off for that fearful lurch of recognition, that chilled sensation enclosing her flesh.

'Take one day at a time,' Harriet had once told her. Harriet had been a great one for clichés, and four years ago she had made it sound so easy. But a day was twenty-four hours and each of them broken up into sixty minutes. How long had it been before she could go even five minutes without remembering? How long had it been since she had lain sleepless in bed, tortured by the raw strength of the emotions she was forcing herself to deny? In the end she had built a wall inside her head. Behind it she had buried two years of her life. Beyond it sometimes she still felt only half-alive...

'Something wrong?'

Meeting Drew's puzzled gaze, she gave an exaggerated shiver. 'Someone walked over my grave,' she joked, veiling her too-expressive eyes.

'Now that you're in London, we'll be able to see each other more often,' Drew remarked tensely and reached for her hand. 'What I'm trying to say, not very well, perhaps, is...I believe I'm in love with you.'

Her hand jerked, bathing them both in sherry. With a muttered apology she fumbled into her bag for a tissue, but a waiter moved forward and deftly mopped up the table. Catherine sat, frozen, wishing that she were anywhere but where she was now, with Drew looking at her expectantly.

He sighed, 'I wanted you to know how I felt.'

'I...I didn't know. I had no idea.' It was all she could think to say, hopelessly inadequate as it was.

'I thought you might have worked it out for yourself.' There was a glimmer of wry humour in his level scrutiny. 'Apparently I haven't been as obvious as I thought I was being. Catherine, don't look so stricken. I don't expect anything from you. I don't believe there is an appropriate response for an occasion like this. I've been clumsy and impatient and I'm sorry.'

'I feel that I've come between you and Annette,' she whispered guiltily.

He frowned. 'That's nonsense. It's only since I left her that I began to realise just how much I enjoyed being with you.'

'But if I hadn't been around, maybe you would have gone back to her,' she reasoned tautly. 'You're a very good friend, but I'm...'

He covered her hand again with his. 'I'm not trying to rush you, Catherine. We've got all the time in the world,' he assured her evenly, and deftly flipped the subject, clearly registering that further discussion at that moment would be unproductive.

They were in the River Room Restaurant when she heard the voice. Dark-timbred, slightly accented, like honey drifting down her spine. Instantly her head spun on a chord of response rooted too deep even to require consideration. Her eyes widened in shock, her every sinew jerked tight. The blood pounded dizzily in her eardrums. With a trembling hand she set down her wine glass.

Luc.

Oh, God...Luc. It had been him earlier. It was him. His carved profile, golden and vibrant as a gypsy's, was etched in bold relief against the light flooding through the window behind him. One brown hand was moving to illustrate some point to his two male companions. That terrible compulsion to stare was uncontrollable. The lean, arrogant nose, the hard slant of his high cheekbones and the piercing intensity of deep-set dark eyes, all welded into one staggeringly handsome whole.

His gleaming dark head turned slightly. He looked straight at her. No expression. No reaction. Eyes golden as the burning heart of a flame. Her ability to breathe seized up. A clock had stopped ticking somewhere. She was sentenced to immobility while every primitive sense she possessed screamed for her to get up and run and keep on running until the threat was far behind. For a moment her poise almost deserted her. For a moment she forgot that he was very unlikely to acknowledge her. For a moment she was paralysed by sheer gut-wrenching fear.

Luc broke the connection first. He signalled with a hand to one of his companions, who immediately rose from his seat with the speed of a trained lackey, inclining his head down for his master's voice.

'I've upset you,' Drew murmured. 'I should have kept quiet.'

Her lashes dropped down like a camera shutter. The clink of cutlery and the buzz of voices swam back to her again. One thing hadn't changed, she acknowledged numbly; when she looked at Luc there was nothing and nobody else in the world capable of stealing her attention. Perspiration was beading her upper lip. Luc was less than fifteen feet away. They said that when you drowned your whole life flashed before you. Oh, for the deep concealment of a pool.

'Catherine——'

Belatedly she recalled the man she had been lunching with. 'I've got a bit of a headache,' she mumbled. 'If you'll excuse me, I'll get something for it.'

Up she got, on jellied knees, undyingly grateful that she didn't have to pass Luc's table. Even so, leaving the restaurant was like walking the plank above a gathering of sharks. An unreasoning part of her was expecting a hand to fall on her shoulder at any second. Feeling physically sick, she escaped into the nearest cloakroom and ran cold water over her wrists.

Drying her hands, she touched the slender gold band on her wedding finger. Harriet's gift, Harriet's invention. Everyone but Peggy thought she was a widow. Harriet had coined and told the lie before Catherine had even left hospital. She could not have publicly branded Harriet a liar. Even so, it had gone against the grain to pose as something she wasn't, although she was ruefully aware that, without Harriet's respectable cover-story, she would not have been accepted into the community in the same way.

Her stomach was still heaving. Calm down, breathe in. Why give way to panic? With Luc in the vicinity, panic made sense, she reasoned feverishly. Luc was very unpredictable. He threw wild cards without conscience. But she couldn't stay in here forever, could she?

'I think there must be a storm in the air,' she told Drew on her return, her eyes carefully skimming neither left nor right. 'I often get a headache when the weather's about to break.'

She talked incessantly through the main course. If Drew was a little overwhelmed by her loquacity, at least he wasn't noticing that her appetite had vanished. Luc was watching her. She could feel it. She could feel the hypnotic beat of tawny gold on her profile. And she couldn't stand it. It was like Chinese water-torture. Incessant, remorseless. Anger began to gain ground on her nerves.

Luc was untouched. It was against nature that he should be untouched after the scars he had inflicted on her. There was no justice in a world where Luc continued to flourish like a particularly invasive tropical plant. Hack it down and it leapt up again, twice as big and threatening.

And yet some day...somehow...some woman had to slice beneath that armour-plating of his. It had to happen. He had to learn what it was to feel pain from somebody. That belief was all that had protected Catherine from burning up with bitterness. She would picture Luc driven to his knees, Luc humanised by suffering, and then she would filter back to reality again, unable to sustain the fantasy.

Religiously she stirred her coffee. Clockwise, anticlockwise, clockwise again, belatedly adding sugar. Her mind was in turmoil, lost somewhere between the past and the present. She was merely one more statistic on the long Santini casualty list. It galled her to acknowledge that demeaning truth.

'I've been cut dead.' Drew planted the observation flatly into the flow of her inconsequential chatter.

'Sorry?' she said, all at sea.

'Luc Santini. He looked right through me on the way out.'

She was floored by the casual revelation that Drew actually *knew* Luc. Yet why was she so surprised? Even if he was in a much smaller category, Drew was in the same field as Luc. Huntingdon's manufactured computer components. 'Is th-that important?' she stammered.

'It'll teach me not to get too big for my boots,' Drew replied wryly. 'I did do some business with him once, but that was years ago. I'm not in the Santini league these days. Possibly he didn't remember me.'

Luc had a memory like a steel trap. He never forgot a face. She was guiltily conscious that Luc had cut Drew because of her presence and for no other reason. And she wasn't foolish enough to pretend that she didn't know who Luc was. The individual who hadn't heard of Luc Santini was either illiterate or living in a grass hut on a desert island.

Drew sipped at his coffee, clearly satisfied that he had simply been forgotten. 'He's a fascinating character. Think of the risks he must have taken to get where he is today.'

'Think of the body-count he must have left behind him.'

'That's a point,' Drew mused. 'To my knowledge, he's only slipped once. Let me see, it was about four... five years ago now. I don't know what happened, but he damned near lost the shirt off his back.'

Obviously he had snatched his shirt back again and, knowing Luc, he had snatched someone else's simultaneously. On that level, Luc was unashamedly basic. An eye for an eye, a tooth for a tooth, and perhaps interest into the bargain. In remembrance she stilled a shudder.

As they left the hotel, Drew said in a driven undertone, 'I've made a bloody fool of myself, haven't I?'

'Of course you haven't,' she hastened to assure him.

'Do you want a taxi?' he asked stiffly. 'I'd better get back to the office.'

'I think I'll go for a walk.' She was ashamed that she hadn't handled the situation with greater tact, but the combination of his confession and Luc, hovering on the horizon like a pirate ship, had bereft her of her wits.

'Catherine?' Before she could turn away, Drew bent down in an almost involuntary motion and crushed her parted lips briefly with his own. 'Some day soon I'm going to ask you to marry me, whether you like it or not,' he promised with recovering confidence. 'It's nearly five years since you lost your husband. You can't bury yourself with his memory forever. And I'm a persistent man.'

A second later he was gone, walking quickly in the other direction. Tears lashed her eyes fiercely. Waves of delayed reaction were rolling over her, reducing her self-control to rubble. He was such a kind man, the essence of an old-fashioned gentleman, proposing along with the first kiss. And she was a fraud, a complete fraud. She was not the woman he thought she was, still grieving for some youthful husband and a tragically short-lived marriage. Drew had her on a pedestal.

The truth would shatter him. In retrospect, it even shattered her. For two years she had been nothing better than Luc Santini's whore, in her own mind. Kept and clothed in return for her eagerness to please in his bed. Luc hadn't once confused sex with love. That mistake had been hers alone. The polite term was 'mistress'. Only rich men's mistresses tended to share the limelight. Luc had ensured that she'd remained strictly off stage. He had never succumbed to an urge to take her out and show her off. She hadn't had the poise or the glitter, never mind the background or the education. Even now, the memories were like acid burns on her flesh, wounding and hurting wherever they touched.

Choices. Life was all about choices. Sometimes the tiniest choice could raise Cain at a later date. At eighteen Catherine had made a series of choices. At least, she had *thought* she was making them; in reality, they had most of them been made for her. Love was a terrifying leveller of pride and intelligence when a woman was an insecure girl. Before she had met Luc, she wouldn't have believed that it could be a mistake to love somebody. But it could be, oh, yes, it could be. If that person turned your love into a weapon against you, it could be a mistake you would regret for the rest of your days.

From no age at all, Catherine had been desperate to be loved. With hindsight she could only equate herself with a walking time-bomb, programmed to self-destruct. Within hours of her birth, she had been abandoned by her mother and her reluctant parent had never been traced. Nor had anybody ever come forward with any information.

She had grown up in a children's home where she had been one of many. She had been a dreamer, weaving fantasies for years about the unknown mother who might eventually come to claim her. When that hope had worn thin in her teens, she had dreamt of a towering passion instead.

Leaving school at sixteen, she had worked as a helper in the home until it had closed down two years later. The Goulds had been related to the matron. A young, sophisticated couple, they had owned a small art gallery in London. Giving her a job as a receptionist, the Goulds had paid her barely enough to live on and had taken gross advantage of her willingness to work long hours. Business had been poor at the gallery and it had been kept open late most nights, Catherine left in charge on the many evenings that her employers went out.

Luc had strolled in one wet winter's night when she'd been about to lock up. His hotel had been near by. He had walked in off the street on impulse, an off-white trenchcoat carelessly draped round his shoulders, crystalline raindrops glistening in his luxuriant black hair and that aura of immense energy and self-assurance splintering from him in waves. She had made her first choice then, bedazzled and bemused by a fleeting smile...she had stopped locking up.

A silver limousine purred into the kerb several yards ahead of her now, penetrating her reverie. She hadn't even noticed where she'd been walking. Looking up, she found herself in a quiet side-street. The rear door of the car swung open and Luc stepped out on to the pavement, blocking her path. 'May I offer you a lift?'

CHAPTER TWO

CATHERINE focused on him in unconcealed horror, eyes wide above her pale cheeks. 'I'm... I'm not going anywhere——'

'You're simply loitering?' Luc gibed.

'That I would need a lift,' she completed jerkily. 'How did you know where I was?'

A beautifully shaped brown hand moved deprecatingly.

'How?' she persisted.

'I had you followed from the hotel.'

Oxygen locked in her throat. Had she really thought this second meeting a further coincidence? Had she really thought he would let her go without a single question? A car pulled up behind the limousine, two security men speedily emerging. Like efficient watchdogs, one of them took up a stance to Luc's rear, the other backing across the street for a better vantage point. For Catherine, there was an unreality to the scene. She was reminded of how vastly different a world she had inhabited over the past four years.

'Why would you want to do that?' she whispered tautly.

Black spiky lashes lowered over glittering dark eyes. 'Perhaps I wanted to catch up on old times. I don't know. You tell me,' he invited softly. 'Impulse? Do you think that is a possibility?'

Involuntarily she backed towards the railings behind her. 'You're not an impulsive person.'

'Why are you trembling?' He moved soundlessly closer, and her shoulders met wrought iron in an effort to keep the space between them intact.

'You come up out of nowhere? You gave me one heck of a fright!'

'You used to have the love of a child for surprises.'

'You might not have noticed, but I'm not a child any more!' It took courage to hurl the retort, but it was a mistake. Luc ran a raking, insolent appraisal over her, taking in the purple bullclip doing a haphazard task of holding up her silky hair, the lace-collared blouse and the tiered floral skirt cinched at her tiny waist with a belt. Modestly covered as she was, she still felt stripped.

'I see Laura Ashley is still doing a roaring trade,' he said drily.

He was so close now that she could have touched him. But she wouldn't raise her eyes above the level of his blue silk tie. He wore a dove-grey suit with an elegance few men could emulate. Superb tailoring outlined his lean length in the cloth of a civilised society. However, what she sensed in the atmosphere was far from civilised. It was nameless, frightening. A silent intimidation that clawed cruelly at her nerve-endings.

'We don't have anything to talk about after all this time.' The assurance left her bloodless lips in a rush, an answer to an unvoiced but understood demand.

Negligently he raised a hand and a fingertip roamed with taunting slowness from her delicate collarbone where a tiny pulse was flickering wildly up to the taut curve of her full lower lip. Her skin was on fire, her entire body suddenly consumed by a heatwave.

'Relax,' he cajoled, carelessly withdrawing his hand a split second before she jerked her head back in violent repudiation of the intimacy. Flames danced momentarily in his dark eyes and then a slow, brilliant smile curved his hard mouth. 'I didn't intend to frighten you. Come... are we enemies?'

'I'm in r... rather a hurry,' she stammered.

'And you still don't want a lift? Fine. I'll walk along with you,' he responded smoothly. 'Or we could get into the car and just drive around for a while... even sit in a traffic jam. Believe me, I'm in an unusually accommodating mood.'

'Why?' Valiantly moving away from the hard embrace of the railings, Catherine straightened her shoulders. 'What do you want?'

'Well, I don't expect you to do what we used to do in traffic jams.' Slumbrous dark eyes rested unrepentantly on the tide of hot colour spreading beneath her fair skin. 'What do you think I might want? Surely, it's understandable that I should wish to satisfy a little natural curiosity?'

'What about?'

'About you. What else?' An ebony brow quirked. 'Do you think I am standing here in the street for my own pleasure?'

Catherine chewed indecisively at her lower lip. She could feel his temper rising. Time was when Luc would have said 'get in the car' and she would have leapt. He was smiling, but you couldn't trust Luc's smiles. Luc could smile while he broke you in two with a handful of well-chosen words. Without speaking, she reached her decision and bypassed him. Luc was exceptionally newsworthy and she could not afford to be seen with him, lest her past catch up with the present that Harriet had so carefully reconstructed for her.

A security man materialised at her elbow and opened the door of the limousine. Ducking her head, she slid along the cream leather upholstery to the far corner. The door slammed on them, sealing them into claustrophobic privacy.

'Really, Catherine... was that so difficult?' Luc murmured silkily. 'Would you like a drink?'

Her throat was parched. She fought for her vanished poise. 'Why not?'

Her palms smoothed nervously down over her skirt, rearranging the folds. Her skin prickled at his proximity as he bent forward to press open the built-in bar. For the longest moment of her existence, the black springy depths of his hair were within reach of her fingers. The mingled aroma of some elusive lotion and that indefinable but oh, so familiar scent that was purely him assailed her defensively flared nostrils. As he straightened again, she was disturbingly conscious of the clean movement of rippling muscles beneath the expensive fabric that sheathed his broad shoulders. And an ache and an agony were reborn treacherously within her.

Her hands laced tightly together. In the unrelenting silence, she believed she could hear her own heartbeat, speeding and pounding out the evidence of her own betrayal. She was horrified by the sensual imagery that had briefly driven every other thought from her mind. If her memory was playing tricks on her, her body was no less eager to follow suit.

Luc extended her glass, retaining hold of it long enough to force her to look at him. It was a power-play, a very minor one on Luc's terms but it made her feel controlled. She took several fast swallows of her drink. It hurt her tight throat and she hated the taste, but once she had been naïve enough to drink something she detested because she believed that was sophistication.

'Feel better now?' Luc enquired lazily, lounging back with his brandy in an intrinsically graceful movement. 'Do you live in London?'

'No,' she said hurriedly. 'I'm only here for the day. I live in... in Peterborough.'

'And you're married. That must be a source of great satisfaction to you.'

The ring on her wedding finger began to feel like a rope tightening round her vocal chords. She decided to overlook the sarcasm.

'When did you get married?'

'About four years ago.' She took another slug of her drink to fortify herself for the next round of whoppers. 'Shortly after——'

Her brain had already registered her error. 'It was a whirlwind romance,' she proffered in a rush.

'It must have been,' he drawled. 'Tell me about him.'

'It's all very pedestrian,' she muttered. 'I'm sure you can't really be interested.'

'On the contrary,' Luc contradicted softly. 'I am fascinated. Does your husband have a name?'

'Luc, I——'

'So, you remember mine? An unsought compliment...'

She stared down into her glass. 'Paul. He's called Paul.' Fighting the rigid tension threatening her, she managed a small laugh. 'Honestly, you can't want to hear all this!'

'Indulge me,' Luc advised. 'Are you happy living in...where was it? Peterhaven?'

'Yes, of course I am.'

'You don't look very happy.'

'It doesn't always show,' she retorted in desperation.

'Children?' he prompted casually.

Catherine froze, icicles sliding down her spine, and she could not prevent a sudden, darting, upward glance. 'No, not yet.'

Luc was very still. Even in the grip of her own turmoil, she noticed that. And then without warning he smiled. 'What were you doing with Huntingdon?'

The question thrown at her out of context shook her. 'I...I ran into him while I was shopping,' she hesitated and, with a stroke of what seemed to her absolute brilliance, added, 'My husband works for him.'

'You do seem to have enjoyed a day excessively full of coincidences.' Stunning golden eyes whipped over her flushed, heart-shaped face. 'The unexpected is invariably the most entertaining, isn't it?'

She set down her glass. 'I r... really have to be going. It's been... lovely meeting you again.'

'I'm flattered you should think so,' Luc murmured expressionlessly. 'What are you afraid of?'

'Afraid of?' she echoed unsteadily. 'I'm not afraid of anything!' She took a deep, shuddering breath. 'We have nothing to talk about.'

'I foresee a long day ahead of us,' Luc commented.

Catherine bent her head. 'I don't have to answer your questions,' she said tightly, struggling to keep a dismaying tremor out of her voice. Fight fire with fire. That was the only stance to take with Luc.

'Think of it as a small and somewhat belated piece of civility,' Luc advised. 'Four and a half years ago, you vanished into thin air. Without a word, a letter or a hint of explanation. I would like that explanation now.'

Stains of pink had burnished her cheeks. 'In a nutshell, getting involved with you was the stupidest thing I ever did,' she condemned.

'And telling me that may well prove to be your second.' Dark hooded eyes rested on her. 'You slept with me the night before you disappeared. You lay in my arms and you made love with me, knowing that you planned to leave...'

'H-habit,' she stammered.

Hard fingers bit into her wrist, trailing her closer without her volition. 'Habit?' he ground out roughly, incredulously.

Her tongue was glued to the dry roof of her mouth. Mutely she nodded, and recoiled from the raw fury and revulsion she read in his unusually expressive eyes. 'You're hurting me,' she mumbled.

He dropped her wrist contemptuously. 'My compliments, then, on an award-winning performance. Habit inspired you with extraordinary enthusiasm.'

She reddened to the roots of her hair, attacked by the sort of memories she never let out of her subconscious even on temporary parole. To remember was to hate herself. And that night she had known in her heart of hearts that she would never be with Luc again. With uncharacteristic daring, she had woken him up around dawn, charged with a passionate despair that could only find a vent in physical expression. Loving someone who did not love you was the cruellest kind of suffering.

'I don't remember,' she lied weakly, loathing him so much that she hurt with the force of her suppressed emotions. He made her a stranger to herself. He had done that in the past and he was doing it now. She was not the Catherine who understood and forgave other people's foibles at this moment. She had paid too high a price for loving Luc.

'Habit.' He said it again, but so softly; yet she was chilled.

Quite by accident, she registered, she had stung his ego, stirring the primitive depths of a masculinity that was rarely, if ever, challenged by her sex. She wasn't the only woman to make a fool of herself over Luc. Women went to the most embarrassing lengths to attract his attention. They went to even greater lengths to hold him. The reflection was of cold comfort to her.

Women were leisure-time toys for Luc Santini. Easily lifted, just as easily cast aside and dismissed. On the rise to the top, Luc had never allowed himself to waste an ounce of his single-minded energy on a woman. Women had their place in his life... of course they did. He was a very highly sexed male animal. But a woman never held the foreground in his mind, never came between him and his cold, analytical intelligence.

'I have to be going,' she said again and yet, when she collided with that gleaming gaze, she was strangely reluctant to move.

'As you wish.' With disorientating cool, he watched her gather up her bag and climb out of the car on rubbery legs, teetering dangerously for an instant on the very high heels she always wore.

Dragging wayward eyes from his dark, virile features, she closed the door and crossed the street. She felt dizzy, shell-shocked. All those lies, she thought guiltily; all those lies to protect Daniel. Not that Luc could be a threat to Daniel now, but she felt safer with Luc in ignorance. Luc didn't like complications or potential embarrassments. An illegitimate son would qualify as both.

A little dazedly, she shook her head. Apart from that one moment of danger, Luc had been so...so cool. She couldn't say what she had expected, only somehow it hadn't been that. In the Savoy, she could have sworn that Luc was blazingly angry. Obviously that had been her imagination. After all, why should he be angry? Four years was a long time, she reminded herself. And he hadn't cared about her. You didn't constantly remind someone you cared about that they were living on borrowed time. At least, not in Catherine's opinion you didn't.

Her mind drifted helplessly back to their first meeting. She had rewarded his mere presence at the gallery with a guided tour *par excellence*. She had never been that close to a male that gorgeous, that sophisticated and that exciting. Luc, bored with his own company and in no mood to entertain a woman, had consented to be entertained.

He had smiled at her and her wits had gone a-begging, making her forget what she was saying. It hadn't meant anything to him. He had left without even advancing his name but, before he had gone, he said, 'You shouldn't be up here on your own. You shouldn't be so friendly with strangers either. A lot of men would take that as a come-on and you really wouldn't know how to handle that.'

As he'd started down the stairs, glittering golden eyes had glided over her one last time. What had he seen? A pretty, rounded teenager as awkward and as easily read as a child in her hurt disappointment.

In those days, though, she had been a sunny optimist. If he had happened in once, he might happen in again. However, it had been two months before Luc reappeared. He had walked in late on and alone, just as he had before. Scarcely speaking, he had strolled round the new pictures with patent uninterest while she'd chattered with all the impulsive friendliness he had censured on his earlier visit. Three-quarters of the way back to the exit, he had swung round abruptly and looked back at her.

'I'll wait for you to close up. I feel like some company,' he had drawled.

The longed-for invitation had been careless and last-minute, and the assumption of her acceptance one of unapologetic arrogance. Had she cared? Had she heck!

'I've been shut in all day. I'd enjoy a walk,' he had murmured when she'd pelted breathlessly back to his side.

'I don't mind,' she had said. He could have suggested a winter dip in the Thames and she would have shown willing. Taking her coat from her, he had deftly assisted her into it, and she had been impressed to death by his instinctive good manners.

As first dates went, it had been...different. He had walked her off her feet and treated her to a coffee in an all-night café in Piccadilly. She hadn't had a clue who he was and he had enjoyed that. He had told her about growing up in New York, about his family, the father, mother and sister who had died in a plane crash the previous year. In return she had opened her heart about her own background, contriving to joke as she invariably did about her unknown ancestry.

'Maybe I'll call you.' He had tucked her, alone and unkissed, into a cab to go home.

He hadn't called. Six, nearly seven agonising weeks had crawled past. Her misery had been overpowering. Only when she had abandoned all hope had Luc shown up again. Without advance warning. She had wept all over him with relief and he had kissed her to stop her crying.

He could have turned out to be a gangster after that kiss... it wouldn't have mattered; it wouldn't have made the slightest difference to her feelings. She was in love, hopelessly, crazily in love, and somewhere in the back of her mind she had dizzily assumed that he had to be too. How romantic, she had thought, when he presented her with a single white rose. Later she had bought a flower press to conserve that perfect bloom for posterity...

What utterly repellent things memories could be! Luc didn't have a romantic bone in his body. He had simply set about acquiring the perfect mistress with the same cool, tactical manoeuvres he employed in business. Step one, keep her off balance. Step two, convince her she can't live without you. Step three, move in for the kill. She had been seduced with so much style and expertise that she hadn't realised what was happening to her.

Pick an ordinary girl and run rings round her. That was what Luc had done to her. She might as well have tied herself to the tracks in front of an express train. Every card had been stacked against her from the start.

Glancing at her watch in a crowded street, she was stunned to realise how late it was. Lost in her thoughts she had wandered aimlessly through the afternoon. Without further ado, she headed for the bus-stop.

Drew's housekeeper, Mrs Bugle, was putting on her coat to go home when Catherine let herself into the apartment. 'I'm afraid I was too busy to leave dinner prepared for you, Mrs Parrish,' she said stiffly.

'Oh, that's fine. I'm used to looking after myself.' But Catherine was taken aback by the formerly friendly woman's cold, disapproving stare.

'I want you to know that Mrs Huntingdon is taking this divorce very hard,' Mrs Bugle told her accusingly. 'And I'll be looking for another position if Mr Huntingdon remarries.'

The penny dropped too late for Catherine to speak up in her own defence. With that parting shot, Mrs Bugle slammed the front door in her wake. A prey to a weary mix of anger, embarrassment and frustration, Catherine reflected that the housekeeper's attack was the finishing touch to a truly ghastly day.

So now she was a marriage-wrecker, was she? The other woman. Mrs Bugle would not be the last to make that assumption. Annette Huntingdon's affair was a well-kept secret, known to precious few. Dear God, how could she have been so blind to Drew's feelings?

Harriet had been very much against her brother's desire for a divorce. She had lectured Drew rather tact-lessly, making him more angry and defensive than ever at a time when he was already hurt and humiliated by his wife's betrayal.

Had she herself been too sympathetic in an effort to balance Harriet's well-meant insensitivity? When Drew chose to talk to her instead, had she listened rather too well? She had felt desperately sorry for him but she hadn't really wanted to be involved in his marital problems. All she had done was listen, for goodness' sake...and evidently Drew had read that as encouragement.

What she ought to be doing now was walking right back out of this apartment again! But how could she? After paying Mrs Anstey a month's rent in advance, she had less than thirty pounds to her name. Peggy had raged at her frequently for not demanding some sort of a wage for looking after Harriet, whose housekeeper had retired shortly after Catherine had moved in. However, Harriet, always ready to give her last penny away to someone more needy than herself and, let's face it, Catherine acknowledged guiltily, increasingly silly with what little money she did have, could not have afforded to pay her a salary.

And it hadn't mattered, it really hadn't mattered until Harriet had died. With neither accommodation nor food to worry about, Catherine had contrived to make ends meet in a variety of ways. She had registered as a child-minder, although, between Harriet's demands and Daniel's, that had provided only an intermittent income for occasional extras. She had grown vegetables, done sewing alterations, boarded pets...somehow they had always managed. But the uncertainties of their future now loomed over her like a giant black cloud.

As she unpacked, she faced the fact that she would have to apply to the Social Services for assistance until she got on her feet again. And when Drew returned from Germany, she decided, she would tell him about her past. If what he felt for her was the infatuation she suspected it was, he would quickly recover. Either way, she would lose a friendship she had come to value. When she fell off her pedestal with a resounding crash, Drew would feel, quite understandably, that he had been deceived.

The doorbell went at half-past six. She was tempted to ignore it, lest it be someone else eager to misinterpret her presence in the apartment. Unfortunately, whoever was pressing the bell was persistent, and her nerves wouldn't sit through a third shrill burst.

It was Luc. For a count of ten nail-biting seconds, she believed she was hallucinating. As she fell back, her hand slid weakly from the door. 'Luc...?' she whispered.

'I see you haven't made it back to Peterborough yet. Or was it Peterhaven?' Magnificent golden eyes clashed with startled blue. 'You didn't seem too sure where you lived. And you're a lousy liar, *cara*. In fact, you're so poor a liar, I marvel that you even attempted to deceive me. Yet you sat in that car and you lied and lied and lied...'

'Did I?' she gasped, in no state to put her brain into more agile gear.

'Do you know why I let you go this afternoon?' He sent the door crashing shut with one impatient thrust of his hand.

'N-no.'

'If you had told me one more lie in the mood I was in, I would have strangled you,' Luc spelt out. 'Where do you get the courage to lie to me?'

It was nowhere in evidence now. Helplessly she stared at him. He was so very tall and, in the confines of a hall barely big enough to swing the proverbial cat in, he was overpowering. He had all the dark splendour of a Renaissance prince in his arrogant bearing. And he was just as lethally dangerous. As he slid a sun-bronzed hand into the pocket of his well-cut trousers, pulling the fabric taut across lean, hard thighs, she shut her eyes tight on the vibrantly sensual lure of him.

But her mouth ran dry and her stomach clenched in spite of the precaution. Had she really expected to be quite indifferent? To feel nothing whatsoever for this man she had once loved, whose child she had once borne in fearful isolation? Now she knew why she had fled his car in such a state, both defying and denying the existence of responses she had fondly believed she had outgrown with maturity.

A woman met a male of Luc Santini's calibre only once in a lifetime if she was lucky. And forever after, whether she liked it or not, he would be the standard by which she judged other men. She was suddenly frighteningly aware that, in all the years since she had walked out of that Manhattan apartment, no other man had stirred her physically. It had been no sacrifice to ignore the sensuality which had in the past so badly betrayed her. Now she was recognising that facing Luc again had to be the ultimate challenge.

The silence went on and on and on.

'Cristo, cara!' The intervention was disturbingly low-pitched. 'What is it that you think of? You look as though you're about to fall down on your knees and pray for deliverance...'

Her lashes flew up. 'Do I?' It was called playing for time by playing dumb. What was he doing here? What did he want from her? Which lies had he identified as lies? Dear God, did he suspect that she had a child? How could he suspect? she asked herself. Even so, she turned white at the very thought of that threat.

Without troubling to reply, he strode past her to push open the kitchen door and glance in. In complete bewilderment, she watched him repeat the action with each of the remaining doors, executing what appeared to be an ordered search of the premises. What was he looking for? Potential witnesses? Her mythical husband? Or a child? Her flesh grew clammy with fear. In the economic market, Luc was famed for his uncanny omniscience. He noticed what other people didn't notice. He could interpret what was hidden. If he had ever taken the time to focus that powerful intelligence on her disappearance, he would have grasped within minutes that there was a strong possibility that she was pregnant.

'Did you enjoy yourself trailing my security men all over town for three hours this afternoon?' Luc enquired dulcetly, springing her from her increasingly panic-stricken ruminations.

'Trailing your...?' As she registered his meaning, her incredulity spoke for her.

'Zero for observation, *cara*. You don't change. You wander around in a rosy dream-state like an accident waiting to happen.' He strolled fluidly into the lounge, his wide mouth compressing as he took open stock of his surroundings. 'No verdant greenery, not a floral drape or a frill or a flounce anywhere in sight. Either you haven't lived here very long or he has imposed his taste on yours. *Dio*, he had more success than I...'

The last was an aside, as disorientating as the speech which had preceded it. Unwittingly, she went pink as she recalled scathing comments about her preference for nostalgia as opposed to the abrasively modern décors he favoured. It was an unfortunate reference, summoning up, as it inexplicably did, stray and rebellious memories of baths by candlelight and an over-the-top lace-strewn four-poster bed...

The vast differences between them even on that level were almost laughable. Two more radically differing personalities would have been hard to find. Her dreams had been the ordinary ones of love and marriage and children.

But Luc hadn't had dreams. Dreams weren't realistic enough to engage his attention. He lived his life by a master plan of self-aggrandisement. He achieved one goal and moved on to the next. The possibility of failure never occurred to him. It was, after all, unthinkable that Luc would ever settle for less than what he wanted. As she thought unavoidably of how much less than her dreams she had settled for, bitterness coalesced into a hard, unforgiving stone inside her.

'Feel free to make yourself at home.' Her sarcasm was so out of character that Luc whipped round in surprise to stare at her.

'Don't talk to me like that,' he breathed almost tautly.

'I'll talk to you whatever way I want!' she dared.

'Be my guest,' Luc invited. 'You won't do it more than once.'

'Want to bet?' Her ability to defy him was gathering steam on the awareness that neither Daniel nor any trace of him could betray her in this apartment.

'If I were you, I wouldn't risk it,' Luc responded. 'You have this appalling habit of backing the wrong horse. And the odds definitely aren't in your favour.'

Courageously, she lifted her chin. 'I am not afraid of you.'

'You ought to be.'

Her Joan of Arc backbone suffered a sudden jolt in confidence. 'Are you trying to threaten me?' she asked shakily.

'To my knowledge, I've never *tried* to threaten anyone.' It was an assertion backed by immovable cool.

She bent her head. 'I've got nothing to say to you.'

'But I have plenty to say to you.'

'I don't want to hear it.' Jerkily she crossed her arms to conceal the fact that her hands were shaking, and moved over to the window, her back protectively turned on him.

'When I talk to people, I prefer them to look at me,' Luc imparted with irony.

'I don't want to look at you.' She was dismayed to realise that she was perilously close to tears. If wishes were horses, she would have been a thousand miles from this confrontation.

'Since I arrived, I've been having a marvellous conversation with myself.' The sardonic criticism of her monosyllabic responses drove much-needed colour into her cheeks. 'Perhaps I should approach this from a different angle.'

Taking a deep breath, she spun back to him. 'I want you to leave.'

An ebony brow elevated. 'The carpet or me?'

She flung her head back, sharp strain etched into every delicate line of her features, but she said nothing, could not trust her voice to emerge levelly or her gaze to meet directly with his.

'May we dispense with the imaginary husband, whose name you have such difficulty in recalling?' Luc murmured very quietly. 'I don't believe he exists.'

'I don't know where you get that idea.' Wildly disconcerted by the question thrown at her without warning, she was dismally conscious that her reply lacked sufficient surprise or annoyance to be convincing.

'I won't play these games with you.' The victim of that hooded dark stare holding her by sheer force of will, she felt cornered. 'I play them everywhere else in my life, but not with you. I saw you with Huntingdon outside the hotel. No doubt you believe that that ring lends a certain spurious respectability to your present position in his life. It doesn't,' he concluded flatly.

Desperation was beginning to grip her. 'You misunderstood what you saw.'

'Did I? I don't think so,' Luc murmured. 'Relax, he's still all in one piece... but he's halfway to Germany in pursuit of a contract he's not going to get.'

Her lower lip parted company with the upper. 'I b-beg your pardon?'

'You are not, I believe, hard of hearing.'

Unbearable tension held her unnaturally still. 'What have you got to do with that contract?'

'Influence alone,' Luc delivered. 'And influence will be sufficient.'

'But why? I mean, Drew?' she whispered strickenly.

'Unfortunately for him, this is his apartment.' Luc sent her a glittering glance, redolent of unashamed threat. 'And when a man trespasses on my territory, it must hurt. If it does not, who will respect the boundaries I set? Surely you do not expect me to reward him for bedding my woman?'

CHAPTER THREE

CATHERINE went white. Luc was hitting her with too much all at once. It was as if she were drowning and unable to breathe. Shock was reverberating with paralysing effect all the way down from her brain to her toes.

Luc surveyed her without a tinge of remorse. And this time she could sense the savage anger he was containing. A dark aura that radiated violent vibrations into the thickening atmosphere. It was an insidiously intimidating force, for Luc had never lost his temper with her before. Luc rarely unleashed his emotions. People who let anger triumph invariably surrendered control of the situation. Luc would not be guilty of such a gross miscalculation. Or so she had once believed...

She tried and failed to swallow. The tip of her tongue nervously crept out to moisten her dry lips. 'I am not your woman,' she said unsteadily.

Black spiky lashes partially screened a blaze of gold. 'For two years you were mine, indisputably mine, as no other woman ever has been. Some things don't change. In the Savoy, you couldn't take your eyes off me.'

Catherine was so appalled by the accusation that she momentarily forgot the threat to Drew. 'That's nonsense!'

'Is it?' She was reminded of a well-fed tiger indulgently watching his next meal at play. His brilliant gaze was riveted to her. 'I don't believe it is. And why should we argue about it? You have the same effect on me. I'm not denying it. A certain *je ne sais quoi*, unsought and, on many occasions since, unwelcome, but still in existence after six and a half years. Doesn't that tell you something?'

A furrow between her brows, Catherine was struggling to follow what he was telling her, but every time she came close to comprehension she retreated from it in disbelief.

'Plenty of marriages don't last that long,' Luc pointed out smoothly. 'I want you back, Catherine.'

In the bottomless pit of the silence he allowed to fall, she was sure she could hear her own heartbeat thundering fit to burst behind her breastbone. Her throat worked convulsively but no sound emerged, and that was hardly surprising when he had deprived her of the power of speech. Shock had gone into counter-shock, and her capacity to think straight had gone into cold storage.

'You have to be the most incredibly modest woman of my acquaintance. Do you really think I would go to these lengths for anything less?' Strolling over to the table, Luc uncapped one of the decanters, lifted a glass off the tray and poured a single measure of brandy.

'I can't believe that you can say that to me,' she mumbled.

'Console yourself with the reflection that I have not said one quarter of what I would like to say.' Luc slotted the glass between her nerveless fingers, cupped them helpfully round to clasp it, the easy intimacy of his touch one more violently disorientating factor to plague her. 'I feel sure that you are grateful for my restraint.'

Dimly she understood how a rabbit felt, mesmerised by headlights on the motorway. Those golden eyes could be shockingly compelling. The brandy went down in one appreciative gulp and she gasped as fire raced down her throat. It banished her paralysis, however, and retrieved her wits. 'You... you actually think that Drew is keeping me?' she demanded with a shudder of distaste. 'Is that what you're insinuating?'

'I rarely insinuate, *cara*. I state.'

'How dare you?' Catherine exclaimed.

Luc dealt her an impassive look. 'I find it particularly unsavoury that he should be a married man, old enough to be your father.'

Restraint, she acknowledged, was definitely fighting a losing battle. Fierce condemnation accompanied that final statement. 'There's nothing unsavoury about Drew!' she protested furiously. 'He's one of the most decent, honourable men I've ever met!'

'Only not above cheating on his wife with a woman half his age,' Luc drawled in biting conclusion. 'A little word of warning, *cara*. After tonight, I don't ever wish to hear his name on your lips again.'

Catherine was too caught up in an outraged defence of Drew to listen to him. 'He wouldn't cheat on his wife. He's been separated from her for almost a year. He'll be divorced next month!'

'I know,' Luc interposed softly, taking the wind from her sails. 'He should have stayed home with his wife. It would have been safer for him.'

'Safer?' she whispered, recalling what he had said some minutes earlier. 'You threatened him——'

'No. I delivered a twenty-two-carat-gold promise of intent.' The contradiction was precise, chilling.

'But you didn't mean it, you couldn't have meant it!' she argued in instinctive appeal.

Dark eyes lingered on her reflectively and veiled. 'If you say so.' A broad shoulder lifted in a very Latin shrug of dismissal. 'We have more important things to discuss.'

Her stomach executed a sick somersault. Under that exquisitely tailored suit dwelt a predator of Neanderthal proportions, ungiven to anything as remote as an attack of conscience. 'It's absolutely none of your business,' she conceded tightly, 'but I'm not having an affair with Drew.'

'Everything that concerns you is my business.'

It went against the grain to permit that to go past unchallenged, but she was more concerned about Drew. 'Why should you want to damage Huntingdon Components? What has he ever done to you?'

'You ask me that?' It was a positive snarl of incredulity. 'You live in his apartment and you ask me that?'

'It's not what it seems.'

'It is exactly what it seems. Cheap, nasty.' His nostrils flared as he passed judgement.

'Like what I had with you?' She couldn't resist the comparison.

'Cristo!' He threw up both hands in sudden lancing fury. 'How can you say that to me? In all my life, I never treated a woman as well as I treated you!'

The most maddening quality of that assurance was its blazing, blatant sincerity. He actually believed what he was saying. Her teeth ground together on a blistering retort.

'And what did I receive in return? You tell me!' he slashed at her rawly, rage masking his dark features. 'A bloody stupid scrawl on a mirror that I couldn't even read! I trusted you as though you were my family and you betrayed that trust. You stuck a knife in my back.'

She should have been better prepared for that explosion, but she wasn't. His legendary self-control had evaporated right before her stricken eyes, revealing the primitive depth of the anger she had dared to provoke. 'Luc, I——'

'Stay where you are!' The command cracked like a whiplash across the room, halting her retreat in the direction of the door. 'You were with me two years, Catherine. Two years,' he repeated fiercely, anger vibrating from every tensed line of his lean, powerful physique. 'And then you vanish into thin air. In nearly five years, what do I get? Hmm? Not so much as a postcard! So, I look for you. I wonder if you're starving somewhere. I worry about how you're managing to live. I think maybe you've had an accident, maybe you're dead. And where do I find you?' he grated in soaring crescendo. 'In the Savoy with another man!'

Her feet were frozen to the carpet under that searing onslaught. She had never seen Luc betray that much emotion. Dazedly, she watched him swing away from her, ferocious tension etched into the set of his broad shoulders and the angle of his hard, taut profile. She could not quite credit the evidence of what she was seeing, never mind what he had said.

He had worried about her? He had actually worried about her? In her mind she fought to come to terms with that revelation. When she had left him, sneaking cravenly out of the service entrance like a thief, she had foreseen his probable response to her departure. Disbelief... outrage... contempt... acceptance. The idea of his worrying about her, looking for her, had never once occurred to her.

In a strange way which she could not understand, she found the idea very disturbing, and it was in reaction to that that she chose to say nothing in her own defence. One fact had penetrated. Luc had no suspicion of Daniel's existence. That fear assuaged, she could only think of Drew.

'Leave Drew alone,' she said. 'He needs that contract.'

'Is that all you have to say to me?' There was a formidable chill in his dark eyes.

She swallowed hard. 'Losing that contract could ruin him.'

A grim smile curved his lips. 'I know.'

'If you're angry with me, take it out on me. I can't believe you really want to harm Drew,' she confided.

'Believe it,' Luc urged.

'I mean...' she made a helpless movement of her small hands, eloquent of her confusion '...you walk in here and you say...you say you want me back, but there's absolutely no question of that,' she completed shakily.

'No?'

'No! And I don't understand why you're doing this to me!' she cried.

'Maybe you should try.'

She refused to look at him. He had hurt her too much. In Luc's presence she was as fearfully wary as a child who had once put her hand in the fire. The memory of the pain was a persistent barrier. 'I won't try,' she said with simple dignity. 'You're an episode which I put behind me a long time ago.'

'An episode?' he derided incredulously. 'You lived with me for two years!'

'Nineteen months, and every month a mistake,' Catherine corrected, abandoning her caution by degrees.

'Madre de Dio.' A line of colour demarcated his high cheekbones. 'Hardly a one-night stand.'

Visibly she flinched. 'Oh, I don't know. I often used to feel like one.'

'How can you say that to me? I treated you with respect!' he ground out.

'That was respect?' A chokey laugh escaped her. She felt wild in that instant. If she had been a tigress, she would have clawed him to death in revenge. Her very powerlessness taunted her cruelly. 'When I look at you now, I wonder why it took me so long to come to my senses.'

'Since I arrived, you have looked everywhere but at me,' Luc said drily, deflatingly.

'I hate you, Luc. I hate you so much that if you dropped dead at my feet I'd dance on your corpse!' she vented in a feverish rush.

'The near future promises to be intriguing.'

'There isn't going to be one for us!' Catherine had never lost her head with anyone before, but it was happening now. As if it were not bad enough that he should stand there with the air of someone handling an escaped lunatic with enviable cool, he was ignoring every word she said. 'I'm not about to fall into line like one of your employees! Come back to you? You have to be out of your mind! You used me once, and I'd sooner be dead than let you do it again! I loved you, Luc. I loved you much more than you deserved to be loved——'

'I know,' he interposed softly.

A hectic flush carmined her cheeks, fury running rampant through her every skin-cell. 'What do you mean...you know? Where do you get the nerve to admit that?'

Unreadable golden eyes arrowed into her and lingered intently. 'I thought it might be in my favour.'

'In your favour? It makes what you did to me all the more unforgivable!' Catherine ranted in a fresh burst of outrage. 'You took everything I had to give and tried to pay for it, as though I were some tramp you'd picked up on a street-corner!'

His jawline clenched. 'I might have made one or two unfortunate errors of judgement,' he conceded after a very long pause. 'But, if you were dissatisfied with our relationship, you should have expressed that dissatisfaction.'

'I beg your pardon? Expressed it?' Catherine could hardly get the words out, she was so enraged. 'God forgive you, Luc, because I never will! Let me just make one little point. You can go out there and you can buy anything you want, but you can't buy me. I'm not available. I'm not up for sale. There's no price-tag attached, so what are you going to do?'

Trembling violently, she turned away from him, emotion still storming through her in a debilitating wave. She had never dreamt that she could attack Luc like that, but somehow it had simply happened. Yet in the aftermath she experienced no sense of pleasure; she felt only pain. A tearing, desperate pain that seemed to encompass her entire being. Just being in the same room with him hurt. She had sworn once that she would not let him do this to her. She would not let hatred poison the very air she breathed. But that wall inside her head was tumbling down brick by brick, and the vengeful force of all the feelings she had buried behind it was surging out of control. With those feelings came memories she fiercely sought to blank out...

That day he had given her the rose, he had escorted her down to a limousine. Cinderella had never had it so good. There had been no glass slipper to fall off at midnight. He had swept her off her feet into a world she had only read about in magazines. He had revelled in her wide eyes, her innocence, her inability to conceal her joy in merely being with him. For five days, she had been lost in a breathless round of excitement. Fancy night-clubs where they danced the night away, intimate meals in dimly lit restaurants...and his last evening in London, of course, in his hotel suite.

But even then Luc hadn't been predictable. When he had reduced her to the clinging, mindless state in his arms after dinner, he had set her back from him with a pronounced attitude of pious self-denial. 'I'm spending Christmas in Switzerland. Come with me,' he had urged lazily as though he were inviting her to merely cross the road.

She had been staggered, embarrassed, uncertain, but she had always been hopelessly sentimental about the festive season. Initially she had said no, uneasy about the prospect of letting Luc pay her way abroad.

'I don't know when I'll be back in London again.' A lie, though she hadn't known it then, as carefully processed as she had been by the preparation of two-month absences between meetings. What Luc didn't know about giving a woman withdrawal symptoms hadn't yet been written.

Convinced that she might lose him forever by letting old-fashioned principles come between them, she had caved in. She had been so dumb that she had expected them to be staying in a hotel in separate rooms. Even in the grip of the belief that she would walk off the edge of the world if he asked her to, she hadn't felt that she had known him long enough for anything else. He had returned to New York. Elaine Gould had been stunned to see a photo of her with Luc in a newspaper the next day. Elaine had tried to reason with her in a curt, well-meaning way. Even her landlady, breathlessly hung on the latest instalment of her romance, had given the thumbs-down to Switzerland. But she had been beyond the reach of sensible advice.

Six hours in an isolated Alpine chalet had been enough to separate her from a lifetime of principles. No seduction had ever been carried out more smoothly. No bride could have been brought to the marital bed with greater skill and consideration than Luc had employed. And, once Luc had taken her virginity, he had possessed her body and soul. She hadn't faced the fact that she knew about as much about having an affair as Luc knew about having a conscience. The towering passion had been there, the man of her dreams had been there, but the wedding had been nowhere on the horizon. She had given up everything for love... oh, you foolish, reckless woman, where were your wits?

'Catherine.' As she sank back to the present, she shivered. That accent still did something precarious to her knees.

'What were you thinking about?'

Blinking rapidly against the sting of tears, she breathed unsteadily, 'You don't want to know.'

'If you come back to me,' Luc murmured expressionlessly, 'I'll let Huntingdon have the contract.'

'Dear God, you can't bargain with a man's livelihood!' she gasped in horror.

'I can and I will.'

'I hate you! I'd be violently ill if you laid a finger on me!' she swore. Her legs were wobbling and she couldn't drag her eyes from his dark, unyielding features.

Unexpectedly, a smile curved his sensual mouth. 'I'll believe that when it happens.'

'Luc, please.' When it came down to it, she wasn't too proud to beg. She could not stand back and allow Drew to suffer by association with her. She could not disclaim responsibility and still live with herself. Luc did not utter idle threats. 'Please think of what you're doing. This is an ego-trip for you...'

A dark brow quirked. 'I've seldom enjoyed a less ego-boosting experience.'

'I can't come back to you, Luc... I just can't. Please go away and forget you ever saw me.' The wobble in her legs had spread dismayingly to her voice.

He drew closer. 'If I could forget you, I wouldn't be here, *cara*.'

Catherine took a hasty step backward. 'Don't you remember all those things I used to do that annoyed you?' she exclaimed in desperation.

'They became endearing when I was deprived of them.'

'Stay away from me!' Hysteria was creeping up on her by speedy degrees as he advanced. 'I'll die if you touch me!'

'And I'll die if I don't. I ought to remind you that I'm a survivor,' Luc drawled almost playfully, reaching for her, golden eyes burning over her small figure in a blaze of hunger. 'You won't remember his name by tomorrow.'

She lunged out of his reach and one of her stiletto heels caught in the fringe of the rug, throwing her right off balance. Her feet went out from under her and she fell, her head bouncing painfully off the edge of something hard. As she cried out, darkness folded in like a curtain falling and she knew no more.

'You can see the area I'm referring to here.' The consultant indicated the shading on the X-ray. 'A previous injury that required quite major surgery. At this stage, however, I have no reason to suspect that she's suffering from anything more than concussion, but naturally she should stay in overnight so that we can keep an eye on her.'

'She's taking a hell of a long time to come round properly.'

'She's had a hell of a nasty bump.' Meeting that narrowed, fierce stare, utterly empty of amusement, the older man mentally matched his facetious response to a lead balloon.

The voices didn't make any sense to Catherine, but she recognised Luc's and was instantly soothed by that recognition. A shard of cut-glass pain throbbed horribly at the base of her skull and, as she shifted her head in a pointless attempt to deaden it, she groaned, her eyes opening on bright light.

Luc swam into focus and she smiled. 'You're all fuzzy,' she mumbled.

A grey-haired man appeared at the other side of the bed and tested her co-ordination. Then he asked her what day it was. She shut her eyes again and thought hard. Her brain felt like so much floating cotton wool. Monday, Tuesday, Wednesday...take your pick. She hadn't a clue what day it was. Come to think of it, she didn't even know what she was doing in hospital.

The question was repeated.

'Can't you see that she's in pain?' Luc demanded in biting exasperation. 'Let her rest.'

'Catherine.' It was the doctor's voice, irritatingly persistent, forcing her to lift her heavy eyelids again. 'Do you remember how you sustained your injury?'

'I've already told you that she fell!' Luc intercepted him a second time. 'Is this interrogation really necessary?'

'I fell,' Catherine whispered gratefully, wishing the doctor would go away and stop bothering her. He was annoying Luc.

'How did you fall?' As he came up with a third question, Luc expelled his breath in an audible hiss and simultaneously the sound of a beeper went off. With a thwarted glance at Luc, the consultant said, 'I'm afraid I'll have to complete my examination in the morning. Miss Parrish will be transferred to her room. Perhaps you'd like to go home, Mr Santini?'

'I'll stay.' It was unequivocal.

Catherine angled a sleepy smile over him, happily basking in the concern he was showing for her well-being. Letting her lashes lower again, she felt the bed she was lying on move. Nurses chattered above her head, complaining about what a wet evening it was, and one of them described some dress she had seen in Marks. It was all refreshingly normal, even if it did make Catherine feel as though she were invisible. Without meaning to, she drifted into a doze.

Waking again, she found herself in a dimly lit, very pleasantly furnished room that didn't mesh with her idea of a hospital. Luc was standing staring out of the window at darkness.

'Luc?' she whispered.

He wheeled round abruptly.

'This may seem an awfully stupid question,' she muttered hesitantly. 'But where am I?'

'This is a private clinic.' He approached the bed. 'How do you feel?'

'As though someone slugged me with a sandbag, but it's not nearly as bad as it was.' She moved her head experimentally on the pillow and winced.

'Lie still,' Luc instructed unnecessarily.

She frowned. 'I don't remember falling,' she acknowledged in a dazed undertone. 'Not at all.'

Luc moved closer, looking less sartorially splendid than was his wont. His black hair was tousled, his tie crumpled, the top two buttons of his silk shirt undone at his brown throat. 'It was my fault,' he said tautly.

'I'm sure it wasn't,' Catherine soothed in some surprise.

'It was.' Dark eyes gleamed down at her almost suspiciously. 'If I hadn't tried to pull you into my arms when you were trying to get away from me, it wouldn't have happened.'

'I was trying to get away from you?' Nothing in her memory-banks could come to terms with that startling concept.

'You tripped over a rug and went down. You struck your head on the side of a table. *Madre de Dio, cara*... I thought you'd broken your neck!' Luc relived with unfamiliar emotionalism, a tiny muscle pulling tight at the corner of his compressed mouth. 'I thought you were dead... I really thought you were dead.' The repetition was harsh, not quite steady.

'I'm sorry.' A vaguely panicky sensation was beginning to nudge at her nerve-endings. If Luc hadn't been there, it would have swallowed her up completely. Yet his intent stare, his whole demeanour was somehow far from reassuring. Other little oddities, beyond her inability to recall her fall, were springing to mind. 'The nurses...that doctor...they were English. Are we in England?' she demanded shakily.

'Are *we*——?' He put a strange stress on her choice of pronoun, his strong features shuttered, uncommunicative. 'We're in London. Don't you know that?' he probed very quietly.

'I don't remember coming to London with you!' Catherine admitted in a stricken rush. 'Why don't I remember?'

Luc appraised her for a count of ten seconds before he abandoned his stance at a distance and dropped down gracefully on to the side of the bed. 'You've got concussion and you're feeling confused. That's all,' he murmured calmly. 'Absolutely nothing to worry about.'

'I can't help being worried—it's scary!' she confided.

'You have nothing to be scared of.' Luc had the aspect of someone carefully de-programming a potential hysteric.

Her fingers crept into contact with the hand he had braced on the mattress and feathered across his palm in silent apology. 'How long have we been in London?'

Luc tensed. 'Is that important?' As he caught her invasive fingers between his and carried them to his mouth, it suddenly became a matter of complete irrelevance.

Watching her from beneath a luxuriant fringe of ebony lashes, he ran the tip of his tongue slowly along each individual finger before burying his lips hotly in the centre of her palm. A quiver of weakening pleasure lanced through her and an ache stirred in her pelvis. It was incredibly erotic.

'Is it?' he prompted.

'Is...what?' she mumbled, distanced from all rational thought by the power of sensation.

Disappointingly, he laid her hand back down, but he retained a grip on it, a surprisingly fierce grip. 'What is the last thing you remember?'

With immense effort, she relocated her thinking processes and was rewarded. Remembering the answer to that question was as reassuringly easy as falling off the proverbial log. 'You had the flu,' she announced with satisfaction.

'The flu.' Black brows drew together in a frown and then magically cleared again. '*Si*, the flu. That was nineteen eighty——'

She wrinkled her nose. 'I do know what year it is, Luc.'

'*Senz'altro.* Of course you do. The year improves like a good vintage.' As she looked up at him uncomprehendingly, he bent over her with a faint smile and smoothed a stray strand of wavy hair from her creased forehead.

'It seems so long ago, and, when I think about it, it seems sort of hazy,' she complained.

'Don't think about it,' Luc advised.

'Is it late?' she whispered.

'Almost midnight.'

'You should go back to the hotel . . . are we in a hotel?' she pressed, anxious again.

'Stop worrying. It'll all come back,' Luc forecast softly. 'Sooner or later. And then we will laugh about this, I promise you.'

His thumb was absently stroking her wrist. She raised her free hand, powered by an extraordinarily strong need just to touch him, and traced the stubborn angle of his hard jawline. His dark skin was blue-shadowed, interestingly rough in texture. He had mesmeric eyes, she reflected dizzily, dark in shadow or dissatisfaction, golden in sunlight or passion. Vaguely she wondered why he wasn't kissing her.

In that department, Luc never required either encouragement or prompting. When he came back from a business trip, he swept through the door, snatched her into his arms and infrequently controlled his desire long enough to reach the bedroom. And when he was with her it sometimes seemed that she couldn't cook or clean or do anything without being intercepted.

It made her feel safe. It made her feel that where there was that much passion, surely there was hope. Only of late she had listened less willingly to another little voice. It was more pessimistic. It told her that expecting even the tiniest commitment from Luc where the future was concerned was comparable with believing in the tooth-fairy.

'I've only forgotten a few weeks, haven't I?' she checked, hastily pushing away those uneasy thoughts which made her so desperately insecure.

'You have forgotten nothing of import.' Brilliant eyes shimmered over her upturned face, meeting hers with the zap of a force-field, and yet still, inconceivably to her, he kept his distance.

'Luc——' she hesitated '—what's wrong?'

'I'm getting very aroused. *Dio*, how can you do this to me just by looking at me?' he breathed with sudden ferocity. 'You're supposed to be sick.'

She didn't know which of them moved first but suddenly he was as close as she wanted him to be and her fingers slid ecstatically into the springy depths of his hair. But, instead of the forceful assault his mood had somehow led her to anticipate, he outlined her parted lips with his tongue and then delved between, tasting her with a sweet, lancing sensuality again and again until her head was spinning and her bones were melting and a hunger more intense than she had ever known leapt and stormed through her veins.

With an earthy groan of satisfaction, Luc dragged her up into his arms and, although the movement jarred her painfully, she was more than willing to oblige him. Thrusting the bedding impatiently away from her, he lifted her and brought her down on his hard thighs without once removing his urgent mouth from hers.

Excitement spiralled as suddenly as summer lightning between them. Wild, hot and primeval. His hand yanked at the high neck of the white hospital gown, loosening it, drawing it away from her upper body. Cooler air washed her exposed skin as he held her back from him, lean hands in a powerful grip on her slender arms. A dark flush over his hard cheekbones, he ran raking golden eyes over the fullness of her pale breasts, the betraying tautness of the pink nipples that adorned them.

Reddening beneath that unashamed, heated appraisal, she muttered feverishly, 'Take me back to the hotel.'

Luc shook her by saying something unrepeatable and closing his eyes. A second later, he wrenched the gown back up over her again, stood up and lowered her into the bed. Tucking the light covers circumspectly round her again, he breathed, '*Chiedo scusa*. I'm sorry. You're not well.'

'I'm fine,' she protested. 'I don't want to stay here.'

'You're staying.' He undid the catch on the window and hauled it up roughly, letting a cold breeze filter into the room. 'You're safer here.'

'Safer?'

'Do you believe in fate, *cara*?'

Her lashes fluttered in bemusement and she turned her head on the pillow. Luc, who had been aghast and then vibrantly amused by her devotion to observing superstitions such as not walking under ladders, avoiding stepping on black lines...Luc was asking her about fate? He looked deadly serious as well. 'Of course I do.'

'One shouldn't fight one's fate,' Luc mused, directing a gleaming smile at her. 'You believe that, don't you?'

She had never had an odder conversation with Luc and she was so exhausted that it was an effort to focus her thoughts. 'I think it would be almost impossible to fight fate.'

'I've no intention of fighting it. It's played right into my hands, after all. Go to sleep, *cara*,' he murmured softly. 'We're flying to Italy in the morning.'

'I-Italy?' she parroted, abruptly shot back into wakefulness.

'Don't you think it's time we regularised our situation?'

Catherine stared at him blankly, one hundred per cent certain that he couldn't mean what she thought he meant.

Luc strolled back to the bed and sank down in the armchair beside her, fixing dark glinting eyes on her. 'I'm asking you to marry me.'

'Are you?' She was so staggered by the assurance that it was the only thing she could think to say.

He scored a reflective fingertip along the line of her tremulous bottom lip. 'Say something?' he invited.

'Have you been thinking of this for long?' she managed jerkily, praying for the shock to recede so that she could behave a little more normally.

'Let's say it crept up on me,' he suggested lightly.

That didn't sound very romantic. Muggers crept up on you; so did old age. A paralysing sense of unreality assailed her. Luc was asking her to marry him. That meant she had been living with a stranger for months. That meant that every disloyal, ungenerous thought she had ever had about him had been wickedly unjustified. Tears welled up in her eyes. Lines of moisture left betraying trails down her pale cheeks.

'What did I say? What didn't I say?' Luc demanded. 'OK, so this is not how you imagined me proposing.'

'I never imagined you proposing!' she sobbed.

With a succinct expletive, he slid his hands beneath her very gently and tugged her on to his lap, hauling off the light bedspread and wrapping it round her. She sniffed and sucked in oxygen, curving instinctively in the heat of him. 'I'm so h-happy,' she told him.

'You have a very individual way of being happy, but then,' a caressing hand smoothed through her silky, tumbled hair, 'you have an individual way of doing most things. We'll get married in Italy. And now that we've decided to do it, we don't want to waste time, do we?'

She rested her head against his chest as he lounged back into a more comfortable position to accommodate her. He was being so gentle and once she had honestly believed that he didn't know how to be. Had her fall given him that much of a shock? Certainly something had provoked an astonishing alteration in Luc's attitude to her... or had she really never understood Luc at all? Did it matter if she couldn't understand him? She decided it didn't.

Luc was planning the wedding. The royal 'we' did not mislead her. She could have listened to him talk all night, but the kind of exhaustion that was a dead weight on her senses was slowly but surely dragging her towards sleep.

CHAPTER FOUR

THE sapphire-blue suit was unfamiliar but it had 'bought to please Luc' stamped in its designer-chic lines. The shoes? Catherine grimaced at the low heels which added little to her diminutive height. She must have been in a tearing hurry when she chose them. They weren't her style at all, but they were a perfect match for the suit. Since co-ordinating her wardrobe had never been one of her talents, she was surprised by the discovery. Luc must have ransacked her luggage to pull off such a feat.

He had been gone when she'd woken, securely back within her bed. Her clothes had arrived after breakfast. Although the effort involved had left her weak, she had been eager to get dressed. A nurse had lightly scolded her for not asking for assistance, adding that Mr Ladwin, the resident consultant, would be in to see her shortly. Catherine couldn't help hoping that Luc arrived first. The prospect of a barrage of probing questions which she wouldn't be able to answer unnerved her.

So, a few weeks had sort of got lost, she told herself bracingly. A few weeks didn't qualify as a real loss of memory, did it? Subduing the panicky sensation threatening, she sat down in the armchair. Of course it would come back and, as Luc had pointed out, it wasn't as though she had forgotten anything important.

Even so, the silliest little things kept on stirring her up. When had she had her hair cut to just below her shoulders? And it was a mess, a real mess! Heaven knew when she had last had a trim. Then there were her hands. She might have been scrubbing floors with them! And there was this funny little dent on her wedding finger, almost as if she had been wearing a ring, and she never put a ring on that finger...

She didn't even recognise the contents of her handbag. She had hoped that something within its capacious depths might jog her memory. She had hoped in vain. Even the purse had been unfamiliar, containing plenty of cash in both dollars and sterling but no credit cards and no photos of Luc. Even the cosmetics she presumably used every day hadn't struck a chord. And where was her passport?

Luc's proposal last night already had a dream-like quality. Luc hadn't been quite Luc as she remembered him. That was the most bewildering aspect of all.

When she had broken an ankle in Switzerland last year, Luc had been furious. He said she was the only person he knew who could contrive to break a limb in the Alps without ever going near a pair of skis. He had stood over her in the casualty unit, uttering biting recriminations about the precarious height of the heels she favoured. The doctor had thought he was a monster of cruelty, but Catherine had known better.

Her pain had disturbed him and he had reacted with native aggression to that disturbance in his usually well-disciplined emotions. Telling her that he'd break her neck if he ever saw her in four-inch stilettos again had been the uncensored equivalent of a major dose of sympathetic concern.

But last night, Luc hadn't been angry...Luc had asked her to marry him. And how could that seem real to her? Her wretched memory had apparently chosen to block out a staggeringly distinct change in her relationship with Luc. Her very presence in London with him when he always jetted about the world alone fully illustrated that change in attitude. But what exactly had brought about that change?

She could not avoid a pained recall of the women Luc had appeared with in newsprint in recent months. Beautiful, pedigreed ladies, who took their place in high society without the slightest doubt of their right to be there. Socialites and heiresses and the daughters of the rich and influential. Those were the sort of women Luc was seen in public with—at charity benefits, movie premières, Presidential dinners.

'I don't sleep with them,' Luc had dismissed her accusations, but still it had hurt. She had looked into the mirror that day and seen her own inadequacy reflected, and she had never felt the same about herself since. It was agonising to be judged and found wanting without ever being aware that there had been a trial.

The door opened abruptly. Luc entered with the consultant in tow. Sunk within the capacious armchair, tears shimmering on her feathery lashes, she looked tiny and forlorn and defenceless in spite of her expensive trappings.

Luc crossed the room in one stride and hunkered down lithely at her feet, one brown hand pushing up her chin. 'Why are you crying?' he demanded. 'Has someone upset you?'

If someone had, they would have been in for a rough passage. Luc was all Italian male in that instant. Protective, possessive, ready to do immediate battle on her behalf. Beneath the cool façade of sophistication, Luc was an aggressively masculine male with very unliberated views on sexual equality. His golden eyes were licking flames on her in over-bright scrutiny. 'If someone has, I want to know about it.'

'I seriously doubt that any of our staff would be guilty of such behaviour.' Mr Ladwin bristled at the very suggestion.

Luc dropped a pristine handkerchief on her lap and vaulted upright. 'Catherine's very sensitive,' he said flatly.

Catherine was also getting very embarrassed. Hastily wiping at her damp cheeks, she said, 'The staff have been wonderful, Luc. I'm just a little weepy, that's all.'

'As I have been trying to explain to you for the past half-hour, Mr Santini,' the consultant murmured, 'amnesia is a distressing condition.'

'And, as you also explained, it lies outside your field.'

Catherine studied the two men uneasily. The undertones were decidedly antagonistic. Ice had dripped from every syllable of Luc's response.

Mr Ladwin looked at her. 'You must feel very confused, Miss Parrish. Wouldn't you prefer to remain here for the present and see a colleague of mine?'

The threat of anything coming between her and the wedding Luc had described so vividly filled Catherine with rampant dismay. 'I want to leave with Luc,' she stressed tautly.

'Are you satisfied?' Luc enquired of the other man.

'It would seem that I have to be.' Scanning the glow that lit Catherine's face when she looked at Luc Santini, the older man found himself wondering with faint envy what it felt like to be loved like that.

Mr Ladwin shook hands and departed. Luc smiled at her. 'The car's outside.'

'I can't find my passport,' she confided abruptly, steeling herself for the disappearance of that smile. Luc got exasperated when she mislaid things.

'Relax,' he urged. 'I have it.'

She sighed relief. 'I thought I'd lost it...along with my credit cards and some photos I had.'

'You left them behind in New York.'

She smiled at the simplicity of the explanation. Her usual disorganisation appeared to be at fault.

'Why were you crying?'

She laughed. 'I don't know,' she said, but she did. 'Has someone upset you?' he had demanded with a magnificent disregard for the obvious. Nobody could hurt her more than Luc and, conversely, nobody could make her happier. Loving Luc put her completely in his power and, for the first time in a very long time, she no longer felt she had to be afraid of that knowledge.

A brown forefinger skimmed the vulnerable softness of her lower lip. 'When I'm here, you don't have to worry about anything,' he censured.

Since meeting Luc, worry had become an integral part of her daily existence. The sharp streak of insecurity ingrained in her by her rootless childhood had been roused from dormancy. But it wasn't going to be like that any more, she reminded herself. As Luc's wife, she would hold a very different position in his scheme of what was important. Depressingly, however, when she struggled to picture herself in that starring role, it still felt like fantasy.

'Why do you want to marry me?' Her hands clenched fiercely together as she forced out that bald enquiry in the lift.

'I refuse to imagine my life without you.' He straightened the twisted collar of her silk blouse and tucked the label out of sight with deft fingers. 'Do you think we could save this very private conversation for a less public moment?' he asked lazily.

Catherine made belated eye-contact with the smiling elderly couple sharing the lift with them and reddened to her hairline. She had been too bound up in her own emotions to notice that they had company. Catherine Santini. Secretly she tasted the name, savoured it, and the upswell of joy she experienced was intense.

'Life doesn't begin with "once upon a time", *cara*, and end "and they all lived happily ever after", Luc had once derided. But, regardless, Luc had just presented her with her dream, gift-wrapped and tagged. Evidently if you hoped hard enough and prayed hard enough, it could happen.

As she crossed to the limousine, the heat of the sun took her by surprise. Her eyes scanned the climbing roses in bloom at the wall bounding the clinic's grounds and her stomach lurched violently. 'It's summer,' she whispered. 'You had the flu in September.'

With inexorable cool, Luc pressed her into the waiting car. Her surroundings were then both familiar and reassuring, but still she trembled. Luc hadn't said a word. Of course, he had known. He had known that she had lost more than a few weeks, had seen no good reason to increase her alarm. Everything now made better sense. No wonder Mr Ladwin had been reluctant to see her leave so quickly. No wonder she didn't recognise her clothes or her hairstyle or the change in Luc. She had lost almost a year of her life.

'Luc, what's happening to me?' she said brokenly. 'What's going on inside my head?'

'Don't try to force it.' His complete calm was wondrously soothing. 'Ladwin advised me not to fill in the blanks for you. He said you should have rest and peace and everything you wanted within reason. Your memory will probably come back naturally, either all at once or in stages.'

'And what if it doesn't?'

'We'll survive. You didn't forget me.' Satisfaction blazed momentarily in his stunning eyes before he veiled them.

The woman who could forget Luc Santini hadn't been born yet. You could love him passionately, hate him passionately, but you couldn't possibly forget him. Hate him? Her brow creased at that peculiar thought and she wondered where it had come from.

'Are you thinking of putting off the wedding?' she asked stiffly. It was the obvious thing to do, the sensible thing to do. And what she most feared was the obvious and the sensible.

'Is that what you want?'

Vehemently she shook her head, refusing to meet his too perceptive gaze. How could she still be so afraid of losing him? He had asked her to marry him. What more could he do? What more could she want?

He didn't love her, he still didn't love her. If she was winning through, it was by default and staying power. She wasn't demanding or difficult, spoilt or imperious. She was loyal and trustworthy and crazy about children. She had had no other lovers. Luc would have a problem coming to terms with a woman who had a past to match his own. And in the bedroom... her skin heated at the acknowledgement that she never said no to him, could hardly contain her pleasure when he touched her. Most importantly of all, perhaps, she loved him, and he was content to be loved as long as she never asked for more than he was prepared to give. All in all, he wasn't so much marrying her as promoting her and, though her pride warred against that reality, it was better than severance pay.

'The wedding will take place within a few days,' Luc drawled casually and, picking up the phone, he began the first of several calls. Finding himself the focus of her attention, a smile of almost startling brilliance slashed his hard mouth and he extended a hand, drawing her under the shelter of his arm. 'You look happy,' he said approvingly.

Only a woman who was fathoms deep in love could lose a year of her life and still be happy. Kicking off her shoes, she rested blissfully back into the lean heat of him, thinking she had to be the luckiest woman alive.

Maybe if she worked incredibly hard at being a perfect wife, he might fall in love with her.

'We're in a traffic jam,' she whispered teasingly, tugging at the end of his tie, feeling infinitely more daring than she had ever felt before. The awareness that they would soon be married was dissolving her usual inhibitions.

Luc tensed into sudden rigidity and stumbled over what he was saying. Leaning over him, bracing one hand on a taut thigh, Catherine reached up and loosened his tie, trailing it off in what she hoped was a slow, seductive fashion.

'Catherine... what are you doing?'

Luc was being abnormally obtuse. Colliding with golden eyes that had a stunned stillness, she went pink and, lowering her head, embarked on the buttons of his shirt. Hiding a mischievous smile, she understood his incredulity. Undressing Luc was a first. Initiating love-making was also a first. She ran caressing fingertips over warm golden skin roughened by black curling hair. His audible intake of oxygen matched to the raw tension in his muscles encouraged her to continue.

There was so much pleasure in simply touching him. It was extraordinary, she thought abstractly, but, although sanity told her it couldn't be possible, she felt starved of him. As she pressed her lips lovingly to his vibrant flesh and kissed a haphazard trail of increasing self-indulgence from his strong brown throat to his flat muscular stomach, he jerked and dropped the phone.

'Catherine...' he muttered, sounding satisfyingly ragged.

Her small hand strayed over his thigh. As she touched him he groaned deep in his throat and a sense of wondering power washed over her. He was trembling, his dark head thrown back, a fevered flush accentuating his hard bone-structure. All this time and it was this easy, she reflected, marvelling at the sheer strength of his response to her.

'Catherine, you shouldn't be doing this.' He was breathing fast and audibly, the words thick and indistinct.

'I'm enjoying myself,' she confided, slightly dazed by what she was doing, but telling the truth.

'*Per amor di Dio*, where's my conscience?' he gasped as she ran the tip of her tongue along his waistband.

'What conscience?' she whispered, lost in a voluptuous world all of her own as she inched down his straining zip.

'*Cristo*, this is purgatory!' Taking her by surprise, Luc jackknifed out of reach at accelerated speed. 'We can't do this. We're nearly at the airport!' he muttered unsteadily.

'We're in a traffic jam.' In an agony of mortification more intense than any she had ever known, she stared at him, her hauntingly beautiful eyes dark with pain.

With a succinct swear-word, he dragged her close, taking her mouth with a wild, ravishing hunger that drove the breath from her lungs and left her aching for more. Every nerve-ending in her body went crazy in that powerful embrace. Plastered to every aroused line of his taut length, the scent of him and the taste of him and the feel of him went to her head with the potency of a mind-blowing narcotic.

Dragging his mouth from hers, he buried his face in her tumbled hair. The sharp shock of separation hurt. His heart was crashing against her crushed breasts. She could literally feel him fighting to get himself back under control. A long, shuddering breath ran through him. 'You're not strong enough for this, Catherine. You're supposed to be resting,' he reminded her almost roughly. 'So, have a little pity, hmm? Don't torture me.'

'I'm not ill. I feel great.' She ignored the throbbing at the base of her skull.

With a hard glance of disagreement, he set her back on the seat. 'You're quite capable of saying that because you think that's what I want to hear. How could you feel great? You must feel lousy, and, the next time I ask, lousy is what I want to hear! Is that clear?'

'As crystal.' Bowing her head, she fought to suppress the silent explosion of amusement that had crept up on her unawares. Why was she laughing? Why the heck was she laughing? Her body was shrieking at the deprivation he had sentenced them both to suffer. It wasn't funny, it really wasn't funny, but if she went to her dying day she would cherish the look of disbelief on his dark features when she, and not he, took the initiative for a change.

She had shocked Luc, actually shocked him. Who would ever have dreamt that she could possess that capability? It made her feel wicked...it made her feel sexy...and his reaction had made her feel like the most wildly seductive woman in the world. And wasn't it sweet, incredibly sweet of her supremely self-centred Luc to embrace celibacy for her benefit?

Once, she was convinced, Luc would have taken her invitation at face value, satisfying his own natural inclinations without further thought. That he *had* thought meant a great deal to her. That brand of unselfish caring was halfway to love, wasn't it? In a state of bliss, Catherine listened to him reeling off terse instructions to some unfortunate, no doubt quailing at the other end of the phone line. She wanted to smile. She knew why Luc was in a bad mood.

They traversed the airport at speed in a crush of moving bodies, security men zealously warding off the reporters and photographers Luc deplored. He guarded his privacy with a ferocity that more than one newspaper had lived to regret.

'Who's the blonde, Mr Santini?' someone shouted raucously.

Without warning, Luc wheeled round, his arm banding round Catherine in a hold of steel. 'The future Mrs Santini,' he announced, taking everyone by surprise, including Catherine.

There was a sudden hush and then a frantic clamour of questions, accompanied by the flash of many cameras. Luc's uncharacteristic generosity towards the Press concluded there.

They were crossing the tarmac to the jet when it happened. Something dark and dreadful loomed at the back of her mind and leapt out at her. The sensation frightened the life out of her and she froze. She saw an elderly woman with grey hair, her kindly face distraught. 'You mustn't do it...you mustn't!' she was pleading. And then the image was gone, leaving Catherine white and dizzy and sick with only this nameless, irrational fear focused on the jet.

'I can't get on it!' she gasped.

'Catherine.' Luc glowered down at her.

'I can't...I can't! I don't know why, but I can't!' Hysteria blossoming, she started to back away with raised hands.

Luc strode forward, planted powerful hands to her narrow waist and swung her with daunting strength into his arms. In the grip of that incomprehensible panic, she struggled violently. 'I can't get on that jet!'

'It's not your responsibility any more.' Luc held her with steely tenacity. 'I'm kidnapping you. Think of it as an elopement. Good afternoon, Captain Edgar. Just ignore my fiancée. She's a little phobic about anything that flies without feathers.'

The pilot struggled visibly to keep his facial muscles straight. 'I'll keep it smooth, Mr Santini.'

Luc mounted the steps two at a time, stowed Catherine into a seat and did up the belt much as though it were a ball and chain to keep her under restraint. He gripped her hands. 'Now breathe in slowly and pull yourself together,' he instructed. 'You can scream all the way to Rome if you like but it's not going to get you anywhere. Think of this as the first day of the rest of your life.'

Gasping in air, she stared at him, wide-eyed. 'I saw this woman. I remembered something. She said I mustn't do it...'

'Do what?'

'She didn't say what.' Already overwhelmingly aware of the foolishness of her behaviour, her voice sank to a limp mumble. 'I had this feeling that I shouldn't board the jet, that I was leaving something behind. It was so powerful. I felt so scared.'

'Do you feel scared now?'

'No, of course not.' She flushed. 'I'm sorry. I went crazy, didn't I?'

'You had a flashback. Your memory's returning.'

'Do you think so?' She brightened, was faintly puzzled by his cool tone and the hard glitter of his gaze. 'Why was I so scared?'

'The shock and the suddenness of it,' he proffered smoothly. 'It couldn't have been a comforting experience.'

The flight lasted two hours. They were not alone. There was the steward and the stewardess, the two security men, a sleek executive type taking notes every time Luc spoke, and a svelte female secretary at his elbow, passing out files and removing them and relaying messages. And the weird part of it all was that if Catherine looked near any of them they hurriedly looked away as if she had the plague or something.

Sitting in solitary state, she beckoned the stewardess. 'Could I have a magazine?'

'There are no magazines or newspapers on board, Miss Parrish. I'm so sorry.' The woman's voice was strained, her eyes evasive. 'Would you like lunch now?'

'Thanks.' It was quite peculiar that there shouldn't even be a magazine on board. Still, she would only have flicked through it. Sooner or later, she would have to tell Luc that she was dyslexic. She cringed at the prospect. She had never expected to be able to fool Luc this long. But somehow he had always made it so easy for her.

If there was a menu in the vicinity, he ordered her meals. He accepted that she preferred to remember phone messages rather than write them down for him, and was surprisingly tolerant when she forgot the details. He never mentioned the rarity with which she read a book. Occasionally she bought one and left it on display, but he never asked what it was about. And why did she go to all that trouble?

She remembered how often she had been called stupid before the condition was diagnosed at school. She remembered all the potential foster parents who had backed off at the very mention of dyslexia, falsely assuming that she would be more work and trouble than any other child. She also remembered all the people who had treated her as though she were illiterate. And if Luc realised he was taking on a wife to whom the written word was almost a blur of disconnected images, he might change his mind about marrying her.

When they landed in Rome, he told her that they were completing their journey by helicopter. 'Where will we be staying?' she prompted.

'We won't be staying anywhere,' he countered. 'We're coming home.'

'Home?' she echoed. 'You've bought a house?'

Luc shifted a negligent hand. 'Wait and see.'

'I haven't been there before, have I? It's not something else that I've forgotten, is it?'

'You've never been in Italy before,' he soothed.

She hated the helicopter and insisted on a rear seat, refusing the frontal bird's-eye view that Luc wanted her to have. The racket of the rotors and her sore head interacted unpleasantly, upsetting her stomach. She kept her head down, only raising it when they touched down on solid ground again.

Luc eased her out into the fresh air again, murmuring, 'Lousy?'

'Lousy,' she gulped.

'I should've thought of that, but I wanted you to see Castelleone from the air.' Walking her way from the helipad, he carefully turned her round. 'This is quite a good vantage point. What do you think?'

If he hadn't been supporting her, her knees would have buckled at the sight which greeted her stunned eyes. Castelleone was a fairy-tale castle with a forest of towers and spires set against a backdrop of lush, thickly wooded hills. Late-afternoon sunlight glanced off countless gleaming windows and cast still reflections of the cream stone walls on the water-lily-strewn moat. She should have been better prepared. She should have known to think big and, where Luc was concerned, think extravagant. He might have little time for history but with what else but history could he have attained a home of such magnificence and grandeur?

'It wasn't for sale when I found it, and it wasn't as pretty as it is now...'

'Pretty?' she protested, finding her tongue again. 'It's beautiful! It must have cost a fortune.'

'I've got money to burn and nothing else to spend it on.' Idle fingertips slid caressingly through her hair. 'It's a listed building, which is damnably inconvenient. The renovations had to be restorations. Experts are very interfering people. There were times when I wouldn't have cared if those walls came tumbling down into that chocolate-box moat.'

'You're joking!' she gasped.

'Am I? Have you ever lived with seventeenth-century plumbing, *cara*? It was barbaric,' Luc breathed above her head. 'The experts and I came to an agreement. The plumbing went into a museum and I stopped threatening to fill in the moat. We understood each other very well after that.'

'You said it wasn't for sale when you first saw it.'

'For everything there is a price, *bella mia*.' With a soft laugh, he linked his arms round her. 'The last owner had no sentimental attachment to the place. It had been a drain on his finances for too long.'

'Did you ever tell me about it?'

'I wanted to surprise you.' He guided her towards the elaborate stone bridge spanning the moat. Tall studded doors stood wide on a hall covered with exquisitely painted frescoes.

'I've never seen anything so beautiful,' she whispered.

'Admittedly not everyone has a foyer full of fat cherubs and bare-breasted nymphs. I'll concede that if I concede nothing else,' Luc said mockingly. 'The original builder wasn't over-endowed with good taste.'

'If you don't like it, why did you buy it?' she pressed, struggling to hold back her tiredness.

He moved a broad shoulder. 'It's an investment.'

'Does that mean you plan to sell it again?' Her dismay was evident.

'Not if you feel you can live with all those naked women.'

'I can live with them!'

'Somehow,' he murmured softly, 'I thought you would feel like that.'

Luc appraised her pallor, the shadows like bruises below her eyes, and headed her to the curving stone staircase. 'Bed, I think.'

'I don't want to go to bed. I want to see the whole castle.' If it was a dream that Luc should want to marry her and live in this glorious building, she was afraid to sleep lest she wake up.

'You've had all the excitement you can take for one day.' Luc whipped her purposefully off her feet when she showed signs of straying in the direction of an open doorway. 'Why are you smiling like that?'

'Because I feel as though I've died and gone to heaven and——' she hesitated, sending him an adoring look '—I love you so much.'

Dark blood seared his cheekbones, his jawline hardening. Unconcerned, she linked her arms round his throat. 'I'm not a plaster saint,' he breathed.

'I can live with your flaws.'

'You'll have to live with them,' he corrected. 'Divorce won't be one of your options.'

She winced, pained by that response. 'It isn't very romantic to talk about divorce before the wedding.'

'Catherine... as you ought to know by now, I'm not a very romantic guy. I'm not poetic, I'm not sentimental, I'm not idealistic,' he spelt out grimly.

'You make love in Italian,' she said in a small voice.

'It's the first language I ever spoke!'

For some peculiar reason, he was getting angry. She decided to let him have his own way. If he didn't think sweeping her off to a castle in Italy and marrying her within days was romantic, he had a problem. It might be wise, she decided, to share a little less of her rapture. But it was very difficult. Feeling weak and exhausted didn't stop her from wanting to pin him to the nearest horizontal surface and smother him with grateful love and kisses.

At the top of that unending staircase, Luc paused to introduce her to a little man called Bernardo, who rejoiced in the title of major-domo. Catherine beamed at him.

'Do you think you could possibly pin those dizzy feet of yours back to mother earth for a while?' Luc enquired sardonically.

'Not when you're carrying me,' she sighed.

Thrusting open a door, he crossed a large room and settled her down on a bed. It was a four-poster, hung with tassels and fringes and rich brocade. She rested back with a groan of utter contentment, lifted one leg and kicked off a shoe, repeated the action with the other. It was definitely her sort of bed.

His expressive mouth quirked. 'I've arranged for a doctor to see you in half an hour. Do you think you could manage to look less as though you've been at the sherry?'

'What do I need another doctor for?'

A smile angled over her. 'Amnesia is a distressing condition, or so the story goes. I've never seen you like this... at least,' he paused, 'not in a long time.'

'You've never asked me to marry you before,' she whispered shyly.

'A serious oversight. You've never tried to seduce me in the back of a limousine before, either.' Golden eyes rested on her intently and then, abruptly, he took his attention off her again. 'I don't think you'll find Dr Scipione too officious. He believes that time heals all.' He strolled back to the door, lithe as a leopard on the prowl. 'Bernardo's wife will come up and help you to get into bed.'

'I don't need——'

'Catherine,' he interrupted, 'one of the minor advantages of being my wife is being waited on hand and foot, thus saving your energy for more important pursuits.'

Her eyes danced. 'And one of the major ones?'

Hooded dark eyes wandered at a leisurely pace over her, and heat pooled in her pelvis, her stomach clenching. 'I'll leave that to your imagination, active as I know it to be. *Buona sera, cara.* I'll see you tomorrow.'

'Tomorrow?' She sat up in shock.

'Rest and peace.' Luc made the reminder mockingly and shut the door.

She stared up at the elaborately draped canopy above her. You were flirting with him, a little voice said. What was so strange about that? She couldn't ever recall doing it before. As a rule, she guarded and picked and chose her words with Luc in much the same fashion as one trod a careful passage round a sleeping volcano. Only at the beginning had she been naïve enough to blurt out exactly what was on her mind.

But she wasn't conscious of that barrier now, hadn't been all day or even last night. She was no longer in awe of Luc. When had that happened? Presumably some time during this past year. And yet Luc had said he had never seen her like this in a long time. What was this? This, she conceded, hugging a pillow dripping lace and ribbons to her fast-beating heart, was being wonderfully, madly and utterly without restraint . . . happy.

CHAPTER FIVE

THE rails of clothing in the dressing-room bedazzled Catherine. Encouraged, the little maid, Guilia, pressed back more doors: day-wear, evening-wear, leisure-wear, shelves of cobwebby, gorgeous lingerie and row upon row of shoes, everything grouped into tiny bands of colour. Co-ordination for the non-colour-clever woman, she thought dazedly. Luc had bought her an entire new wardrobe.

Such an extensive collection could not have been put together overnight. Overwhelming as the idea was, she could only see one viable explanation—Luc must have been planning to bring her to Italy for months! As her fingertips lingered on a silk dress, Guilia looked anxious and swung out a full-length gown, contriving to be very apologetic about the suggested exchange.

'*Grazie*, Guilia.'

'Prego, signorina.' With enthusiasm, Guilia whipped out lingerie and shoes and carried the lot reverently through to the bedroom. Catherine recognised a plant when she saw one. Guilia was here to educate her in the nicest possible way on what to wear for every possible occasion. Luc excelled on detail. Guilia had probably been programmed to bar the wardrobe doors if presented with a pretty cabbage-rose print.

It was eight in the evening. She had slept the clock round, slumbering through her first day at Castelleone. Last night, Bernardo's wife, Francesca, had fussed her into bed with the warmth of a mother hen. Dr Scipione had then made his début, a rotund little man with a pronounced resemblance to Santa Claus and an expression of soulful understanding.

Only when he had gone had she realised that she had chattered her head off the whole time he was there. He had only made her uneasy once by saying, 'Sometimes the mind forgets because it wants to forget. It shuts a door in self-protection.'

'What would I want to protect myself from?' she laughed.

'Ask yourself what you most fear and there may well lie the answer. It could be that when you fully confront that fear your mind will unlock that door,' he suggested. 'I suspect that you are not ready for that moment as yet.'

What did she most fear? Once it had been losing Luc, but since Luc had asked her to marry him that old insecurity had been banished forever. And the truth was that a little hiccup in her memory-banks did not currently have the power to alarm her—despite a nagging anxiety which she resolutely banished.

Attired in the fitting cerise-hued sheath, which was tighter over the fullness of her breasts than Guilia seemed to have expected, judging by the speed with which she had whipped out a tape-measure, Catherine sat down at the magnificent Gothic-styled dressing-table and smiled at the familiarity of the jewellery on display there. Her watch, stamped with the date she had first met Luc; clasping it to her wrist, she marvelled at how long it seemed since she had worn it. A leather box disclosed a slender diamond necklace and drop earrings; a second, a shimmering delicate bracelet. Christmas in Switzerland and her birthday, she reflected dreamily.

Leaving the bedroom, she peered over the stone balcony of the vast circular gallery. Bernardo's bald-spot was visible in the hall far below. She hurried downstairs and said in halting Italian, '*Buona sera*, Bernardo. *Dov'é* Signor Santini?'

Bernardo looked anguished. He wrung his hands and muttered something inaudible. Abruptly she turned, her eyes widening. Raised voices had a carrying quality in the echoing spaces around them.

One of the doors stood ajar. A tall black-haired woman, with shoulder-pads that put new meaning into power-dressing, was ranting, presumably at Luc, who was out of view. Or was she pleading? It was hard to tell.

Catherine tensed. She had no difficulty in recognising Rafaella Peruzzi. She was the only person Catherine knew who could argue with Luc and still have a job at the end of the day. She inhabited a nebulous grey area in Luc's life, somewhere between old friend and employee. She was also Santini Electronics' most efficient hatchet-woman. She lived, breathed, ate and slept profit . . . and Luc.

She had grown up with him. She had modelled herself on him. She was tough, ruthless and absolutely devoted to his interests. At some stage she had also shared a bed with Luc. Nobody had told Catherine that. Nobody had needed to tell her. Rafaella was a piece of Luc's past, but the past was a hopeful present in her eyes every time she looked at him. The women who blazed a quickly forgotten trail through his bedroom didn't bother Rafaella. Catherine had.

'You've got six weeks left. Enjoy him while you can,' she had derided the first time Catherine met her. 'With Luc, it never lasts longer than three months, and, with the clothes-sense you've got, honey, another six weeks should be quite a challenge for him.'

Luc was talking very quietly now. Rafaella vented a strangled sob and spat back in staccato Italian. Catherine moved away, ashamed that she hadn't moved sooner, and uneasily certain of the source of the drama. Yesterday, Luc had publicly announced his marital plans. Rafaella was reeling. Her pain seared Catherine with a strange sister pain. There but for the grace of God go I.

Luc was the sun round which Rafaella revolved. She could not resist that pull even when it scorched her; she could not break free. Though she knew that she was overstepping the boundaries that Luc set, she would still interfere. That was Rafaella. Stubborn, persistent, remorseless in enmity. Sometimes what disturbed Catherine most about Rafaella was her similarity to Luc. By the law of averages, she had thought uneasily more than once, Luc and Rafaella ought to have been a match made in heaven.

A door slammed on its hinges with an almighty crash. Bernardo had made himself scarce. Catherine wasn't quick enough. Rafaella stalked across the hall and circled her like a killer shark drawn by a lump of raw meat, rage and hatred splintering from her diamond-hard stare.

'You bitch!' She launched straight into attack. 'He wouldn't believe me when I told him, but I'll be back when I can prove it. And when I get the evidence you'll be out with the garbage, because he'll never forgive you!'

'Rafaella.' Luc was poised fifty feet away, lithe and sleek as a panther about to spring, his features savagely set.

She shot him a fierce, embittered glance. 'I wanted a closer look at the only truly honest woman you've ever met! She must be on the endangered species list. And, *caro*,' she forecast on her passage to the door, 'you're in for a severe dose of indigestion.'

Bernardo reappeared out of nowhere and surged to facilitate her exit. Catherine slowly breathed again. Rafaella, out of control and balked of her prey, was an intimidating experience. And she was astounded by her threats. What wouldn't Luc believe? What did Rafaella intend to prove? What would Luc never forgive her for?

'What on earth was she talking about?' she whispered tautly.

Smouldering tension still vibrated from Luc. She could read nothing in the steady beat of his dark eyes. For an instant it seemed to her that that stare both probed and challenged, but she dismissed the idea when a faintly sardonic smile lighted his expression. 'Nothing that need concern you.'

But it *did* concern her, she reasoned frustratedly as he curved a possessive arm to her slim shoulders and guided her into the magnificently proportioned *salone*. 'And Rafaella need not concern you either,' he completed.

'Why?' she prompted uncertainly.

'As of now, she no longer works for me,' Luc drawled with a chilling lack of sentiment.

Catherine was immediately filled with guilt. Rafaella lived for her career. If she hadn't been hanging about in the hall, the incident which had so enraged Luc would never have occurred. 'She was terribly upset, Luc. Shouldn't you make allowances for that?' she muttered after a long pause, resenting the ironic twist of fate that had set her up as the brunette's sole defender.

'What is wrong with you?' Luc demanded, abrasive in his incredulity. 'In the same position, she'd slit your throat without a second's hesitation. She walks into my home, she insults me, she insults you . . . and you expect me to take that lying down? I don't believe this!'

'She lost her head and it wouldn't have happened if . . . if . . .' she fumbled awkwardly beneath his piercing scrutiny '. . . she didn't love you.'

'Love like that I can do without,' he responded, unmoved.

'Sometimes,' she whispered, 'you can be very unfeeling, Luc.'

His superb bone-structure clenched, something more than irritation leaping through him now. 'Which translates to a ruthless, insensitive bastard, does it not?' he sizzled back at her.

Nobody criticised Luc. Rafaella might argue with him, but she would not have dreamt of criticising him. From being an infant prodigy in a very ordinary, poorly educated family in awe of his intellectual gifts, Luc had stalked into early adulthood, unfettered by any need or demand to consider anyone but himself. But he was in the wrong and she was helplessly tempted to tell him that plainly, had to bite back the words. He could not treat Rafaella as an old friend one moment and a humble employee the next. It had not been a kindness to keep Rafaella so close when he was aware of her feelings for him. It had only encouraged her to hope.

'I didn't say that,' she said tightly. 'Don't shout me down.'

'I am not shouting you down. You fascinate me. You belong up on a cloud with a harp!' he derided with acid bite. 'You haven't the slightest conception of what makes other human beings tick.'

Catherine lifted her chin. 'I only said that Rafaella deserves a little compassion——'

'Compassion? If you were bleeding to death by the side of the road, she'd sell tickets!' he grated. 'She's out because I don't trust her any more. I understand her too well. The first opportunity she gets, she'll stick a knife in your back, even if it costs her everything she has.'

Her flesh chilled involuntarily at the deadly certainty with which he voiced that belief.

'The subject is now closed. Are you coming to dinner?' he concluded drily.

'Will you give her a reference?'

There was a sharp little silence. Luc spun back, clashed with the hauntingly beautiful blue eyes pinned expectantly to him. '*Per amor di Dio*... all right, if that's what you want!' he gritted, out of all patience.

He wasn't built to recognise compromise. Compromise was a retrograde step towards losing, and losing didn't come gracefully to Luc. Catherine tucked into her dinner with unblemished appetite. Luc poked at his appetiser, complained about the temperature of the wine, sat tapping his fingers in tyrannical tattoo between courses and cooled down only slowly.

'What did you think of Dr Scipione?' he enquired over the coffee.

'He was very kind. Is he the local doctor?'

An ebony brow quirked. 'He lives in Rome. He's also one of the world's leading authorities on amnesia.'

'Oh.' Catherine almost choked on her dismay. 'I treated him as if he was just anybody!'

'Catherine, one of your greatest virtues is the ability to treat everyone from the lowliest cleaning-lady up in exactly the same way,' he murmured, unexpectedly linking his fingers with hers, a smile curving the formerly hard line of his lips. 'Let us at least agree that your manners are a great deal better than mine. By the way, I have some papers for you to sign before we can get married. We should take care of them now.'

She accompanied him into the library where he had been with Rafaella earlier. It was packed with books from floor to ceiling, and a massive desk sat before the tall windows. Fierce discomfiture gripped her when she saw the sheaf of documents he lifted. Forms to fill in...bureaucracy. With Luc present, her worst nightmare had full substance.

'This is the...' Luc handed her a pen but she didn't absorb his explanation. There was a thunderbeat of tension in her ears. 'You sign here.' A brown forefinger indicated the exact spot and stayed there.

The paper was a grey and white blur. Covertly she bent her head. 'I just s-sign?' she stammered, terrified that there was something else to do that he wasn't mentioning because he would naturally assume that she could easily see it and read it for herself.

'You just sign.'

She inscribed her signature slowly and carefully. Luc whipped the document away and presented her with a second. 'And here.'

More hurriedly, less carefully, she complied. 'Is that it?' Struggling to conceal her relief at his nod of confirmation, she lifted the document. 'You once told me never to sign anything I couldn't read,' she joked unsteadily.

'I was more obtuse than I am now.' He studied her. The strain etched in her delicate profile was beginning to ease but her hand was shaking perceptibly. 'It's in Italian, *cara*,' he told her very gently.

'I wasn't really looking at it.' Clumsily she put it down again.

Before she could turn away, lean hands came down to rest on her tense shoulders, keeping her in front of him where he lounged on the edge of the polished desk. 'I believe it's more than that,' he countered quietly. 'Don't you think it's time that we stopped playing this game? Whether you realise it or not, it's caused a lot of misunderstanding between us.'

Her face had gone chalk-white. 'G-game?'

He sighed. 'Why do you think I choose your meals for you when we dine out?'

'I . . . I dither; it saves time,' she muttered, making an abrupt move to walk away, but he was impervious to the hint.

'And I'm just naturally insensitive to what you might choose for yourself?' he chided. 'Catherine, I've been aware that you have trouble reading since the first week

I spent with you in London. I saw through all those painfully elaborate little stratagems and, I have to admit, I was pretty shocked.'

Her stricken gaze veiled as tears lashed her eyelids in a blistering surge. She wanted the ground to open up and swallow her. His deep voice, no matter how calm and quiet it was, stung like a whip on her most vulnerable skin. Her throat was convulsing and she couldn't speak. All she wanted to do was get away from him, but his arms banded round her slim waist like steel hawsers.

'We are going to have this all out in the open,' Luc informed her steadily. 'Why didn't you tell me right at the beginning that you were dyslexic? I didn't realise that. You were ashamed of it and I didn't want to hurt your feelings, so I pretended as well. I ignored it but, in my ignorance of the true situation, I hoped very much that you would do something about it.'

'I can't!' she gasped. 'They did all they could for me at school but I'll never be able to read properly!'

'Do you think I don't know that now? Will you stop trying to get away from me?' he demanded, subduing her struggles with determined hands. 'I know that you're dyslexic, but I didn't know it then. I thought——'

'You thought I was just illiterate!' she sobbed in agonised interruption. 'I'll never forgive you for doing this to me!'

'You're going to listen to me.' He held her fast. 'I was at fault as well. I took the easy way out. What I didn't like, I chose not to see. I should have tried to help you myself. Had I done that, I would have realised what was really wrong. But you should have told me,' he censured.

'Let go of me!' she railed at him, shaken by tempestuous sobs of humiliation.

'Don't you understand what I'm trying to tell you?' He gave her a fierce little shake that momentarily roused her from her distress. 'If I had known, if I had understood, I wouldn't have been angry when you made no effort to improve your situation! I'm not getting through to you, am I?'

'You're ashamed of me!' she accused him despairingly.

Sliding upright, he crushed her into his arms and laced one hand into the golden fall of her hair to tip her head back. 'No, I'm not,' he contradicted fiercely. 'There is nothing to be ashamed of. Einstein was dyslexic, da Vinci was dyslexic. If it was good enough for them, it's good enough for you!'

'Oh, Luc!' A laugh somewhere between a hiccup and a sob escaped her as she looked up at him. 'Good enough? I probably have it worse than they did.'

'I don't know how I could have been so blind for so long,' he admitted. 'You have no sense of direction, you can't tell left from right, the tying of a bow defeats you, and sometimes you're just a little forgetful.' There was a teasing, soothing quality to that concluding statement.

She was still shaking. Her distress had been too great to ebb quickly. She buried her face in his jacket, weak and uncertain, but beyond that there was this glorious sense of release from a pretence that had frequently lacerated her nerves and kept her in constant fear of discovery.

'You don't mind, you really don't mind?' she muttered.

'All that I mind is that you didn't trust me enough to tell me yourself, but, now I know, we can speak to an educational specialist—I'm sure you can be helped.' Tipping her head back, he produced a hanky and automatically mopped her up, smiling down at her, and something about that smile made her heart skip an entire beat. 'It wasn't brave to suffer in silence, it was foolish. I would have understood your difficulties. We live in a world in which the capacity to interpret the written word is taken for granted. How did you manage to work in the art gallery? I've often wondered that,' he confided.

'Elaine taped the catalogue for me.'

He finger-combed her hair back into a semblance of order. 'Secrets,' he said, 'create misunderstandings.'

'That's the only one I have,' she sighed. 'You're always tidying me up and putting me back together again.'

'Maybe I enjoy doing it. Have you thought of that?' he teased, his husky voice fracturing slightly as she stared up at him.

All the oxygen in the air seemed to be used up without warning. Desire clutched at her stomach in a lancing surge. Her breasts felt constrained within their silken covering as her sensitive flesh swelled and her nipples peaked into tight aching buds. The sensations were blindingly physical, unnervingly powerful, and she trembled.

He withdrew his hand from her hair and stepped back. 'It's late. You should go to bed,' he muttered harshly. 'If you don't, I'll take you here.'

A heady flush lit her cheeks. She backed away obediently on cotton-wool legs. She couldn't drag her eyes from his dark-golden beauty. The view was spiced by her intrinsic awareness of the savage sexual intensity contained below that surface calm and control. She wanted him. She wanted him so much that it scared her. In her memory there was nothing to equal the force of the hunger she was experiencing now. It confused her, embarrassed her.

'I'm expecting an important call,' he added, and, as she looked at him in surprise, said succinctly, 'Time zones.'

She couldn't picture Luc sitting up to take a phone call, no matter how important it was. People called at his convenience, not their own. Still watching him, she found the door more by accident than design and fumbled it open. 'I really am feeling marvellous,' she assured him in a self-conscious rush before she ducked out into the hall.

Although she had bathed earlier, Catherine decided to have a refreshing shower. Fifteen minutes later, liberally anointed with some of the scented essences she had found on a shelf in the *en suite* bathroom, she donned the diaphanous peach silk nightdress lying across the bed and slid between the sheets to lie back in a breathless state of anticipation and wait for Luc.

The minutes dragged past. She amused herself by thinking lovingly of how reassuring he had been about her dyslexia. He was right. She should have confided in him a long time ago. He would have understood. She saw that now, regretted her silence and subterfuge, and felt helplessly guilty about misjudging him so badly.

Somewhere in the midst of these ruminations, she dozed off and dreamt. It was the strangest dream. She was writing on a mirror, sound-spelling 'Ah-ree-va'...and she was crying while she did it, reflections of what she was writing and her own unhappy face making the task all the more difficult. There was so much pain in that image that she wanted to scream with it, and she woke up with a start in the darkness, tears wet on her cheeks.

Somebody had switched the light out. She made that connection, bridging the gap between a piece of the past she had forgotten and the present. She slumped back against the pillows, clinging to the dream, but there was so little of it to hold on to and build on. It was the pain she recalled most, a bewildered, frantic sense of pain and defeat.

Padding into the bathroom, she splashed her face and dried it. Who had switched the light off? It must have been Luc. He had come to her and she had been fast asleep. She lifted a weak hand to her forehead where the pounding in her temples was only slowly steadying. It was impossible to stifle a sudden, desperate, tearing need to be with him.

She approached the door in her bedroom which she assumed connected with his. Finding it locked, she frowned and crept out on to the gallery, dimly wondering what time it was. The bedroom itself was in darkness when she entered, but a triangle of light was spilling from the open bathroom door. She could hear a shower running and she smiled. It couldn't be that late. She scrambled into the turned-back bed as quietly as a mouse.

The shower went off and the light almost simultaneously. A second or two later the bedroom curtains were drawn back. Luc unlatched one of the windows and stood there in the moonlight, magnificently naked, towelling his hair dry.

He was asking to catch his death of cold but the urge to announce her presence dwindled. Whipcord muscles flexed taut beneath the smooth golden skin of his back. Her mouth ran dry. Feeling mortifyingly like a voyeur, she closed her eyes. The mattress gave slightly with his weight and three-quarters of the sheet was wrenched from her.

As he rolled over, punching a pillow and narrowly missing her head, he came into sudden contact with her. *'Dio!'* Jerking semi-upright, he lunged at the light above the bed before she could prevent him.

One hand braced tautly on the carved headboard, he stared down at her in shock. 'Catherine?'

She could feel one of those ghastly beetroot blushes crawling in a tide over her exposed skin. Somehow his tone implied that the very last place he expected to find her was in his bed. 'I couldn't sleep.'

He slid lower on the mattress, surveying her intently, his cheekbones harshly accentuated. 'No more could I. Come here.' He reached out with a determined hand and brought her close, not giving her time to respond to what was more of a command than a request. 'I want you,' he admitted roughly. 'Do you have any idea how much I want you?'

'I'm here,' she whispered, suddenly shy of him.

Bending his dark head, he muttered something ferocious in Italian and crushed her lips apart with a savage urgency that took her very much by surprise. His tongue ravished the tender interior of her mouth. She might have been a life-saving draught to a male driven to the edge of madness by thirst. He bruised her lips and drank deep and long until her head swam and she couldn't breathe. Fire as elemental as he was leapt through her veins.

Her hands found his shoulders. He was burning up as though he had a fever, his skin hot and dry, his long, hard body savagely tense against hers. Lean fingers fumbled with an unusual lack of dexterity at the silk that concealed her from him. With a stifled growl of frustration, he drew back and tore the whisper-fine fabric apart with impatient hands.

'Luc!' Catherine surfaced abruptly from a drowning well of passion and fixed shocked eyes on him as he knelt over her, trailing the torn remnants from her and tossing them carelessly aside. As she made an instinctive attempt to cover herself from his devouring scrutiny, he caught at her wrists and flattened them to the bed.

'Please.' It was a word he very rarely employed and there was a note in that roughened plea that stabbed at her heart and made her ache.

Brilliant golden eyes ran over her in a look as physical as touch, exploring the burgeoning swell of her breasts, the smoothness of her narrow ribcage, the feminine curve of her hips and the soft curls at the juncture of her thighs.

'Squisita...perfetta,' he muttered raggedly as he drew her towards him, and his mouth swooped down to capture a taut nipple.

Her back arched as a whimper of formless sound was torn from her throat. He suckled her tender flesh with an intensely erotic enjoyment that drove her wild. He bit with subtle delicacy, his hand toying with the neglected twin, shaping, tugging, exciting until she was writhing beneath his ministrations. She wanted his weight on her and he denied her, lifting his head only to trail the tip of his tongue teasingly down between her breasts, traversing the pale skin of her ribs and dipping into the hollow of her navel.

Her hands dug into his hair and tightened in immediate protest as he strung a line of wholly determined kisses from the bend of her knee to the smooth inner skin of her thigh, tensing tiny muscles she didn't know she possessed. And then her neck extended and her head fell back on the pillows. A cry fled her lips, all thought arrested as she sank into the seduction of pure sensation and was lost in the frantic clamour of her own body.

At the peak of an excitement more of agony than pleasure, Catherine cried out his name, and his hands curved hard to her hips as he rose above her, silencing her with the tormenting force of his mouth. Against her most tender flesh, he was hot and insistent. For a split second he stared down at her, desire and demand stamped in his dark, damp features, and then he moved, thrusting deep as a bolt of lightning rending the heavens.

Pain clenched her, unexpected enough to dredge her briefly from the driving, all-enveloping hunger for satisfaction that he had induced. He stilled, dealt her a look in which tenderness and triumph blazed, more blatant than speech, and pressed a fleeting benediction of a kiss to her brow. He muttered something about doubting her and never doubting her again.

She was in no condition to absorb what he was saying. With tiny, subtle, circling movements of his hips, he was inciting her to passion again, accustoming her to his fullness. All conscious thought was suspended. She was lost in the primal rhythm of giving all and taking everything, driven mindless and powerless towards that final shattering release. When it came in wave after wave of unbelievable pleasure, it was sublime.

His harsh groan of masculine satisfaction still echoing in her ears, she let her hands rove possessively over his sweat-dampened skin. Obtrusive questions licked at the corners of her mind. Had it ever been that profound, that overwhelming before? She remembered excitement, but not an excitement that swept her so quickly into oblivion. She remembered his hunger, but not a hunger that threatened to rage out of control in its raw intensity. She remembered the sweet joy of fulfilment, but not a fulfilment that stole her very soul with its fiery potency.

And she also remembered...sadly...that Luc was invariably halfway to the shower by now, shunning with that essential detachment of his the aftermath of passion when she had so desperately wanted him to stay in her arms.

He was holding her now as if at any moment she might make a break for freedom, and the awareness provoked a deep rush of tenderness within her. She rubbed her cheek lovingly against a strong brown shoulder. He shifted languorously like a sleek cat stretching beneath a caress, as unashamedly physical in his enjoyment as any member of the animal kingdom.

'I had a very strange dream.' She broke the silence hesitantly, afraid that the magic might escape. 'I don't know if it was a memory.'

Tension snaked through his relaxed length. 'What was it?'

'You'll probably laugh.'

'I promise I won't. Tell me.'

'I was writing on a mirror,' she whispered. 'Can you imagine that? I never write anything but my name unless I can help it, and there I was, writing on this mirror!'

'Amazing,' he murmured softly.

'It wasn't. It felt scary,' she muttered, half under her breath. 'It probably has nothing to do with my memory at all. What do you think?'

'I think you're talking too much.' Rolling over, he carried her with him on to a cool spot on the bed. 'And I would much rather make love, *bella mia*.' He nipped teasingly at the velvet-soft lobe of her ear and forged an erotic path along the slender arch of her throat as she involuntarily extended it for his pleasure. Her hair splayed out across the pillow and he studied the chopped ends wryly and looked down at her. 'You've been using scissors to hack at your hair again.'

'I can't think why,' she confessed with a slight frown. 'I'll go and get it cut tomorrow.'

'Someone can come here to take care of it,' he countered.

'I want to see Rome.'

'Bumper-to-bumper traffic and unbelievable heat and noise and pollution. Not to mention the tourists.' He extracted a long lingering kiss before she could protest, and then he started to make love to her again. This time he was incredibly gentle and seductive, utilising every art to enthrall her. Pleasure piled on pleasure in layers of ever-deepening delight. Incredibly, it was even more exciting than the first time.

A single white rose lay on the pillow when she opened her eyes. She discovered it by accident, her hand feeling blindly across the bed in automatic search for Luc. Instead she found a thorn and, with a yelp, she reared up, sucking her pricked finger. And there it was. The rose. She wanted to cry, but that was soppy. The dew still dampened the petals. She tried to picture her supremely elegant Luc clambering through a rosebed and failed utterly. A gardener had undoubtedly done the clambering. Luc wouldn't be caught dead in a flowerbed. All the same, it was the thought which counted and, for an unromantic guy, he really was trying very hard to please. In the end, it was that reflection rather than the rose that flooded her eyes with tears.

CHAPTER SIX

THE heat had reduced Catherine to a somnolent languor. She heard footsteps, recognised them. The cool of a large parasol blocked out the sun and shadowed her. She turned her head, rested her chin on her elbow and watched Luc sink down on the edge of the lounger beside her. In an open-necked short-sleeved white shirt and fitting black jeans that accentuated slim hips and long, lean thighs, he looked stunning enough to stop an avalanche in its tracks. A sun-dazed smile tilted her soft lips. He also looked distinctly short-tempered.

Since wedding fervour had hit Castelleone, the peace, the privacy and the perfect organisation which Luc took for granted had been swept away by a chattering tidal wave of caterers and florists and constantly shrilling phones. Luc's enthusiasm had waned with almost comical speed once he'd realised what throwing a reception for several hundred people entailed.

'I feel like throwing them all out,' he admitted grimly.

'You wanted a big splash,' she reminded him with more truth than tact.

'I thought it was what you expected!' he condemned.

'A couple of witnesses and a bunch of flowers would have done me,' she confided, feeling too warm and lazy to choose her words.

He threw up expressive hands. 'Now she tells me!'

The rattle of ice in glasses interrupted them. Luc leapt up and carefully intercepted Bernardo before he could come any closer. Catherine absorbed this defensive exercise with hidden amusement. Anyone would have been forgiven for thinking that her bare back was the equivalent of indecent exposure. Yesterday, a low-flying light plane had provoked an embargo on topless sunbathing and a no doubt fierce complaint to the local airfield. She wondered why it had taken her all this time to notice just how shockingly old-fashioned Luc could be about some things.

He cast her a sardonic glance. 'I love the way you lie out here as though there's nothing happening.'

'Bernardo knows exactly what he's doing.' With an excess of tact, she did not add that if Luc stopped wading in to interfere and organise, imbuing everyone with the feeling that their very best wasn't good enough, the last-minute arrangements would be proceeding a lot more smoothly. Having given the intimidating impression that he intended to supervise and criticise every little detail, he was not receiving a moment's peace.

Tomorrow, she reflected blissfully. Tomorrow, she would be Luc's wife. The 'died and gone to heaven' sensation embraced her again. Whole days had slid away in a haze of hedonistic pleasure since her arrival in Italy. Never had she enjoyed such utter relaxation and self-indulgence. Her sole contribution to the wedding had been two dress-fittings. Her gown, fashioned of exquisite handmade lace, was gorgeous. It was wonderful what could be achieved at short notice if you had as much money as Luc had.

'Tomorrow, I'll be rich,' she mused absently.

After an arrested pause, Luc flung back his gleaming dark head and roared with laughter. 'You're probably the only woman in the world who would dare to say that to me *before* the wedding.'

She gave him an abstracted smile. Luc? Luc was wonderful, fantastic, beautiful, incredible, divine... With unwittingly expressive eyes pinned to him, she ran out of superlatives, and he sent her a glittering look that made her toes curl. That detachment which had once frozen her out when she got too close was steadily becoming a feature of the past.

Last night, Luc had actually talked about his family. And he never talked about them. The death of his parents and sister in that plane crash had shattered him but he had never actually come close to admitting that fact before. And she was quite certain that he would never admit the guilt he had suppressed when they died. On the rise to the top, Luc had left his family behind.

He had given them luxury, but not the luxury of himself. Business had always come first. He had sent them off on an expensive vacation in apology for yet another cancelled visit and he had never seen them alive again. When he had talked about them last night, it had been one of those confiding conversations that he could only bring himself to share with forced casualness in the cloaking darkness of the bedroom. Until now, she had never understood just how very difficult it was for Luc to express anything which touched him deeply.

Sliding up on her knees, she lifted her bikini top. His dark eyes travelled in exactly the direction she had known they would, lingering on the unbound curves briefly revealed. A heady pink fired her cheeks but, as she arched her back to do up the fastener, the all-male intensity of his appraisal roused an entirely feminine satisfaction as old as Eve within her.

'You like me looking at you,' he commented, lazily amused.

She bent her head, losing face and confidence. 'You're not supposed to notice that.'

'I can't help noticing it when you look so smug.'

Leaning lithely forward, he scooped her bodily across the divide between the loungers with that easy strength of his that melted her somewhere deep down inside. He laced an idle hand into her hair and claimed her mouth in a provocative sensual exploration. The world lurched violently on its axis and went into a spin, leaving her light-headed and weak. It didn't matter how often he touched her, it was always the same. There had always been this between them, this shatteringly physical bond.

And once it had scared her. In her innocence, she had believed it one-sided, had assumed that Luc could, if he wanted, discover the same pleasure with any other woman. She was not so quick to make that assumption now. In the long passion-drenched hours which had turned night into day and day into night, the depth of Luc's hunger had driven her again and again to the brink of exhaustion.

He released her mouth with reluctance. 'You make me insatiable.' The sexy growl to that lancing confession did nothing to cool her fevered blood and she rested her head on his shoulder. 'Somehow, I doubt,' he murmured, 'that it'll take that long for you to become pregnant.'

'Pregnant?' she squeaked, jerking back from him, her first reaction one of shock and, curiously, fear.

His hands steadied her before she could overbalance and he nuzzled his lips hotly into the hollow of her collarbone where a tiny pulse beat out her tension. 'Don't tell me you believed in the stork story,' he teased. 'Believe it or not, what we've been doing in recent days does have another more basic purpose above and beyond mere pleasure.'

She was trembling. 'Yes, but——'

'And we haven't been taking any steps to forestall such a result,' he reminded her with complete calm.

That awareness was only hitting Catherine now. It shook her that a matter which had once been shrouded with such importance could have slipped her mind so entirely. There had been no contraceptive pills in her possession. Evidently she was no longer taking them. Remembering to take them had once been the bane of her existence, invoking horrid attacks of panic when she realised that she had forgotten one or two. If Luc realised just how many near misses they had had, he would probably feel very much as she did now.

That background hadn't prepared her very well for Luc's smoothly talking about having a baby as if it was the most natural thing in the world. Which of course it was...if you were married. In the circumstances, she decided that her initial sense of panic at his comment had been quite understandable. Where reproduction was concerned, she had to learn a whole new way of thinking.

Seemingly impervious to the frantic readjustments he had set in train, Luc ran a caressing hand down her spine and eased her closer. 'Didn't you notice that omission?' he said softly.

'No,' she muttered with instinctive guilt.

'I want children while I'm young enough to enjoy them.'

It crossed her mind that he might just have mentioned that before taking the decision right over her head, as it were. But equally fast came a seductive image of carrying Luc's baby and she was overcome by the prospect and quite forgot to be annoyed with him. 'Yes,' she agreed wistfully.

Engaged on cutting a sensual path across her fine-boned shoulder, Luc murmured huskily, 'I knew you'd agree with me. Now, instead of rushing to look into every baby carriage that passes by, you can concentrate on your own.'

'Do I do that?' she whispered.

'You do,' he said wryly.

Once anything to do with babies had left Luc arctic-cold. Naturally she couldn't help but be surprised that he should want a child with such immediacy. But when she thought about it for a minute or two, it began to make sense. Luc was entering marriage much as he entered a business deal, armed with expectations. He wanted an heir, that was all. You couldn't empire-build without a dynasty. But still she couldn't summon a smile to her face and she couldn't shake off that irrational fear assailing her.

Common sense ought to have reasoned it away. She loved Luc. She loved children. Where was the problem? Yet still the feeling persisted and her temples began to throb. When the phone buzzed on the table and Luc reached for it impatiently, she was starting to feel distinctly shaky and sick into the bargain.

Luc was talking in Japanese with the languid cool of someone fluent in a dozen languages. A frown pleating his dark brows, he sighed as he replaced the phone. 'Business,' he said. 'I have to go inside to make a few calls. I'll be as quick as I can.'

Sunlight played blindingly on the surface of the pool several feet away. As a faint breeze sent a glimmering tide of ripples across the water, the effect was almost hynotic. Catherine's head ached too much to think. She wondered ruefully if she had had too much sun.

A sound jerked her out of an uneasy doze. A child emerged from below the trees. His stubby little legs pumped energetically in pursuit of the ball he was chasing. As it headed directly for the water, Catherine flew upright, consumed by alarm. But he caught the ball before it reached the edge, and as he did so one of the maids came racing down the slope from the castle.

'Scusi, signorina, scusi!' she gasped in frantic apology for the intrusion as she scooped the child up into her arms. He gave a wail of protest. As he was hurried away, still clutching his ball, Catherine stopped breathing.

The thumping behind her forehead had for a split second become unbearable, but now it receded. She didn't even notice the fact. She was in a benumbed state that went beyond shock into incredulous horror.

Daniel... Daniel! The sybaritic luxury of the pool with its marble surround vanished as she unfroze.

Snatching up the phone, she pressed the button for the internal house line. A secretary answered. 'This is Miss Parrish.' She had to cough to persuade her voice to grow from a thread into comprehensible volume. 'I want you to get me a number in England and connect me. It's urgent,' she stressed, straining to recall Peggy's maiden name and the address of her home and finally coming up with them.

Shaking like the victim of an accident, she sat down before her legs gave out beneath her. What sort of a mother could forget about her son? Oh, dear God, please let me wake up, please don't let this nightmare be real, she prayed with fervour.

The phone buzzed and she leapt at it.

'Hello? Hello?' Peggy was saying.

'It's Catherine. Is Daniel there?'

'He's out bringing in the hay. I cried off to make refreshments,' Peggy chattered. 'Our phone was out for a couple of days and we didn't realise. Have you been frantic, trying to get through?'

'Well——'

'I thought you would've been,' Peggy interrupted with her usual impatience. 'I tried to ring you a few times from the call-box in the village but I always struck out. I suppose you've been out scouring the pavements in search of a job if you've decided against working for Mrs Anstey.'

'I——'

'Daniel's having a fabulous time. The weather's been terrific. We were planning to camp out tonight but, of course, if you want to speak to him...'

'No, that's OK.' I've been kidnapped. I'm in Italy. I'm getting married tomorrow. The revelations went unspoken. Peggy would think she was a candidate for the funny farm. In any case, she would be home before they were back in London. Nobody need ever know, she thought in that first frantic flush of desperation.

'Catherine, somebody's just driven into the yard. Wow, fancy car. Can I ring you back?'

'No...no, I'm out...I mean, I'm ringing from somewhere else. Give my love to Daniel.' She dropped the phone as though it burnt, and tottered backwards on to the lounger.

The hideous, absolutely inexcusable events of the past week were suddenly all crowding in on her. She flinched and she shrank and she cringed over the replay. Humiliation scored letters of fire into her soul. From rock-bottom there was only one way to go, and that was up, as she relived what Luc had done to her.

And really, there wasn't anything that Luc *hadn't* done. While she was in no condition to know what was happening to her, he had moved in for the kill. Plotting and intrigue were a breath of fresh air to that Borgia temperament of his. It had been as easy as stealing candy from a baby. Baby. *Baby*! She blenched and recoiled from that terrifying train of thought, completely unable to deal with it on top of everything else.

For a week she had been unaware that she was living four years in the past. He had left nothing within her possession that might jog her memory. Not a newspaper or a television set or a calendar had been allowed anywhere within a mile of her.

Every detail had been bloodlessly, inhumanly precise. It had Luc stamped all over it. He hadn't made a single error. She had been baited, hooked and landed like a fish. Only even a fish would have had more sense of self-preservation. A fish wouldn't have scrambled up the line, thrown itself masochistically on to the gutting knife and looked forward to the heat of the grill...but she had.

What Luc wanted, he took. Scruples didn't come into it. Costs didn't come into it. The end result was all that interested him. He had believed that she had planned to marry Drew and, with Drew's freedom so close, time had been a luxury Luc hadn't had. No doubt if she had thrown herself gratefully at his feet that night marriage would never have been mentioned. But in resisting Luc, she had challenged Luc. And he could not resist a challenge.

Her teeth ground together and her stomach heaved. That degrading fish image wouldn't leave her alone. Her small hands clenched into fists. Rage shuddered through her; rage that knew no boundaries; rage so powerful that it boiled up in a violent physicality she had not known she could experience.

At that precise moment, Luc appeared, striding down the steps set into the slope, and she remembered the episode in the back of the limousine and death would have been too quick a release for him to satisfy her. Springing upright, she grabbed up a glass and threw it at him. As it smashed several feet to the left of him, he stilled.

'You filthy, rotten, cheating, conniving swine!' she railed at him, snatching up the second glass and hurling it with all her might. 'You rat!' she ranted, and the phone went in the same direction. 'You louse!' she launched, bending in a frenzy to take off a shoe, her rage only getting more out of control at her failure to hit a fixed target. 'Bastard!' She broke through her loathing for that particular word and punctuated it with her other shoe. 'I want to kill you!'

'Poison would be a better bet than a gun.' Luc spread a speaking glance over the far-flung positions of the missiles, entire and smashed. 'Marksmanship wouldn't appear to be one of your hidden talents.'

Her rage reached explosive, screaming proportions. 'Is that all you've got to say?'

'It seems fairly safe to assume that you've retrieved your memory,' he drawled. 'I'm not sure it would be safe to assume anything else.'

'No, it wouldn't be!' His complete cool was maddening her even more. 'If you were dying of thirst, I wouldn't give you a drink! If you were starving, I wouldn't feed you! If you were the only man left alive on this earth and I was the only woman, the human race would grind to a halt! You deserve to be horsewhipped and keelhauled and hung, and if I was a man I'd do it!'

'And if you were a man, you wouldn't be in this situation,' Luc input helpfully as she paused to catch her breath.

'I'm going to report you to the police!' Catherine blazed at him, satisfied to have at last found a realistic threat.

Luc angled his dark head back, piercing golden eyes resting on her. 'What for?'

'W-what for?' she stammered an octave higher. 'What for? You kidnapped me!'

'Did I drug you? Physically abuse you? Have you witnesses to these events?'

'I'll make it up; I'll lie!' she slashed back at him.

'But why did you stand so willingly at my side at the airport when I announced our marriage plans?' Luc enquired with the same immovable, incredibly outrageous cool.

'You've kept me a prisoner here all week!' In desperation, she set off on another tack, determined to nail him down to a crime on the statute books.

An ebony brow quirked. 'With locked doors? I don't recall refusing to let you go anywhere.'

'Physical abuse, then!' Catherine slung through gnashing teeth. 'I'll get you on that!'

Luc actually smiled. 'What physical abuse?'

Catherine drew herself up to her full five feet and one quarter inch and shrieked. 'You know very well what I'm talking about! While I...while I was not in my right mind, you took disgusting advantage of me!'

'Did I?' he murmured. 'Catherine, it is my considered opinion that over the past week you've been more in your right mind than you've been for almost five years.'

'How dare you?' she screamed at him, fit to be tied. 'How dare you say that to me?'

A broad shoulder shifted in an elegantly understated shrug. 'I say it because it is the truth.'

'The truth according to who?' she shouted ferociously. 'You take that back right now!'

'I have not the slightest intention of withdrawing that statement,' he informed her with careless provocation. 'When you calm down, you will realise that it is the truth.'

'When I calm down?' she yelled. 'Do I look like I'm about to calm down?'

Luc ran a reflective appraisal over her. 'If you could swim a little better, I would drop you in the pool.'

'You're not even sorry, are you?' That was one reality that was sinking in. It did nothing to reduce her fury.

He sighed. 'Why would I be sorry?'

'Why? Why?' She could hardly get the repetition out. 'Because I'm going to make you sorry! I should have known you wouldn't have a twinge of conscience about bringing me here!'

'You're quite right. I haven't.'

'You act as though I'm some sort of a thing, an object you can lift and lay at will!' As his wide mouth curled with amusement, she understood why people committed murder.

His lashes screened his expressive eyes. 'If you are an object to me, then I am an object to you in the same way.'

For a second she glared at him uncomprehendingly and then caught his meaning. 'I'm not talking about sex!' she raged.

'No,' he conceded. 'I had noticed that once the charge of physical abuse was withdrawn——'

'I didn't withdraw it!' she interrupted.

'You were careful to change the subject,' he countered. 'You want me every bit as much as I want you.'

'You conceited jerk! I was sick! I hate you!'

'You'll get over that,' he assured her.

'I'm not going to get over it! I'm leaving, walking out, departing...' she spelt out tempestuously.

'A fairly typical response of yours when the going threatens to get rough, but you're not doing a vanishing act this time.'

'I'm leaving you!' she shouted wildly.

'Watch the glass!' Luc raked at her rawly.

But it was too late. A sharp pain bit into her foot and she vented a gasp. Striding forward, Luc wrenched her off her feet, moved over to the nearest seat and literally tipped her up, a lean hand retaining a hold on one slender ankle. 'Stay still!' he roared at her. 'Or you'll push the glass in deeper.'

Sobbing with thwarted temper and pain, she let him withdraw the sliver and then she cursed him.

'I knew you would do that.'

'Let go of me!' she screeched.

'With all this broken glass around? You just have to be kidding,' he gibed, wrapping an immaculate hanky round her squirming foot. 'When did you last have a tetanus jab?'

'Six months ago!' she spat, infuriated beyond all bearing by the ignominy of her position. 'Did you hear what I said? I'm leaving!'

'Like hell you are.' Jerking up the sarong that had fallen on the ground, he proceeded to her utter disbelief to wrap it round her much as if she were a doll to be dressed.

She thrust his hands away. 'Don't you dare touch me! What do you mean—"Like hell you are"? You can't keep me here!'

Casting the sarong aside, he took her by surprise by lifting her and, when she fought tooth and nail with every limb flailing, he flung her over his shoulder.

'Let me go!' she shrieked, hammering at his back with her fists. 'What do you think you're doing?'

'Putting you under restraint for your own good. You're hysterical,' he bit out. 'And I've had enough.'

'*You've* had enough?' Her voice broke incredulously. 'Put me down!'

'*Sta' zitta*. Be quiet,' he ground out.

Gravity was threatening the bra of her bikini. She became more occupied with holding it in place than thumping any part of him she could reach. He was heading for the stone staircase that led up to the french doors on the first-floor gallery. 'I hate you!' she sobbed, tears of mortification, unvented fury and frustration flooding her eyes without warning.

A minute later Luc dumped her on her bed with about the same level of care as a sack of potatoes might have required. 'And hating me isn't making you happy, is it?' he breathed derisively. '*Per dio*, doesn't that tell you something?'

'That you're the most unscrupulous primitive I've ever come across!' she spat through her tears. 'And I'm leaving!'

'You're not going anywhere.'

'You can't stop me!' And you certainly can't make me marry you!' she asserted with returning confidence, wriggling off the bed and hobbling over to a chair to pull on the flimsy négligé lying there, suddenly feeling very exposed in what little there was of the bikini. 'And, now that Drew's got his precious contract, you can't hold that over me any more!'

'He signs for it one hour after the wedding.'

Catherine was paralysed in her tracks. Jerkily she turned round. Shimmering golden eyes clashed with hers in an almost physical assault. 'I had foreseen the possibility that this might occur.'

'He...he hasn't got it yet?' She could hardly get the stricken question past her lips.

'I'm such a conniving bastard, I'm afraid,' Luc purred like a tiger on the prowl.

'You can't want me when I don't want you!' she gasped.

'I've already disproved that fallacy,' he said drily. 'And, when we reach our destination in England tomorrow, I have no doubt that you will be in a more receptive frame of mind.'

All Catherine caught was that one magical word. 'England?' she repeated. 'You're taking me back to England after the wedding?'

'A change of scene is usual.'

Evidently he believed that, once that ring was on her finger, it would have the same effect as a chain holding a skeleton to a dungeon wall. But, once she was back in England, he couldn't hold her. While she was here, he had her passport and she wouldn't have liked to bet on her chances of escape from a walled estate patrolled by security staff, aided in their task by an impressive range of electronic devices.

If she didn't go through with the wedding, Drew would suffer. She shuddered with inner fury at that unavoidable conclusion. The seductive fantasy of leaving Luc without a bride on his much-publicised wedding-day faded. She should have known better than to think it could be that easy. All the same, the prospect of being back in England tomorrow was immensely soothing. He could hardly force her to stay with him.

'Catherine,' Luc drawled. 'Don't even think it.'

'I have nothing to say to you,' she muttered tightly. 'I've already said it all.'

'We have to talk.' A knock sounded on the door. He ignored it. 'I won't allow you to spoil the wedding.'

A gagged and bound bride might raise an eyebrow or two, she reflected fiercely as the knock on the door was repeated.

'Avanti!' Luc called in exasperation.

Bernardo appeared, a secretary just visible behind him. 'Signorina Peruzzi.' He gestured with the cordless phone apologetically. 'She says it is a matter of great urgency that she speak with you, *signor*.'

'I will not take a call from her,' Luc dismissed. 'Leave us, Bernardo.'

The door shut again.

'He speaks English,' Catherine realised. 'Only you must've told him not to around me.'

'The staff are under the illusion that the request was made because you are keen to improve your Italian.'

She covered her face with shaking hands, what composure she had retained threatening all of a sudden to crumble. 'I loathe you!'

'You are angry with me,' he contradicted steadily. 'And I suppose you have some reason for that.'

'You suppose?' Wild-eyed, she surveyed him over the top of her white-boned fingers. Reaction was setting in.

'You belong with me, Catherine. Use the brain God gave you at birth.' The advice was abrasive. 'You have been happy, happier than I have ever known you to be, here.'

'I was living in the past!'

'But why did you choose to return to that particular part of the past?' His sensual mouth twisted. 'Ask yourself that.'

'I didn't choose anything!' she protested. 'And what I ended up with isn't real!'

'It can be as real as you want it to be.'

The sense of betrayal was increasing in her. He had betrayed her. But, worst of all, she had betrayed herself. She had betrayed everything she believed in, everything that she was, everything that she had become after leaving him. In one week she had smashed four years of self-respect. In one week she had destroyed every barrier that might have protected her.

'Can you turn water into wine as well?' she demanded wildly, choking on her own humiliation. 'You must have been laughing yourself sick all week at just how easy it was to make a fool of me!'

A muscle pulled tight at his hard jawline. 'That is not how it has been between us.'

'That's how it's always been between us!' she attacked shakily. 'You plot and you plan and you manipulate and you make things happen just as you want them to happen.'

'I didn't plan for you to lose your memory.'

'But you didn't miss a trick in making use of it!' she condemned. 'And I've been through all this before with you. When we came back from Switzerland, my employers had mysteriously vacated their flat and shut down the art gallery, leaving me out of a job! Coincidence?' she prompted. 'I don't think so. You made that happen as well, didn't you?'

A faint darkening of colour flared over his cheekbones, accentuating the brilliance of his dark eyes. 'I bought the building,' he conceded in a driven tone.

'And it made it so much easier for you to persuade me to come to New York.' Her breath caught like a sob in her throat.

'I wanted you very much. And I was impatient.' He looked at her in unashamed appeal. 'I am what I am, *bella mia*, and I'm afraid I don't have the power to change the past.'

'But I had. Don't you understand that?' Moisture was hitting her eyes in a blinding, burning surge and she could not bear to let him see her cry. 'I had!' she repeated in bitter despair.

'Catherine... what do you want me to say in answer?' he demanded. 'If you want me to be honest, I will be. All that I regret in the past is that I lost you.'

'You didn't lose me... you drove me away!' she sobbed.

He spread eloquent, beautifully shaped hands. 'All right, if semantics are that important, I drove you away. But you might try to see it from my point of view for a change. You shoot a crazy question at me out of the blue one morning over breakfast——'

'Yes, it was crazy, wasn't it?' she cut in tremulously. 'Absolutely crazy of me to think that you might actually condescend to marry me!'

'I didn't know there was going to be no court of appeal!' he slashed back at her fiercely. 'So I said the wrong thing. It was cruel, what I said. I admit that. If you want an apology, you should have stayed around to get it because I don't feel like apologising for it now! I came back to the apartment an hour and a half after I left it that morning. I didn't go to Milan. And where were you?'

She was shattered by the news that he had returned that morning. It shook her right out of her incipient hysteria.

'Yes, where were you?' Luc pressed remorselessly. 'You'd gone. You'd flounced out like a prima donna, leaving everything I'd ever given you, and if you wanted your revenge you got it then in full!'

With a stifled sob, she fled into the bathroom and locked the door, folding down on to the carpet behind it to bury her face in her hands and cry as though her heart was breaking. The past and the present had merged and she could not cope with that knowledge.

CHAPTER SEVEN

WHAT a fool Catherine had been, what a blind, besotted fool! The instant Luc had asked her to marry him, her wits had gone walkabout. So many little things had failed to fit but she had suppressed all knowledge of them, trusting Luc and determined to let nothing detract from her happiness. If it had been his intent to divert her from her amnesia, he could not have been more successful.

How dared he suggest that she had somehow chosen to return to a period of the past when they had still been together? That night in Drew's apartment, Luc had trapped her between two impossible choices. Either she sacrificed Drew or Daniel. With every fibre of her being she would have fought to keep Daniel from Luc.

But Drew also had a strong hold on her loyalty, both in his own right and in his sister's right as well. She owed Harriet a debt she could never repay for helping her when she had hit rock-bottom. How could she have chosen between Daniel and Drew? Faced with the final prospect of telling Luc that he had a son, she had shut her mind down on Daniel to protect him.

Luc poisoned all that he touched. And if he was prepared to marry her simply to ensure her continuing presence in his bed, why shouldn't he accept Daniel as well? Luc, she sensed fearfully, would want his son. Five years ago, Daniel would have been a badly timed, unwelcome complication. Luc had not over-valued her precise importance to him. She was convinced that he would have expected her to have an abortion. But times had changed...

Daniel was innocent and vulnerable, a little boy with a lion-sized intellect often too big for him to handle. Once Luc had been a little boy like that . . . and look how he had turned out. Hard as diamonds. Cold, calculating and callous. Did she want to risk that happening to Daniel? Daniel already had too many of Luc's traits. They had been doled out to him in his genes at birth.

He was strong-willed, single-minded and, if left to his own devices unchecked, exceedingly self-centred. Catherine had spent four and a half years endeavouring to ensure that Daniel grew up as a well-rounded, normal child rather than a remote, hot-house-educated little statistician, divorced by his mental superiority from childish things.

She hated Luc, oh, God, how she hated him! Enshrouded in lonely isolation, she clung ferociously to the hatred that was her only strength. She squashed the sneaking suspicion that Luc was not as callous and cold as she had once believed he was, tuned out the little voice that weakly dared to hint that Luc might have changed. Anger and self-loathing warred for precedence inside her as she cried.

So what if she had to go through the wedding first? As soon as they landed in London, she would leave him. She had done it before; she would to it again, and this time she wouldn't be so dumb. She would take her jewellery with her and sell it. With the aid of that money, she could make a new life for herself and Daniel. She would do it for Daniel's sake.

Misery crept over her with blanket efficiency. It hadn't been real; none of it had been real. She had been living out a fantasy. The background had been so cruelly perfect. A castle for the little girl who had once dreamt about being a princess. A white wedding for the teenager who had once believed in living happily ever after. But, for the woman she was now, there was nothing, less than nothing. And wasn't that her own fault? A grown woman ought to have been able to tell the difference between fantasy and reality.

A certain *je ne sais quoi*, he had called it. A certain three-letter word would have been less impressive but more accurate. Sex. Luc's fatal flaw and probably his only weakness. A certain *je ne sais quoi*, unsought and on many occasions since unwelcome, he had admitted. And you really couldn't blame him for feeling like that, could you? It must be galling to acquire that much wealth and power and discover that you still lusted after a very ordinary little blonde with none of the attributes necessary to embellish your image.

'Catherine? Are you OK?' Luc demanded, startling her.

'You b-bloody snob!' she flared on the back of another sob.

Silence stretched.

'What the hell are you talking about?' he blazed from the other side of the door. 'If you don't come out of there, I'll smash the lock!'

'Force is your answer to everything, isn't it?' Abruptly galvanised into action by the mortifying awareness that he had been listening to her crying, she stood up, stripped off, and walked into the shower, hoping the sound of it would make him go away.

Sex, she thought, loathing him. The lowest possible common denominator. And, after a five-year drought, her value had mushroomed. In fact it had smashed all known stock-market records. In return for unlimited sex, Luc was graciously ready to lower his high standards and marry her. Well, bully for him, and wasn't she a lucky girl?

Little wonder he didn't understand what all the fuss was about. He was sensationally attractive, super-rich and oversexed. Nine out of ten women would contrive to live with his flaws. Unfortunate that she was the tenth. Unfortunate for him, that was!

He might get a bride, but he wasn't getting a wife. He would live to regret forcing her to go through with the wedding. When she took off within hours of it, the public embarrassment would be colossal. Then she could stamp the long-overdue account 'paid in full'. Getting mad got her nowhere; getting even would restore her self-respect. Luc might have set her up, but he had set himself up as well.

Pay-back time was here. She would go down in history as the woman of principle who had rejected one of the world's most eligible bachelors. It was perfect, she decided, the old adrenalin flowing again. Shame she wouldn't be able to stay around to take advantage of the publicity. She could see the headlines. Why I couldn't live with Luc Santini.

Tying a towelling robe round her, she abandoned the entrancing imagery with regret and padded back to the bedroom, a woman with a mission now, a woman set on revenge and nobody's victim.

A cork exploded from a bottle like a pistol shot. His dark head thrown back as he let the excess champagne foam down into his mouth, Luc was a blaze of stunning black and gold animal vibrancy in the strong sunlight. He straightened and poured the mellow golden liquid expertly into a pair of glasses, white teeth flashing against brown skin as a brilliant smile curved his mouth. 'Force is not my answer to everything.' Magnificent lion-gold eyes skimmed over her. 'You look like a lobster. You've been in there so long, you must have used up all the hot water in the castle.'

She hadn't expected him to still be waiting for her. The filthy look she gave him ought to have withered him. Naturally it didn't. It drifted impotently off him like a feather trying to beat up a rock. Crossing the carpet with feline grace, he pressed a glass into her hand. 'You're not in love with Huntingdon,' he drawled. 'If you were, you would have slept with him.'

Just looking at him drained her. Her nerves were suddenly in shreds again. Her hands weren't steady. It was an unequal contest. She wasn't ready for another confrontation and he knew it, conniving and ruthless swine that he was! She marvelled at his arrogance in believing that he could bring her back to heel within the next twenty-four hours. That was, of course, what he was banking on.

'You wouldn't understand a man like Drew if you lived to be a thousand.' Her cheeks had gone all hot, and she tossed back the champagne in the hope of cooling down her temperature.

'He attracts you because he's a loser. You feel sorry for him.'

Her teeth gritted. 'Drew is not a loser.'

'He's run a healthy family firm off its feet with a series of bad business decisions,' Luc traded succinctly.

'And any day of the week, he's still a finer man than you'll ever be!' she launched shakily.

The superb bone-structure hardened. 'You're in a privileged position, *cara*. I would allow no one else to say that to me with impunity.'

The chill she had invoked was intimidating. A shiver ran down her backbone. She felt like a reckless child rebuked for embarrassing the adults. But his contempt for Drew deeply angered her. Yet, at heart, she knew he was right. Drew had never been ambitious or hungry enough to become successful. He had allowed his family to live at a level beyond their means, draining the firm of capital that should have been reinvested for the future. However, those facts didn't lower Drew in her estimation. He was not a born wheeler-dealer and he never would be. When she thought of the dreadful week of worry Drew had had to endure waiting for that contract, she tasted the full threat of Luc's savagery. No...no, she reflected tautly, she would never have cause to regret concealing Daniel's existence from Luc.

'You've hurt Drew,' she whispered, thinking that, once she was gone, Drew would be safe from all interference. She saw no reason to disabuse Luc of his conviction that she had had a relationship with Drew. It infuriated her that Luc should believe he had the right to stare at her with such chilling censure. 'And you don't own me.'

Confusingly, his wide mouth curled into a sudden, almost tender smile. 'I don't need to own you. You are mine, body and soul. So, you strayed a little, got lost, but you didn't stray as far as I'd feared, and now you are back where you belong.'

Seething temper gripped her. 'I don't belong with you!'

'Why do you fight me?' he demanded softly. 'Why do you fight yourself?'

As she collided unwarily with ebony-fringed dark eyes, a squirming helpless sensation kicked at her stomach. It was hard to withstand that burning, blatant self-assurance of his. 'I'm not fighting myself.'

'Come here,' he invited very quietly. 'And prove it.'

The magnetic force of his will was concentrated on her. Her body shivered, though she was not cold, her heart raced, though she was not exerting herself, in reaction to the sheer physical pull he could exert. It crossed her mind crazily that he ought to be banned like a dangerous substance.

He strolled closer and refilled her glass in the throbbing silence. 'You're afraid to,' he noted. 'Indeed, you behave as though you are afraid of me. I don't like that. I don't want a little white ghost with fear in her eyes in my bed tomorrow night. I want that scatty, loving, happy creature you've been all week.'

He was so close now she couldn't breathe. 'I don't love you.'

'If I weren't so certain that you loved me, I wouldn't be marrying you.'

She backed off hastily from his proximity. 'I wouldn't have thought it would have mattered a damn to you either way!'

'If you take refuge in the bathroom again, I'll break the door down,' he delivered conversationally. 'You started this and I'll finish it. I want to know why you're putting up barriers again.'

'Why?' she echoed breathlessly. 'Why? After what you've done?'

A brown hand inscribed a graceful arc. 'What have I done? I spend all these years looking for you and, the moment I find you again, I ask you to marry me. Isn't that a compliment?'

'A c-compliment?'

'It is certainly not an insult, *bella mia*.'

'But I don't want to marry you!'

'I'm becoming fascinated by what must go on in your subconscious mind,' he confessed huskily.

God, he was incredibly attractive. He could talk his way round a lynch mob, she conceded in panic. What she was experiencing right now came down to hormones. That was all. Luc was turning up the heat, stalking her like the pure-bred predator he was. If she lost her head for a second, she would be flat on her back on that bed. Somehow he contrived to say the most outrageous things charmingly. Or maybe it was just that her brain had packed up in disgust at her own frailty.

'You can't persuade me differently with sex either!' she asserted, her spine meeting unexpectedly with a wall that concluded her retreat.

Dancing golden eyes, alight with mockery, arrowed over her. He took her glass from her hand and set it aside. 'We don't have sex, we have intensely erotic experiences,' he countered, his wine-dark voice savouring the syllables.

'Sex!' She hurled the reiteration like a forcefield behind which she might hide. 'And I'm not some tramp... Are you listening to me?'

'I might listen if you say something I want to hear, but you've been rather remiss in that department this afternoon.' Instead of moving closer, he stayed where he was, confusing her. 'And I'm not about to make it easy for you by persuading you into bed.'

She straightened from the wall jerkily, no longer under threat, pink flying into her cheeks. 'You couldn't persuade me.'

'I wouldn't try. I'm saving you up for an intensely erotic experience tomorrow night,' he murmured softly, before closing the door behind him.

She darted after him and turned the key. Then she slumped. Heavens, he was so modest, such a shrinking violet. Wiping her damp forehead, she lay down on the bed, acknowledging, now that he was gone, just how much the past hours of stormy emotion had taken out of her. She had time for a nap before dinner.

She was terribly hot and sticky and thirsty when she woke up. Filling a glass to the brim with flat champagne, she drank it down much as she would have treated lemonade. Had someone been banging on the door a while ago, or was that her imagination?

Nobody's victim, eh? Her earlier fighting thoughts came back to haunt her. Luc had walked the last round. He had switched back to the intimate playful mood of the last few days and she hadn't expected that; she hadn't been prepared. He was in for a heck of a shock when she took her leave at the airport. He hadn't given serious consideration to a single thing she said. Her temper sparked again.

It maddened her to have to admit it, but hating Luc did not make her immune to his physical attraction. It was a hangover from the bad old days—what else could it be? Once she had believed he was a bit like the measles. If you caught him once, you couldn't catch him again.

Evidently the chemistry didn't work like that. Here she was, in full possession of her senses, no longer the doormat *doppelgänger* of recent days, and still she was vulnerable. It enraged her. When he had taken that glass from her and she had thought... she had been in the act of melting down the wall in anticipation.

Pacing about the room in a temper, she helped herself to more champagne. When she had loved Luc, she had just about been able to live with the effect he had on her. When she didn't even like him, never mind love him, it was inexcusable. And as for him—what he deserved was a cheap little tramp, the sort of female prepared to barter sexual favours for his bank balance, the sort of female he ought to understand. That was exactly what he deserved...

She was rifling the dressing-room when the banging on the door interrupted her. Opening it a crack, she found Guilia, for some reason backed by Bernardo, who was holding a large bunch of keys. Her maid looked all hot and flushed and anxious.

'I won't be needing any help tonight. *Grazie*, Guilia.'

'But *signorina*——'

'Dinner will be served in one half-hour,' Bernardo said with a look of appeal.

'I'm sorry, but dinner will have to wait.' Catherine shut the door again. Didn't they all speak great English? When she recalled the sign language she had been reduced to using several times during the week, she cursed Luc. Why had Bernardo looked so shattered at the idea of dinner's having to be held back?

Luc would probably create. Well, so what? It would do him no harm to cool his heels for once. He would appreciate her appearance all the more when she did wander in. Dinner, she decided fiercely, would be fun...fun...fun! However, lest the staff receive the blame for her tardiness, she would be as quick as she possibly could be.

The shimmering tunic top of a black evening suit was extracted from the wardrobe first. It would just cover her hips and, if she wore it back to front, the neckline would be equally abbreviated. Sheer black stockings, no problem. She had every colour of the rainbow. A very high pair of black court shoes were withdrawn next and finally a pair of long black gloves.

Dressed, she walked a slightly unsteady line into the bathroom to go to town on her face. Sapphire and violet outlined her eyes dramatically. Putting on loads of blue mascara, she dabbed gold glitter on her cleavage and traced her lips with strawberry pink. She was starting to enjoy herself. Having moussed her hair into a wild, messy tangle, she went through her jewellery.

She had three diamond bracelets. One went on an ankle, the other two on her wrists over the gloves. A necklace and earrings completed the look. Sort of Christmassy. It was astonishing how cheap diamonds could look when worn to excess. And her wardrobe, shorn of Guilia, had far more adventurous possibilities than Luc could ever have dreamt. The reflection that greeted her in the mirror was satisfyingly startling.

She picked a careful passage down the staircase, aware that she had been a little free with the champagne. Bernardo literally couldn't take his eyes from her as she crossed the hall. He froze, stared, tugged at his tie.

'Evening, Bernardo,' she carolled on her way past. 'It's a hot night, isn't it?'

And it's about to get hotter, she forecast with inner certainty. Abruptly, Bernardo flashed in front of her, spreading wide both doors of the salon. 'Signorina Parrish.'

Why on earth was he announcing her? Did he think Luc wouldn't recognise her under all this gloop? Have her thrown out as a gatecrasher? Taking a deep breath, she launched herself over the threshold. A whole cluster of faces looked back at her, some standing, some sitting. Horror-stricken, she blinked, stage fright taking over. The outfit had been for private viewing only. Behind her, Bernardo was subduing a fit of coughing.

Now that she came to think of it—and thinking was exceedingly difficult at that moment—Luc had mentioned something casual about some close friends coming to stay the night before the wedding. The minute she had shown her nerves at the prospect, he had dropped the subject. Right now, he was undoubtedly wishing he hadn't. Right now, he was remembering that she had a head like a sieve. Right now, as his long lean stride carried him towards her, his eyes were telling her that he wanted to kill her, inch by painful inch, preferably over a lengthy period. And that he intended to enjoy every minute of it when he got the chance.

'Say, I thought it was fancy dress,' she muttered and attempted to sidle out again, but Luc snaked out a hand and cut off her escape.

'She's so avant-garde,' a youthful female voice gasped. 'Mummy, why can't I wear stuff like that?'

'Designer punk,' someone else commented. 'Very arresting.'

'And I wouldn't mind being arrested with her.' A tall, very good-looking blond man sent her a sizzling smile. 'Luc, I begin to understand why you kept this charming lady under wraps until the very last moment. I'm Christian . . . Christian Denning.'

Catherine shook his hand with a smile. He had bridged an awkward silence. A whirl of introductions took place. There were about thirty people present, an even mix of nationalities, fairly split between the business élite and the upper crust. It was a relief when she finally made it into a seat to catch her breath.

'You have the most fabulous legs.' Christian dropped down on to the arm of her sofa. 'Why do I have the feeling that Luc would rather have kept the view an exclusive one?'

'Have you known Luc for long?' she asked in desperation.

'About ten years. And I saw you at a distance once in Switzerland, seven years ago,' he confided in an undertone. 'That was as close as I was allowed to get.'

A wave of heat consumed her skin. This was someone who had to have a very fair idea of what her former association with Luc had been. 'Was it?' She tried to sound casual.

'Luc's very possessive,' he responded mockingly. 'But he must have snatched you right out of your cradle. I must remember to tease him about that.'

Luc strolled over. 'Enjoying yourself, Christian?'

'Immensely. There isn't a man in the room who doesn't envy me. Why did I have to wait this long to meet her?'

'Perhaps I foresaw your reaction.' Luc reached for Catherine's hand. It was time to go into dinner. 'Everybody likes you,' he breathed, pressing his mouth with fleeting brevity to her bare shoulder, fingertips skating caressingly down her taut spinal cord. 'You forgot they were coming, didn't you?' He was smiling at her, she registered dazedly. '*Cara*, if you had seen your face when you realised what you had done! But in this gathering you don't look quite as shocking as you no doubt thought you would.'

On that point, he was correct. There was no conventional garb on display. At this level, the women were more interested in looking different from each other. She might look startling to her own eyes and to those of anyone who knew her, but nobody was likely to suspect that she had deliberately dressed up as some sort of pantomime hooker. Had it been her intent to embarrass Luc in company, she would not have succeeded and, since that had not been her intent, she was relieved until it occurred to her that he would endure more than embarrassment when she walked out on him at the airport. A sneaking twinge of guilt assailed her. Immediately she was furious with herself. Luc had set the rules and she was playing by *his* rules now. He had given her no other choice. What transpired, therefore, was of his own making.

A middle-aged woman with a beaky nose took a seat to the left of her at the dining-table and asked, 'Do you hunt?'

'Only when I lose something,' Catherine replied abstractedly.

Someone hooted with amusement as though she had said something incredibly witty. A wry smile curved Luc's mouth. 'Catherine's not into blood sports.'

'She must be planning to reform you, then,' a blonde in cerise silk said with smiling sarcasm. 'Blood sports are definitely your forte.'

'And yours, sister, dear,' Christian interposed drily.

The long meal was not the ordeal she had expected but it was impossible for her to relax. Luc was in an exceptionally good mood, which somehow had made her feel uncomfortable. She was flagging by the time the Viennese coffee was served in the *salone*. Christian's sister settled down beside her and she struggled to recall her name. Georgina, that was it.

'I didn't see you with Luc in Nice last week,' Georgina remarked.

'I wasn't there.'

Georgina contrived to look astonished. 'But he was with Silvana Lenzi. Naturally, I assumed... Oh, dear, have I said something I oughtn't?'

'You've said exactly what you intended to say, young lady,' the kindly woman with the beaky nose retorted crisply, and changed the subject.

Across the room, Luc was laughing with a group of men. Catching her eye, he gave her a brilliant smile. Hurriedly, she glanced away. Her nails dug into the soft flesh of her palm. She really couldn't understand why she should feel so shattered. Luc had not spent the past four and a half years without a woman in his bed. Celibacy would come no more naturally to him than losing money.

The South American film actress was notorious for her passionate affairs. He certainly hadn't been boldly going where no man had gone before, Catherine thought with a malice that shook her. She was speared by a Technicolor picture of that beautiful, lean, muscular, suntanned body of his engaged in intimate love-play with the gorgeous redhead. It made her feel sick. She felt betrayed.

Obviously she had had too much to drink. It had unsettled her stomach, confused her thoughts. If she felt betrayed, it was only because she had been the chosen one this week and the awareness was bound to distress her. Really, she didn't care if he had been throwing orgies in Nice. His womanising habits were a matter of the most supreme indifference to her.

A few minutes later, Luc interceded to conclude her evening. She was tired. He was sure everyone would excuse her. With his usual panache, he swept her out of the *salone*. She shook off his arm with distaste.

'It's ten minutes to midnight.' Impervious to hints, he was reaching for her. 'Isn't it supposed to be bad luck for me to see you after midnight?' he teased, glittering golden eyes tracking over her in the most offensively proprietorial way.

Without even thinking about it, Catherine lifted her arm and slapped him so hard across one cheekbone that she almost fell. 'That's for Nice!' she hissed, stalking up the staircase. 'And if I see you after midnight, it won't be just bad luck, it'll be a death-trap!'

'Buona notte, carissima,' he said softly, almost amusedly.

Incredulous at the response, she halted and turned her head.

He stared up at her and smiled. 'You're crazy, but I like it.'

'What's the matter with you?' she snapped helplessly.

He checked his watch. 'You have six minutes to make it out of my sight. If you start talking, you'll never make it.'

Her fingermarks were clearly etched on one high cheekbone. The sight of her own handiwork filled her with sudden shame. She really didn't know what had come over her. 'I'm sorry. I shouldn't have done that,' she conceded.

'I'd forgive you for anything tonight. Even keeping me awake,' he advanced huskily.

That did it. She raced up to her room as though all the hounds in hell were pursuing her.

The beautiful breakfast brought to Catherine on a tray couldn't tempt her. The hair-stylist arrived, complete with retinue, followed by the cosmetics consultant and then the manicurist. The constant female chatter distanced her from the proceedings. As the morning moved on, she felt more and more as if she were a doll playing a part. She had nothing to do. Everyone else did it for her. And finally they stood back, hands were clapped, mutually satisfied smiles exchanged and compliments paid...the doll was dressed.

It wasn't real, not really real, she told herself repeatedly and stole another glance at her reflection, for it so closely matched that teenage dream. Certainly she had never before looked this good. No wonder they were all so pleased with themselves.

The little church was only a mile from the castle. It had been small and plain and dark when she had seen it earlier in the week. Today it was ablaze with flowers that scented the air heavily. She was in a daze. She went down the short aisle on the arm of a Spanish duke she had only met the night before. It's five years too late, five years too late; this doesn't mean anything to me now, she reasoned at a more frantic pitch as Luc swung round to take a long unashamed look at her. But somehow from that moment she found it quite impossible to reason at all.

'The most beautiful bride I've ever seen.' Luc brushed his lips very gently across hers and the combination of a rare compliment and physical contact sent her senses reeling dizzily.

Sunlight was warming her face, glinting off the twist of platinum on her finger next, and Christian was dropping a kiss on her brow, laughingly assuring her that Luc had said her mouth was out of bounds.

In the limousine, he caught her to him and took her mouth with all the hunger he had earlier restrained. Her bouquet dropped from her fingers, fell forgotten to the floor, and her arms went round his neck, her unsteady fingers linking in an unbroken chain to hold him to her.

CHAPTER EIGHT

VIOLINS were thrumming in Catherine's bloodstream. She drifted round the floor in a rosy haze of contentment.

'Catherine?'

'Hmm?' she sighed dreamily into Luc's shoulder, opening her eyes a chink and vaguely surprised to recognise that the light, cast by the great chandeliers above, was artificial. In her mind she had been waltzing out under the night stars. 'Candles would have been more atmospheric,' she whispered, and then, 'You're thinking of the fire hazard and the smoke they would have created.'

'I'm trying very hard not to. I know what's expected of me,' Luc confessed above her head, and she gave a drowsy giggle. A lean hand tipped her face back, lingered to cup her chin. 'It's time for us to leave.'

'L-leave?' she echoed, jolted by the announcement.

His thumb gently eased between her parted lips and rimmed the inviting fullness of the lower in a gesture that was soul-shatteringly sensual. A heady combination of drowning feminine weakness and excitement spread burning heat through her tautening muscles. He might as well have thrown a high-voltage switch inside her. Dark eyes shaded by ebony lashes glimmered with gold. 'Leave,' he repeated, the syllables running together and merging. 'Fast,' he added as an afterthought.

'Everybody's still here.' She trembled as the hand resting at her spine curved her into contact with the stirring hardness of his thighs. 'Oh.'

'As you say, *cara*...oh,' he murmured softly. 'Our guests will dance quite happily to dawn without me. I have other ambitions.'

Her body was dissolving in the hard circle of his arms. She would have gone anywhere, done anything to stay there. The very thought of detaching herself long enough to get changed scared her. She was waking up out of the dream-like haze which had floated her through the day. And waking up was absolutely terrifying.

Had she really been stubborn enough to cling to the conviction that she hated him? It hadn't been hatred she'd felt when she saw him at the altar. It wasn't hatred she felt when he touched her. It was love. Love. She was blitzed by that reality. Her emotions had withstood the tests of pain and disillusionment, time and maturity. Why? But she knew why; scarcely had to answer the question. And in the beginning there was Luc...and there ended her story.

He steered her out of the ballroom, quite indifferent to the conversational sallies of several cliques in their path. In the shadow of the great staircase, he moulded her against him, his mouth hard and urgent, long fingers framing her cheekbones as he kissed her, at first roughly, then lingeringly with a slow, drugging sexuality that devastated her.

A low-pitched wolf-whistle parted them. Hot-cheeked, still trembling with the force of the hunger Luc had summoned up, she let her hands slide down from his shoulders, steadying herself.

Christian was regarding them from several feet away, a smile of unconcealed amusement on his face. Dealing him an unembarrassed glance, Luc directed her upstairs with the thoughtful precision of someone who doubted her ability to make it there without assistance. Guilia was waiting to help her out of her gown.

Dear God, Catherine thought in numbed confusion, was there a strong streak of insanity in her bloodline? Nothing less than madness could excuse her behaviour over the past twenty-four hours. Did all women lie to themselves as thoroughly as she had? Luc knew her better than she knew herself. He knew her strengths and insecurities, her likes and dislikes, even, it seemed, her craven habit of avoiding what she couldn't handle and denying what she was afraid of...

Why did she deceive herself this way? She had been like a child with an elaborate escape-plan, a child who secretly wanted to be caught before she did any real damage. Almost seven years ago she had given her heart without the slightest encouragement, and that heart was still his. And that love was something she couldn't change, something that was simply a part of her, something that it was quite useless to fight. Luc was her own personal self-destruct button. But leaving him less than five years ago had still been like tearing her heart from her body.

'I need you,' he had said once in the darkness of the night in Switzerland. The admission had turned her over and inside out. She would have walked on fire for him just for those three little words. But he had never said them again, never even come close to saying them once he had been secure in the knowledge that she adored him.

It hadn't been very long before he'd begun to smoothly remind her that what they had wouldn't last forever. He had hurt her terribly. He had taught her to walk floors at night, to feel sick at a careless word or oversight, to panic if a phone call was late...to live from day to day with this dreadful nagging fear of losing him always in the background. Inside, where it didn't show, he had killed her by degrees.

'He was very bad for you,' Harriet had scolded. 'You're not cut out to cope with someone like that. But you did what you had to do. You protected Daniel. Be proud that you had that much sense.'

Whenever she had wavered, as waver she had for far longer than she wanted to recall, Harriet had been the little Dutch boy, sticking her finger in the dam-wall of her emotions, preventing the leak from developing into a torrent that might prompt her into some foolish action. Oh, yes, she had thought about phoning him times without number. She had always chickened out. Once she had even stood in the post office a couple of days before his birthday, crazy enough to consider sending him a card because she knew that since his family's death there was nobody else but her to remember. Harriet had had her work cut out and no mistake. That first year keeping her away from Luc had been a full-time occupation.

But Catherine had been lucky enough to have had Daniel on whom to target her emotions. How could anyone understand what Daniel meant to her? The first time she held him in her arms she had wept inconsolably. Nobody but Harriet had understood. Daniel had been the first living person she had ever seen to whom she was truly related. Between them, Daniel and Harriet had become the family she had never had.

Why had she planned to leave Luc again? This time she was honest with herself about her most driving motivation. She was terrified of telling him about Daniel, as terrified as she had been when she had realised she was pregnant. Luc did not have and clearly never had had the smallest suspicion that she might have been pregnant.

It was all so horribly complicated and she had so much to lose. Daniel believed his father was dead. He had asked very few questions and she really hadn't understood that he actually resented not having a father until that day at Greyfriars when he had raged at her, naïvely sharing his secret belief that his father, had he still been alive, would have been able to work miracles.

Daniel would accept Luc with very little encouragement. How Daniel would react to the discovery that his mother had lied to him was another question entirely. And could she trust Luc with Daniel? Daniel was very insecure right now, very breakable. If Luc could not accept him wholeheartedly, Daniel would know it. In addition, he was illegitimate. That couldn't be hidden and, sooner or later, it would hit the newspapers. Luc would find that intolerable.

And on what basis did she dare to assume that Luc saw their marriage as a permanent fixture? Luc was so unpredictable. Did she turn Daniel's life upside-down in the hope that Luc could come to terms with the decision she had made five years ago, and the fact that he had a four-year-old son?

Yesterday she had believed she had a choice. Today she accepted that she had merely talked herself into taking the easy way out and running away again. It wouldn't work this time. And the irony was that she didn't want it to work anyway. She loved Luc. She wanted to hope. She wanted to trust. She wanted to believe that somehow all this could be worked out. And that meant telling Luc about Daniel.

There was no time to be lost. The day after tomorrow, Peggy would be driving down to London. How did she tell him? The enormity of the announcement she had to make sunk in on her, another razor edge to hone her nerves. She would tell him on the flight to London...it wouldn't be very private, though. She would tell him whenever they arrived at their destination, wherever that was. But the more she dwelt on the coming confrontation, the more panic-stricken she became at the prospect.

'You're very pale.'

In the limousine, she didn't feel up to that narrowed, probing gaze. How would Luc react? That was all she could think about. Yesterday she had been telling herself that he was cold, callous and calculating in an effort to shore up her reluctance to tell him about Daniel. Yesterday she had been determined to hate him, determined to see him as a threat to Daniel. Now she had come down out of the clouds again, but the view was no more encouraging. She had deceived him. She had lied by omission. Those who crossed Luc lived to regret the miscalculation. Since she had never put herself in that position before, how could she possibly predict how he would react?

'And very quiet,' Luc continued.

She gulped. 'I was just thinking.'

'About what?'

'Nothing in particular.' She veiled her troubled eyes in case he did what he had done before and read her mind. Do it now, do it now, she urged herself. You know what you're like. The longer you leave it, the bigger mess you'll make of it. 'What time do we arrive in London?'

'Didn't I tell you? The air-traffic controllers in Rome are having a twenty-four-hour stoppage,' he imparted with the utmost casualness. 'We fly to London early tomorrow morning.'

'We're not going to the airport?' she gasped.

'A friend has offered us the use of his villa overnight.'

Her hands clenched convulsively together. Reprieve, the coward in her thought. An opportunity to be alone with him and tell him, her conscience insisted. The limousine was already turning through tall gates.

A housekeeper greeted them on the steps. When Luc refused the offer of supper, they were shown upstairs to a bedroom suite. It was full of mirrors and exotic silks and the most enormous bed. This was her wedding night, she reflected in despair. How could she tell him tonight? It would ruin the whole day, she reasoned weakly.

He came up behind her and buried his mouth hotly against the soft, sensitive spot where her shoulder met her throat, and her knees buckled. 'We should have supper,' she managed shakily.

'Are you hungry?'

'Well——'

'Supper wouldn't satisfy my hunger either,' he breathed approvingly. Slowly, heart-stoppingly, he turned her round. 'What's wrong with you?' he enquired, completely without warning.

'W-wrong?'

'You have the look of a murderer caught burying the body,' he murmured thoughtfully. 'Or is that my imagination?'

'Your imagination.' Avoiding his far too perceptive eyes, she tried to sidetrack him by reaching up and starting to undo his tie.

'My imagination rarely plays tricks on me.' He watched her struggling with his tie. With an expressive sigh, he covered her small shaking hands with one of his. 'You don't trust me, do you? I won't hurt you ever again, *bella mia*. I promise you that.'

Unbearably touched and suddenly rent with guilt, her eyes clouded over.

'I was only twenty-seven when I met you.' He ran a questing fingertip along the taut curve of her cheek. 'And I didn't want to meet someone like you. I set out to get you on my terms and I knew it wasn't what you wanted or what you deserved. You loved me too much, *cara*. You let me get away with murder. So, I took you for granted.' His superb bone-structure was prominent beneath his suntanned skin, his eyes very dark. 'I thought you would always be there. And then one day you were gone and I realised that even you had your breaking point. I realised that a little too late for it to make any difference.'

'Luc, I——'

He brushed his fingers in a silencing motion against her lips. 'I don't want to talk about the past now. It casts shadows. Maybe tomorrow, maybe the next day, hmm?' he cajoled. 'But not tonight.'

She turned her mouth involuntarily into the warm palm of his hand, tears wet on her cheeks. He appealed to her for understanding and Luc was not given to appeals. Strain clenched his dark features. The break with the tradition of keeping his own counsel hurt.

He trailed his tie off, shed his jacket with a lithe twist of his shoulders and pulled her into his arms, emanating now all the raw self-assurance that came so naturally to him. 'I scarcely slept last night,' he admitted softly. 'And I intend to keep you awake all night as punishment.'

His breath warmed her cheek and then his tongue slid between her lips, thrusting them apart to explore the moist interior she so freely offered him. The floor under her feet seemed to fall away, and she clung to him while he took her mouth again and again with a stormy intensity that stirred a dulled ache in the pit of her stomach. Her silk dress pooled on the carpet without her even being aware that he was expertly removing it. Lean fingers slid caressingly over her hip, encountering lace, and, disregarding the fragile barrier, he made her jerk and moan beneath his marauding mouth.

He laughed soft and deep in his throat, ceasing the provocation only to pick her up and carry her over to the bed, following her down in fluid motion, reacquainting her with every sleek line of his lean body. His shirt had come adrift and she ran her hands up over his smooth brown back, feeling every muscle tauten to her reconnaissance. He ground his hips sensuously slowly into hers, and for mindless seconds she was ruled by the hunger he could evoke and completely lost.

He looked down at her, dark eyes aflame with gold satisfaction and desire. 'Remember that first night in Switzerland?' he whispered huskily. 'You were so exquisitely shy.' He strung a line of kisses across her delicate collarbone. 'So innocent. I was a bastard, *bella mia*. It should have been our wedding night.'

'I pretended it was.'

A faint flush of colour irradiated the high cheekbones that intensified his raw attraction. He captured the fingers lacing into his black silky hair and pressed them to his lips, dense lashes concealing his gaze. 'I'd never made love to a virgin before. I wanted it to be special for you. That's why I took you to Switzerland.'

'It was special,' she managed unsteadily. 'Very special.'

'Grazie... grazie tanto, cara,' he teased. 'It was so special for me that I had to keep you all to myself, being of a naturally selfish disposition.'

She had never seen him so relaxed, not this last week, not ever. But for a split second he reminded her so powerfully of Daniel. The same beautiful dark eyes, the same wide mouth that could yank at her heart-strings with the faintest smile. Her breath caught in her throat, but he was brushing aside the lace cups of her bra, letting his tongue and then his mouth circle the taut pink nipples he had uncovered, and her mind became a complete blank, her fingers clenching together as sensation began to build, drawing every tiny muscle tight beneath his ministrations.

There was a mirror above the bed. She blinked bemusedly and then the imagery of his brown hands on her paler skin and his dark head bent so intimately over her took over. 'There's a mirror up there,' she whispered.

'How shocking.' His voice was indistinct, abstracted. 'Tell Christian he has outrageous bad taste next time you see him.'

'This is his villa?'

Luc eased back from her reluctantly, rolled off the bed and proceeded to strip. She couldn't take her eyes from him. Wide shoulders tapered down to a narrow waist, lean hips and long, muscular thighs. He was very aroused, superbly male, supremely beautiful.

'Looking at me like that does nothing for my self-control.' He came down beside her again, dispensed with the wispy lingerie and curved her into his arms. The dark hair hazing his chest rubbed against her tender breasts, one lean thigh hooking over hers as he stared down at her, so much unashamed hunger in his probing appraisal that she was breathless. 'You wouldn't have done it.'

'Done what?'

'Walked away at the airport.' A wry smile challenged her shock. 'I wouldn't have let you go. Did you think I didn't know? Sometimes I know what you think before you think it.'

Having devastated her, he took advantage by ravishing her swollen mouth with a fierce, driving sweetness. Time and thought were banished. She got drunk on the taste of him. The warm masculine scent of him flooded her, making her even more light-headed. She could feel herself sliding out of control. Breathing hurt her lungs. Tiny sounds she was barely conscious of broke from her lips, and when his hand touched her where she most ached for fulfilment, she went wild, writhing with his burning caresses, hungrily searching out for herself the compulsive heat of his mouth.

It was agony and ecstasy but he wouldn't give her what she sought as she blindly arched her hips in a silent expression of need as old as time. She was twisting in the heat of a fire that demanded assuagement. Her fingernails raked his back in torment and protest. And then, in the shuddering, explosive tension of his body, she felt the flames leap and scorch through him as well. Suddenly he was all aggressor, all savage demand, spreading her out like a sacrifice to some primitive god and falling on her, hands bruising her thighs as he took her with all the strength he possessed in a driving surge of passionate intensity.

It went on and on and on, more and then incredibly more until she was sobbing her pleasure out loud, lost to everything but the remorseless demands of her own body. The release came in a frenzied explosion of exquisite sensation that left her awash with the bliss of satiation.

'Dio!' he groaned in harsh satisfaction, shuddering in the possessive circle of her arms, burying his damp face in her hair. *'Te amo,'* he muttered, almost crushing her beneath his weight. *'Te amo.'*

She stilled. I love you. I love you, he had said.

'Scusi.' He rolled over and sprawled back in an indolent tangle of sun-darkened limbs against the white percale sheeting. 'Now I finally know what it's like to be a sex object,' he sighed without particular concern in the winging smile he angled at her. 'You made me lose control. That's my department.'

She smiled, a fat-cat-got-the-cream smile. He probably didn't even know he'd said it. That was fine. The last thing she wanted to do was to make an issue out of it. She had lived off 'I need you' for almost two years once. She could manage a good decade on 'I love you'. Moving over, she scattered a trail of kisses across a sweat-slicked broad shoulder. 'I love you... I love you... I love you,' she whispered feverishly.

He caught a hand into her tousled hair. 'I know, I know, I know,' he said playfully.

He hadn't bitten the bait. When did he? She was too impatient. If he had meant it, he would tell her in his own good time. If? It didn't help to be aware that such a confession at the height of sexual excitement was recorded the world over as a statutory and meaningless phrase. But didn't she have rather more to worry about right now? Daniel rose like Mount Everest in the back of her mind.

'Luc...how do you feel about children?'

He tugged her down on top of him, claimed a kiss, clearly not very focused on the concept of dialogue. 'I never thought of them until recently.'

'Do...do you like them?'

'Like them?' Ebony brows slashed together in a frown. 'What sort of a question is that? I expect I will like my own. I have no real interest in other people's.'

It wasn't very encouraging. She made no demur when his hands started to roam lazily over her again. Indeed, she needed that closeness, that hunger of his to control the fear that was steadily rising inside her. Luc would be furious. But what frightened her most was the unknown quantity of how he would react after the fury.

'You can sleep during the flight.' Luc smiled down into her heavy eyes, satisfaction and amusement mingling in his scrutiny.

They were about to leave the VIP lounge when a small grey-haired man, closely followed by a security guard, came in.

'Antonio?' Luc crossed the room to greet him with pleated brows.

The low-pitched exchange of Italian had an odd edge of urgency that made Catherine glance in their direction. The older man gave something to Luc, withdrew a handkerchief to mop his perspiring brow and, by his manner, was clearly apologising. He looked as though he was reporting a death. She stifled a yawn, and her attention slewed away again.

'Who was that?' she asked as they boarded the jet.

'One of my lawyers.' His intonation was curiously clipped.

She hated take-off; always had. She didn't open her eyes until they were airborne. Luc wasn't beside her. On the other side of the cabin, he was scanning a single sheet of paper. As she watched he scrunched it up between his fingers and snatched up the newspaper lying on the desk in front of him. He signalled to the steward with a snap of his fingers. A large whiskey arrived pronto. Draining it in one long, unappreciative gulp, he suddenly sprang up, issuing a terse instruction to the steward who left the cabin at speed.

'Catherine...come here.' He moved a hand in an oddly constrained arc.

Releasing her belt, she got up. His set profile was dark, brooding. He indicated the seat opposite. 'Sit down.'

When she collided with his eyes her heart stopped beating and her mouth ran dry. The suppressed violence that sprang out at her from that hawk-like stare of intimidation was terrifying.

'I will not lose my head with you,' he asserted in a controlled undertone. 'There must be an explanation. I still have faith, but it hangs by a thread.'

'You're scaring me.'

He continued to study her, a kind of flagellating stare that threatened to strip the skin from her facial bones. 'Last week, Rafaella told me something I refused to believe. After your disappearance five years ago, she stayed in the apartment we shared for some weeks. I didn't want it to be empty if you phoned or chose to return.'

Uncertainly she nodded.

'And last week she informed me that during her stay a call came from some doctor's surgery, asking why you hadn't been back for a check-up.'

She bent her head and studied the desk-top, goose-flesh prickling at the nape of her neck, an impending sense of doom sliding over her.

'From that call and certain trivia she subsequently uncovered in the apartment,' Luc continued in the same murderously calm tone, 'Rafaella deduced that you were pregnant at the time of your departure.'

She flinched, froze, watched the desk-top blur.

'She assumed—that is, if her story is true—that you had decided on an abortion. She told me that at the time she saw no good reason to share this knowledge with me. So she cultivated a short memory.'

Catherine wanted God to pluck her out of the sky and put her somewhere out of Luc's reach. Her vocal cords were in arrest. Her brain had stopped functioning.

'Naturally her assumption was that, if there was a child, it was not mine. Halston figured largely as the culprit,' he extended, his tone quieter and quieter, every word slow and precise and measured. 'Perhaps you can now understand why I was so angry with her. After this length of time the story struck me as fantastic and wholly incredible. I didn't believe a word of it. I defended you.'

The weight of the world's sins seemed to sit on her bowed shoulders. She was shrinking inwardly and outwardly.

'This is now your cue to tell me that not a word of her story is true. You see, Rafaella is persistent. When I refused her calls, she communicated with one of my lawyers in Rome, giving him the details of what she apparently discovered in England,' he spelt out. 'Antonio spent a most troubled night before rousing the courage to bring those facts to me. He was hastened to a decision when an article purporting to relate to you was printed in an English newspaper.'

'I...I didn't think of it coming out like this!' she burst out strickenly. 'I intended to tell you when we arrived in England...' Her voice trailed away.

'Look at me.' He ground out the command fiercely. 'Are you telling me it is true? That you were pregnant? That there is a child?'

Like a puppet she nodded twice, shorn of speech by the violent incredulity splintering from him in waves.

'And...you...married...me?' He was rising slowly from behind the desk, having trouble in getting the question past his compressed lips.

'What did you expect me to do?' she muttered frantically.

'What did I expect? What did I expect?' he roared at her, a hand like a vice closing round her wrist to trail her bodily out of her seat.

'You're hurting me!'

'He'd better not be mine!' he bit down at her rawly.

The tension broke her and she sobbed, 'Of course he is. Of course he's yours. Why would you want anything else?'

He punched a fist into the palm of his other hand with a sickening thud and swung violently away from her. Barbaric fury throbbed from every tensed line of his long, taut body. 'If I touch you, I'll kill you. *Cristo*, get out of my sight before I lose control!'

'Luc, please,' she said brokenly.

He spun back to her, fluid as a cat on his feet even in rage. 'If he hadn't been mine, maybe...just maybe I could have forgiven you, because then at least I could have understood why you ran away. But this!' He spread brown hands eloquently wide in a slashing movement. 'This I don't understand at all!'

'If you would just calm down,' she interposed pleadingly.

'Calm down? I find out I have a son of almost five whom I don't know and I never even dreamt existed, and you ask me to calm down?'

'I should have told you last night.'

'Last night?' he grated in disbelief. 'Last night, while you were playing the whore in my arms, I'd definitely have strangled you! I don't give a damn about last night or last week! I'm talking about five years ago when you were pregnant!'

The brutality of his attack on her behaviour the night before cut with the efficacy of a knife through her heart. 'S-stop shouting——'

'If I don't shout I'll get physical! And I've never struck a woman in my life and I will not start now,' he shot at her furiously.

It took immense will-power for her to drag her thoughts into order. The sheer force of his rage had shattered her, and his contention that he would have preferred to learn that Daniel was another man's child was quite incomprehensible to her.

'Why didn't you tell me five years ago?' The repetition scorched back at her.

'I meant to... I tried to——'

'I don't remember you trying,' he cut in ruthlessly.

She sucked in air convulsively. 'I was afraid to tell you.'

He uttered a succinct swear-word he had never used in her presence before. It blazed with his derision.

'All right,' she whispered, and, mustering the tattered shreds of her composure, she mastered herself sufficiently to continue. 'You won't like what I'm about to say...'

'I don't like you,' he breathed with chilling effect. 'Nothing that you could say could be any worse than the revulsion I feel now.'

Unintentionally she burst into tears, hating herself for the weakness, but she felt as if she were an animal caught in a trap.

'I couldn't bring myself to tell you,' she formulated shakily, 'because I knew you wouldn't want him and I was scared that I would let you talk me into getting rid of him.'

'You dare to foist the blame on me!' he raked back at her with contempt.

In a benumbed state, she moved her head back and forth. 'You always made it so obvious that you didn't want to commit yourself to me in any way. I honestly believed that you would see a termination as the only practical solution.'

'Where my own flesh and blood is concerned, I am not practical! And what does commitment to you have to do with commitment to my unborn child?' he demanded. 'And what do you know of my feelings about abortion? When did we ever discuss the subject?'

'I... I made an assumption,' she conceded, no longer able to look at him.

'You made one hell of an assumption!'

'At the time, I believed it was the right one,' she whispered.

'And shall I tell you why you made that assumption? Look at me!' he commanded fiercely, and she did, fearfully, sickly, wondering where the axe could possibly fall next. 'I never knew what a temper you had. I never dreamt there could be such bitterness and obstinacy behind that angel face. But I know it now, and I don't need your interpretation, for I have my own! Let me tell you how it was: if I wasn't going to marry you, I would pay for that with the loss of my child!'

'No!' she cried. 'It wasn't like that!'

'It was exactly like that. No ring, no child. I was playing Russian roulette over that breakfast table and I didn't know it!' He looked at her with hatred. 'To think that I tortured myself over what I said to you that day! You had no right to conceal the truth from me. It was my right to know that you were carrying my child. *Cristo*, did you hate me so much that you couldn't even give me a chance?'

Her legs were shaking. She sank down in the nearest seat and covered her face with damp hands. 'I loved you. I loved you so much.'

'*That* was love?' He emitted a harsh laugh of incredulity. 'I lash out at you once. In nearly two years, I lose my temper with you once! Once! And I've been paying for it ever since. It was revenge you took, and I understand revenge very well.'

'I don't think like you,' she said in defeat.

'If you thought like me, you'd have been my wife five years ago! *Si*, I'd have married you.' Lancing dark eyes absorbed her white face with a kind of grim satisfaction. 'I probably wouldn't have done it with the best of grace, but I'd have married you.'

She shrank in retrospect from such a fate. Luc, forced into marriage shotgun-style. It would have been a nightmare. 'I wouldn't have wanted you to marry me feeling like that.'

'*Dio!* What would your feelings or my feelings have had to do with it with a child on the way?'

'I couldn't have lived with you under those circumstances,' she muttered limply.

His mouth twisted chillingly. 'The only truly honest woman I ever met—that's what I told Rafaella about you. It's a wonder she didn't laugh in my face! But then, she has one virtue you don't have. She's loyal even when I turn on her as I did last week.'

'Daniel and I will go away.' Hardly knowing what she was saying, Catherine spoke the thought out loud. 'You won't hear from us again.'

CHAPTER NINE

'YOU'RE not taking him anywhere!'

'You don't want him. You didn't even want him to be yours. That has to be the sickest, cruellest thing you've ever said to me.' Catherine's voice wobbled alarmingly on the contention.

'Sick?' Luc thundered. 'I've lost five years of his life! He's illegitimate. What will he suffer in later years? Don't you realise that all this will hit the papers? Did you think you'd be able to shelter behind the fallacy that you were a widow with a child for the rest of your days? It will come out... of course it will, and how will the child feel then? About you? About me? That is why my first wish was that he should not be mine. For *his* sake, not my own. The papers are already sifting what few facts they have, already hinting that all is not as it appears. Why else was he left in England?'

'The papers?' She was ghost-pale, paralysed by the sheer force of the condemnation coming her way.

'Surely you didn't believe that you could step from nowhere into the life that I lead and conceal the truth? If it hadn't been for Rafaella, his face would already have been splashed all over the gutter Press! When she tracked him down to your friend's home in the Lake District, she got him out before the paparazzi could make a killing.'

'Got him out? To take him where?' she pressed feverishly, registering that the threat of Press interest had been roused far more swiftly than she had naïvely expected.

'She persuaded your friend to bring him south before the Press arrived. They're waiting for us at the house.'

'What house?' she mumbled dazedly.

His strong jawline clenched, a tiny muscle tugging at the hardened line of his mouth. 'I bought it for you as a wedding present. Five years ago... five long, wasted years ago!' he vented rawly.

In the state she was in, it took a little while for the significance of that admission to sink in. 'Five years ago?'

Smouldering dark eyes black as pitch bit into her. 'I was such a fool. I, who prided myself on my superior judgement! Haven't you worked it out yet, *cara*? I was in love with you.'

'F-five years ago?' It was a shattered gasp.

'I didn't know it myself until you had gone.' His inflexion, his whole demeanour, was chillingly cold and harsh. 'The last laugh really was on me. I believed you would return... phone... send a postcard with "x marks the spot" on it... something, anything! I couldn't believe you would stay away forever. I could not have done that to you.' That confession appeared to awaken another scorching tide of anger. His teeth gritted as he stared at her. 'I spent a fortune trying to trace you. In an excess of conscience-stricken self-reproach, I intended to marry you as soon as I found you! So much for the fresh start!'

Slow tears brimmed up in her eyes and rolled down her cheeks. She swallowed back her sobs in the seething silence that throbbed and tortured and taunted. But Luc was not finished with her.

'And when I find you, I close my eyes to the evidence of what you are. I make excuses for you. I cling to an illusion that probably never existed anywhere outside my own imagination. Why?' A savage bitterness stamped his dark taut features. 'It can only be because you're the best lay I've ever had. That is all I will ever allow it to be now.'

'Don't,' she begged brokenly, sensing his destructive determination to smash the bonds between them . . . or had she already done that for herself?

'You did this to me before. I will never let you do it to me again.' The assurance carried all the lethal conviction of an oath.

'What did I do?' she whispered.

'Five years ago I trusted you more than anyone else in this world, Catherine. And you betrayed that trust,' he delivered contemptuously. 'You spent all night in my arms, telling me how much you loved me and then you walked out . . .'

'I was saying goodbye the only way I could.' It was a dulled murmur.

'Of course, it would not occur to you that one of the reasons I was so angry with you the next morning was that I felt that I had been set up!'

'How could you feel that?'

'How could I fail to feel that? And then I didn't want to marry you, I didn't want to marry anyone. My parents did not give me a very entrancing view of the married state. They hated the sight of each other!'

She looked up in shock at that grated revelation. 'You never told me that!'

'You have so many illusions about happy family life, I could never bring myself to tell you the truth.' His dark gaze was unrelentingly grim. 'My parents married because they had to marry. My mother was pregnant. They didn't love each other. They didn't even like each other. They lived together all those years in absolute misery. And the only thing they ever wanted from me was money. As long as the money came, they hadn't the slightest interest in what I was doing. But it took me a long while to face that reality. When that plane went down, the only things I lost were a sister and two parents who never wanted to be parents in the first place.'

Shutting her eyes tightly, she lowered her head. 'I always thought your family loved you.'

'They loved what I could give them,' he contradicted fiercely. 'And you're not so very different, are you? Ten days ago, you were sitting in Huntingdon's apartment ready to marry him. Miraculously, you converted to me!'

'He asked me to marry him that day you saw us. There was never anything between us before that. At least not on my side. I should have been honest about that sooner,' she conceded uncertainly.

'Honest?' he gritted. 'You don't know the meaning of the word. I look forward to you telling my son in another few years that the reason for my late appearance in his life lies with your fear of my intentions towards him before he was even born!'

She flinched at the image he projected.

'What have you told him about me?'

She might as well have been hanging from a cliff by her fingernails. One by one, he was breaking them, loosening their hold, bringing the jagged rocks of retribution closer and closer. She chose to jump. 'Nothing,' she admitted shakily.

'Nothing?' he exclaimed. 'You must have told him something about his father!'

She broke into a faltering explanation of Harriet's cover-story. She could not have said that he absorbed the details. He zoomed in on only one, cutting her short in another surge of shuddering rage when he realised that Daniel thought his father was dead. The last straw had broken the camel's back. That Luc should not know he had had a son was bad enough. But that Daniel should not know about him was unforgivable.

She was desperately confused by what he had told her in anger, confidences which she sensed that in his present mood would never have been made otherwise. He had said that he loved her five years ago. All else receded before that single stated fact. The love she had longed to awaken had been there. And she had been too blind and too insecure to even suspect its existence for herself.

Why had she listened to Harriet? Why, oh, why? But it wasn't fair to blame Harriet. Harriet had judged Luc on the evidence of what Catherine herself had told her. Harriet had influenced her only in so far as she had confirmed what Catherine had already believed. And Luc had just brought down the convictions that had sustained her through the years like a pack of cards.

Enormous guilt weighted her now. She had run away when she should have stood her ground, stayed away when she should have returned. A little voice said that what Luc said so impressively now with the benefit of hindsight was no very good guide to how he might have reacted to her pregnancy without having sustained the shock of first losing her. That voice was quashed because the guilt was greater. Luc would have married her. Daniel would have had a father. Daniel would have had many things and many advantages which she had not had the power to give him.

Luc was right on one count. She had not given him a chance. In her own mind, the result had been a foregone conclusion. Then, she had to admit, it had been easier to run away than face a confrontation. In those days, she had been out of her depth with Luc, unable to hold her own. She could not have dreamt then that Luc could be so bitter or indeed that losing her could have brought him so much pain. For it had been pain that powered that bitterness, that fierce conviction that she had betrayed him for the second time. Luc viewed her response to his lovemaking last night in the same light as he had viewed that long-ago last night in New York.

And she understood facets of his temperament which she had not understood before. The heat in the bedroom, the coolness beyond it. Recently he had begun to break out of that pattern. But he must have learnt early in life not to show his emotions. And he must have been hurt. His parents, by all accounts, had not encouraged or sought his affection. The financial generosity, which in the past had made her feel like an object to be bought, was shown now in a different light. Luc had had a long history before her of giving to those closest to him. It had been expected of him. When his family had died, he had simply continued the same habit with her.

There was so much fear trapped inside her. Luc was more than disappointed in her: Luc was embittered and disillusioned. Five years ago, whether she knew it or not, she had thumped the last nail into her coffin. It had never occurred to Luc that she might have been pregnant because it had equally never occurred to him that, if she was, she might go to such lengths to conceal the fact from him.

But what a disaster it would have been had Luc felt forced to marry her, repeating what he surely would have believed to be his parents' mistake. He had not been ready to make such a commitment of his own free will. It wouldn't have worked, it couldn't have worked, but Luc could not see that. No, at this moment Luc saw only Daniel, and he was already demonstrating a voracious appetite for knowledge of his son. He wanted Daniel. Right now, he did not want Daniel's mother.

Anger was within him still, anger dangerously encased in ice which could shatter again. When Luc came to terms with the awareness that he was a father, how would he feel about her then? He had trusted her. He had blamed himself entirely for her defection in the past. He had wanted to put the clock back, make everything right...she could see that now. And now he had learnt that that wasn't possible. It was very probable, she registered strickenly, that the driving determination of his to take what he wanted had resulted in a too hasty marriage.

'I love Daniel very much,' she murmured tightly.

'You have a fine way of showing it,' he censured. 'You dump him in the back of beyond with some seething feminist——'

'Don't you dare call Peggy that!' Catherine interrupted hotly. 'She's a university lecturer and she's written three books. She's also a very good friend.'

But possibly Peggy wouldn't be a friend any more in the midst of this nightmare that had erupted. Kept in the dark about Luc's identity, railroaded from her family home by Rafaella, and told goodness knew what, Peggy was sure to be furious as well.

Catherine's wedding present was an Elizabethan country house. It wasn't enormous, it wasn't ostentatious and it would have stolen her heart had she been in a less wretched mood...and had Rafaella not been emerging from the front entrance, wreathed in welcoming smiles...

'Not bad as a pressie, not bad at all.' Hands on her slim hips, Peggy scanned the house in the early-evening sunshine, her wryly admiring scrutiny glossing over manicured lawns, a stretch of woodland and the more distant glimmer of a small lake. 'Strewth, Catherine, it's incredibly hard not to be impressed by all this.'

Catherine glanced at her watch helplessly again.

Too observant to miss the betraying gesture, Peggy frowned. 'They'll show up again sooner or later. Stop worrying. Daniel will come round. It's my fault,' she sighed. 'I shouldn't have left him alone with Rafaella for a second. The woman's poisonous.'

Catherine thought back reluctantly to their arrival. Luc had gone straight to greet Rafaella. Catherine had no idea what had passed between them but the brunette had been smiling and laughing, switching on to the ultra-feminine mode she invariably employed around Luc. Then, with a pretty little speech about not wanting to intrude, she had climbed into her car, no doubt smugly aware that she was leaving bedlam in her wake between husband and wife...and mother and son.

Daniel had been sitting like a solemn little old man in one of the downstairs rooms. Her attempt to put her arms round him had been fiercely rejected. 'You tol' me my daddy was dead!' Daniel had condemned and, from that point on, the reunion had gone from bad to worse.

Rafaella had done her work well. Daniel might be a very clever child but his grasp of adult relationships was no greater than any other four-year-old's. He understood solely that his mother had lied to him. Hurt and confused, terribly nervous of meeting this father Rafaella had described in over-impressive terms, Daniel had taken the brunt of his conflicting emotions out on Catherine.

Luc had taken over the same second he chose to join them, crouching down on his son's diminutive level to engage his attention. 'I don't know anything about being a father,' he had confided cleverly. 'I'll probably make mistakes. You'll have to help me.'

'I don't want a daddy who bosses me around all the time,' Daniel had traded in a small voice, but quick as a flash with the return.

'I wouldn't either,' Luc had agreed smoothly.

'I'm not sure I want one,' Daniel had admitted less argumentatively.

'I can understand that, but I am very sure that I want you to be my son.'

'Have you got any other ones?' Daniel asked innocently.

'Only you. That is what makes you so special.'

Catherine had hovered like a third wheel, watching without great surprise as Daniel had responded to Luc. Luc had put in a performance of unsurpassed brilliance, quieting all of Daniel's fears. It had gone on for ages. A series of extremely subtle negotiations on Luc's side and of blossoming confidence and curiosity on Daniel's.

Luc hadn't moved too far, too fast. A mutual sizing-up had been taking place. After an hour, Daniel had been chattering confidingly, flattered by Luc's interest in him, relaxed and unthreatened by his manner. Clover had been mentioned. It had taken Luc precisely five seconds to recognise that the retrieval of an elderly donkey from an animal sanctuary would do much to cement his new relationship with his son. And never let it be said that Luc would look a gift horse or, in this case, a gift donkey in the mouth. A phone call had established that Clover was still in residence.

'I think we should go and get her now, don't you?' Luc had suggested with the innate cool of a master tactician, and Daniel had been so overcome with tears, excitement and gratitude that he had flung himself at Luc, breaking the no-physical-contact barrier he had until that moment rigidly observed.

They had departed before lunch. 'He's a beautiful child,' Luc had murmured, choosing then to notice Catherine for the first time since their arrival. 'And I am very proud that he is mine.'

She still wasn't sure whether that had been a compliment, a veiled apology, a mere acknowledgement of Daniel's attractions or a concealed criticism that he had had to wait this long to meet his own son.

'You should have gone with them,' Peggy told her.

'I wasn't invited. Anyway,' she sighed, 'I needed to talk to you. I thought you'd be furious over all that's happened.'

'Are you kidding? The last two days have been excitement all the way!' Peggy laughed. 'I was staggered when Rafaella showed me that picture of you with Luc at the airport and by that time the first reporter was ringing. Someone in the village must have tipped them off. Lots of people knew I was taking Daniel up to my parents' place. When I go back, I can bask in your reflected glory...'

'There's not a lot of it around at the moment. You'll catch a chill,' Catherine warned ruefully. 'When all of this comes out——'

'When all of what comes out? Don't exaggerate,' Peggy scolded. 'You lived with him, it broke down, and now you're married to him. You can't get a lot of scandalous mileage out of that. Daniel's his, end of story.'

'It's not that simple——'

'Neither was the amount of information you contrived to leave out when you once briefly discussed Daniel's father with me,' Peggy interposed. 'I've met him for about ten minutes now and I'm not sure I'm very much the wiser. Mind you, he has three virtues not to be sneezed at. One, he's generous. I won't add that he can afford to be. Two, he has to be the best-looking specimen I've ever seen live off a movie-screen. That's a sexist observation, Catherine, but, shamefully, that *was* my first reaction. Three, anyone capable of charming Daniel out of a tantrum that fast is worthy of respect.'

'Anything else?'

'When he breezed off with Daniel and left you behind like faithful Penelope, I found myself hoping that Clover would be in a more than usually anti-social state of mind when he has to get close and enthuse. I bet he's never been within twenty feet of a donkey before!'

That so matched Catherine's thoughts that she burst out laughing, but her amusement was short-lived. She sighed. 'If I hadn't lost my memory, I'd have had to tell him about Daniel last week. That wouldn't have been quite so bad.'

'If you ask me, and you won't, so I'll give it to you for free,' Peggy murmured, 'where Daniel's concerned, Luc got what he deserved. If he hadn't made you so insecure you'd have trusted him enough to tell him. And it strikes me that he's bright enough to work that one out for himself.'

If he *wants* to work it out, Catherine reflected unhappily. And nothing Luc had said earlier in the day had given her the impression that he intended to make that leap in tolerant understanding. She walked Peggy back to her car, both dreading and anticipating Luc's return.

Clover arrived first, as irascible as ever, snapping at the gardener, who was detailed to take her to the paddock. Catherine was interrupted in the midst of her thanks to the lady who ran the animal sanctuary and had taken the trouble to deliver Clover back, and was informed with an embarrassed smile that Luc had made a most handsome donation to the sanctuary. Ironically, that irritated her. Why were things always so easy for Luc?

He strolled in after ten with Daniel fast asleep in his arms. On the brink of demanding to know where they had been all day, she caught herself up. The cool challenge in Luc's gaze informed her that he was prepared for exactly that kind of response. Moving forward, she took Daniel from him instead. 'I'll put him to bed.'

She carted her exhausted son up to the bedroom where he had slept for the previous two nights. He stirred while she was undressing him, eyes flying open in sudden panic. 'Where's Daddy?'

'Downstairs.'

'I thought I dreamt him.' Daniel gave her a sleepy, beguiling smile. 'He doesn't know anything about kids but he knows a lot about computers,' he said forgivingly, submitting to a hug and winding his arms round her neck. 'I'm sorry I was bad.'

Her eyes stung. 'I'll forgive you this once.'

'Daddy s'plained everything. It's all his fault we got split up,' he whispered, drifting off again.

From the bottom of her heart, she thanked Luc for that at least. He had put Daniel's needs before his own anger, healing the breach between Catherine and her son before it could get any wider. As it could have done.

Catherine was well aware that, for the foreseeable future, Luc would occupy centre stage with Daniel. Luc had had the power to swerve him even further in that direction. But he hadn't used it.

She went down to the drawing-room. For all its size, it had a cosy aspect of comfort, decorated as it was with the faded country-house look she had always admired. The interior lacked a lived-in quality, though. The housekeeper, Mrs Stokes, had gone to considerable trouble with flower arrangements in empty spaces, but it was so obvious that nobody had lived here in years. Mrs Stokes had told her quite casually that Luc had never even spent a night below this roof before.

And he had bought this house for her, had scarcely come near it after the first few months. Luc had had faith in her, she registered painfully. Luc had been convinced that she would return. What she had forced him to face today was that she had not had a corresponding faith in him. She had asked for nothing, expected nothing and, not surprisingly, nothing was what she had received.

'Is he asleep?' Luc paused on the threshold, leashed vitality vibrating from his poised stance. His veiled dark gaze was completely unreadable.

She cleared her dry throat. 'He went out like a light. You must have tired him out. That doesn't often happen.'

Luc moved a fluid shoulder. 'He doesn't have enough stimulation. He was on his very best behaviour with me, but I suspect displays of temper such as I witnessed earlier are not infrequent.'

'He was upset,' she said defensively.

'He's an extremely bright child. He should start school as soon as possible.'

She paled in dismay. 'I don't want him sent away.'

Luc raised a brow. 'Did I suggest that? He does not have to board. Rome has an excellent school for gifted children. The opportunity to compete with equals would benefit Daniel.' He took a deep breath, cast an almost wary look at her, but she wasn't looking at him. Tight-mouthed, she was staring at the floor. 'He's a little old to be throwing tantrums. That surplus energy could be better employed.'

'You're very critical!' she snapped.

'That wasn't my intention. He's an infinitely more well-balanced child than I was at the same age, but he needs more to occupy him. Unless you plan to continue letting him educate himself from the television set.'

Catherine reddened fiercely but she didn't argue, uneasily conscious that he had some grounds for that comment. 'I did my best.'

'He's basically a very happy, very confident child. I think you did a marvellous job, considering that you were on your own and, as Daniel assured me repeatedly, very short of money.'

The compliment only increased her tension. Luc was so distant, so controlled. She didn't recognise him like this. He was unnerving her. She stole a covert under-the-lashes glance at the vibrancy of his dark golden features, desperate to know how he felt now that he had had time to cool down.

'Was what you said to me this morning true? Or a fabrication of the moment?' he prompted very quietly. 'Did you really believe that I would have demanded that you have an abortion?'

The colour drained from her complexion. 'Put like that, it sounds so——'

'Cruel? Inhuman? Selfish?' he suggested, his beautiful eyes running like flames of dancing gold over her distressed face. 'Presumably that is how you saw me then.'

In bewilderment she shook her head at this incorrect assertion. 'I didn't . . . when something gets in your way, you get rid of it,' she stumbled, conscious that she was not expressing herself very well. 'I just felt that if that was what you wanted, I mightn't have been able to stand up to you. That was what I was most afraid of. I might have let you persuade me...'

Every angle of his strong bone-structure was whip-taut. '*Per amor di Dio*, what did I do to give you such an image of me?'

The scene wasn't working in the way she had hoped it would. Luc was dwelling with dangerously precise intensity on the jumbled mess of imprecise emotions and fears which had guided her almost five years ago. 'It wasn't like that. Can't you understand that the longer I kept quiet about it, the harder it was for me to tell you?'

'What I understand is that you were very much afraid of me and that you were convinced that I would kill my unborn child for convenience. Yet even when I didn't know that I loved you, I cared for you,' he murmured with flat emphasis. 'And even if I hadn't loved you, I still couldn't have chosen such a course of action.'

Tears lashed the back of her eyes. She blinked rapidly. 'I'm sorry.' It was a cry from the heart.

A grim curve hardened his mouth. 'I think it is I who should be sorry. I appear to have reaped what I sowed. And you had no more faith in me yesterday when you married me. You still couldn't summon up the courage to tell me about Daniel.'

'I'm a frightful coward... you ought to know that by now.' It was an uneasy joke that was truth. 'And anyway, I didn't want to spoil the wedding,' she muttered, not looking at him, too aware that it was a pathetic excuse.

The silence stretched, dragging her nerves unbearably tight.

'How much of a chance is there that this last week will threaten to extend the family circle?' he asked tautly.

As his meaning sank in, she licked her dry lips nervously, conscious that she would very soon have confirmation one way or another. 'Very little chance,' she proffered honestly, strangely, ridiculously embarrassed all of a sudden by the subject. Luc's attitude was a far cry from his attitude that day at the pool, and that day seemed so long ago now.

If he wasn't quite tactless enough to heave a loud sigh of relief at the news, he wasn't capable of concealing that she had alleviated a fairly sizeable apprehension. The most obvious aspects of his strong tension dissolved. 'I want you to know that I didn't think of repercussions either those first few days that we were together. I am not that unscrupulous,' he asserted, even managing a faint smile. 'I didn't plan to make you pregnant.'

'That's OK.' Catherine gave a jerky shrug, couldn't have got another word out, she was so desperately hurt by his reaction. The idea of another child had taken surprising root, she discovered belatedly. She saw Luc's withdrawal of enthusiasm as the ultimate rejection. It was only a tiny step further to the belief that he no longer saw their marriage as a permanent fixture. A second child would only have complicated matters.

'I was very careless,' he remarked.

Catherine wasn't listening to him. She was on the edge of bursting into floods of tears and bitter recriminations. A strategic retreat was called for. She cut a wide passage round him. 'I'm tired. I'm going to bed.'

'I won't disturb you.'

It was no consolation at all to discover that Luc's possessions had been removed from the main bedroom at some stage of the evening. He hadn't even given her the chance to throw him out! Grabbing a pillow, she punched it and then thrust her face in it to muffle her sobs.

CHAPTER TEN

'CAN I get you anything else, Mrs Santini?'

Catherine surveyed her plate guiltily. One croissant, shredded into about fifteen pieces, not a toothmark on one of them. 'No, thanks.' She forced a smile. 'I'm not very hungry.'

Her appetite was no more resilient than her heart. Luc had taken Daniel to Paris with him very early this morning. They would be back by evening. In Daniel's hearing, Luc had smoothly suggested that she might like to accompany them. Her refusal had been equally smoothly accepted. The invitation had clearly been for Daniel's benefit alone.

The past four days, she conceded numbly, had been hell upon earth. She had learnt the trick of shortening them. She went to bed early and slept late. Yet she could not fault Luc's behaviour. He was being scrupulously polite and considerate. Indeed, he was making a very special effort. It didn't come naturally to him. She could feel the raw tension behind the cool front. She could taste it in the air. He couldn't hide it from her.

He didn't love her. How could she ever have been foolish enough to believe that he might? Then again, she had a talent for dreaming, for believing what she wanted to believe, she conceded with bitter self-contempt. Luc had chased an illusion for almost five years and he had suddenly woken up to the truth. Daniel had been the catalyst, but even if Daniel hadn't existed Luc would inevitably have realised that he had made a mistake.

In her absence, Luc must have built her up to be something more exciting than she was. When he'd found her again, her reluctance and the challenge of apparently taking her away from another man had provoked that dark, savage temperament of his. All that mattered to him was winning. Having won, he'd found that the battle had not proved to be worth the prize.

He was in a quandary now. It would look exceedingly strange if their marriage broke up too soon. There was also Daniel to be considered. At least, however, there would be no other child. She sat rigidly in the dining chair, a tempest of emotion storming through her slight body.

She was not carrying his child. The proof had come that very night when she had abandoned herself to grief. There would be no other baby, no further tie by which she might hold him. Her sane mind told her that was fortunate, but more basic promptings rebelled against that cooler judgement.

She could not picture life without Luc again. That terrified her. The more distant he was, the more desperate she felt. She couldn't eat, she couldn't sleep, she couldn't do anything. What was there now? she asked herself. What had he left her? Daniel adored him. Daniel could hardly bear Luc out of his sight.

Her future stretched emptily before her. Daniel would start school in Rome. Initially she would be there as well but, little by little, the marriage that had never quite got off the ground would shift into a separation. Luc would make lengthy business trips and she would no doubt do what was expected of her and make regular visits back to England. Certainly it would be impossible for her to withstand continual exposure to Luc as he was now.

It was torture to be so close and yet so far, to shake with wanting him in the loneliness of her bed at night, to exhaust herself by day keeping up a pretence that she was quite happy with things as they were. Damp-eyed, she lifted her head high. She would not let Luc see how much he was hurting her. Pride demanded that she equal his detachment and make no attempt to break it.

Not that she thought she was managing to be totally convincing. In between all the pleases and thank-yous she had never heard so many of before, she occasionally encountered searching stares. His tension spoke for itself. Luc wanted her to let go with finesse. He was willing her not to force some melodramatic scene. Rage and despair constrained her in an iron yoke of silence, creating an inner conflict that threatened to tear her apart. Why couldn't he have left her alone? Why had he had to thrust his way back into her life? Why had he laid a white rose on her pillow? Why had he had to force her to admit that, far from hating him, she loved him? Why? Why? Why?

Angered by her own desperation, she stood up, determined not to spend another day wandering about like a lost soul. For starters, it was time she saw Drew, time she stopped avoiding that issue. After all, she had already contacted his godmother. Mrs Anstey had ranted down the phone at her, refusing her apologies and telling her with satisfaction that she had given the flat to a great-niece, who would be far more suitable. Catherine had taken the verbal trouncing in silence. It had lightened her conscience.

She didn't expect her meeting with Drew to be quite so straightforward. Did she tell him that she was responsible for the nerve-racking experiences he must have endured in Germany? Or did he already know? Would he even want to see her now?

It was early afternoon when she entered the compact offices that housed Huntingdon Components. Drew's secretary phoned through an announcement of her arrival. Drew emerged from his office, his pleasant features stiff and almost expressionless. 'This is a surprise.'

'I felt I had to see you.'

'I'm afraid I don't know quite how to greet Mrs Luc Santini.'

She tilted her chin. 'I'm still Catherine,' she murmured steadily.

He stood at the window, his back half turned to her. 'I tried to call you from Germany. My housekeeper told me that you'd cleared out without even staying the night. She said the bedroom was so tidy that she wasn't too sure you'd been in it at all.'

Catherine bent her head. Luc's security staff were thorough.

'Then I saw that photo of you at the airport with Santini. It was in every newspaper,' he sighed. 'Daniel is the image of him. Harriet lied about your background. I put that together for myself.'

'I'm sorry that I couldn't tell you the truth.'

'It was none of my business when I first knew you. But I preferred competing with a ghost,' he admitted wryly, and hesitated. 'To take off with him like that, you have to be crazy about him...'

Her vague idea of explaining what had really happened died there. Somehow she felt it would be disloyal to Luc. Drew had no need of that information. 'Yes,' she agreed, half under her breath, and then, looking up, asked, 'Did you get your contract?'

Unexpectedly, he smiled widely. 'Not the one I went out for. Quite coincidentally, an even more promising prospect came up. It's secured the firm's future for a long time to come. What's that saying? Lucky at cards, unlucky in love?'

Her eyes clouded over, but she was shaken to realise that Drew was quite unaware that his firm had been under threat and had ultimately profited from the change in contracts. He had undergone no anxiety, and the news that he had achieved that second contract through Luc's influence would not be welcome.

He cleared his throat awkwardly. 'I've agreed to go to counselling with Annette, but I don't know if it will change anything.'

A smile chased the tension from her soft mouth. 'I'm glad,' she said sincerely.

'I still think you're pure gold, Catherine.' His mouth twisted. 'I just hope that he appreciates how lucky he is.'

Not so's you'd notice, she repined helplessly as she climbed back into the limousine. A male, punch-drunk on his good fortune, did not willingly vacate the marital bed and avoid all physical contact. Quite obviously, Luc couldn't bring himself to touch her. The white-hot heat of his hunger had died along with the illusion. But it hadn't died for her. Her love had never been an illusion. She had never been blind to Luc's flaws or her own. She still ached with wanting him. And soon she would despise herself again for that weakness.

It was wrong to let Luc do this to her. It was undignified, degrading...cowardly. Their marriage had been a mistake. Continuing it purely for the sake of appearances demanded too high a cost of her self-respect. Nor could she sacrifice herself for Daniel's sake. Daniel was like Luc. Daniel would survive. It was her own survival that was at risk. She couldn't afford to sit back and let events overtake her as she had done so often in the past. A clean break was the only answer and it was for her to take the initiative.

Dazed by the acknowledgement, she wandered round Harrods in the afternoon. The heavens were falling on her. The ground was suddenly rocking beneath her feet. It was over...over. She had felt this way once before and she had never wanted to feel like this again.

The chauffeur was replacing the phone when she returned to the car. 'Mr Santini's back from Paris, madam. I said we'd be back within two hours, allowing for the traffic.'

Dear heaven, for someone who didn't give two hoots about her, Luc certainly kept tabs on her! She was suddenly very reluctant to go home. It would be better, she reasoned, if Daniel was in bed when she returned.

'We'll be later,' she said. 'I want to stop somewhere for a meal.'

She selected a hotel. She spent ages choosing from the chef's recommendations, chasing each course round the plate and deciding what she would say to Luc, how she would say it and, more importantly, how she would look when she said it. Cool, calm and collected. Not martyred, not distressed, not apologetic. When she told Luc that she wanted an immediate separation, she would do it with dignity.

She was tiptoeing up the stairs, deciding that she would feel fresher and more dignified in the morning, when Luc strode out of the drawing-room. 'Where the hell have you been?' he demanded, making her jump with fright.

'Out.' Carefully not sparing his lean, dark physique a single visually disturbing glance, she murmured, 'I want a separation, Luc.'

'Prego?' It was very faint. She studied him then, unable to resist the temptation. The lights above shed cruel clarity on the sudden pallor defining his hard bone-structure. For some reason, he looked absolutely shattered by her announcement. It also occurred to her that he had lost weight over the last few days.

'We can talk about it tomorrow.' Consumed by raging misery, she lost heart in her prepared speeches about incompatability.

'We talk about it now. You've been with Huntingdon!' The condemnation came slamming back at her with ferocious bite as he mounted the stairs two at time.

He was seething, she registered bemusedly.

'You go slinking back to him the instant my back's turned. I won't let you go,' he swore fiercely. 'I'll kill him if he comes near you!'

'I can't think why. After all——'

'After all *nothing*,' he cut in wrathfully. 'You're my wife.'

Gingerly, she pressed open her bedroom door. 'Your room's next door, I seem to recall,' she reminded him for want of anything better to say.

'I was a fool to take that lying down! How dare you put me out of your bed?' he ground out between clenched white teeth, following her in, slamming the door with a resounding crash.

She blinked. 'I didn't——'

'I should never have stood for it. You played on my guilt!'

Catherine was frowning. 'Mrs Stokes must have moved your luggage. I remember her asking me how many bedrooms Castelleone had. We talked a lot about bedrooms but I really wasn't paying much attention——'

'Is this a private conversation or can anyone join in? I don't know what you're talking about!'

'She must have realised we had separate bedrooms in Italy and she probably assumed we wanted the same set-up here.' She smiled at him sunnily. 'You thought I was responsible?'

A dark flush had risen over his cheekbones. 'I came in very quietly and you were asleep that night. My clothes had gone.'

'I thought you'd told her to move them.' She could hardly credit that a mistake on the housekeeper's part had led to such a misunderstanding. 'Why didn't you say something?'

He looked ever so slightly sheepish. 'I didn't know what to say. All that day I was in shock at what you said to me on the jet.' He shifted a beautifully shaped brown hand in a movement of frustration. 'It only happens with you,' he breathed tautly.

She watched him move fluidly across the room like a restive cat night-prowling on velvet paws. 'What only happens with me?'

His jawline clenched. 'I lose my temper and I say things I don't mean.' Long fingers balled into a fist and then vanished into the pocket of his well-cut trousers. Discomfiture was written all over him. 'But that you should distrust me to such an extent . . . it . . . it hurt.'

So did saying it. She longed to reach out and put her arms round him, but sensed how unwelcome it would be. He was so proud, so defensive and ill-at-ease with words that came so easily to her. He was fluent in every other mood but this one, where deeper emotions intruded. And he was only talking now because anger had spurred him to the attempt.

'I was very insecure when I was pregnant,' she said uncertainly. 'You were breaking me up, Luc. Emotionally I was in a mess. I just didn't have the courage to face you with a complication you didn't want. It never occurred to me that you might choose to insist on marrying me or want to take any responsibility for the child I was expecting . . .'

The muscles in his strong brown throat worked. 'You don't have to justify your decision. I don't blame you for what you did,' he said almost indistinctly. 'I had to lose you before I could appreciate what you meant to me.'

He hadn't vacated the marital bed. He understood what she had done five years ago. He wasn't holding it against her as if she had failed him. He was accepting that, whether he liked it or not, it had been inevitable.

'Actually, if I hadn't been hit by that car,' she muttered, 'I would have phoned you.'

He paled. 'What car?'

She told him about the accident in the car park and the months she had spent in hospital. He was visibly appalled and shaken, but he didn't take her into his arms as she had secretly hoped. He wandered over to the window and looked back at her with glittering dark eyes. 'The first time I saw you, you reminded me of a Christmas-tree angel. Very fragile, not intended for human handling. You were wearing a hideous dress covered with roses and you were so tiny, it wore you. When I smiled at you you lit up like an electric light and you chattered non-stop for fifteen solid minutes,' he extended very quietly. 'You got lost in the middle of sentences. You didn't hear the phone ringing. You didn't notice that a woman came in and walked round while I was there. You were so dizzy, you fascinated me. I'd never met anyone like you before. You want to hear that I was ravished at first glance but I wasn't.'

'I never thought you were.' Her cheeks were hot enough to light a fire.

'That night I didn't think of you in a sexual way,' he was scrupulously careful to tell her.

'Nostalgia's not your thing,' she muttered fiercely.

'But I'd never met anyone with so much natural warmth. Being with you was like standing in the sunshine. When I walked away, I felt as though I'd kicked a puppy...'

Her nails ploughed furrows into her palms.

'It was surprisingly hard to walk away,' he confided in an undertone. 'Over the next two months, you kept drifting into my mind at the oddest times. I slept with another woman and then I would think about you. It was infuriating.'

'I'm not overcome by it either!' she snapped.

'When I was next in London, I didn't intend to look you up again. In fact, I had a woman with me on that trip. I deliberately went to a different hotel that was nowhere near the gallery.'

'Am I supposed to *want* to hear this?'

Tense dark eyes flickered over her and veiled. 'I never slept with her. She got on my nerves and I sent her back to New York. I was callous about it. I was callous in most of my dealings with women in those days. But I found I couldn't be callous with you. You had incredible pulling-power, *cara*. I was back at the gallery the second she left for the airport.'

'Why?' Involuntarily, she was finding that this was compulsive listening, a window on to a once blank wall.

'I didn't know why then. You were so extravagantly pleased to see me, it was as though you'd been waiting for me. Or as though you knew something I didn't. And perhaps you did.' An almost tender smile softened his mouth. 'It was unsettling. It threw me. I haven't asked a woman to go for a walk since I was thirteen. I was in a foul mood and you talked me out of it. You were so painfully honest about yourself and so agonisingly young, but somehow...' he hesitated '...you made me feel ten feet tall.'

'I made you feel so good it took you another two months to show up again!' she protested.

He released his breath in a hiss. 'You were only eighteen. You didn't belong in my world. I didn't want to hurt you. I also never wanted to make love to anyone as badly as I wanted you that night. I was twenty-seven, but I felt like a middle-aged lecher!' he gritted abruptly. 'I didn't plan to see you ever again.'

'Have you any idea how many nights I sat up, waiting for you to call?'

'I knew it.' He sounded grimly fatalistic. 'I could feel you waiting and I couldn't get you out of my head. I also found that I couldn't stay away from you. I believed that once I went to bed with you I would be cured.'

'That's disgusting!' she gasped.

'*Per Dio*, what do you want? The truth or a fairy-tale?' he slashed back at her in sudden anger. 'You think it is easy for me to admit these things? The lies I told to myself? That first night in Switzerland—how is it you describe euphoria? You thought you'd died and gone to heaven? Well, so did I, the first time I made love to you!'

The shocked line of her mouth had softened into a faint smile.

'But naturally I assured myself that I only felt that way because it was the best sex I'd ever had.'

Her smile evaporated like Scotch mist.

'I was in love with you but I didn't want to accept that fact,' he admitted harshly. 'I hated being away from you but I didn't want to take you abroad with me. The papers would have got hold of you then.'

'Would that have mattered?'

'Seven years ago, *cara*, you couldn't have handled a more public place in my life.' He shrugged in a jerky motion. 'And I didn't want to share you with anyone. I didn't want other women bitching at you. I didn't want gossip columnists cheapening what we had.'

She lowered her head. 'And perhaps you didn't want anyone realising that I had a literacy problem.'

'Yes. That both embarrassed and angered me.' He had to force out the admission. 'But I wouldn't have felt like that had I known you were dyslexic. I could have been open about that. In spite of that, wherever you were was home for me. If something worried me, I forgot about it when I was with you. I didn't realise until you had gone just how much I relied on you.'

She was trying very hard not to cry. He pulled her rigid figure into his arms very slowly, very gently. 'I have few excuses for what I did five years ago. But, if it is any consolation to you, I paid; *Dio* . . .' he said feelingly, 'I paid for not valuing you as I should have done. If only I'd intercepted you before you left the apartment that morning! I must have missed you by no more than an hour.'

She bowed her head against his broad chest, drowning in the warm masculine scent of him, feeling weak, shivery and on the brink of melting. 'I hated leaving you.'

'For a while, *bella mia*, I too hated you for leaving.' The hand smoothing through her hair was achingly gentle. 'It was the one and only time I lost interest in making money. I hit the bottle pretty hard...'

She was shocked. 'You?'

'Me. I felt unbelievably sorry for myself. I let everything slide.'

Her brow indented. 'Drew told me that you almost lost the shirt off your back a few years ago. Was that true?'

'It was.'

'Over me?' she whispered incredulously.

'I needed you,' he said gruffly. 'I missed you. I felt very alone.'

Tears swimming in her eyes, she wrapped her arms tightly round him, too upset by the image he invoked to speak.

'I picked myself up again because I believed you would come back,' he shared. 'When I saw you in the Savoy two weeks ago there was nothing I would not have done to get you back.'

'No?' She positively glowed at the news.

'It was not, however, how I pictured our reconciliation. You shouldn't have been with another man. You should have looked pleased to see me, instead of horror-stricken. I'm afraid I went off the rails that day,' he breathed tautly.

'Did you?' She smiled up at him, unconcerned.

He frowned down at her. 'I threatened you. I took advantage of your amnesia to practically kidnap you. You could have been madly in love with Huntingdon and I was determined that you would get over it. When you came round in the clinic and smiled at me, I was lost to all conscience. When I realised you'd lost your memory, all I could think about was getting you out of the country.'

'You were always quick to recognise a good opportunity,' she sighed approvingly.

Long fingers cupped her cheekbones. 'Catherine, what I did was wrong. This week, after I learnt about Daniel and cooled down, which I did very quickly, I felt very ashamed of what I had done. It was completely unscrupulous of me.'

'If you say so.' She wound her arms round his neck, stretching up on tiptoe. 'Personally I think it was thrilling. I waited twenty-four and a half years to be spirited off to an Italian castle, and I wouldn't have missed it for the world.'

'Be serious.' He was alarmingly set on contrition. In fact, the more forgiving she became, the more grim he looked. 'Be honest with me. Can you forgive me for what I have said and done?'

'I forgive you freely, absolutely and forever. Do you want to know why?' she whispered teasingly. 'You're crazy about me...aren't you?' She drew back to stare up at him, suffering a sudden lurch in overwhelming confidence.

Brilliant golden eyes shimmered almost fiercely over her anxious face. 'Only a lunatic would behave the way I did if I wasn't,' he grated. 'Of course I love you!'

'I don't want a separation...I don't even want a separate bedroom,' she swore.

'Relax—you weren't getting either. What I have, I hold.' He lifted her with wonderful ease off her feet. 'But I should never have made love to you before you regained your memory. Unfortunately that night I found you in my bed,' his voice thickened betrayingly, 'I could not resist you.'

'I can't resist you, either.' She sank small determined hands into his black hair and drew his mouth down to hers. He lowered her to the bed without breaking the connection. It was some minutes before she remembered to breathe again.

'It's been torture to stay away from you,' he admitted roughly. 'But I believed that was what you wanted. I went to all that trouble arranging to go to Paris, thinking that you would be tempted to come, and you said no.'

'Serves you right for being so casual about it.'

He shuddered beneath the caressing sweep of her hands. 'Don't do that,' he groaned, pinning her provocative hands to the mattress. 'When you do that, I react like a teenager.'

'Why do you think I do it?' she murmured wickedly.

'*Dio*, I want you so much,' he said raggedly, removing her dress with more speed than expertise. Abruptly he stopped dead, staring down at her. 'It isn't safe, is it? I could make you pregnant.'

'The best things in life are dangerous. It's your choice,' she whispered.

'You wouldn't mind?' He looked dazed. 'By the pool that day, you weren't very enthusiastic about the idea. That's why I worried that it was too late.'

She ran a loving fingertip across his sensual mouth. 'I'm afraid all those intensely erotic experiences in Italy were unproductive.'

He nipped at her fingertip with his teeth, a brilliant smile curving his lips. 'Give me a month's trial.'

'You're so modest.' She blushed under raking golden eyes, heat striking her to the very centre of her body, making her tremble deliciously. He started to kiss her slowly and deeply and hungrily until conversation was the last thing on either of their minds.

What followed was wild, passionate and incredibly sweet. And afterwards he told her how much he loved her in Italian and English and French.

'You've got a certain *je ne sais quoi*,' Catherine conceded against a damp brown shoulder, letting the tip of her tongue slide teasingly across his smooth skin.

Luc's tousled dark head lifted, a sudden lancing grin flashing across his darkly handsome features. 'I understood that I was a habit.'

'You are,' she sighed with a voluptuous little wriggle of glorious contentment. 'An addictive one. Didn't I mention that?'

Jacqueline Baird began writing as a hobby when her family objected to the smell of her oil painting! She immediately became hooked on the romantic genre, which proved to be successful as her first romance was published by Mills & Boon® in 1988. Since then over four and a half million copies of her books have been distributed worldwide.

Jacqueline loves travelling and worked her way around the world from Europe to the Americas and Australia, returning to marry her teenage sweetheart. She lives in Ponteland, Northumbria, the county of her birth, and has two teenage sons. She enjoys playing badminton, and spends most weekends with husband Jim, sailing their Gp.14 around Derwent Reservoir.

THE VALENTINE CHILD

by

JACQUELINE BAIRD

CHAPTER ONE

HIS lips were warm on the tender skin of her throat. Somewhere along the way Nigel had removed his T-shirt and she could feel the heat of his body through her fine silk blouse. She closed her eyes tight and told herself that she was enjoying his kisses. It was Nigel—her friend, her colleague and soon to be her lover.

They were sprawled across the sofa in Zoë's London apartment, the only sound Nigel's heavy breathing. She felt his fingers at the buttons of her blouse and tensed, then forced herself to relax. Hadn't she planned this? She was twenty, and still a virgin! And now she was finally going to be a woman! So why did she feel sick?

The thought stopped her cold, and, shoving at Nigel's chest, she said, 'No, Nigel. Get off.' The ensuing tussle was undignified and bordering on the ridiculous. Zoë struggled from beneath his sprawling body but her elbow caught him in the eye, and his yelp of pain was drowned out by the ringing of the doorbell, followed by loud and rapid knocking.

'Saved by the bell!' Zoë murmured, and dashed across the room. Whoever was calling after midnight was in danger of waking the whole house. Her apartment was one of six in a converted Victorian town house.

She flung open the door, about to demand what all the urgency was for, and stopped. Her mouth fell open and she brushed a small hand through the tumbled mass of her silver-blonde hair, sweeping it out of her eyes to get a better view. It couldn't be... But it was... Justin Gifford.

For a second she saw the old Justin, as he had been before the fatal night of her eighteenth birthday. He was smiling tenderly down at her, his dark eyes filled with some emotion she could not guess at.

'Justin.' She said his name, and raised her hand as though to touch him, but he brushed past her and into the room. She closed the door and turned around. Obviously she had been mistaken about his tender glance, she thought dryly.

'So that's what stopped you.' Nigel's voice broke the tense silence. 'You heard the bell.'

Zoë glanced at Nigel, who was sitting on the sofa, struggling to pull his shirt back on, and then back at Justin.

The comparison was inevitable. Nigel looked like a flushed, frustrated twenty-one-year-old—which he was. Whereas Justin, at thirty-five, and touching six feet tall, exuded an aura of sophisticated, arrogant masculinity that was undeniable. Certain of his place and power in the world as a top barrister with a glittering future, tipped to be one of the youngest judges ever appointed, he dominated those around him without even trying.

He was doing it now! Standing in the centre of the room, a long cashmere overcoat draped casually over his broad shoulders. Beneath it a black wool roll-neck sweater moulded the muscular contours of his broad chest, and black denim jeans did the same for his long legs. His night-black hair was, unusually for him, rumpled in disarray and the contempt in his eyes, as he recognised at a glance what had been going on, was unmistakable.

His gaze swept over her small, dishevelled form and the furious glitter in his deep brown eyes would have made a saint quake...

'Does your lover live with you?' he demanded harshly.

Zoë tensed, and wiped her damp palms nervously down her jean-clad thighs. She wriggled her bare toes in the deep-pile carpet and straightened her shoulders in a vain attempt to add inches to her diminutive stature. She tilted back her head and looked a long way up into angry eyes.

'I don't think that is any of your business, Justin. More to the point, what are you doing here at this hour?' She was proud—her voice sounded firm when inside she was trembling. Nigel was not helping any by pulling his shirt down with one hand and knuckling his eye with the other, looking like a drowsy, sated male.

'I'm making it my business, Zoë.' Justin stepped towards her, his massive frame looming over her. She had nowhere to go; her back was at the door. 'Is that the kind of pipsqueak you prefer?' he demanded scathingly. 'I can't say I admire your taste. Get rid of him. Now.'

'Nigel is my guest——' she spluttered.

'So he doesn't live here?' Justin cut in, and simply grabbed her arm and swung her behind him while roaring at Nigel, 'You—whatever your name is—get out.'

Nigel got to his feet. 'Wait just a minute. Who the hell do you think you are? Zoë and I——'

'There is no Zoë, not for you. Now out, before I throw you out.'

Zoë had seen Justin angry before, but never like this. 'You'd better go, Nigel,' she said quietly. Justin's hand around her wrist relaxed slightly at her surrender to his request...

'It's OK. Justin is my uncle's partner; I'll be all right,' she assured him, and she was free. Involuntarily she rubbed her wrist as she stepped away from Justin's towering presence, looking, if she did but know it, as if she was wringing her hands in agitation.

After a token objection Nigel left, and Zoë didn't blame him. She had first met Justin Gifford as a sad and frightened fourteen-year-old who had just lost her actor parents in an air disaster in California. She had been swept from her boarding-school in Portland, Maine, to be deposited on her only relative, Uncle Bertie Brown, in England.

She remembered as if it were yesterday. Born and brought up in the States, with an American mother and an English father, she had arrived in what to her had been an alien country, to live in a huge old house, "Black Gables", with an uncle she had never met before.

She had been curled up on the window-seat in the garden-room, quietly crying, when a deep voice had said softly, 'Are you all right, little girl?' She had looked up into the darkest brown eyes she had ever seen, set in the tanned, attractive face of Justin Gifford. Tall and built like a quarter-back, with the broken nose to prove it, he had swung her on to his lap and comforted her and she had been smitten with her first ever crush on a member of the opposite sex.

She glanced warily at him; he was positively bristling with rage and Justin in this mood was dangerous. The only other time she had seen him as mad had been the terrible night of her eighteenth birthday party. Justin had arrived at the party with a red-haired woman in tow—Janet Ord—and Zoë had been consumed by jealousy.

Ever since moving in with her uncle and first seeing Justin she had adored him, even though at twenty-eight he'd been twice her age. Justin had spent many a weekend at the house in Surrey and had always treated Zoë with the greatest kindness. They had talked, laughed and played tennis together.

Every year a valentine card had arrived at Black Gables for her with the simple message "Thinking of you, from your tall, dark, handsome friend". The postmark had been from London and, as Justin was the only man she'd known in the city, she had hoarded the cards as tokens of his love. In her girlish heart she'd honestly believed that he loved her as she loved him.

Her birthday party had changed all that. Furious that he had brought a woman with him, Zoë had stayed up until four in the morning waiting for Justin to return from driving Janet home, and then had tried to seduce him.

A grim smile twisted her full lips at the memory. It hadn't worked. Justin had taken one penetrating look at her, dressed in only a flimsy nightie, and had laughed out loud.

'Run along to bed, little girl, before you get more than you bargained for,' he had drawled with mocking amusement.

Instead she had thrown her arms around his neck and pressed her slender body against him, and demanded that he kiss her. She had known he wanted to... What followed was engraved in her mind forever.

'Maybe I will at that,' he had growled as his strong arms had closed around her. His dark head had swooped down, and he'd proceeded to ravage her mouth with hard, passionate kisses.

At first she'd exulted in his fierce passion but he'd made no concession to her youth or innocence and when his large, strong hands had swept all over her trembling body, and she'd felt the full force of his masculine aggression, she'd been suddenly terrified by the savagery she had unleashed and had cried for him to stop.

They had not been friends since. Zoë made a point of not being at Black Gables when she knew Justin was arriving for the weekend. It hadn't been difficult—what with studying at art college and moving to her own apartment, she had rarely seen him over the past couple of years.

'Fasten your blouse, for God's sake!' A deep, grating voice broke into her troubled reminiscences.

'What...?' She glanced down at herself, and felt a tell-tale tide of colour flood her pale face. 'Oh!' she gasped. Her blouse was open to the waist, revealing her firm, high breasts hardly covered by a wisp of white lace. Head bent, with trembling fingers she fastened her blouse. She might not have seen Justin for ages, but she was horrified to realise that he still had the power to make her blush like a lovesick schoolgirl.

Taking a deep breath, she bravely raised her head, her blue eyes clashing with furious brown ones. 'Is it possible you have some explanation for bursting into my apartment in the middle of the night? Or perhaps you've been drinking?' she prompted with all the hauteur she could muster.

In the blink of an eye a shutter seemed to fall over his hard face, masking all expression. 'Sorry, Zoë, you're right of course. You're a grown woman; your private life is none of my business.'

'Big of you to recognise that,' she drawled sarcastically.

'Cut the sarcasm and sit down. I have some bad news.'

'News?' And suddenly she was filled with a dreadful foreboding. She should have realised immediately that nothing short of a major catastrophe would have bought Justin to her apartment in the middle of the night.

She moved towards him; her small hand clasped his forearm. 'What has happened?' Her beautiful face paled; her eyes searched his rugged features. 'Not...?'

'There's no easy way to say this. Bertie has had a massive heart attack and is in Intensive Care at the local hospital. I'll take you to him.'

'Will he be OK, Justin?' Zoë asked the question for the hundredth time of the brooding figure sitting beside her on the banquette in the cold waiting-room of the hospital.

He turned his dark head, compassion in his steady gaze. 'Of course he will be, little one. Your uncle Bertie is a fighter.' And, curving a long arm around her slender shoulders, he drew her into his side. 'Snuggle up and try to rest, hmm?' With his other hand he brushed the tumble of blonde hair from her brow. 'I'll look after you; after all, that's what friends are for.' He smiled softly, giving her shoulder a brief squeeze.

Comforted by his reassuring words and held against the warmth of his hard body, she forgot the humiliation, the embarrassment that had made her avoid him for the past two years. Instead she lifted her sapphire-blue eyes to his harshly handsome face and said, 'Are we friends again?' And they were.

Two weeks later, when Bertie was released from hospital a month before Christmas, Zoë willingly gave up her apartment and returned with her uncle to Black Gables, quite happy to commute every day to her job as a graphic artist at Magnum Advertising in London if it meant spending her free time with her uncle.

Zoë positively danced into the breakfast-room. 'Good morning, Uncle Bertie.' She pressed a swift kiss on the parchment-like cheek of the old man sitting at the pine table. 'You're looking better today,' she said, with a quick smile, though in reality she was worried about him. His once tall, raw-boned figure seemed to be shrinking by the day. His fine head of silver hair appeared lank and somehow lifeless. But she did not betray her worry as she asked, 'Any post for me today?'

'Yes, two, minx.' He smiled fondly back at her. 'And thank you.' He waved a card, with a big red rabbit sitting in a heart on the front, in her face. 'It was kind of you to think of me.'

Chuckling, she took the two envelopes he held out to her and, plonking down on the nearest chair, ripped them open. One was obviously from Bertie. 'You're not supposed to sign them, you know, Uncle,' she admonished, and then went dreamy-eyed over the next valentine card: 'Thinking of you, from your tall, dark, handsome friend.'

She just knew it was Justin and tonight she was going to tell him she had known all along. Finally she was confident enough in herself and her new-found adult relationship with him.

Over the past months he had been a tower of strength, visiting most weekends, and the rapport he shared with Uncle Bertie had naturally spread to include her again. They had shared the occasional dinner date; Justin had taken her to the theatre, and the ballet and, most important of all, at the end of their evenings out he had always kissed her goodnight, and always left Zoë aching for something more. But tonight Justin was taking her to the Law Society's Valentine's Ball at a top London hotel, and she just knew that tonight would be special.

'Not going to work today, young lady?' Uncle Bertie's question broke into her happy reverie.

'No, I have the day off, and I'm going to pamper myself shamelessly because Justin's taking me to the ball.'

'I see . . .' His watery blue eyes crinkled at the corners.

'Good. He's a fine young man. You couldn't do better.'

'I know,' she agreed, with a cheeky grin.

A dozen hours later Zoë heard Justin arrive as she blotted her lipstick for the final time. She seldom bothered much with make-up, having a fine clear skin, but tonight she had gone to town and she was delighted with the result.

Her eyes were huge, her brows and lashes subtly darkened, and a faint touch of colour on her eyelids served to enhance the sparkling blue of her eyes. She had used a light foundation that seemed to make her skin gleam almost translucently. And, daringly, she had coloured her wide, full-lipped mouth in a bright cerise lip-gloss that exactly matched her gown.

The dress was a romantic dream, she thought happily, floating out of her room and down the grand staircase to where Justin and her uncle waited. Designed in cerise satin, demure cap sleeves set off the plunging, heart-shaped, fitted bodice that nipped her waist and ended in black embroidered points over her hips, then flared out into a wide skirt with an underskirt of frothy layers of black net.

The assistant in Harvey Nichols had assured her that the nineteenth-century romantic look was all the rage and, when she stopped halfway down the stairs to glance down at Justin, and saw the flare of admiration in his eyes, she knew she had made the right choice.

Justin—tall, dark and incredibly impressive in a conservative black dinner-suit—moved to the stairs and held out his hand to her. She felt like a princess as he led her down the last few steps.

'You have grown into an amazingly beautiful woman, Zoë. You look absolutely stunning.' His dark eyes gleamed with admiration and some other emotion that Zoë hoped was love.

'Thank you, kind sir,' she said prettily.

A wry smile curved Justin's firm mouth. 'But I knew I should have asked. I'm no good at all at this romance thing.' And, handing her a clear cellophane box, with a shrug of his broad shoulders he added, 'For you. And before you say anything even I know a corsage of red roses will clash with your dress. Sorry...'

'I love them, but you shouldn't have; your valentine card has always been enough for me,' she declared openly, her eyes sparkling with happiness. 'Wait till I get my cape; the corsage will look great on it.'

Dashing back upstairs, she didn't see Justin's dark scowl or hear his muttered, 'What card?'

'Right, I'm ready.' She returned, holding out her velvet cloak for Justin to place around her shoulders. She shivered with delicious anticipation when his strong fingers caressed her flesh as he fastened the cap and solemnly pinned the red roses on the velvet above her breast.

With Uncle Bertie's good wishes, and his admonition to stay in town for the night ringing in her ears, Justin led her out to the car—a sleek black BMW—and slid in beside her.

Justin was the perfect partner; he insisted on dancing every dance with her, and the evening took on a magic all of its own. She could not help but observe the respect and esteem he attracted from his fellow professionals. She overheard in the powder-room that it was rumoured that he was definitely going to be on the next list of judges, and, on returning to the ballroom, she could not resist teasing him unmercifully.

'Such exalted company. Why, m'lud, I fear you give me the vapours.' She fluttered her thick lashes unashamedly.

'I'd like to give you a lot more,' he drawled mockingly, his brown eyes smiling down into hers. 'You little tease.'

'Who—*moi*? Your honour! No, your honour!' She camped it up, pressing a hand to her heart.

'You're asking for trouble, little one,' Justin opined, and swept her into his arms and on to the dance-floor.

'If...or...when...' he spaced the words out as they moved slowly and lazily around the floor to the haunting strains of 'Unchained Melody' '...I...am...made...a...judge...' he curled her small hand in his and held it against his chest while his other hand stroked up her back to bury beneath the silken fall of her pale blonde hair and curve around her nape '... it won't be "Unchained Melody" we dance to, my love.'

He tilted her face up to his and murmured against her ear, 'I'll sentence you to be chained to me for life.' And then his mouth moved over hers in a kiss as light as the brush of a butterfly's wing.

She clung to him, her eyes shining like stars; her breasts, hard against his chest, throbbed with burgeoning arousal while her heart drummed to an erratic beat. 'If only,' she breathed, licking her suddenly too dry lips.

His dark eyes followed the movement of her tongue. 'Not if—when,' he rasped, his arms tightening around her until even through the many layers of her gown Zoë could feel his hardening need, and she finally admitted to herself that nothing had changed—her schoolgirl crush had turned into a woman's love for a man.

'Let's get out of here,' he said urgently.

'But it's only eleven.'

'The way I feel right now, I won't live to midnight.' Their eyes met and clung—no more teasing, no amusement, just a basic primeval need.

'Yes,' she agreed softly.

Back in Justin's apartment, she barely noticed the décor; she had eyes only for Justin.

He stripped off her velvet evening cloak and dropped it to the floor, then, catching her hand, hurried her down a hall through a door and into a large room—his bedroom! She hesitated, eyeing the king-size bed warily. Was she ready for this? But the question was answered by Justin.

'Zoë.' He cupped her small face in his large hands and tilted her head back, his deep brown eyes darkened to almost black. 'Don't be afraid. You know I would never do anything to hurt you. But I feel as though I've waited aeons for you. I can't wait any longer.' His mouth brushed gently over hers. 'I promised myself I would do this properly,' he breathed against her lips.

She reached her slender arms around his neck, her heart melting with love, and felt anything but proper... She gazed up into his dark eyes, and was surprised to see a hint of uncertainty, a touching vulnerability in their black depths. 'Do what?' she encouraged with a dreamy smile.

His hands lowered, one to curve around her waist, the other to go to his jacket pocket. 'Ask you to be my valentine tonight and always. Be my wife,' he husked, and, putting a little space between them, he showed her the velvet ring-box.

Zoë, her eyes misted with tears of joy, took the box and opened it. A gasp of delight escaped her at the sight of the diamond and sapphire ring. 'Put it on for me.' She held it out with a hand that trembled.

Justin slipped the ring on the appropriate finger. 'I take it that's a yes?' he queried huskily before he enfolded her once more in his arms; his dark head bent and he kissed her, long and tenderly.

She parted her lips at his urging; his tongue seductively traced the inside of her mouth and she was lost. She would be anything he wanted her to be.

'Now, do I get to unwrap my valentine? You, my heart,' he mouthed against her cheek as he spread small kisses all over her face, her eyelids, the slender arch of her throat, while his hands deftly found the zip of her dress.

It was no good; she could stand it no longer; she had to get away for a while. Her head was pounding, and if she had to listen to one more stilted condolence on the death of her uncle Bertie she would break down completely.

'Are you all right, Zoë?'

She glanced up into concerned deep brown eyes and tried to smile. 'I will be when this is over.' A supporting arm closed around her tiny waist and she relaxed against the hard, muscled, masculine frame of her husband of two months—Justin. She still had to pinch herself sometimes to believe that she and Justin were actually man and wife.

'Zoë.' Justin's voice snapped her back to the present.

She raised misty blue eyes to his. 'I'm OK.'

'You're not,' he contradicted her bluntly. His hand tightened fractionally on her waist. 'Slope off to your secret seat, and I'll make sure you're not disturbed for a while.' His hand moved to her back and turned her to the door. His dark head bent, she felt the feather-light brush of his mouth against the top of her head and she was out in the large oak-panelled hall.

Justin knew her so well, she thought, slipping quickly through the door opposite and making straight for the window-seat. Curled up behind the curtain, she stared out of the window. The clear, bright light of a mid-May day glinted over the long lush green lawns and on down to the river, which wound like a sinuous silver snake along the bottom of the garden.

Too nice a day for a funeral! She sighed deeply, and a tear rolled slowly down the curve of her cheek. Uncle Bertie—dead...

She wiped away the moisture with the back of her hand. She couldn't have any tears left. She had done her crying for her uncle over the past few months when it had become obvious that it was simply a matter of time before his ruined heart gave out. The funeral today was the last act for a man who had led an exemplary life. The guests across the hall numbered among some of the greatest names in the land, here to pay their respects.

Uncle Bertie had been an eminent judge destined for one of the highest positions in the English judiciary, until he had suffered his heart attack last November.

Zoë closed her eyes and lay back against the wall, her feet tucked beneath her. She was going to miss him, she knew. But—thank God!—she had Justin; she was not alone, and Uncle Bertie had been delighted when she'd married his protégé. So she at least had the solace of knowing that her uncle's last weeks had been happy.

Smiling softly to herself, she glanced at her sparkling engagement ring and the pale gold band beside it. Then she breathed on the window, misting the glass, and, in a childish gesture, drew a heart with her forefinger and inserted the initials ZG and JG with a rather wobbly arrow, remembering the Valentine's ball.

No girl had ever had a more tender, intoxicating initiation into womanhood. Justin was the perfect lover; slowly and carefully he had kissed and caressed, urged and cajoled her through the intricacies of love, and at the final moment had protected her from any untoward consequences.

The next morning, when he had taken her back to Black Gables, he had formally asked Uncle Bertie for her hand in marriage, informed her arrogantly that as his wife-to-be she no longer needed to work, and, of course, she had agreed. Then, a month later, on the arm of her uncle Bertie, she had walked down the aisle of the village church to wed Justin.

She sighed. Who would have thought that two months later Bertie would be dead? Then she heard the voice of Mrs Sara Blacket, the wife of one of the partners in Justin's law firm, speaking.

'It's a magnificent house. Gifford has done very well for himself, even if he did have to marry the old man's niece to get it.'

Why, the cheeky old bat! Zoë thought, and would have moved, but then she recognised another voice—that of Mary Master, the wife of a High Court judge.

'Oh, I don't think Justin married for any mercenary reason. They make a lovely couple, and it's obvious she adores him.'

'I don't dispute the girl loves him, but my Harold told me he'd heard that Bertie Brown, when he realised he was dying, offered Justin his place as the head of chambers on condition that he married the niece. He wanted her settled before he died.'

'I find that hard to believe. In any case, the other partners would have had some say in the matter,' Mary Master argued.

'Bertie was well liked, and which one of them would refuse a dying man's last wish? As Harold said, the girl is exquisitely beautiful, tiny—like a rare Dresden china doll—but young and hardly a match for an aggressively virile male like Gifford.

'His taste in the past was for large, bosomy ladies more his own age. Remember the Christmas dinner two years ago and Justin's redhead partner? Harold told me they were taking bets on whether her boobs would stay covered through to the sweet course.'

'Oh, really, Sara!' Mary exclaimed. 'That's a bit much, and in any case Justin was not dating Zoë at the time. He was a free agent.'

Zoë cringed behind the curtain, her face flaming; she could not believe what the Blacket woman was saying. Didn't want to.

'Believe me or not, Mary, but I wouldn't mind being a fly on the wall when the will is read. Bertie befriended Justin Gifford when he was a teenager and his father died—apparently they were old friends. I'll bet Gifford gets at least half the old boy's estate, if not more. Hardly fair on Zoë, his only living relative.'

'Surely it's not important? They are married—everything they have is divided equally anyway.'

Zoë heard Mary Master reply. The woman's voice was fading—they were obviously leaving the room—but Zoë could not move; she was frozen in shock.

'Exactly my point.' Sara Blacket's piercing voice echoed in the room as she closed the door. 'Gifford is a very ambitious man and by doing what the old man wanted and marrying the American girl he has made doubly sure of getting control of virtually everything. I can't see young Zoë being involved in finance at all—she's the arty type.'

Zoë stared at the heart she had drawn on the glass; the mist was fading, the shape disappearing—a bad omen! Don't be stupid! she told herself, and quickly raised her hand and rubbed the window clean. But she could not clean the doubt in her mind away so easily. Could it be true? Had Uncle Bertie insisted that Justin marry her? No, of course not, her common sense told her. Justin loved her, didn't he?

She slid off the seat and stood up. She was overreacting. Sara Blacket was a nosy, overbearing old gossip whose husband, as the most senior in chambers, had wanted to be head himself. Justin had told her as much. Obviously it was pure sour grapes on Sara's part.

'Zoë? Zoë?' Justin's voice broke into her uncomfortable thoughts, and, smoothing the plain black jersey shift down over her hips, she moved towards the door. It was flung open and Justin walked in, his dark eyes full of concern.

'Ah! There you are. I saw Mary and Sara leave. I take it you didn't get the peace you were looking for,' he said lightly, casually slipping an arm around her shoulders. 'Judge Master is waiting in the study, darling. It's time to say goodbye to the guests, and then the will will be read. Are you up to it or would your rather wait? There's no hurry.'

'Why? Because you know what's in it?' The curt words had left her mouth before she could stop them...

'No. No, I don't.' Justin turned her around to face him, his arms encircling her waist, holding her loosely, his dark eyes scrutinising her pale face. 'I was thinking of you; you look tired. It's been a long day.'

Held in his arms, conscious of his warmth and the tender care in his expression, Zoë hated herself for doubting him for a minute, but she could not control her wayward tongue. She loved Justin, and she needed his reassurance.

'You do love me, Justin?' she asked softly, her eyes catching his, a pleading light in their sapphire depths.

'Of course I do, silly girl; I married you, didn't I?' And his dark head lowered, blocking out the light as his mouth moved over hers in an achingly tender kiss.

She moved closer into his embrace and curved her slender arms around his neck; she felt his arms tighten and she opened her mouth, inviting the kiss to deepen. She sighed into his mouth, their breath mingling there, tongues entwining; she ran her fingers through his thick black hair, her heart pounding. Justin loved her; he was her husband, her love, her life.

Justin slightly parted his long legs, one strong hand curving down over her bottom and urging her between his muscular thighs. She curved into the hot, hard warmth of his body, her breasts flattened against his ribcage, her nipples tingling with the contact then hardening as his other hand swept up to cup possessively over one high, firm breast through the soft wool of her dress.

He broke the kiss long enough to nuzzle her throat, his mouth covering the madly beating pulse in her neck then trailing back to her softly parted lips; a low moan escaped her just as his mouth found hers once more.

As always she trembled, melting against him, her blood pounding through her veins, but suddenly he was easing her away. 'Justin,' she murmured.

'Easy, Zoë. Now is not the time.'

She raised passion-hazed eyes to his rugged face; she recognised the dark blush of desire staining his taut features at the same time as she saw the familiar iron control reassert itself in the black depths of his eyes.

'You're right, as usual,' she agreed, and was swept into a gentle hug, his large hand stroking the back of her head as he pressed her to his broad chest, easing the sexual tension surrounding them into something more manageable.

'Come on, Zoë; the quicker we say goodbye to the guests, the sooner we can get this day over with.'

He was right, but sometimes, just sometimes, Zoë wished that he would get swept away by passion. But the great Justin Gifford, renowned for his cool, lethal voice, his absolute control of any jury, never, ever lost control.

Now, where had that unkind thought come from? Zoë mused as she saw the guests depart. Justin was British and restraint was an accepted characteristic of the people, and she should know! On first arriving here, a typical American teenager, she had found it difficult to adjust to the more formal way of life.

Half an hour later she followed Justin into the study and sat down beside him on the black hide sofa. Mrs Crumpet, the housekeeper, Jud, her husband—also the gardener—and John Smith, the chauffeur, plus the two daily women, stood around in a rather embarrassed silence as Judge Master sat down in the chair behind Uncle Bertie's desk.

It soon became apparent that Bertie hadn't changed his will in years. All the staff were left generous amounts of money and there were pensions for Mr and Mrs

Crumpet and the chauffeur. His law books were to go to Justin and the remainder of the estate was left to Zoë, with the proviso that Justin be her guardian until she was twenty-five.

'You—my guardian.' She smiled at Justin. 'It sounds slightly kinky as we're already married.'

Judge Master laughed. 'Bertie made this will when you were sixteen; he did think about changing it, but, as you and Justin married, there was no real point. It's all in the family anyway.'

The staff left the room, and then Judge Master revealed the extent of the estate. It was not a great deal of money but, with the house, a very nice legacy. She felt Justin tense beside her, and she shot him a puzzled look, but he ignored her, his gaze fixed on Judge Master.

'With the house included, if he didn't make prior arrangements, the death duty will be quite considerable.' Justin was all business, and Zoë felt oddly excluded as the two men talked literally over her head.

'Yes, I did warn him,' the judge responded.

'But you know Bertie—he refused to admit he was dying right up until the end.'

'I shouldn't worry about the tax, though. Zoë is twenty-one in a month, when she will obtain control of her trust fund from her parents. I was talking to the lawyer in New York only a few days ago, and, with the reissue of an old film of her father's about dinosaurs, apparently her trust fund is quite healthy.'

'How healthy exactly?' Justin asked quietly.

'Double what Bertie left, so the tax should not be a problem. Mind you, I would advise you to sell this place; it's far too big for this day and age. Maintenance alone was always a drain on Bertie's funds.'

'Do you mind, gentlemen? I *am* sitting here,' Zoë intervened, and wanted to laugh as the two males in the room turned to look at her as though she were some apparition.

Judge Master was the first to recover. 'Yes, of course. It has been a long day; Justin and I can discuss all this in a day or two, and I'd better be making tracks or Mary will not be pleased.'

Zoë smiled; she liked Judge Master and, after the conversation she had overheard earlier, she appreciated his wife, who had defended her against the infamous Sara Blacket.

Justin rose to his feet and walked across to the cabinet in the corner of the oak-panelled study. 'You will join me in a drink, Judge? I need one.' He picked up a bottle of whisky, opened it and poured a large shot into a crystal tumbler before adding, 'How about you, Zoë?'

She looked across at her husband; his back was to her, his shoulders tense, and, as she watched, his dark head tilted back as he lifted the glass to his mouth and drank. It was unusual for Justin to drink spirits—an occasional glass of wine was more his style.

'Zoë.' Justin turned, glass in hand. 'Do you want one?' he asked again, his expression austere.

'No. You and the judge carry on. I'll go and find Mary.'

Ten minutes later, she stood in the entrance hall and thanked Judge Master for all his help, but her glance kept straying to Justin at her side as she said goodbye to the couple. She had the oddest feeling that although he was there he was not really with her.

The door closed behind Judge and Mary Master and she sighed in relief.

'At last it's all over,' she murmured, her eyes seeking her husband's. He had been a tower of strength all through the death, the funeral, everything. She could never have managed without him, and all she wanted now was to feel the comfort of his arms around her.

Dressed in a perfectly tailored dark suit, a stark white shirt and the obligatory black tie, he looked all powerful, virile male, as though nothing could touch him or those he cared for. He was her rock, her comfort and her lover, and she had never needed him more than now. She stepped towards him.

'I have some work to attend to, Zoë; I'll see you at dinner.'

She shot him a pleading if puzzled glance and could have sworn that he was avoiding her eyes. 'Yes, OK.' But she doubted whether he heard her as she was talking to his back.

CHAPTER TWO

ZOË knocked on the heavy oak door, turned the handle, opened it and entered the study. Justin was sitting behind the huge mahogany desk in what used to be Uncle Bertie's chair, his broad shoulders hunched, his head buried in a mass of papers.

He had removed his jacket and tie, and his white shirt was open at the neck, the sleeves rolled back to reveal sinewy forearms sprinkled with a downy covering of dark hair. He looked stern and somehow remote. She moved silently across the room but he sensed her presence, his proud head lifting.

'Yes?' he said distantly.

'It's eight—dinner is ready.' She shook her head in disgust at his vacant look, her long blonde hair floating around her shoulders in a silvery cloud as she moved to his side and leant against his broad shoulder. Placing one slender arm around his other shoulder, she added, 'You work far too hard, Justin, and it has got to stop.' She pressed a swift kiss on the top of his head. 'Come and eat.'

'I have to work hard if I expect to keep my beautiful wife in the manner to which she is accustomed,' he retorted, his sensuous mouth curving in a brief smile, and, getting to his feet, he spanned her tiny waist with his strong hands and swung her high in the air, as one would a child. 'And that's my mission in life.'

She grinned down into his handsome face, thrilled by the compliment. 'Not any more, you don't, if what Judge Master said about my trust fund is correct,' she teased.

Justin looked up at her, all trace of amusement deserting his hard features, and abruptly he lowered her to the ground. 'Yes, of course. Apparently I've married a woman of means,' he drawled, stepping back and rolling down the sleeves of his shirt. 'The tax man will certainly see it that way,' he added with dry sarcasm, hooking his jacket with one hand as he headed for the door, and flinging over his shoulder, 'Let's eat.'

She stared at his retreating back for a moment, hurt by the obvious sarcasm in his tone. Was it possible that Justin was disappointed not to have received more in the will? No, he couldn't be. He was a comfortably wealthy man in his own right.

Later, sitting opposite each other across the small table in the breakfast-room, sharing a simple, almost silent evening meal of beef goulash and rice followed by ice-cream, the thought haunted her, and by the time they were sipping their coffee she could contain herself no longer.

'Justin, are you upset by the will?' She had to ask. Absolute honesty was essential to a good marriage—or so all the books said—and she wanted their marriage to be perfect.

His black head lifted, his eyes capturing hers across the table. 'No, certainly not. But why do you ask?' he demanded, the hard tone of his voice jarring on her sensitive nerves.

'Earlier, in the study, you didn't seem too amused when...'

His mouth compressed. 'Today is hardly a day for amusement; we have just buried your uncle,' he prompted, in a voice he usually used to destroy some unsuspecting witness.

'Please, Justin, you don't have to remind me. I just thought... Well, maybe you felt left out.' How could she tell him of the conversation she had overheard? Her own doubts...?

'No, I assure you,' he said, lowering his voice, 'as far as the will is concerned, it was exactly as it should be. Bertie was my guide and mentor all through my career and before, and I am greatly honoured that he left me his law books.'

Zoë believed him; she knew his sentiment was genuine and she wanted to say so, but, as often happened though she was reluctant to admit it, her brilliantly clever husband left her tongue-tied. She only had to look into his deep brown eyes, or note the curve of his mouth as he spoke, and his effect on her was immediate. After two months of marriage her pulse still raced at the sight of him. Tonight a lock of black hair had fallen over his broad brow and unconsciously she reached across the table and brushed it back with her fingers.

Justin caught her hand in his and pressed a quick kiss to her palm, his glance flashing knowingly to her face. 'You've had a long, hard day, Zoë. Leave the worrying to me and go to bed, hmm? I'll join you later.' He squeezed her hand before letting it go to resume drinking his coffee.

But the mention of bed reminded her of another problem she had. The house! Because of Uncle Bertie's ill health when they had married there had been no honeymoon; Justin had simply moved in with them, here at Black Gables.

It was a massive old house, totally impractical and virtually impossible to heat. It contained fifteen bedrooms and several reception-rooms, plus a ballroom and a dozen attic rooms. In the extensive grounds were two cottages and a range of outbuildings, some with commercial use but long since left derelict.

Her uncle had insisted on having the master suite decorated for them, but unfortunately for Zoë it was built on the old-fashioned lines of two bedrooms joined by a dressing-room and bathroom. She would have much preferred to share a bed with her husband. Instead, she found that after making love Justin invariably went back to his own room . . .

'About the house, Justin,' she burst out. 'Judge Master suggested we sell it and I'm inclined to agree.'

She was a thoroughly modern girl, having spent the first fourteen years of her life living at home in California and boarding-school in Maine. She had once before broached the subject of separate rooms to Justin, but he had fobbed her off with, 'Best to leave things as they are. There's no point in upsetting Bertie,' and, as a new bride and still in some awe around her dynamic husband, she had let it go. But now . . .

'I mean the separa——'

'It's your house—you can do what you like with it, but I had thought you felt something for the old place. Obviously I was wrong.' He rose from the table, threw down his napkin, and turned to leave.

'I simply meant it's far too big for us, and you have to travel to London every day.' She jumped up, hurrying after him. She did love Black Gables but she loved her husband more, and she could not bear him to be angry with her.

''Zoë.' He spun round, his hands falling on her shoulders, gripping them tightly. 'Shut up and go to bed; now is not the time to discuss these things. Neither of us is thinking straight.' He looked down into her flushed, puzzled face and sighed, his gaze moving from her sapphire eyes to the long, soft fall of her silver-blonde hair, and finally settling on her wide, soft mouth.

'Are we having our first fight?' She tried to joke, but could not hide the tremor in her voice. The events of the day were finally getting to her, and her self-control was perilously close to breaking.

'No, no, of course not, little one,' he hastened to reassure her. 'I'm a bit tense, that's all. It's been a sad and difficult few weeks for both of us.' He lowered his head.

She trembled at the first brush of his lips and all rational thought deserted her, and when Justin carefully turned her around and pointed at the stairs she meekly walked up them.

Slipping out of her clothes, she walked into the dressing-room, and, replacing the black wool dress in the wardrobe continued to their shared bathroom, where she placed her undies in the wash-basket.

She pulled on a shower-cap and stepped into the double shower stall. Turning on the water and adjusting it to a pleasant temperature, she tilted back her head and closed her eyes, welcoming the soothing spray. It had been a long, sorrow-filled day and she was tense and tired. Justin was right as usual. Picking up the soap, she lazily lathered the fragrant cream into her naked body.

Her hands stilled on her small, firm breasts. How much nicer it would be if they were Justin's hands. The sensual thought brought a brief smile to her small face. Justin sharing the shower—dream on! She smiled wryly.

Justin was a magnificent lover, as she had discovered on Valentine's night, but she had also discovered in the weeks before her wedding that he possessed a monumental self-control, refusing to make love to her again until they were married, however much she had tried to tempt him.

Then, on her wedding night, he had, with skill and patience and a sensitivity she could only marvel at, turned her into a molten mass of pure sensation, leading her to an ecstatic explosion of the senses and emotions that she had never imagined in her wildest fantasies. Plus, he had repeated the miracle almost every night since.

But he was conservative with a small C. They only ever made love at night—in bed! The shower was certainly not Justin's scene.

A frown marring her smooth brow, Zoë stepped out of the shower and wrapped a large, fluffy towel around her slender form. Why, tonight, did the thought of Justin's restraint worry her? It never had before. Surely she wasn't letting the bitchy Sara Blacket's comments get to her? Justin loved her; he had said so, hadn't he?

Much later she lay naked in her bed, trying to keep her eyes open, waiting for him. It had crossed her mind to go to his bed, but, as a relative novice at lovemaking, she somehow found the thought of taking the initiative with her formidable husband oddly intimidating.

Her eyes flew open as she heard Justin entering his room, then the sound of running water in the bathroom. She pulled herself up the bed, tucking the sheet around under her arms, and switched on the bedside light. She waited until the noise from the bathroom stopped, then called his name. She needed him tonight, even if only to hold her and reassure her that she was not alone. He was all the family she had left; he was her world...

'What is it, Zoë?' Justin demanded, walking into the room, a small towel riding low on his hips his only covering. 'I thought you'd be asleep by now.' He crossed to the bed, to look soberly down at her small frame outlined beneath the covers then up to the pure, pale oval of her lovely face.

Her heart turned over in her breast at the sight of him. His night-black hair, damp from the shower, was swept severely back from his broad forehead, throwing his rugged features into prominent relief. His deep brown eyes, the cast of his high cheekbones and his slightly olive-tinged complexion revealed his father's Spanish ancestry, though he never spoke much about his family. She knew his parents were dead, and he had a stepsister who was living with some tribe of Indians in the rain-forest on a four-year anthropology study.

'I was waiting for you,' she told him softly, stretching out a slender hand to touch his forearm, her sapphire eyes roaming over him in undisguised want.

His wide shoulders gleamed like gold satin; a thick mat of hair covered his broad chest, and arrowed down in a fine line past his navel to disappear beneath the towel. His long, muscular legs were planted slightly apart, a lighter dusting of hair shading them darker.

'I thought you were never coming,' she murmured, trailing her hand from his arm to thread her fingers through his curling chest hair.

Justin caught her wrist and, easing her hand back behind her head, lowered his big body down beside her and bent his dark head towards hers. 'Oh, I think I will, and very quickly, my darling girl,' he drawled with mocking amusement, but his eyes flashed for an instant with what, to Zoë, looked suspiciously like anger just before his lips brushed over hers in a kiss as light as thistledown.

'I should go to my own bed and let you rest.' He whispered the words against her mouth.

'No. Please, Justin. Don't leave me alone tonight. I need you.'

'Do you? I wonder if you know what it means to actually need someone. You're so hopelessly young,' he said enigmatically, standing and slipping the damp towel from his hips. She was in no doubt that he would stay—he could not hide his state of arousal from her and did not try to as, with a deft flick of his wrist, he flung the covers back, revealing her naked form to his glittering eyes.

'You were waiting for me,' he husked, his heated gaze sweeping over her from where her long hair trailed across the pillow, lingering on her softly parted lips, then again on the pale, round orbs of her perfect breasts, then moving down to the tiny waist and softly flaring hips, and the soft blonde curls at the juncture of her thighs. 'God, but you're beautiful, Zoë. Perfection in miniature,' he growled.

She could feel her whole body blush but she didn't care; he was her husband. 'Not so much of the miniature,' she teased, and stretched out her arms to him in a female gesture as old as time.

He gave her one long look, his face wearing an oddly restrained expression in the shadowy light. Then he dropped to his knees by the side of the bed.

'Justin?' she queried tentatively. Then his hand circled her ankle and his black head bent and his lips brushed a trail of kisses from her ankle to her knee, then her thigh.

She trembled with exquisite emotion as his other hand stroked slowly up over her flat stomach and higher, to close over one firm breast. He rolled the aching tip between his long fingers with delicate eroticism, and she moaned her delight. She felt like some Eastern slave girl, spread on the bed for her master's delectation, but surprisingly she didn't care...

But soon the hedonistic pleasure was not enough. She wanted to kiss him, touch him, rouse him to the same all-consuming need that engulfed her.

She stretched her hand to his shoulder, her slender fingers clawing his hard flesh. 'Please, Justin.'

But Justin knew exactly what he was doing to her, the burning fire he was igniting in her body, and refused to be rushed. With hands and mouth he kissed and caressed while withholding from her the ability to reciprocate, until she was whimpering, crying out her need...

Then and only then did he rise and, nudging her legs further apart, eased his length between them. As he supported his weight on his elbows either side of her head, his mouth sought hers again. The kiss was a passionate statement, his tongue moving in her mouth, echoing his masculine possession...

Her eyes flew open and she saw his rugged face, the skin flushed and taut across his cheekbones, his lips curled back in a feral grimace as he fought to stay in control. Then he moved deeper and deeper inside her, harder, faster, and her eyes closed again as every part of her clenched around him then exploded in a surging tide of shattering pleasure. She felt his great frame shudder and the fierce, pulsing heat of him filled her as he found his own release.

For a long time the only sound in the room was their erratic, rasping breath; neither was capable of speech, until eventually Justin rolled on to his back and curved an arm around her shoulders, tucking her into his side.

'Justin, my love.' She sighed, turning her head to press a soft kiss to his sweat-dampened chest.

'Enough, Zoë. Lie still,' he ordered raggedly.

They were the first words he had spoken in ages, she realised, but, lying satiated beside him, she didn't mind. She loved her silent lover... Anyway, she made enough noise for both of them, she thought, slightly shocked at how Justin always managed to get her to beg for his possession. But then why shouldn't he? He was an experienced, sophisticated lover, and he was only making sure that she was satisfied, she rationalised contentedly. But her contentment plunged five minutes later...

'I'll leave you to sleep now, darling,' Justin murmured. Removing his arm from her shoulder, he swung his feet to the floor.

'Stay,' she drawled huskily.

But Justin stood up. Unselfconscious in his nudity, he turned to look down at where she lay in the rumpled bed. She gazed languidly up at him; her blue eyes, slumberous and dark with loving, met his. Then, as she watched, she saw his iron self-control reassert itself. His heavy lids dropped over his half-closed eyes as he moved slightly, avoiding her gaze.

'Much as I'd like to, it isn't sensible; I have to be up at six in the morning to be in London for eight. I would only disturb you, Zoë, and you need your rest.' He was talking to somewhere over her left shoulder—as usual! The thought was frightening...

Zoë sat up in bed and reached out a detaining hand, placing it on his naked thigh. 'I could come to London with you.' His hand lifted hers from his thigh and she had the oddest notion that he resented her touch. 'We could move to your apartment n-now——' she swallowed the lump that formed in her throat "—now Uncle Bertie's gone.'

Suddenly it seemed imperative to her that they discuss the future, and she didn't know why. 'We can put this house on the market—it's far too big; it's an anachronism in this day and age. Never mind one child—we would need a dozen even to begin to fill it——'

'So that's what this is all about?' Justin cut in. "I thought we agreed—no babies for a year or two. You would not be trying to blackmail me into changing my mind by threatening to sell the house?' he demanded hardly. 'Because, if so, you can forget it.'

'No, no, nothing like that,' she quickly denied. But as she searched his face he looked so cool and remote that once more Sara Blacket's words echoed in her brain, filling her with a dawning fear that she did not want to recognise. Instead she continued, 'I simply thought that the house could be a conference centre or a nursing home—something like that. It is very expensive to keep up; Judge Master said so himself.' She knew she was babbling but she wanted to keep Justin with her.

He leant forward, brought her small hand to his lips and brushed her knuckles with a kiss. 'You're probably right and if you want to sell it I'll arrange it, but it's not something one can do in five minutes.' And, pressing another kiss on the back of her hand, he added, 'And let me worry about the expense, little one. You try and get some sleep.'

She should have been reassured, but somehow she wasn't. Maybe it was the way he avoided her eyes, or perhaps the way he allowed her hand to fall from his, but she had the strangest notion that he was simply pacifying her as he would a troublesome child.

'I will if you stay with me,' she said slowly. She was testing him, and hated herself for it, but the events of the day had severely dented her confidence in her husband's love and she needed some sign from him, freely given, to allay her doubts and fears.

'I need my sleep even if you don't. I'm a lot older than you, remember.'

'Please, Justin, I need you tonight, simply to hold me. What with the funeral...' She didn't want to plead, but somehow it had become essential to her peace of mind and her trust in him that just this once he stayed all night. To her relief and delight he agreed.

'Let me dispose of the protection.' He grinned. 'I'll be back in a second.'

And he was. Zoë yawned widely and snuggled into the hard warmth of her cautious husband's arms. 'You're not old,' she whispered, a smile twitching her swollen lips. It was ridiculous—a more virile, powerful man than her husband would be hard to find, and yet somehow the fact that he should worry about his age made him seem touchingly vulnerable. It never bothered her.

Justin, true to his word, had the house valued by a prestigious estate agent with a view to selling the place. But to Zoë's amazement Justin informed her, before they actually put it on the market, that she was to have her twenty-first birthday party at Black Gables. It was all arranged; the guests had already been invited.

Apparently Justin had done it at Bertie's request. It had been his last wish that the party go ahead whether he was there to see it or not. Zoë was not absolutely convinced that it was the right thing to do only three weeks after her uncle's death, but, as usual, she gave in to her dynamic husband's wishes.

The next few weeks she passed in a kind of limbo, torn between grief for her uncle and her inability to get really close to her husband.

Justin was very busy as the new head of chambers, and she saw less and less of him. She tried to tell herself it was natural—he had more work to get through. But sometimes in the evening, after yet another solitary dinner, a devilish, tiny voice from the deeper reaches of her mind would rise up to taunt her with the thought that he had married her to please Bertie and get the firm. He had the firm and Bertie was no longer around to see if he neglected his wife. She found it more and more difficult to dismiss her suspicions, however much she tried.

Justin was no help. He rarely talked about his work but he did inform her that he would be staying in town on Monday evenings. He had taken over the job of boxing coach with a group of young offenders at an East End boys' club. Very laudable—and she believed him even as she missed him. But her inability to dismiss completely the conversation she had overheard on the day of her uncle's funeral was a constant source of unease.

She was a practical girl—with egotistical film-star parents she had had to be from a very young age. She knew she was being silly, letting Sara Blacket's catty remarks get to her. Justin loved her. They were married for heaven's sake!

But, however much she tried to convince herself, the doubt lingered. It didn't help that Justin seemed to spend longer and longer in London. He was working far too hard, but nothing she said could make him change.

She was smiling as she spun the wheel of her Mini Metro and headed up the drive to come to a halt, with a screech of brakes, outside the front door of the house. She had spent the day in London, and had had the rare pleasure of lunching with her husband at an exclusive restaurant before raiding Harvey Nichols. The bag lying on the passenger seat contained the most exotic gown she had ever owned.

She picked up the carrier-bag and chuckled as she dashed out of the car and into the house. She could not wait to see Justin's face when he saw her new dress. She wouldn't give a cent for his iron control tomorrow night—her birthday party. The gown was guaranteed to knock him dead. But why did she need to? The question hovered on the fringes of her mind, undermining her confidence.

Not bad—not bad at all, she thought, posing naked in front of the mirrored wall of the bathroom, sucking in her stomach, her small breasts rising enticingly. Were they bigger than usual? she wondered idly. Probably Justin's expert massage was to blame. She giggled and, with a happy smile illuminating her small face, spun round as the object of her thoughts strolled in.

'I didn't hear you,' she said delightedly. She had not seen him since last night and her eyes drank in the sight of the large, splendid bulk of him, clad in a plain black towelling robe that stopped mid-thigh, the deep V of the front exposing his broad, hairy chest. Her heart jumped in her breast as, eyes shining, she walked towards him. 'You must have got back when I was in the shower.'

'Mmm,' Justin grunted, his gaze sweeping slowly over her silver-blonde hair, the perfect oval face, the finely arched brows, the huge, thick-lashed eyes, the small, straight nose and the wide full-lipped, rosy mouth, curved in a warm smile of welcome. His gaze lingered on the lips, then moved almost as if against his will down to the high, full breasts, the tiny waist and flat stomach, the softly flaring hips, his eyes darkening to black in the process.

Zoë, seeing his reaction and thrilled by it, moved closer and slipped a hand under the lapel of his robe. 'Thank you for the card and the roses. I love them,' she husked, thinking of the magnificent bouquet of red roses that had been delivered to the house earlier.

'My pleasure, birthday girl,' he drawled none too steadily.

She felt him tense as her fingernail scraped supposedly accidentally over a small, pebble-like male nipple. Perhaps she had been wrong about Justin; perhaps her fantasy of them in the shower was not so unlikely, she thought, excitement sizzling in her veins.

'Shall I help you to shower?' she asked throatily, glancing up at his tough face through the thick veil of her lashes in what she hoped was a seductive fashion.

His eyes flashed gold lightning as his arm swept around her waist and hauled her into his hard body, while his other hand caught her wandering one beneath his robe. 'You little devil,' he rasped, before covering her mouth with his own in a long, hard kiss.

When he finally released her she was dazed and breathless and aching. 'Justin...' She sighed his name. But, to her chagrin, he spun her round, patted her naked bottom, and almost pushed her out of the door.

'Tempting though the offer is, it's late. The guests will be arriving any minute. Get dressed and allow me to do the same.'

'Spoilsport,' she shouted back cheekily, regaining her equilibrium and shooting him a flirtatious glance over her shoulder.

Justin tossed back his black head and laughed out loud. 'Hold the thought till later, darling, when I have time to do it justice, hmm?'

His parting words filled her with confidence as she stood in front of the cheval-glass, turning this way and that, a complacent grin lighting her face. So much for a Dresden doll, she thought triumphantly. Tonight no one would be in any doubt she was all woman.

The black dress was like nothing she had ever owned before—a sophisticated designer original with tiny, narrow straps supporting the pure silk bodice. She wore no bra because the back was non-existent except for a very broad, sequin-encrusted belt in gold, which nipped her tiny waist and pushed her firm breasts higher—almost empire-style—revealing the curve of the milky white orbs and a tantalising shadowy cleavage.

The skirt was straight to her ankles and figure-hugging, with a teasing fish tail at the back. Matching four-inch-heel satin sandals on her feet gave her an illusion of height, as did the heavy sweep of her blonde hair piled up on the top of her head in a chignon, a few strands of hair pulled free to curl enticingly around her face and the back of her neck.

She did not need foundation, simply a good moisturiser and the lightest trace of blusher to add colour to her fine pale skin. She had paid more attention to her eyes, and, with the careful use of a coloured eyeshadow and the addition of a brownish-black mascara to her long lashes, she knew she had never looked better.

'My God! What on earth are you wearing?'

Justin's horrified cry broke into her reverie. She turned slowly around and spread her arms wide. 'Don't you like it?' she asked as she pirouetted again, then stopped in front of him, grinning wickedly up into his stunned face.

He looked magnificent in a black dinner-suit, white silk shirt and black bow-tie—all elegant, sophisticated male—and for once Zoë thought she matched him. But, if the look in his dark eyes was anything to go by, maybe she was wrong. She saw the muscle in his strong throat move as he swallowed hard. 'Justin?' she queried.

'Like it... ? It's indecent. You will give every man in the place a heart attack—me included.' His dark gaze lingered on her shadowy cleavage. 'Why not wear the romantic thing you wore on Valentine night?' he suggested hoarsely.

'Don't be so staid,' she teased, adding, 'In any case, it's too late to change now.' She slipped her arm through his. 'Let's go down; we can't keep our guests waiting.'

'Wait.' He closed his large hand over hers and turned her towards him. 'I have something for you.' His eyes dipped to her breast and then returned to her face. One dark brow arched sardonically. 'Though I didn't have a neckline like that in mind when I bought it,' he said drily, slipping his free hand into his jacket pocket and withdrawing a long jewel case. He held it out to her.

She opened the box and gasped. 'It's unbelievable,' she cried, her eyes dazzled by the blaze from a magnificent diamond choker set with sapphires falling like tear-drops all around—a perfect match for her engagement ring.

'Happy birthday, Zoë.'

She looked up into her husband's dark, serious eyes, her own filling with moisture. How could she have ever doubted that he loved her? she thought wryly.

'I love it, Justin, as I love you. You darling man.' And, reaching up, she kissed the highest point she could reach—his chin. He pulled back almost as though he was embarrassed by her show of emotion. 'Please put it on for me,' she said in a voice that was not quite steady as she lifted the necklace from its bed of velvet and held it out to him.

He took it, his smouldering gaze intent upon her small face, then, moving behind her, fastened the necklace around her slender neck. Turning her back to face him, he said with arrogant certainty, 'I *knew* they would match your eyes.'

She put a hand to her throat. 'Thank you,' she murmured, her heart bursting with love.

'There is more,' he said softly, a tender grin quirking the corners of his sensuous mouth as he delved once more into his jacket pocket and withdrew a smaller case. 'From Bertie.'

She swallowed the lump that rose in her throat. 'How?' she whispered, taking the proffered box.

'He sent for the jeweller two months ago and chose it himself. I promised I would give it to you at the appropriate time.'

She opened the box and lifted out a delicate gold watch of startling beauty. The time markings on the face were etched in diamonds and the surround was encrusted in diamonds and sapphires. 'I wish he could have been here,' she whispered, fastening the watch around her slender wrist and raising tear-drenched eyes to her husband.

'He is in spirit, love.' Justin pulled her into his arms and gave her a quick hug. 'Dry your eyes and let's go.'

Ten minutes later Zoë, once again in control of her emotions, followed her husband into the formal drawing-room. 'I feel guilty allowing you to arrange all this for me—the party, the caterers.' She glanced at the watch on her wrist; any moment now the guests would be arriving. 'The guests.' And she stopped, her mouth falling open. She had forgotten to tell Justin...

'Justin, I—er—I hope you don't mind but——' She glanced at him leaning negligently against the French marble fireplace, the epitome of the sophisticated male animal, and hesitated.

'But what?' He arched one dark brow enquiringly.

'You know when I worked at Magnum Advertising? Well, I have kept in touch with some of the staff—an occasional lunch in town—and——' she took a deep breath '—a few of them are hiring a minibus and coming to the party,' she finished in a rush.

'Why not? Your uncle insisted on inviting everyone from the doorman at chambers to the Lord Chief Justice—a few more won't matter.' In two lithe strides he was beside her. 'Stop worrying. It is your party—enjoy it.'

She took a deep breath to steady her fluttering nerves. 'I'll try.'

'But for God's sake don't breathe like that in that apology for a gown!' he exclaimed irritably, and would have said more, if the thunderous expression on his dark face was anything to go by. But at that moment the doorbell chimed...

CHAPTER THREE

As Zoë stood in the huge old panelled hall with Justin at her side, his proprietorial arm around her waist, her doubts of the past few weeks vanished. She had never been happier as they greeted the constant flow of guests.

She welcomed Judge Master and his wife Mary with a kiss on their cheeks, while Justin looked indulgently on. She was not quite as enthusiastic with Sara Blacket and her husband, but soon she was having difficulty keeping track of who every one was.

Then, to her surprise, a tall, rangy stranger appeared, looking for all the world like a cowboy. She hesitated for a second, then let out a startled cry of joy. It had been seven years but there was no mistaking Wayne Sutton, the Texan. He had been a friend of her parents for years and she remembered him as being particularly kind to her when she was a child in California.

'Wayne, I can't believe it...' She grinned up into his deeply tanned, handsome face. 'How did you get here?'

'I walked on water of course,' he teased with masculine arrogance.

It would not have surprised her if he had. From being a rising young executive when her parents were alive he was now the head of one of the major studios in Hollywood, yet he couldn't have been much over forty.

'Let me look at *you*,' Wayne drawled provocatively and, casually pulling her out of her husband's arms, he held her hands wide and gave her a long, lingering scrutiny. 'You're more beautiful than your mother ever was. How about becoming a film star——?'

'Hands off!' Justin cut in, hauling her back to his side. 'The lady is spoken for, Wayne.' The two men held each other's gaze, sizing each other up rather like two stags at bay.

Zoë's puzzled eyes shot from one to the other. 'You know each other?'

'Wayne and I spoke on the telephone last week,' Justin said curtly. 'And he is here tonight in his capacity as the executor of your trust fund. Nothing more.'

'No business tonight, Wayne.' She deliberately spoke to the Texan, not at all happy with Justin's tone of voice. She reached up and kissed Wayne's cheek. 'I should scold you,' she teased. 'To think that you've spoken to my husband and yet not once have you got in touch with me!' She pouted, flirting outrageously.

'Hey, honey, that's not true. Surely you got my Valentine's cards? Damn it! I paid the agency in London enough for the service. I knew you would miss not getting one from your dad, so I kind of took his place.'

Her smile faltered. All these years it had been Wayne and not Justin... 'Yes, yes, of course. Thank you, Wayne; I appreciated the gesture; I just forgot.' She felt the colour rise in her face and quickly changed the subject. 'But come on; you're here to enjoy yourself—bar's second door on the left and there's champagne everywhere.' She indicated the hovering waiters balancing trays loaded with glasses of champagne.

'Whatever you say, gorgeous.' Wayne winked. 'Now, let me find the bourbon.' And he walked off towards the bar.

Justin's skin darkened with colour. 'There was no need to kiss the man.'

'Why, I do believe you're jealous!' Zoë teased. She was stupidly hurt to discover after all these years that the cards had not come from Justin, but she was determined not to show it.

'It's that damned dress,' Justin bent down to murmur in her ear. 'Every time you reach up, I have palpitations in case you pop out the top.'

She glanced up, her eyes clashing with his. His show of possession was flattering, and she laughed out loud, her humour restored. To the people watching, the stern barrister's responding laughter came as something of a shock.

For the rest of the introductions Zoë relaxed easily in her husband's hold, until she felt Justin tense, his fingers tightening imperceptibly on her waist. She shot him a sidelong glance; his rugged features were set in an impassive mask. She looked back to the couple in front of her. She knew the man, Bob Oliver, a junior partner in the law firm; her glance shifted to his red-headed companion, and immediately she knew the reason for Justin's sudden tension. Janet Ord had been his companion at Zoë's eighteenth birthday...

'Bob and Janet, how nice to see you again; it must be three years.' She tried to lighten the atmosphere. She was Justin's wife and she wanted to show him that she was adult enough to realise that it was only to be expected that eventually she would bump into one of his old girlfriends. The law, and those who pursued it in England, comprised quite an insular community.

'Good to see you, Bob—Janet.'

She heard Justin's voice, cool and clipped, and wondered at the unmistakable frostiness in his tone. But at that moment the busload of friends from Magnum Advertising arrived, and she forgot all about Justin's peculiar reticence with his junior partner and Janet. A few hours later she was to remember and wonder how she could have been such a fool...

She looked around the crowded room, her blue eyes shining like stars. The party was going brilliantly; the caterers had done a superb job on the buffet and the large formal dining-room was subjected to a constant stream of guests. In the small ballroom, opened for the first time in years for the occasion, an enthusiastic quintet played a good mixture of popular and rock music.

'Quite a triumph,' Justin murmured, turning her into his arms and grinning down at her. 'Though I should be angry with you. You never mentioned the pipsqueak Nigel was one of your guests.'

'I could say the same,' she teased back, confident in his love. 'You never mentioned that the luscious Janet was invited.'

His grin vanished, his face going peculiarly rigid. 'I did not invite the lady. I ruined your eighteenth party by inviting that woman—do you really think I would be so unthinking as to repeat the mistake?'

Inexplicably she shivered.

'Zoë, you're cold. It's that damned dress.'

'No, no. A ghost walking over my grave.' She tried to smile. Or was it an omen? she wondered.

'Bob invited Janet as his partner. Do you mind?' Justin bit out, his dark gaze intent on her upturned face.

'No, of course not, silly.' She shrugged off her fanciful thoughts. 'Come on, let's dance.' And, curving her slender arms around his waist, she swayed in towards him.

Justin needed no second bidding, and she hid a secret smile as she noted his muffled sigh of relief when he urged her on to the dance-floor. Poor man! He was obviously afraid that she would take offence and sulk as she had three years ago.

They danced, Justin stroking one hand up her bare back while the other rested lightly on her hip. She flattened her palms on his shirt-front and gave herself up to the dreamy music, swaying to the rhythm of the golden oldie 'As Time Goes By'.

His hand moved from her hip to her buttock as he pulled her closer, one long leg edging between hers. She felt him stir against her, his hold tighten, and the familiar heat flowed through her. His dark head bent; his lips brushed lightly over her brow. She tilted her head back; their eyes met and desire lanced between them, as sharp and piercing as a laser-beam.

'How long will this damn party last?' he muttered as his hand moved up her back, his fingers spreading to clasp her nape while his other hand dropped to stroke her thigh.

She made no response; instead she simply gazed dazedly up at him, her pulse racing. Her husband's control was slipping, she thought bemusedly. They were lost in a world of their own; the crowd, the laughter faded away, and there was only passion and need. Then Justin kissed her...

It was the cheers of the guests and the heavy beat of a rock and roll number that brought them back to their senses.

Justin's head jerked back, his dark face flushed with passion and a good deal of embarrassment as he shot a frustrated glance at the assembled throng. 'I need a drink. *We* need a drink,' he muttered, his arms falling to his sides. 'I knew that dress was a disaster area. I should never have allowed you to wear it,' he growled angrily.

She regained her composure—for once, before her dynamic husband—and her lips twitched in the beginnings of a smile. 'Why, I do believe, Mr Gifford——' she held his gaze, fluttering her long eyelashes like some Southern belle '—your behaviour is most unbecoming for a barrister and soon-to-be judge,' she drawled in mock-horror, and then spoilt it by giggling.

'Witch!' Justin chuckled. 'I'll get you later; meanwhile I think we should circulate. It will be much easier on my libido.'

She glanced around the dance-floor, rubbing one foot against her ankle: four-inch heels gave her height, but they played havoc with her feet. She had danced with dozens of men, including the Lord Chief Justice. She had done her duty, and with a cheerful smile to everyone in general she escaped out into the hall, and went on through the garden-room, where a few close couples were in conversation, and into the old-fashioned Victorian conservatory.

Good! She was alone. She sank down on to a bamboo chair—part of a group placed around a centre table. She slipped off her shoes, put her feet inelegantly on the glass table in front of her and let her head fall back against the soft cushion. Five minutes' rest and then back to the fray, she promised herself.

It was a beautiful summer night and through the glass roof a million stars glittered in the midnight-blue sky. She sighed deeply, contentedly. Twenty-one on the twenty-first of June—there must be a lucky omen in there somewhere, she mused, not that she needed luck; she had it all...

'Hiding, Zoë.' A feminine voice interrupted her reverie. She glanced up and muffled a groan as Janet swayed unsteadily before her.

'No. Simply resting for a minute or two.'

'I don't blame you.' The redhead collapsed in the opposite chair, a glass in one hand and a half-full bottle of champagne in the other.

Zoë thought, So much for my five minutes' peace. 'I hope you're enjoying the party,' she prompted with a tinge of sarcasm. The woman was obviously three sheets to the wind.

'Great party.' Janet giggled and took a swig of the champagne, ignoring the glass and drinking from the bottle. 'But, parties aside, I can understand your needing a rest. Just—J-ustin is one dynamic lover—a tiger in bed.' She took another swig of the champagne.

Zoë didn't want to hear any more. It was one thing to accept that your husband had had lovers in the past, but quite another to have one of the same describe his powers in bed. 'Yes, well . . .' she mumbled, praying that the other woman would leave or pass out. But her wish wasn't granted.

'Def-f-f . . . Definit-t-t . . .' Janet slurred the words. 'A three-times-a-night man, and day, and anywhere.' Her high-pitched laughter grated across Zoë's nerves like a dentist's high-powered drill.

'"A three-times-a-night man" . . .' Zoë whispered, shocked to the core. She knew what it meant, and could not believe they were talking about the same person. They made love most nights but Justin was always in control, and they never did it more than once. Well, except for the night of the funeral, she qualified in her mind.

Suddenly her confidence in her husband's love took a nosedive. She remembered the conversation she had overheard—Sara Blacket's opinion that Justin preferred large, luscious women.

She looked across at Janet. Had she been the redhead at the dinner Mrs Blacket had mentioned? It was possible. Janet was a very attractive, very well-endowed sexy woman of about Justin's age; add to that the fact that they had once worked in the same chambers and three years ago they had arrived as a couple at her eighteenth birthday and it made sense. Justin and this woman had been lovers not for a few weeks, as Zoë had mistakenly imagined, but for years . . .

'He's not the sort to go without, not our Justin.'

Zoë raised huge blue eyes to the other woman's face; she was still talking, but Zoë felt as if she had been hit by a truck. 'No?' she queried numbly.

'Even the night before he got married I had to throw him out of my place at two in the morning—couldn't have him exhausted for his wedding... No, sir... So keep your strength up, girl; you'll need it.' And, leaning across the table, she held out the bottle of champagne. 'Have a drink...'

Zoë blindly shook her head. She could not believe Janet. She didn't want to, but as Janet rambled on she was filled with a certain dread.

'Don't get me wrong, I like Justin.' Janet fell back against the seat. 'He's ambitious; he could have stayed with our firm—become a top international lawyer, loads of money. But he preferred the establishment. He wants the prestige of the ermine. Already head of your late uncle's firm, he will be a faithful husband. He has no choice if he wants to make judge. You have nothing to worry about. Nothing at all...'

Deep inside Zoë something shattered—something rare and pure, an intrinsic part of her—her faith and love in her husband. She sat as though carved in stone, robbed of her pride and self-respect by the casual words of a drunken woman. She bit her lip to prevent the scream of anguish that was filling her head; she could almost hear the dull beat of her too trusting heart echoing in a black void.

'There you are, Janet. I've been looking all over for you.' Bob's voice intruded in the silence. His handsome, boyish face wreathed in smiles, he took the bottle from Janet's hand and placed it on the table, and, grabbing her arm, pulled her to her feet. 'You've had enough.'

Only then did he see Zoë.

'The party girl, having a breather.' He put a finger to his lips. 'Shh. We'll leave you to it.'

Bob's smiling face swam before her eyes, and she tried to smile. 'It's OK Bob; I just have to put my shoes on and I'll be back inside.'

The effort it took her to get the words out was more than she could stand. She slid her feet off the table and bent over, her head almost in her lap, more to hide the tears in her eyes than from any real desire to find her shoes.

She heard the other two depart, and her arms fell towards the floor, her hands shaking; she felt around in the semi-darkness for her sandals.

Slipping her feet back into the sandals, she stood up. The faint noise of the party filtered through her stunned brain. Her party. Her twenty-first, on the twenty-first... So much for lucky omens! If twenty-one was coming of age, she had come of age with a vengeance in the last ten minutes, she thought bitterly, dashing the tears from her cheeks with an angry, shaking hand.

Janet's revelation and all Zoë's niggling doubts and fears of the past few weeks coalesced into one absolute certainty: whatever reason Justin had for marrying her, it had not been love...

She straightened her shoulders and took a deep breath; she could hear her name being called. Now was not the time to give way to the pain gnawing at her heart. Instead she smoothed the soft silk of her dress down over her hips, adjusted the bodice and, with head held high, a smile plastered on her face, walked back into the garden-room.

'There you are, Zoë. I was looking all over for you.'

It was Wayne, thank God! Right at that minute she didn't think she could have faced Justin.

'Sorry to be a party-pooper, but I have to get back to London; I have a breakfast meeting in the morning. But I would like to arrange a meeting with you, Zoë. We have a lot to discuss—the trust, the transfer of the cash.

And I want to fly back Thursday; I must be at the studio on Friday.'

'Wayne, please.' The idea came to her in a flash. She glanced up into his tanned, attractive face. She could trust this man—that much she was sure of. She placed her hand on his arm, her wide blue eyes, unbeknown to her, betraying her pain and anguish. 'It was lovely to see you, but there's no need for us to meet in London. Don't transfer anything. I'll be in the States in a few days and I'll call you at the studio.'

'Zoë, what's wrong?' The Texan's tanned hand touched her shoulder in a gesture of comfort. 'You're shivering—something has upset you. I know I haven't seen you in years, but you can trust me; your parents were my friends. If anyone has hurt you, tell me, and I'll punch their lights out.'

His kindness and insight were almost her undoing. 'Please, Wayne, don't ask questions, and promise you won't mention any of this to...to—' she couldn't say his name '—to my husband.'

'You've got it, honey. I'll wait for your call.' And, bending down, he planted a swift kiss on her cheek. 'Chin up, kid. Remember your parents were great actors; you can do it.'

'Wayne, you're wonderful. Come on, I'll see you out.' And with her arm linked in his she made it to the hall and thc front door. Thcy said goodbye with another brief kiss, and she was just about to turn around when Justin's voice reached her.

'Zoë, darling, I was beginning to think I had lost you.'

You have, you bastard! Pain and rage almost blinded her, but she bit her tongue and said nothing, suffering Justin's hand on her arm as he turned her around.

'The Lord Chief Justice and his wife are about to leave; they want to say goodnight.'

'But of course. You can't afford to upset Justice Speak,' she said with biting sarcasm.

'Zoë...' Justin began.

'Lovely party.' Justice Speak strolled up, his wife clinging to his arm. 'Sorry to leave, but at our age we need our rest.' He chuckled.

'Thank you for coming, and for the wonderful present—I shall cherish it always,' Zoë responded politely, and she wasn't lying. She did love the exquisite gold miniature they had given her.

'Glad you like it, my dear. Your uncle Bertie advised me—rang me the week before he died and told me you loved art. Great friend, sorry to lose him.' The old man's voice was gruff. 'He was so proud of you, young woman, and so pleased he had got you and Justin together; he could die content.'

Moisture filled her eyes—for her uncle, but also for herself. Dear heaven! Even Justice Speak knew her marriage had been arranged. Did everyone? Was she the only idiot who had not seen the truth?

'There, there, girl, don't upset yourself. Bertie would have loved to have seen the old house lit up and full of laughter again. I don't suppose you knew his wife, but she was a wonderful woman—loved entertaining on the grand scale; after she died Bertie rather let the place go.' The old man chattered on. 'Can't say I blame him—different era, don't you know! But you gave him a new lease on life; he adored you.'

Justin's arm curved around her waist and she stiffened immediately. Wiping the tears from her eyes, she forced a smile to her lips. 'Yes, I know; this party was his idea. So thank you once again for coming,' she managed to say firmly.

The goodnights said, a steady stream of guests began leaving until by two in the morning only her friends from Magnum Advertising were left. Zoë was reluctant for them to go and insisted on sharing another couple of bottles of champagne. The idea of getting drunk held great appeal. It might anaesthetise her feelings, so that she would not feel the pain she knew was waiting for her the moment she relaxed.

She was sitting on the sofa listening to one of Nigel's shaggy-dog stories—something he was renowned for—and sipping her drink, when Justin walked into the room, having dismissed the band.

He took in the scene at a glance—Zoë and Nigel on the sofa, two of the girls sprawled on the floor at their feet. Pat and Pam, Zoë's luncheon friends, were almost asleep on the other sofa. His dark gaze sought hers but she avoided his eyes. She couldn't bear to look at him. She sensed him move towards her, and only looked up when he spoke.

'Sorry, folks, the driver is insisting on leaving. Time to go.'

'We have the room. They can stay the night.'

'I don't think so, Zoë. They have to work tomorrow.'

'The master has spoken,' Nigel quipped, getting to his feet and performing a rather drunken salute. But the rest followed suit.

Zoë smiled grimly, her gaze colliding with her husband's and moving as quickly away again. Nigel was closer to the truth than he knew. 'Yes, indeed,' she concurred, standing up, and, ignoring Justin's narrow-eyed scrutiny, she followed the last of the guests to the hall and bid them goodnight.

'What was all that about?' Justin demanded hardly, catching her arm when she would have walked straight past him to the stairs.

She glanced down at his long fingers curled around her arm, and then tilted back her head to stare a long way up into his harsh face. 'I don't know what you mean,' she said flatly, proud of her self-control when really she felt like tearing his eyes out. 'I'm tired; I'm going to bed. Lock up, won't you?'

'Zoë, don't lie to me. Something is wrong.' He moved closer and she flinched.

'You're being ridiculous,' she snapped; she could not stand his questioning much longer.

'I think not.' He was inches away, his tall figure dwarfing her. She could almost see his analytical mind going over the events of the evening. 'The party was great, you were enjoying yourself, and then I lost sight of you for a while. When I saw you again you were kissing Wayne, and then you could barely speak to me, and for the rest of the night you flirted with Nigel while treating me as if I were some kind of ogre. What happened, Zoë? Did someone say something to upset you?'

She could have wept. 'Upset' wasn't the word. 'Destroyed' maybe! She glared at him, hurt and fury warring within her. He looked so cool, so in control, even concerned! Uncle Bertie had once told her that the truly great barristers could just as easily be actors, the court the stage, and the judge and jury the audience, and, by God, Justin should have received an academy award for the part he had played for years!

'Answer me, Zoë.' His fingers tightened on her arm.

'No one upset me; I had a wonderful evening and you have an over-active imagination,' she declared flatly. She had to get away; his closeness, the subtle scent of him were draining her will-power. 'You're also hurting my arm.'

His hand fell away immediately. 'Sorry,' he apologised and, stuffing his hands in his pockets, his voice terse, he added, 'Perhaps you're right. Go to bed; I'll be up in a minute.'

Glad to escape, she kicked off her shoes and ran up the stairs. She closed the bedroom door behind her and quite deliberately locked it. She tore off her clothes and left them where they fell; her jewellery she dropped in a heap on the dressing-table along with the key and then she dashed into the bathroom and locked the door to Justin's room before stepping into the shower.

She lifted her head and allowed the fierce pressure of the water to wash over her, in the vain hope that it would wash away her tormented thoughts. Her tears mingled with the spray and, hating her own vulnerability, she turned off the water and stepped out of the shower. She wrapped a large soft towel around her naked body, sarong-style, and sank down on the small bathroom stool, burying her head in her hands. Her long, wet hair, hanging in tangled rats' tails down over her shoulders, dripped, unnoticed, on her rapidly cooling flesh.

Sara Blacket had been right all along. Justin had married her to please her uncle and further his career. His real preference was for large, luscious ladies and Janet Ord had confirmed the fact in a few short sentences.

Zoë groaned out loud. Justin! 'A three-times-a-night man'. How could she have been so naïve? The pain in her heart was worse than any knife wound—it went through flesh and blood to her very soul. Justin—her husband, her lover, who had only spent the whole night with her once since their wedding night—the night of the funeral—and even then she had had to beg him to stay and comfort her. She felt so stupid. So *used*...

With hindsight it was all so obvious. Justin made love to her with a skill and sophistication she was helpless to resist—had never wanted to resist. But now she realised how naïve she had been. She had thought the fact that Justin always brought her to a shattering climax before finding his own release was the ultimate act of love by a considerate husband. Now she saw it for what it was—a clinical manipulation of her body and her love for him, while never losing his own iron control.

Being brutally honest with herself, she knew deep down inside that she had recognised that Justin held some part of himself back, but had refused to face the knowledge until now. She had masked it by telling herself that it was solely a cultural difference. She had spent her formative years used to the easy friendship and the exuberant, extrovert types of people who had made up her parents' circle of friends. Justin's attitude was simply very British and nothing to worry about—the stiff upper lip, and all that, not the most tactile of people.

She raised her head and shivered; the water running from her hair was freezing her tender flesh, but she welcomed the numbness. She heard a sound and glanced at the door to Justin's room—the handle was moving. She thanked God that she had locked the door; she could not face him—not tonight. She hadn't the strength. She had a terrible suspicion that if he took her in his arms and kissed her she would be the same spineless pushover she had always been where he was concerned.

Sadly she realised her own weakness. Every night in Justin's arms was her idea of heaven. She could have forgiven him the steely control, the separate beds, even his ambition and conniving with Uncle Bertie to marry her. But what she could not forgive—could not live with!—was Janet Ord's last revelation.

No man who had any respect at all for his prospective bride—never mind love—would ever spend the eve of his wedding making love to another woman. To Zoë it was far worse than an unfaithful husband. If a married man went astray one presumed that he had at least tried to honour his commitment. Justin had not even tried; he had betrayed her on the eve—no, not the eve but the *morning* of her wedding, if Janet was to be believed... and Zoë did believe her.

'"*In vino veritas*,"' Zoë sighed, getting to her feet, her mind made up. Nigel had been right when he'd called

Justin 'the Master'. Justin, except for one brief mistake three years ago, had masterminded her whole life for virtually the last seven years.

But no more... Her rose-coloured spectacles were smashed to smithereens, and she could see Justin for what he was—a ruthlessly ambitious, mature male who had taken one look at a shy fourteen-year-old girl and deliberately used her schoolgirl crush to bind her to him in matrimony and further his career in the process. She could not blame him for her uncle's heart attack, but he had certainly used it to his own advantage.

It had forced her back into his sphere of influence and it had been Justin who'd suggested that she give up her fledgling career in advertising immediately after he had made love to her on Valentine's night. She could not believe how stupid she had been. How corny can you get? she thought cynically. Justin had seduced her with red roses and soft words, the Ritz, romance and champagne, and she had swallowed the whole fantasy, believing in the omens of love...

Well, they said life went in seven-year cycles, she thought fatalistically. It was certainly true for her. At seven, boarding-school in Maine; at fourteen, England and Justin. Now, at twenty-one...back to America...

Who knew? she mused. Perhaps her subconscious mind had accepted the end of her marriage and had been working out the solution within minutes of Janet Ord opening her mouth, maybe even earlier—when Sara Blacket had planted the first seeds of doubt in her heart.

With stark clarity she saw her impulsive declaration to Wayne—that she would see him in the States in a matter of days—as the best and only solution.

Tightening the towel around her breasts, and flicking her wet hair from her eyes, she moved like an old woman to the door and into her room.

CHAPTER FOUR

ZOË clutched at the door-frame with one hand and her towel with the other. Her heart almost stopped beating, and her eyes widened in angry shock at the sight before her.

In the dim glow of the bedside light Justin was sprawled across her bed. The pillows bunched behind his back to keep him semi-upright, he had a glass of champagne in his hand, a wicked light in his deep brown eyes, his only concession to modesty a pair of black silk boxer shorts. 'Short' being the operative word...

'I thought the black dress was a turn-on,' he drawled throatily, 'but that towel takes some beating.' Playfully crooking a finger, a sensual smile curving his wide mouth, he added, 'Come to bed, birthday girl. Let's celebrate.'

A few hours ago she would have been overjoyed at such a blatant statement of intent from her restrained husband, but with Janet's revelation in the forefront of her mind all she felt was a furious rage.

Obviously she had not hidden her distress as well as she had thought. Justin had picked up on it, she told herself with a new cynical awareness that she had not realised she possessed. Or why else would he, for the first time ever, be lying in wait for her? Except to get her in his arms and mindless as usual.

Her gaze slid slowly over him. He lay there, a sophisticated male animal, all rippling muscle and confident virile charm, expecting her to fall gratefully into his arms.

Well, the manipulative swine was in for a rude awakening.

'Celebrate? I think not,' she bit out, her lashes flickering over wild blue eyes to hide her fury. She deliberately turned, proceeded across the room to the dressing-table, and sat down on the softly padded stool, her glance resting on the key she had thrown down earlier.

'How did you get in?' She had locked the door, she knew she had...

'I know you didn't intend to lock me out, darling, and I also know all the locks in the master suite are the same. Open with the same key. *Et voilá*! Here I am.'

'I'm not in the mood for you or French, so please leave.'

'Zoë, what's wrong?' Justin swung his feet to the floor and in a couple of lithe strides was standing behind her.

'I'm tired. I want to sleep,' she said curtly, his towering presence at her back causing her stomach to knot with tension. If he touched her she'd scream...

'Funny—half an hour ago, you were almost begging Nigel and his friends to stay longer,' he reminded her silkily. 'A more suspicious husband might have cause for alarm.'

His hands curved over her naked shoulders, and she stiffened. She looked up, her gaze colliding in the mirror with dark, piercing eyes.

She had thought that every ounce of feeling for Justin had been destroyed by the knowledge she had gained this evening, but she was horrified to discover that, despite knowing that he had never loved her, that he had married her for ambition and at her uncle's request, his closeness and the touch of his hand could still arouse an aching longing inside her. She despised her own weakness, and in a fury of hurt and humiliation she jumped to her feet and swung away from him.

'A more suspicious wife might wonder why a new husband would prefer his own bed to his wife's,' she shot back scathingly.

An unfathomable expression flickered in his eyes; as she watched his mouth tightened. 'I didn't prefer my own bed tonight, but it doesn't seem to have done me much good,' he opined drily, an odd grating in his usually deep, modulated tone.

'About as much good as it does me, knowing you married me at my uncle Bertie's request, and simply to further your overriding ambition in law.' Not bothering to hide the bitterness in her voice, she spun to face him, head high. Her blue eyes shooting flames, she instantly dismissed his shocked expression as simply more play-acting.

'That is a ridiculous notion and patently untrue,' he denied harshly.

At one time Zoë might have believed him, but not any more. 'No?' One brow arched derisively. 'You mean Uncle Bertie never suggested to you that marrying me would please him?' If Zoë had any lingering doubts they vanished as Justin's glance seemed to waver, a dull flush streaking his high cheekbones.

'Zoë, I don't know what you have heard or who has been gossiping but it wasn't like that and you know it.'

'Oh, sure I know it! Next you'll be telling me you love me—something you have studiously avoided saying, and I was too stupid to see it.'

The one time she had asked him if he loved her—the day of the funeral—he had answered with, 'Of course I do, silly girl; I married you, didn't I?' At the time she had been reassured; now she saw it for the evasion it was.

'Zoë, what is going on here? It's not like you to deliberately try and start an argument.'

'You're right, it isn't, and I'm not about to argue with you now.' He was standing before her, all aggrieved, near-naked male, and she didn't trust herself not to reach out and stroke the muscular chest, to give in weakly to his overwhelming sex appeal. 'Just go,' she said sadly, tearing her eyes away from his powerful body.

'That's it!' The words exploded into the air like gunfire, and she stepped back in shocked surprise.

But Justin moved in on her. 'I don't know who has been filling your pretty little head with nonsense, but you and I are going to have a talk,' he grated between clenched teeth, and, taking her arm in a tight grip, marched her across to the bed.

'Let go of me!' she snapped angrily, trying to break free. But his fingers merely tightened on her tender flesh and she had to bite her lip to prevent a cry of pain.

'Sit down,' Justin ordered, pushing her down on the bed.

'Resorting to violence now, you hypocritical swine?' she accused scathingly.

'Be quiet,' he barked, and the leashed fury in his tone made her shiver inwardly as he stood towering menacingly over her. 'At the beginning of this evening everything between us was fine; in fact, it was only lack of time that prevented you and me sharing this bed earlier—you were aching for me.' An arrogant, knowing smile played across his mouth.

'I——' She tried to deny it, but he cut her off.

'Don't bother to lie,' he said curtly. 'I'm a man, Zoë; I know when a woman's responding to me. Just tell me what happened between then and now that you should accuse me of some ulterior motive for marrying you and deliberately give me the brush-off as if I had some anti-social disease, damn it!'

She looked up, her gaze slanting over his broad chest and on to his hard face and the dark, probing eyes which looked as if they could read her mind. His anger was genuine, but probably simply because she had found him out, she thought cynically.

'Do you deny you discussed marrying me with Uncle Bertie?' she asked, and, without giving him time to answer, carried on, 'Or that our marriage helped you become head of chambers?' She did not see his brown eyes leap with rage; she was too engrossed with her own, furious pain. 'Or that you kept your mistress—lover—call her what you like—right up to our wedding and probably beyond?'

'Stop right there!' Justin snarled. He leaned over her, his hands on either side of her on the bed, imprisoning her, forcing her to lean back with her hands behind her for support. He was so close that she could see the beginnings of dark stubble on his chin.

'Janet—that's what this is all about. She has been spreading her poison, and you, my trusting little wife, believed her,' he drawled in a dangerously quiet voice. 'Such loyalty! I think you owe me an apology and an explanation.'

He was actually serious! She could see that. The nerve of the beast. 'Try the "tiger in bed" for starters,' she spat back.

Her throat ached from the prolonged effort of holding back the tears, and her pulse raced as she fought to retain her composure. She was helplessly aware of her own embarrassing position—naked except for a towel—and Justin—much the same, with his keen eyes surveying her insolently from head to breast and lower. She felt the heat ignite in her stomach and silently cursed her body's unwelcome response to him.

'I don't believe it! You're jealous,' he marvelled. 'That's what all this is about.'

'In your dreams!' she cried furiously. 'I don't give a damn if you spend the rest of your life with the woman. I never want to see you again.'

The colour drained from his face. 'Zoë, you don't know what you're saying.' He looked at her seriously. 'You're my wife; I love you...' And that was the unkindest cut of all for Zoë—his declaration of love had come too late and sounded like the excuse it was.

'Since when?' she snorted. 'Since I found out the truth about you, you manipulative, chauvinistic pig?' She struggled to sit up, pushing at his chest. Surprisingly he moved and sat alongside her on the bed; she saw him clench and unclench his hands as if weighing up the prospect of putting them around her neck.

'Not the best response to a declaration of love,' he drawled, and smiled, not very pleasantly. '"Underwhelmed" would be an accurate description, though I think I can understand. Knowing Janet, she can be a very persuasive if poisonous lady.'

'You should know—you're the expert on the woman,' she cried. She could not stand much more. What was the point? she thought morosely, and made to stand up but Justin's arm fell around her shoulders, his hand gripping her upper arm tightly, as if by the pressure of his fingers he could convince her.

'I promise you, Zoë, Janet means nothing to me. I'm thirty-five; there have been other women in my life I admit, but not as many as you seem to think, and certainly nothing serious.' He sounded very calm and controlled and it only served to infuriate her further.

'Says you,' she spat.

The brown eyes narrowed angrily, but his voice remained cool and reasonable as he continued, 'I had an affair with Janet—if one could call it that. Two adults sharing an evening out and sex occasionally, that was all it was, and it was finished long before you and I married.'

She tilted her head to the side and stared at him, eyes wide and wild. 'You swine!' she hissed, her face alive with hatred.

'You're being childish, Zoë——'

'Long before we were married?' she cut in incredulously. 'You take me for a child, a complete idiot!' Her temper ran out of control and her voice shook. 'Maybe, if I was crazy enough about you, I could forget your cosy-cosy arrangement with my uncle; maybe live with the fact that you never loved me as I loved you. But as for the rest . . .' The words came out harsh with pent-up emotion. 'To have a woman tell me that my husband is a "three-times-a-night man" and more! This same husband who cannot bear to spend a night in the same bed as me. You make me sick . . .'

Zoë shook her head; she tried to go on, but her voice seemed to have dried up. Her heart pounded in her chest and she felt physically sick. But what did it matter? What more was there to say? Except that she was leaving him, and that much must be self-evident to Justin. But to her amazement he threw back his head and laughed out loud.

'You are jealous, sexually jealous, you silly girl. You have no need to be. Janet was obviously just trying to upset you and you fell for it.'

She couldn't believe the man; he was a lawyer, supposedly intelligent, and he actually thought it was a huge joke, even to the extent that there was smug satisfaction in his grinning countenance. A red haze blurred her vision and she struck out at his face with a wildly swinging hand. 'Well, fall for this, buster!' she yelled. 'I'm leaving you. You're the lawyer... Fix the divorce...'

Suddenly his hand tightened around her shoulders. 'This has gone far enough,' he muttered savagely. 'If you won't listen to reason, I'll have to convince you another way.' His other hand captured her chin and forced her head up and his mouth swooped on hers, prising her lips apart, savaging her soft mouth.

With her bent back over his arm, his hand sliding from her chin to tangle in her long hair, he held her fast as he ground his mouth over hers with ruthless passion. She lashed out at him with her fists and tried to drag her head away, a low moan escaping her at the pain he was inflicting.

Justin laughed, a harsh, guttural sound in the silence of the room. 'And I thought I was being considerate.' His tone was ironic, but the blazing fury in his eyes as he stared at her belied his cool voice.

'Considerate? Don't make me laugh,' she yelled hysterically, and struggled to escape, her arms flailing wildly, but he was far too quick and, catching her arms at the wrist, with a swivel of his hard body she was pinned back against the bed, her hands forced above her head in one of his.

She cried out, but his mouth swallowed the sound, his teeth biting into her lips while his other hand tore the towel from her body. She felt his long fingers close around her breast and shuddered.

His dark head lifted as he stared down at the pale skin laid bare to his hot eyes. His strong fingers moved slowly, squeezing the soft flesh; his thumb brushed the hardening tip, and his eyes flicked to her face.

'No, no.' She tremblingly shook her head and tried to fight him, her body bucking against him. She would not let him do this to her—never again, she vowed, even as her traitorous flesh cried out for his familiar touch.

'Yes, my love,' he drawled sardonically in a strangely thickened voice. 'You say you're leaving. You implied I never wanted you. Our lovemaking was less than perfect for you.' He straddled her thighs, his long, near-naked body poised over her. 'I intend to prove you wrong.'

And his head came down to take the place of his fingers at her breast.

'No. I don't want you.' She thought bitterly of Janet even as her heart thudded in her breast. 'Try Janet. I'm sure...' She ended on a groan, hurting with the intolerable pressure of trying to resist him when a slow-burning fire was licking through her body.

He flashed a glance at her wildly shaking head and she arched again, trying to throw him off, but only succeeded in prolonging the agony as her breasts brushed against the hard wall of his chest. He drew a harsh breath, forcing her head back to the bed with the pressure of his mouth, and when he finally freed her swollen lips she was shaking all over.

'Anyone can have Janet, but only I have you,' he snarled close to her ear. 'And that's the way it's going to stay.'

'No, no, no...' she breathed raggedly.

'Yes, yes, yes,' he mocked harshly as his body shifted to crush her deeply in the bed.

There was no doubt that Justin wanted her. Zoë, twisting and struggling beneath him, trying to dislodge the hardening weight of his body, recognised that fact even before he responded by thrusting one of his legs between hers. But she also knew that whatever his reasons, it wasn't love.

Her wide, angry eyes clashed with his, and what she saw in the black depths was a wild, savage, almost desperate hunger, and it shook her to the core. Gone was the controlled Justin she knew...

'I won't let you go. I can't,' he groaned, his mouth claiming hers once more as his hand trailed down across her breasts to the soft mound at her thighs.

Frantically she tried to struggle free, but the mental bonds were as strong if not stronger than the physical. She moaned as Justin buried his head at her throat, trailing moist kisses down to her breast while his hand parted her legs. She could feel the rigid, masculine length of him poised near the juncture of her thighs and she gasped as his long fingers slid between her silken, feminine folds. She was lost...

'Justin...'

His fingers moved intimately against her and she melted, liquid and hot, but he made no move to take possession. Instead he lifted his head from her breast, and stared down into her passion-flushed face.

'You can't win, Zoë, so stop fighting.' He groaned. His head lowering, he kissed her long and deeply.

'Fighting'? She clung to him, the nails of one hand biting into his shoulder, while those of the other scraped over his flat belly, tearing at his shorts. 'Who's fighting...?' She moaned as Justin shrugged out of his shorts and fell back on her, slipping between her parted thighs. She could no more control her body's reaction to him than fly to the moon.

'You want me...' he growled, and she could not deny it as he sheathed himself deeply inside her, covering her cry of excitement with his mouth.

Zoë glanced at the sleeping man beside her. His black hair was wet with sweat and plastered against his skull; his strong-featured face looked years younger in repose, the thick black lashes brushing his cheeks, masking the usually piercing, intelligent eyes.

She stirred restlessly in the bed, her body aching in places and muscles she doubted she had ever used before, or ever would again... The early morning sun shone through the windows, flooding the room with the palest of primrose light.

It was going to be a nice day. The inconsequential thought flashed in her mind. The English always moaned about the weather, and yet she had never found it too bad; in fact, she had adapted to the climate with no bother at all.

Maybe that was her trouble—she had been far too pliable, adapting to her uncle and Justin in much the same way as she had to the weather, a young girl desperate to be accepted by the only family she had left. A psychiatrist would probably have a field-day with the past seven years of her life.

She lifted her hand to her head and swept the tangled mass of her sweat-wet hair from her brow. She was naked, exhausted, sated, and yet unable to sleep. The last few hours had been a revelation to her. Justin had made love to her with a demanding, savage intensity that surpassed anything that had gone before.

To her amazement, and shame, she had matched him every time. Lost in a mindless frenzy, she had held him, shared with him, and followed him down a dozen erotic paths she had never dreamed of, until finally, with the light of dawn just breaking, he had fallen asleep.

She glanced once more at him. A twisted smile curved her full lips but never reached her icy blue eyes. The irony did not escape her—only the threat of divorce could persuade her husband to spend all night in her bed. Nor could she avoid concluding that Janet had been right about her husband. He was a three-times-a-night man and more. But it also underlined the fact that Janet had been telling the truth...

A tear slowly trickled down her cheek; she sniffed and, turning, buried her head in the pillow. A strong arm fell over her waist and hauled her into the hard warmth of a masculine body. She swallowed hard; the last thing she wanted was that Justin should find her crying.

She lay tense and silent, expecting any second to hear him speak, but after a while she realised it had simply been a reflex action—he was still asleep. She stifled a yawn and closed her eyes; she was tired, so very tired.

At least in sleep she would not feel the pain of his betrayal, was her last conscious thought.

The following night the pain was still eating into Zoë's heart, tearing at her stomach, preventing her from eating. She shoved her chair back from the dinner-table and stood up.

'Do you want coffee in the study?' She addressed the question to somewhere over Justin's left shoulder. She could not bear to look at him. Dinner had been a miserable, silent affair and she could not wait to get away.

'So you *are* speaking to me; I'm flattered,' he drawled sarcastically. 'I was beginning to wonder, after your stony silence all evening.'

'Answer the question. Anything else you have to say to me can be said through a lawyer,' she flung back, and stepped back as Justin leapt to his feet, knocking his chair over in his haste.

'Zoë, I will not tolerate that kind of talk from you. You are my wife, and my wife you are going to stay. I thought I made that perfectly clear last night.' His black eyes clashed with her contemptuous blue ones. 'But if you want another demonstration I will be happy to oblige.'

'Sex. You think that solves everything.'

'I didn't hear you complaining.'

'Oh! I'm going for the coffee.' And with a toss of her head she walked out of the room and to the kitchen. She knew that Mrs Crumpet was off tonight; she had said goodbye to the lady a few hours earlier, knowing she would not see her again.

Everything was arranged. She had awakened at lunchtime to discover from Mrs Crumpet that Justin had gone to London. She had been glad; the thought of facing him after the night they had spent together had filled her with anger and humiliation.

She had spent the rest of the day quietly and efficiently packing her clothes; the cases were safely stowed in her wardrobe. Her flight was booked on the morning Concorde to New York, and if she could just get through the next few hours without breaking down she would be home free...

'Zoë, we have to talk.' She was just reaching for the coffee-cups from the top shelf of the cupboard and her hand shook at the sound of her husband's voice. 'Here, let me.' He reached over her head and picked up the cups.

She could feel his warm breath on the back of her neck, and slowly, reluctantly, she turned around. Her back was against the kitchen units; Justin was much too close. 'Thank you,' she mumbled, edging warily along the counter and out of his reach.

His long body tensed. 'For God's sake, Zoë, I'm not about to leap on you in the kitchen! There's no need to behave like a frightened rabbit,' he said bitingly. 'Look at me.'

'I'm making the coffee.' She watched the percolator for what seemed like an awfully long time.

'OK, have it your own way. But we will talk.'

She heard the scrape of the pine kitchen chair on the quarry-tile floor and knew that Justin had sat down. She imagined that she could feel his eyes burning into her back and her hand shook when lifting the coffee-jug. She carefully poured the aromatic liquid, filling two cups.

Slowly she turned, a cup in each hand. He was sitting, his elbows on the table, his head in his hands, a dejected slant to his wide shoulders, and for a second she felt a bitter regret for all she had lost. But, as if sensing her scrutiny, he straightened up immediately.

'I'll have my coffee here; it's been a hell of a day in court and I need it,' he said flatly.

'Yes, I'm sure.' They were talking like two strangers—stiltedly, meaninglessly. She placed a cup in front of him and took the seat opposite, and gratefully lifted her own cup to her suddenly parched lips. This was probably the last time she would ever speak to him at any length, she realised, and the thought hurt. Even though she knew it was for the best, she frowned.

'I'm sorry, Zoë.' He looked at her frowning face, his eyes wary. 'I should not have behaved as I did last night. You have every right to be angry——' He broke off and she looked straight at him, her sapphire eyes wide with a hurt she could not disguise.

How could he be so insensitive? He was apologising for making love to her! Not, as she had expected, for marrying her for all the wrong reasons. 'Yes, yes, I damn well have...' She swore furiously.

'It won't happen again, I promise.' He held her gaze, his features taut. 'I—I lost control.'

'You don't see it, do you?' Shaking her head, she stared at him. 'I couldn't give a damn about your control or lack of it.'

'What? Then why?' He contemplated her from beneath half-lowered lids as though her anger were some strange phenomenon.

She drained her cup and stood up. Last night she had not had the nerve to ask about his final betrayal—had not wanted it confirmed—but twenty-four hours and a lot of heart-searching later she had no such qualms.

'Where were you the night before our wedding?' she demanded, and, glancing down, saw the guilty colour rise in his face.

'Janet, was it?' he asked, his mouth turning down. 'I might have guessed.'

'You have not answered the question,' she prompted icily. 'But your face says it all. You spent the night in her apartment until she threw you out at two in the morning.'

'It was not like that,' he said savagely. 'Nothing happened.' He leapt to his feet and, walking around the table, caught her arm as she would have walked out of the door. 'I can explain.' He spun her round to face him. 'If you would just give me the chance.'

Zoë watched him; he looked oddly vulnerable, still wearing the three-piece suit he had worn for the office, but his tie was loose and his hair rumpled. 'Go ahead; it should be interesting,' she sneered.

'I was at Janet's apartment on the eve of our wedding, but you have to understand that I hadn't seen the woman for over six months. She had been on a case in Hong Kong. She returned to England that day and called me. She had heard I was marrying you, and was upset.'

His dark eyes burned down into hers, a rare anxiety in their depths. 'God knows why. I hadn't slept with the woman in over a year. She was a friend, nothing more. I wouldn't have asked you to marry me otherwise, Zoë. Unfortunately Janet seemed to think differently and proceeded to get blind drunk, maudlin and suicidal in that order. I had a terrible time getting away from her.'

She didn't believe him for one second. Justin was a formidable, mature male by any standards; if he wanted to get rid of someone he could with one cutting phrase. He was renowned for it. Never mind about all the rest—his conniving with her uncle, his lack of desire for her when apparently he was a sex maniac with other women. He must think she was a complete fool.

But the worst part was that, deep inside, she wanted to believe him, to swallow her pride and forgive him. She opened her mouth, about to tell him so, when the telephone rang.

'Oh, hell!' Justin swore violently and, letting go of her arm, marched across the kitchen to the wall-mounted telephone and picked up the receiver.

'Yes, Gifford here,' he barked.

But Zoë was glad of the distraction. Without him holding her and the mesmerising quality of his dark gaze muddling her mind she knew what she had to do. Get away... She turned towards the door.

'Zoë.' He called her name. She glanced back over her shoulder; one of his hands was stretched out to her, the other over the mouthpiece. 'Come here.'

Why not? It would be the last time, she told herself, and crossed to his side. He curved his long arm around her waist and hauled her in tight to his body. 'I have to drive back to London. A client has got in a bit of a bind.' He said urgently, 'I'll probably be back very late. I won't disturb you. But we will continue this discussion over breakfast, yes?' His mouth curved into a wary smile. 'Please?'

'Yes,' she affirmed. 'About nine, in the conservatory; the weather forecast is good for tomorrow.' And she would be long gone...

'Fine.' He gave her a relieved look and, bending, pressed a swift, hard kiss on her lips.

She responded—she could not help herself—but she laughed without amusement as she walked upstairs. How could she sink so low? Discuss the weather with an Englishman and he was instantly reassured of one's reliability, she thought wryly, completely ignoring the fact that neither Justin nor she was totally English.

CHAPTER FIVE

THE VIP lounge for the Concorde flight to New York was filling up slowly. Zoë sat in a comfortable, soft-cushioned sofa, her head back and her eyes closed. She had done it; she had left her husband.

It had been ridiculously easy. With her bags already packed, she had simply crept out of the house at the crack of dawn, and free-wheeled her car down the drive so that the noise would not wake Justin.

She had known he was asleep because she had lain awake all night and heard him come home well after three in the morning. She had listened to him enter her room and feigned sleep when he'd stood over her and whispered her name. Much later she had stealthily crossed to his room, and heard the deep, even tenor of his breathing, before slipping quietly away.

'Zoë. What are you doing here?'

The sound of a familiar voice startled her, and her eyes flew open to rest on the rangy figure of the tall Texan as he strolled across the lounge towards her. 'Same as you—catching a plane, I hope.' Her attempt at humour was pathetic, and her smile wobbled dangerous. 'I—I got away earlier than expected,' she added hesitantly.

'And does your husband know?' Wayne asked quietly, sympathy softening his hard face as he lowered his considerable length on to the sofa beside her.

She shook her head, moisture flooding her lovely eyes, too choked to speak.

'Want to tell me about it?' His arm slid comfortingly around her shoulders, and the sheer will-power that had carried her through the past two days finally deserted her. Zoë turned her face into his broad chest and let the tears fall.

Neither of them saw the powerfully built, black-haired man enter the lounge and stop just inside the door; nor did they see the look of devastation in his eyes before he turned and left.

Zoë pulled on her cut-off jeans and slipped a Lycra bandeau around her breasts. She found a large, brightly coloured bath-towel and slung it over her shoulder; she picked up a paperback, and a sun-block cream, then wandered out of the house on to the wide sundeck.

Her gaze swept along the sandy beach; a couple of joggers lifted their hands and waved. She waved back, a tiny smile lighting her huge eyes. She breathed deeply, relishing the scent of sand and the sea, the pacific rollers rhythmically lapping the beach—a soothing music to her trouble mind.

On arriving in America two months ago, she had gratefully accepted Wayne's offer of accommodation at his Malibu beach-house. He had listened to her tearful story of her ill-fated marriage, had comforted her, and in a more practical way had handed over to her the quite substantial amount of money in her trust fund.

She dropped the book and the sun lotion on the table, and the towel on a nearby lounger, before stretching her scantily clad body out on top of it. She had acquired a light tan in the past few weeks, but this was to be her last day in the Californian sun. Tomorrow she was moving to Maine. It was for the best; she had to make a life for herself—she placed a protective hand over her stomach—especially now that she knew she was pregnant.

Wayne was an extremely attractive man, and a true friend, but she had realised very quickly that she did not fit into the free-and-easy, party-going lifestyle that her parents had enjoyed and Wayne still pursued. She had been a teenager when she'd left America; she had returned from England a badly hurt, disillusioned young woman, and somewhere along the way she had fallen between the two lifestyles.

She was luckier than most—she had money—but her own pride and sense of self-worth would not allow her to sit around doing nothing for very long. She had to make a new start.

She liked Wayne, but over the last few weeks she had had a sneaking suspicion that he would not be averse to something more. She was finished with men for good, but she had no desire to lose Wayne's friendship, so, as tactfully as she could, she had told him that she was moving to Maine. Her excuse that the Californian climate was too hot for her he appeared to accept, and anyway she had gone to school in Portland; she loved the area.

Once Wayne had realised that she was serious he had done everything he could to help her. He had flown her up to Portland in his own private jet, and in a whirlwind drive up the coast she had fallen in love with the tiny village of Rowena Cove, situated on a spindly peninsula pointing out into the sea midway between Brunswick and Bath.

She had viewed and signed a lease on a lovely old white-painted, double-fronted eighteenth-century house. Dark green shutters framed windows that looked out over Casco Bay and the clincher for her had been a large, airy attic, fitted out as a studio.

Zoë stretched and yawned widely. The afternoon heat was wonderful but she was too fair to tan easily; she would have to go in shortly. She sat up and hitched up her top. Her clothes were packed and ready; the house she had leased was part-furnished and even had a daily housekeeper—a Mrs Bacon from the village—so she would not be entirely alone.

A shadow darkened her lovely eyes. Not so long ago she had thought that she would never be alone again; she had been a fool to herself, loving a ruthless, ambitious man: Justin. Simply thinking of him took all the sunshine out of the day. It still hurt. She had the horrible conviction that it always would...

Two days ago when the local medical centre had confirmed her pregnancy she had been elated and terrified in equal proportion. But, once she had recovered from the initial shock, reaction had set in.

In her heart of hearts she knew she should tell Justin—he was the father and entitled to know. She had even considered swallowing her pride and returning to England to try and make some kind of marriage for the sake of their unborn child.

But she was no longer the girl who had fled so hastily from England; she had had time to think, to absorb the pain of her husband's betrayal. She accepted that Justin did not, nor ever had loved her, and, thinking clearly and realistically, she dared not take the risk of returning to England.

Justin was a powerful man in the judicial system of the country, a high-flyer with all the right connections. If he decided he wanted the child and not her, she knew that if it came to a custody battle, she would not stand a chance, and she wasn't prepared to take the risk.

'So this is your hide-away.' The deep, melodious voice echoed on the still air.

For a second she thought she was hallucinating as her startled gaze fell on the man ascending the steps from the beach to the deck. Justin here? In California? She couldn't believe it...

But it was true. He stopped a mere foot away from where she sat frozen in shock. His brown eyes took in every detail of the way she looked—her long blonde hair falling around her face in a tangled mass, the skimpy green band around her full breasts, her cut-off jeans hanging low on her hips. She knew she looked a mess—bare-legged, barefoot and, if he did but know it, pregnant.

A guilty tide of red flooded up her face, but she tilted her chin defiantly and forced herself to withstand his insulting perusal, her own eyes cold as ice. 'A hide-away? I think not... You're here.' She was proud of her steady voice, but she had to clasp her hands together to hide their trembling.

He looked thinner, she thought. His thick black hair curled over the collar of a cream silk shirt, and a leather belt low on his hips supported matching chinos. He needed a haircut, she thought inconsequentially, but nothing could detract from his air of ruthless power nor his vibrant sexuality.

Except herself, she realised sadly, he had never had any trouble controlling his sexy body around her... Which only confirmed what she had been forced to accept when she'd left him. He had never really cared about her.

'Or should I call it a love-nest?' he sneered contemptuously.

'Love-nest?' she parroted, tearing her gaze away from his hard body. What on earth was he talking about? 'Are you off your trolley?'

'I must have been to believe in you, you wanton, adulterous little whore.' His dark eyes flared with rage, his Latin ancestry overcoming his usual, practised British restraint. 'My God! The man is even older than I am, and has apparently been lusting after you since you were a child. It's disgusting.'

Zoë caught her breath, a reciprocal anger flooding her veins. How dared he try to smear her simply to cover his own guilt? But, thinking fast, she guessed where he had got the perverted idea from immediately, and in a cold fury she challenged him.

'Ah! The valentine cards—the last one you claimed you had sent me. But then they do say an honest lawyer is hard to find,' she prompted sarcastically.

'Bitch.' He reached for her, his eyes savage, and for a second she was terrified, but she refused to show it.

Instead, with studied indifference, she arched one delicate eyebrow. 'Really, Justin...it isn't like you to be so unimaginative.'

His hands fell to his sides, his fists clenched, the knuckles gleaming white as he fought to regain his superhuman control, and he won... 'Defending yourself—you have changed,' he ground out between his teeth. 'I take it lover-boy isn't here?'

His dark eyes roamed over her with contempt, demanding a response, but she refused to give him the satisfaction. His face tightening, he watched her in tense, hostile silence for a long, long moment...

Finally a derisory smile curved his hard mouth, and he stepped back. 'Never mind; it's of no importance to me any more,' he said with insulting arrogance. 'I have some papers for you to sign, and then I see no reason why we should ever meet again.'

Zoë wrapped her arms protectively around her body, cold despite the fierce heat of the afternoon sun. She knew he did not love her, but to hear him say he never wanted to see her again was like twisting a knife in her already bleeding heart. The decision was made for her. He would never know she was pregnant. The child would be hers and hers alone, she vowed silently.

As for the rest... That he could be so devious as to try and blame her... To insinuate that she and Wayne...

It was despicable and he wasn't going to get away with it. 'And I see no reason for your presence here in the first place,' she finally retaliated. 'There is such a thing as a mail service.'

'And you would know all about servicing males, my sweet wife,' he mocked silkily. 'Wayne, Nigel and God knows how many more I don't know about.'

Zoë stared at him, deliberately holding his eyes. 'For a man who aspires to be a judge you are singularly lacking in insight.'

'Where you are concerned I would have to agree,' he conceded cynically, his eyes sliding over her with cool insolence, stripping away her brief garments, exposing her naked flesh beneath. Humiliatingly she felt a hardening in her breasts but forced herself not to react.

'I was fooled by your display of innocence, but not any more.' His knowing gaze roamed from the soft swell of her breasts, clearly outlined beneath the fine fabric, up to her flushed face.

'Look at you, and this place.' His glance encompassed the magnificent beach-house and returned to her, his eyes wandering insolently over her yet again. 'You're almost naked, sprawled on a lounger, the archetypal sybarite.'

It was his iron control and his reserve that infuriated her almost as much as his words; only Justin could insult a person so thoroughly without batting an eyelid.

'Forget your fancy language—a lazy, luxury-loving nymphomaniac would have done,' she spat back furiously. She had had enough; she jumped to her feet. 'What did you come for, Justin? I'm not in the mood for games.'

'What are you in the mood for?' he demanded, catching hold of her wrist with sudden violence and pulling her against the hard, male warmth of his body.

She stiffened, instantly aware of his masculine heat, his personal scent. His mouth brushed hers, and she ached to surrender to the longed-for pleasure of his touch. But she refused to give in to her baser urges. That way lay hell! Instead, she jerked her head back and stared up into his calculating eyes.

'Please say what you have to say and leave.' He was much too close, and it took all of her strength to breathe evenly, to control her heavily beating heart.

His eyes darkened. 'I'm not some casual mate you can dismiss with a word,' he grated, tightening his grip on her wrist, and for a moment she felt the force of his rage at her casual dismissal.

'Your fabled control is slipping again, Justin, darling,' she mocked.

'I think not,' he said tightly, his fingers lacing through hers, his thumb stroking the palm of her hand with deliberate provocation. 'But you, Zoë——' his eyes cruelly captured hers as the arm around her waist moved lightly over her near-naked back in a deliberately arousing caress '—you never could say no,' he taunted silkily.

She took a deep, shuddering breath. She had been stupid to bait him. 'I've learnt.'

'Shall we test that?' Justin suggested huskily, but Zoë was too quick for him, and, freeing herself from his grasp, she put the lounger between them.

'No. Our marriage is over; we have nothing more to say to each other.' And for good measure she added, 'And Wayne will be back very soon.'

At the mention of Wayne Justin straightened and stared at her, his hard body taut. Then his dark eyes closed briefly, and when he opened them the cold bleakness of his gaze made her shiver. 'You're right of course. Let's get down to business. I have the papers in my car. I won't be a minute.'

She watched as he strode down the steps, and a shaft of pain lanced through her. In a few minutes she would sign the divorce papers. She looked around the sun-kissed beach, at the gentle sway of the ocean, her eyes misting with tears. She dashed her hand across her eyes. She would not cry.

Slipping into the house, she hastily pulled a large, baggy shirt over her trembling body and fastened the buttons to her neck before returning to the deck.

She watched Justin walk towards her with a briefcase in one hand; he placed it on the table and sprung the lock.

'There was no need to cover up for me. I have seen it all before,' he remarked, casually eyeing the over-long shirt. 'I can't say I admire your lover's taste in shirts.'

Actually it was her own shirt—one she wore when painting. She opened her mouth to say so and closed it again. Let him think she had a lover—what did it matter? 'Just give me the divorce papers and tell me where to sign.'

'Divorce? Oh, no, Zoë. I'm not making it that easy for you.'

Their eyes met and held and her heart lurched in her breast. Was it possible that he wanted her back? 'Then why are you here?' she asked quietly.

He laughed without humour. 'What do you think? That I want you back?' His too intelligent brain had read her mind. 'You were good in bed, but not that good, and I don't go in for used goods, my dear. But I am your guardian until you're twenty-five.'

She had forgotten all about Uncle Bertie's will. 'But under the circumstances surely——?'

Justin cut in, 'Exactly. I see no reason to continue the guardianship.' He spread some papers on the table. 'If you will read these and sign where indicated. You'll find Black Gables is to be sold at a decent price and after probate all the monies accruing to you will be placed in a bank of your choice. Any further communication between us can be conducted by your American lawyer.'

Justin the lawyer was in total control as he raised cold eyes to her face. 'I'll take a walk while you read the relevant documents, and if you have any questions I'll be more than happy to answer them.'

She could not believe what she was hearing. 'And why no divorce?' She was not aware that she had asked the question out loud.

'I have a career to think of. There is no way I will divorce you, and as you have no grounds for divorcing me you must wait the five years as set down in English law.'

She could feel the anger welling up inside her. She had no grounds? The arrogance of the man was incredible. 'You bastard,' she said softly, shaking her head. How had she ever thought she loved such a man?

Snatching the papers from the table, she didn't bother reading them, but simply signed where indicated and thrust them back at him. 'Now get out.'

Leaving him standing, she dashed back into the house, sliding the glass doors closed behind her.

Zoë drove slowly along the main street of Rowena Cove and up the hill leading out of the village. She turned left into a drive leading towards the sea and parked outside the dark green door of her home. For a long moment she simply sat behind the wheel of her practical, four-wheel-drive Range Rover and stared out across the cold waters of the bay.

Three and a half years ago, when she had moved to this house at the top of the hill, she had fallen in love with the place. It was true that in the summer mid-coast Maine was flooded with visitors, but at this time of year—a crisp day in March—the locals had Rowena Cove pretty much to themselves.

Her mind went back to the first winter, and the birth of her son. A fierce snowstorm had blocked the roads out of the village and her beloved boy had been born at home with the help of a local sailor's wife, Margy. Since that day they had become firm friends. Two years ago they had gone into business together, running a small gift shop specialising in hand-painted cards. Amazingly the business had flourished. In the summer they designed Christmas cards, in the fall, valentine cards.

She choked back a sob. Val, her son, loved playing with Margy's daughter Tessa—or he had until his illness had prevented him. She glanced distractedly around the yard. A magpie landed on a tree-stump and was speedily joined by another one. One for sorrow, two for joy... A bitterly ironic smile twisted her lips. There was no mirth, no laughter any more, and she no longer believed in omens.

Her son had been born fit and healthy at twelve-thirty on the morning of Valentine's day. She had called him Valentine after checking the meaning in the baby book. Derived from the Latin, meaning strong, powerful, healthy... The last was the cruellest cut of all.

She glanced over her shoulder at her son, belted into the back seat and fast asleep. His beautiful black curls fell over his forehead, his long lashes, so like his father's, rested on the curve of his cheek, and she was stricken with pain and guilt.

She opened the car door and got out. The cottage door was open and Mrs Bacon was standing on the step, a worried frown creasing her already lined face.

'You're days late; is everything all right?'

Zoë simply shook her head and, opening the rear door, leant in and lifted the sleeping boy into her arms. She hugged him close, burrowing her face in his sweet-smelling hair; he was so precious that she could not bear to lose him, and she was not going to. She would go anywhere, do anything, sacrifice everything she owned, but her son would live, she vowed silently. Straightening her back, a grim determination in her stride, she walked into the hall.

'I'm putting him straight to bed, Mrs B,' she murmured as she passed the older woman and headed for the stairs.

An hour later, bathed and changed into a soft blue jogging-suit, she took a last peek at her sleeping son, dropped a soft kiss on his tousled head, and went back downstairs. In the kitchen Mrs B was waiting, a pot of tea at the ready.

Zoë collapsed on the ladder-backed chair at the pine table and, zombie-like, took the cup Mrs B offered, and seconds later she was greedily drinking the refreshing brew. She didn't have to speak—her face said it all. Devoid of make-up, white as a sheet, her eyes circled in purple shadows, she was a picture of devastation.

'You know what's wrong?' Mrs B prompted quietly.

'Yes, and I still can't accept it,' she said almost to herself. 'It's too incredible for words. Why us?' The cry was from her heart.

The housekeeper shook her head, the sympathy in her hazel eyes plain to see.

'At Christmas Val was a healthy boy—maybe a little tired, but I thought it was simply the aftermath of the cold he had earlier. When he started pre-school in January, I thought maybe that was what was tiring him out.

'I took him to Dr Bell——' she lifted red-rimmed eyes to her companion '—you know I did, and he gave him junior vitamins and a blood test. Then he said he was anaemic.

'I took him to Portland and then to New York University Hospital; he had blood transfusions, but still he was anaemic. Last week we stayed in hospital together while they carried out further investigations. So where did I go wrong? What else could I have done?'

'Don't blame yourself, Zoë; you have done everything you could.'

Zoë straightened in the chair. 'It's odd—money never meant very much to me, probably because I always had enough. I can pay the best in the world to treat my son, and it isn't going to do a damn bit of good.' She thumped her fist on the table in an agony of frustration. 'It is so unfair...'

Mrs B caught her hand in hers. 'Steady, girl,' she soothed gently. 'Tell me what's wrong.'

Zoë threw back her head, laughing, on the edge of hysteria. 'You won't believe it; I didn't at first. I thought it was some kind of sick joke. My son, my baby Val, has apparently got Fanconi's anaemia.

'Before you say anything, I know it sounds like an Italian pizza house. It would be funny if it wasn't so serious.' And, dropping her arms on the table, she laid her head on them and wept...

She didn't hear the doorbell, or the murmur of voices in the corridor; she was too lost in her own despair.

'Hey, come on, partner.' A pudgy arm reached around her shoulders, and she lifted her head to meet the soft brown eyes of Margy.

'Margy, has Mrs B told you?'

'Yes, and nothing is as bad as it seems, believe me, I know. Medical science is a miraculous thing, as is the power of prayer. Pull yourself together. Where is the fighting spirit, the human dynamo that has made our business a success? Use the same energy and determination and you and Val will beat this together.'

'You're right, I know, but sometimes, just sometimes, the strength goes——'

'More tea?' Mrs B cut in. 'Because if not, and you don't want anything else, I need to get home.'

'No, thanks, Mrs B, and thank you for being here today. I'm truly grateful,' Zoë said quietly.

Five minutes later the two friends retired to the living-room, where Mrs B had left a welcoming log fire burning, and, after opening a bottle of wine, they relaxed in the comfortable armchairs.

Zoë quietly sipped the wine and gazed into the red-gold flames, trying to sort her thoughts into some kind of order. She could do nothing about the churning in her stomach; it was plain anxiety, and likely to be with her for evermore.

'So what exactly did Professor Barnet say?'

She raised her head, her blue eyes gazing over Margy's dark head, the sweet, rounded face full of sympathy and understanding, and thanked God that she had such a good friend.

'I saw him the day we arrived, and then the team took over and carried out all kinds of investigations on Val. I had another appointment to see Professor Barnet and hear the results, but when I walked into his consulting rooms it was a Dr Freda Lark, his replacement; apparently he was involved in a pile-up on the freeway the night before and suffering from concussion.'

She took a sip of her wine. 'It was weird but, in a way, probably better. She hadn't had time to read the file thoroughly. So she gave it to me straight. Val is suffering from Fanconi's anaemia.'

She took another swallow of wine, her eyes meeting Margy's. 'I know—I'd never heard of it either. Apparently it's extremely rare; they were not sure what causes it, but the treatment——'

She stopped and swallowed the lump in her throat, determined not to cry again.

'The treatment is transfusions, which Val has already had, followed by, in twelve days' time, a course of chemotherapy.' Just the word horrified her; she licked her dry lips, 'And the best chance for success is a bone-marrow transplant.'

'Oh, God! Does Val know—understand?'

'Yes, and sort of,' Zoë said sadly. 'The reason we were late back was that I was screened immediately and I waited for the result to see if it matched.' She drained her glass and, picking up the bottle, refilled it. 'I don't.' A despairing sigh escaped her as she handed the bottle to her friend.

Margy took the bottle but put it on the floor. 'You must tell him; you have no choice.'

Zoë knew she was not referring to Val. She had confided the circumstances of her marriage and separation to Margy years ago.

'I know... Dr Lark, unaware of my marital state, was quite adamant. "Bring your husband in as soon as possible and any brothers and sisters; the most likely match is the immediate family."' Dully Zoë repeated the doctor's words, but not all of them... The rest she was keeping to herself...

'There is the phone.' Margy indicated the instrument on the table with a wave of her hand. 'Call him now, Zoë.'

'Ring Justin? Just like that? No, I can't.'

'Why? Are you frightened he won't come? Doesn't he like children?'

Zoë thought for a moment, remembering her years in England, which had been mostly happy if she was honest with herself.

'Truthfully, I don't really know. He did suggest that we wait a year before having any of our own. But then

Justin was very good to me when I was a teenager. In fact, when I think about it, he did tell me the reason he stayed late in London every Monday night was that he taught boxing at a boys' club. He got a blue at Oxford for boxing. And, before you ask, I have no idea why it's a *blue*.'

'There you are, then! He must like kids. Ring the man.'

Zoë twirled the stem of her glass around her fingers. 'Actually, I thought if you didn't mind, Margy...' She glanced across at her friend. 'I know it's an imposition, but I wondered if you would do me an enormous favour.'

'If you want me to ask him, forget it. This is something you have to do yourself.'

'No, no, nothing like that.' A brief smile lifted the corners of her mouth but quickly vanished. 'I wondered if you would look after Val for the weekend. Much as I hate to leave him for any time at all, I thought I'd fly to England on Friday and ask Justin in person, and hopefully bring him back with me on Monday.

'I know it's a lot to ask, but you're the only person I trust to look after Val. He loves Tessa...' She was pleading, but it was so vitally important.

Margy dashed across to her and wrapped her arms around her, hugging her tightly. 'Yes, of course. What are friends for? And don't worry about a thing. Take the plane and catch the man. Hog-tie him if you have to but get him back here.'

CHAPTER SIX

ZOË brushed a stray tendril of damp hair from her brow and glanced around the crowded airport, panic building in her chest. Was she doing the right thing? Did she have a choice? They were calling her flight for London; this was it...

She did not notice the admiring glances of the male passengers as she walked across the tarmac to the waiting Concorde. Her silver-blonde hair, scraped back in a ponytail, bounced between her shoulder-blades as she walked. She was dressed in a smart wool suit of pale cream and khaki tweed. The jacket fell, loosely sculptured, over a plain cream waistcoat and khaki silk shirt; the short, straight skirt fitted snugly over her slim hips and ended an inch above her knees. High-heeled, matching shoes flattered her shapely legs and added to her petite height of five feet.

She had the face of an angel, and a figure men would die for, but it wasn't just sex appeal that she possessed; there was something in her face, in the shadows lurking in the sapphire-blue eyes—a deep-rooted sadness that made every man within range want to comfort and protect her.

Zoë would have been horrified if she had known the impression she created. Ever since her twenty-first birthday and the break-up of her marriage she had decided that she had to harden up or she was going to be an exceptionally vulnerable person.

She thought she had succeeded and living in America had helped. In a country where women were proud of their independence and determination she had found it easier to adjust to being a single mother, to balancing family with an interesting career at no loss to either.

She removed her jacket, folded it neatly over the back of her seat and sat down. She placed her shoulder-bag on the floor in front of her and, dropping her head back against the cushion, closed her eyes.

The past few months had tested her character to the limit, but her steely determination had never wavered. She was like a lioness with her cub—she would do anything to protect her most cherished possession, her son Val, and if that meant leaving him for a few days to seek out his father so be it... Even though she was already missing Val dreadfully.

She was unaware of the elderly gentleman who sat down beside her, only opening her eyes when the voice of the stewardess broke into her reverie.

'Would you like a drink, madam?'

'No, thank you.' She tried to smile. 'And please don't disturb me for the rest of the flight. I don't want to eat, I simply want to rest. OK?'

The girl gave her a peculiar look. 'Certainly, madam. Have a nice flight.'

Zoë sighed and, turning her head to the window, closed her eyes again, her mind a seething mass of troubled thoughts. In a handful of hours—with luck—she would be face to face with Justin once again. The thought was frightening, but what she had set out to do absolutely terrified her...

She went over in her head one more time her conversation with Dr Lark. She had not dared tell Margy the whole story, sure that she would disapprove. Dr Lark was a wife and mother herself, and, after confirming that the immediate family was the best bet for a bone-marrow donation, she had elaborated on the theme.

'So long as you love children, and if there is no medical reason why you can't have more, then, if you want to give your son every chance available, and if you are prepared to explore every avenue open to you, I suggest you and your husband get you pregnant as quickly as possible. The long-term prognosis for your son is not good, but a baby as young as a one or two can donate bone marrow. I know if I was in your position I wouldn't hesitate.'

She knew Professor Barnet would never have suggested such a course of action because he knew her marital status. But Dr Lark, unaware of the true state of Zoë's marriage, had had no such reservations.

She shifted restlessly in her seat. The girl who had fled England at twenty-one would never have attempted to seduce her imposing husband, but the woman Zoë had become over the intervening years was determined to do just that...

She had debated the morality of her intention over a clutch of sleepless nights until her head had spun. She was still not absolutely sure that she was doing the right thing, but her mind was made up, and deep down inside she consoled herself with the knowledge that she would love another child.

She didn't know if Justin was involved with another woman and she didn't really care. All she cared about was getting him into bed at the first possible moment—and not necessarily a bed.

Luckily the next few days were the optimum time for her to conceive, and she was taking no chances. She guessed that once she told him about Val his rage at her deceit in hiding his son from him, and his contempt for her, would make any chance she had of seducing him virtually nil. That was why she had no intention of telling him until after she had done her utmost to get him into bed. After all—she rationalised her decision—Justin had used her. Now it was her turn to use him...

The warning-lights instructing passengers to fasten their seatbelts flashed on, and minutes later the aeroplane touched down at Heathrow Airport.

Once through Customs, she picked up her suitcase and marched briskly out of the building and into a waiting taxi. She had booked in advance at the Savoy, and an hour later she was sitting on the bed in her hotel room, the telephone in her hand.

Her first set-back came when she dialled Justin's chambers in the Inner Temple and to her astonishment discovered that he no longer worked there.

She chewed her bottom lip, deep in thought. Apparently her estranged husband was now a well-known international company lawyer with offices in a highly prestigious block in the heart of the city. What had happened to make him change his career plan? she wondered uneasily.

But, dismissing the troublesome thought, she glanced at the number she had been given, and dialled it. Another set-back—Justin was not in his office, and was not expected back that day.

She glanced at her watch. Fool—she'd forgotten to set it forward and it was almost six in the evening. She made one more call, long-distance to Margy in Rowena's Cove. Five minutes later, with her son's 'I love you, Mom,' ringing in her ears, she brushed the moisture from her eyes and with a renewed sense of urgency and determination stripped off her clothes and quickly washed and changed.

It was a very different woman who stepped into a taxi at the hotel entrance and gave the address of Justin's apartment. A fine jersey wool dress, the exact colour of her astonishing blue eyes, clung to every curve of her body. The simple cross-over-style bodice revealed a shadowy cleavage and fastened with two buttons at her waist; the skirt, a wrap-over that revealed an enticing glimpse of leg when she moved, ended just above her knee.

Her make-up was light but carefully applied to hide the purple smudges of worry under her eyes that marred her otherwise perfect complexion. She had left her long pale blonde hair loose, simply clipped back behind each ear with two pearl-trimmed combs. A tantalising scent added to the sophisticated image, along with a fake fur jacket draped elegantly across her shoulders.

She was dressed for seduction; braless, her only underwear was briefs and a garter belt—mere wisps of cream silk lace—and the finest silk stockings. Navy shoes with four-inch heels and a matching shoulder-bag completed her outfit.

She nervously clutched her bag and her stomach sank as the lift whooshed her up to the fourth floor of the mansion block where Justin had his apartment. She stepped out of the lift and walked to the door, taking a deep breath, and, with a quick pat of her hair, rang the bell.

The woman who answered the door was beautiful, Zoë thought dismally. She was tall and elegant, with long black hair falling in a mass of curls over her shoulders, huge, thick-lashed, dark eyes, and a complexion the colour of golden honey. Suddenly Zoë hoped desperately that Justin *had* moved apartment. A man with a woman like this waiting for him was hardly likely to be sidetracked by a petite blonde.

'Yes, can I help you?' Even the voice was a husky purr.

'I was looking for Justin Gifford; he used to live here. But perhaps he has moved?' she asked hopefully. She knew she was no competition for this stunning woman.

'No, you have the right address.' The woman's eyes narrowed in puzzlement on Zoë's pale face. 'Are you a colleague of his? You look vaguely familiar.'

'Yes—yes, I am.' She jumped at the excuse; she could not give up at the first hurdle—her son's life might depend on it.

'In that case, if it's important, you'd better come in and wait; I'm expecting him back any minute.'

Grasping the strap of her shoulder-bag as if it were a lifeline, Zoë had never been more aware of her diminutive stature as she followed the elegant back of the gorgeous woman down a short hall and into a large living-room. Her hope of seducing Justin was looking more unlikely by the minute. Perhaps she would do better just to tell him about Val and trust to his good nature to do the right thing.

The woman called over her shoulder as she crossed to a drinks cabinet, 'I didn't catch your name.'

'Zoë. Zoë Gifford,' she murmured, glancing around the elegant room. A huge, curved black hide sofa was placed in front of an open fire with two large wing-back chairs set at either side of it. The only new addition she noticed was an exquisite Chinese rug in shades of pink and gold that broke the uniformity of the wall-to-wall beige carpet.

'My God, you've got some nerve, you bitch!'

Zoë's head shot up at the loud exclamation, startled by the venom in the woman's voice. 'Pardon me?'

'Don't come the innocent act with me. You destroyed Justin once and there is no way I will allow you to repeat the exercise.'

'I destroyed...?' she cried in amazement. Who the hell did this woman think she was talking to? The pain at the break-up of her marriage, the worry and torment over her son all coalesced together in one great, frustrating fury. She shot her a scathing glance. 'I don't know who you are, and I don't want to know. But——'

'Leave now before I——'

'Jess, what's all the yelling...?'

Slowly Zoë turned towards the door, her heart in her mouth; she would have known that voice anywhere. Justin... Heaven knew she had heard it in her dreams, cried the name in her sleep a thousand times!

But the grim-faced stranger standing less than two feet distant, towering head and shoulders over her, was not the man she remembered. The night-black hair was liberally sprinkled with grey, the brown eyes cautiously hooded and hard in a harsh face, the grooves bracketing his mouth deeper, the lips thinner, denoting years of iron control.

'Zoë?' He drawled her name enquiringly.

She stood frozen like a statue before him, simply because her legs were incapable of movement. He was watching her, waiting for her to speak. She swallowed painfully and, gripping the strap of her shoulder-bag so tightly that her nails dug into her palms, raised her eyes to his. 'Hello, Justin,' she managed, her voice high and nervous.

'This is a surprise. To what do I owe the honour?' he asked cynically.

'Justin, get her out of here. You don't want to talk to her.' Jess spoke before Zoë could form a reply.

'Jess, I believe you have a lecture to attend. I suggest you leave. I am perfectly capable of handling the situation without any help from you.'

Zoë almost felt sorry for the other woman. Justin at his commanding, arrogant best was a formidable adversary, as she knew to her cost. When she had first run away to America she had been hurt and angry, but after his denouement of her character and morals at their last meeting in California her anger had turned to hatred.

She was here now for her son, and him alone. Otherwise she would not have willingly put herself within a million miles of Justin Gifford.

'Don't say I didn't warn you.' The woman shot a vitriolic glance at Zoë before storming out of the room, and some moments later Zoë jumped at the sound of the front door slamming.

'You will have to excuse Jess—she's very protective,' Justin said smoothly, before closing the space between them. 'And forgets her manners sometimes. Allow me.' His hands fell on her shoulders. She stiffened in instant rejection to his touch.

'Your jacket,' he prompted silkily, and slid the fake fur from her shoulders, his gaze flickering slowly over her slender curves, then sliding back to settle on her wide, wary blue eyes.

'Very nice, if a little slim,' he opined coolly.

Her eyes sparkled with resentment, but she dared not retaliate. She was here for a purpose. 'Thank you,' she said in a low voice.

He inclined his black head in acknowledgement and walked past her across the room to a drinks cabinet. He turned and glanced back at her. 'A drink? Whisky, brandy? You look as if you could use one.' His dark gaze raked over her from head to foot and back to her pale face.

'For heaven's sake sit down,' he said harshly, with the first show of emotion he had revealed since seeing her, and she realised that he was not as in control as he appeared. 'You look as if you're going to take flight at any second, yet you must have a purpose in being here.'

'Thank you,' she said inanely yet again. Her brain seemed to have stopped working. She forced her legs to carry her to the hide sofa, and sank on to it with relief. Seeing him again had reawakened all the old pain, the bitter sense of betrayal, and she knew she shouldn't have come.

Margy had been right. She should have simply called him from America, explained the circumstances and trusted to his compassion and better nature. Obviously he had a woman living with him—a very beautiful woman—and her idea of seducing him into, she hoped, making her pregnant before revealing the existence of Val hadn't a hope in hell of succeeding.

She briefly closed her eyes. But she was still going to try; it was a ridiculous long shot, but no sacrifice was too great for her son. She lifted her head, a determined gleam in her sapphire eyes, and found Justin standing in front of her, holding a glass of amber liquid in his hand.

'Thank you yet again,' she said easily, and took the glass, raised it to her lips, and swallowed it down. It burnt her throat and hit her empty stomach like a fire ball. She coughed and spluttered, the glass wavering precariously in her grasp.

He took it from her hand and smacked her on the back with some force. 'That was twenty-year-old cognac, meant to be savoured, not sloshed down like water,' he informed her drily, lowering his muscular length down beside her on the sofa.

'I realise that now,' she said curtly when her coughing fit had subsided enough for her to speak. She glanced sideways at him. He had changed—he was leaner and harder, she thought. But considering that he was now almost forty he looked remarkably good. But then he had been a mature male when she had met him whereas she had been a girl. She knew she had changed more than he had; from twenty-one to nearly twenty-five was a big jump from a girl to a mature woman and mother.

He was wearing an immaculately tailored grey pin-stripe suit, a white shirt and a silk tie in muted grey stripes—conservative to his fingertips. But it did not stop the powerful force of his sexuality hitting her just as hard as it had all those years ago the first time she had seen him. The old, familiar ache in her stomach, the rapid rise of her pulse—nothing had changed.

Justin had stopped patting her back, but whether by accident or design his long arm lay along the back of the sofa almost but not quite touching her shoulders; for a second she was tempted to relax back against him and pour out her desperate fear for their son.

'So, Zoë——' his smile was sardonic '—what are you doing here? I can't believe it's because you finally missed me,' he drawled cynically.

'No. I was passing through London and I thought it might be nice to look you up. I called your chambers and they said you had left.' She forgot her own troubles for a moment, intrigued to know what had happened to her husband in the past few years. 'Why, Justin? I thought you were all set to become a judge.'

'I seem to remember you thought a lot of things about me, Zoë—none of them true, and I find your presence here today incredible to say the least.' His aura of hospitality vanished in a flash. His dark eyes narrowed assessingly on her small face. 'Cut the old pals act, Zoë, and give me the real reason for your visit,' he commanded arrogantly. 'I'm a busy man; I have no time for games.'

'Perhaps I thought we could be friends—we were once,' she said lightly. She could hardly blurt out that she had hated him for the past four years, she thought wryly, especially when she was planning on getting him into bed.

'You want to be my friend?' His eyes hardened. 'Now, why, I wonder, do I find that so difficult to believe?' He smiled at her mockingly over the rim of his glass and she felt a wave of heat surge up her cheeks. Deceit did not come easily to her.

'I know my appearing out of the blue like this must be a shock to you,' she offered. Gathering her scattered wits about her, she made a concentrated effort to disarm him. She turned slightly towards him and, fixing him with her dazzling blue eyes, continued, 'But in the past few years I have grown and matured a little, I hope, and it seems pointless for the two of us to be enemies.'

She forced a casual smile and deliberately lowered her tone. 'We did share a lot together.' She lifted one shoulder languidly against the beautiful blue jersey, exaggerating her cleavage. She saw his eyes flick down to her breasts and quickly away, and her heart leapt; she was getting to him, she knew.

'We had some fun,' she went on. Her knee brushed his thigh and she felt him tense. Heady with success, she ploughed on. 'And I'm sure Uncle Bertie would turn in his grave if he knew his two favourite people couldn't even speak to each other.'

She felt guilty using her uncle but desperate need called for desperate measures, and nothing was sacred in the fight for her son's life.

'Interesting and succinctly argued, my dear Zoë. You have grown up.' His arrogant glance trailed from the silky main of pale blonde hair down to where the low V of her dress exposed the tantalising curve of her firm breasts. 'I find I rather like the idea of you and me as friends—much more civilised,' he opined, with a hint of mocking amusement in his deep brown eyes.

'Yes, yes, it is,' she agreed, grateful for his easy compliance while not questioning it. His arm around the back of the sofa fell to her shoulders, and her stomach tightened in revulsion at his touch. Or was it revulsion?

'Good, I'm glad we agree, and it is good to see you.' He smiled lazily. 'It must be almost four years—we have a lot to catch up on.' Idly his long fingers massaged her shoulder, but her reaction was anything but idle. She tensed as she felt the old familiar ache ignite deep inside her, and his thigh brushing hers made her catch her breath.

'You must tell me what you've been doing with yourself.' His hand slid down to her arm. 'You've obviously lost weight—you were always slender, but now you're almost gaunt.'

'It's the fashion,' she muttered, angry with herself for her total inability to remain immune to the man's sensual charm. Hadn't she learnt her lesson in their ill-fated marriage? She was there for a purpose—a chance to save her son's life—and she would do whatever she had to, but no way was she falling under Justin's spell again. Once was more than enough.

'Whatever.' He shrugged dismissively. 'You still look good and I'm not pressed for time tonight; give me five minutes to shower and change and I'll take you out to dinner.'

'Out to dinner' was not what she had in mind—a crowded restaurant would not help her plan at all. 'There's no need to take me out,' she demurred. 'You must have had a long day. Why not show me the kitchen and I'll rustle up an omelette or something?'

Justin stood up. 'What a very obliging woman you have turned out to be, Zoë.' A sardonic gleam of amusement flashed down at her and, clasping her hand, he pulled her to her feet. 'You still wear your wedding-ring,' he noted abruptly, turning her left hand over in his.

Zoë glanced up at him, her sapphire eyes catching his, and she trembled at the flash of some undefined emotion in their dark depths and tried to pull away. His grasp tightened for a moment as if he would detain her, his gaze oddly intent on her lovely face, then suddenly she was free.

'I wouldn't dream of allowing you to mar your soft hands with anything so mundane as cooking,' he drawled. 'My housekeeper will have prepared something. Help yourself to another drink. I won't be a moment.'

She watched his departure with mixed feelings. Her plan was going well. But why was Justin being so obliging? She had fully expected to have to battle her way into his company. Instead he had almost immediately invited her to dinner. Strange!

Uneasily she crossed to the drinks cabinet and helped herself to a small cognac. She needed it... She sipped the fiery liquid, her confidence slowly rising. No! Not so strange, she told herself firmly. After all, they were both mature, sophisticated adults. Well, Justin certainly was, she amended wryly, making her way back to the sofa and sitting down. She wasn't half so sure about herself...

She smoothed the skirt of her dress over her thighs with a trembling hand. What could be more natural than two adults sharing a dinner? And if it led to something more then that was perfectly acceptable, she told herself staunchly. She wasn't a child, and she had slept with Justin countless times...

She drained the glass and placed it on a nearby table. The hair on the back of her neck prickled and she looked up as the man occupying her thoughts walked in, a bottle of champagne in one hand and two glasses in the other.

'Quite like old times—my wife waiting for me.' His dark eyes roamed leisurely over her reclining figure with a blatant sensual insolence that made her feel as if he had stripped her naked.

She fought down the slow flush spreading through her body at his scrutiny, her confidence dipping alarmingly and a feeling of helplessness overtaking her as she stared at him. He had obviously showered and changed. Huge and casually dressed in a soft blue shirt and jeans, with a black lambswool sweater draped elegantly over his broad shoulders, his black hair damp and curling on his brow, he looked years younger and his likeness to Val was heartbreaking.

She swallowed nervously, looking away. Why was it that of all the men in the world Justin was the only one to make her heart race and her nerves quiver? It wasn't fair. Bitterness rose like gall in her throat; she should hate him that he was so vibrantly male, so *alive*, and her precious child...

No, she must not think negative thoughts, she reprimanded herself, and glanced back at Justin. He was watching her, waiting... His dark, steady gaze was so like Val's that she was hit by an overwhelming sense of guilt.

He placed the glasses on the table and finally his deep voice broke the long silence. 'A toast, I thought—to celebrate.' He deftly opened the champagne; the cork popped and bounced off the ceiling, the foaming liquid spurted from the bottle, but quickly the two glasses were filled, and he lowered his long body down beside her on the sofa. 'We can be friends! Isn't that right?' he questioned silkily.

She shied away nervously; there was something about him that she couldn't put a finger on. And his smile, as he handed her a glass of champagne, didn't quite reach his eyes.

'A toast. To old friends, hmm?'

The words were polite, even banal. Justin appeared relaxed, affable, but beneath his sophisticated exterior she had an odd premonition that something dark and dangerous lurked. Her fingers brushed his as she took the glass, an electric sensation shooting up her arm. She flinched.

'Careful, Zoë,' he prompted, his free hand closing over her wrist. 'Allow me.' In an intimate gesture he urged her hand holding the glass to her mouth while he lifted his own glass. His dark eyes caught and held hers. 'To a civilised friendship, my dear.'

She tensed. His face, only inches from hers, was playing havoc with her veneer of sophisticated control, and she was sure that he must be able to sense it. So, with a calm she was far from feeling, she placed her small hand on his arm, her expression beguiling. 'To a long and civilised friendship,' she responded sweetly, and took a healthy sip of the champagne.

There was nothing civilised about the murderous rage leaping in her companion's eyes, but, luckily for Zoë, she never saw it. By the time she was brave enough to face him again he had finished his drink, his large frame sprawled back on the sofa, a lazy smile in his brown eyes.

'So tell me, what have you been doing with yourself the last few years? You don't have much of a tan for a Californian.'

'Oh, I don't live in California!' she exclaimed, glad to get on to a neutral topic. 'I have a house in Maine, in a lovely little fishing village. Actually, the area is rather like England——'

'Could be why it's known as New England,' he interrupted with a mocking grin.

Her answering smile was completely spontaneous, and for the next few hours she felt as if she had stepped back in time. Over a delicious if simple dinner of a typically English dish—hotpot—he was a charming, witty host.

'Not your nouvelle cuisine,' he said wryly as he carried a tray with a coffee-pot and two cups into the living-room, where Zoë was already relaxing once again on the sofa. 'But ideal for a cold March day.'

The coffee finished, Zoë, sipping a glass of cognac, allowed her eyes to roam over Justin. He was lounging back beside her, his long legs stretched out before him; she noted the stretched denim over his muscular thighs and—whether it was the wine or the food or simply because she was feeling relaxed for the first time in weeks she wasn't sure—a sharp tug of sexual awareness lanced painfully through her.

'You never did tell me why you changed careers,' she blurted, taking another drink of her cognac—anything to get her mind away from the slight friction of his thigh against her own, the overt sensuality of the man. Forgetting for the moment that she was supposed to be seducing him, she suddenly realised that he had skilfully discovered all about her home and career, and a couple of times she had almost slipped up and mentioned Val. But he had revealed very little about himself.

She glanced back at him. He was gazing down at his drink, idly twisting the glass between his long fingers, his expression hidden from her.

'I don't think I was ever cut out to be a judge—as you so rightly told me the last time we met.'

'Oh, but...'

'Don't worry.' His hand slid casually to rest on her thigh, and he squeezed it reassuringly. Except that, to Zoë, it was not reassuring—quite the opposite: intensely arousing. 'It had nothing to do with you. For years I went along with what Bertie wanted for me simply because he had been good to me and I wanted to please him. But I realised a few months after his death that it was his ambition I was following, not my own. So I went back to international law.'

'Do you like it?' she asked breathlessly; his hand, idly stroking her thigh, was playing havoc with her nervous system.

'I love it. I get to travel; I make vast amounts of money.'

Then she remembered Janet; he had once worked with the woman in that field. She tensed. 'And I suppose you work with Janet again?'

'Good God, no!' he exclaimed, easing up, his arm somehow finding its way around her shoulder. 'She put herself in a clinic and dried out and then married Bob. They have two children.'

'Dried out?' she queried.

'Surely you knew the woman was an alcoholic? Everyone else did.'

She had a vivid image of Janet drinking from the champagne bottle at her twenty-first, and the thought that she had allowed Janet's drunken revelations to persuade her to run out on Justin was oddly disturbing, but, banishing her unease, she responded.

'I never guessed. But Janet—with a family—the mind boggles.' She grinned, inexplicably lighter of heart.

'Is it so strange for a woman to want a home and family, Zoë? Are you really such a determined career girl? The girl I married was longing to have a baby. I often wondered—if I hadn't insisted on waiting a year—if I had made you pregnant—would you have run away so easily?'

The colour drained from her face. He was getting too near the truth, and she lowered her eyes, unable to meet his dark, enquiring gaze. The anger, the hatred and bitterness she had felt because he had married her but never loved her were no excuse for what she had done. She was flooded with guilt and remorse and combined with too much liquor it was a lethal combination.

She opened her mouth to tell him about Val, but before she could confess Justin continued, 'Jess and I debated the point once. She's of the opinion that a child only makes a bad relationship worse. I'm not so sure.'

The mention of Jess acted like a bucket of cold water over Zoë, reminding her exactly why she was here, and time was running out if her plan was to work. His girlfriend might be back any minute.

'Yes, well, it is all rather academic now,' she said lightly, and, turning towards him, she deliberately placed her small hand on his chest. She tilted her head back to look up into his harshly attractive face.

'Don't let's talk about the past. I'm much more interested in the present.' And, forcing a regretful smile to her lips and widening her blue eyes appealingly, she added, 'I'm glad we can be friends, Justin.'

She inched her hand higher to where the top buttons of his shirt were open to reveal the strong line of his throat. Her fingers grazed his skin and she felt him tense. 'It is rather late; Jess will be back soon.' She was fishing, but she needed to know. 'I'd better get back to my hotel.'

His dark eyes glittered dangerously down into hers as he caught her hand and held it trapped against his chest. 'Jess won't be back tonight, and you don't have to go—you can stay here.'

He lifted her hand to his mouth, his lips kissing her fingertips, his eyes coolly assessing on her upturned face. 'You understand that I'm not into celibacy?' The corners of his hard mouth quirked in a sensuous smile. 'If that's going to be a problem for you, say so. I will understand,' he said smoothly.

She understood all right. He was offering her what she had set out to get. It was there in the flare of desire in his eyes, quickly masked by his hooded lids. He sucked one of her fingers into his mouth and she trembled, her pulse galloping.

He was still the only man who could arouse the sensual side of her nature. His touch still had the power to turn her will to mush. It was galling to admit. It left a bitter sense of self-loathing in her troubled conscience but it didn't make it any the less true.

She should have been ecstatic but instead all she felt was a profound sadness. This man had been the love of her life, and he had confirmed what she had always known. He was a man who betrayed the women in his life without a qualm.

'But Jess . . .' She needed to hear him confirm his duplicity. It would help to ease her own sense of guilt.

'Don't worry your head about Jess. She's a woman of the world, Zoë, the same as you.' And, lifting her on to his lap, he bent to her mouth.

Much later she was to wonder if she had actually seduced her husband, or if it had been the other way around . . .

CHAPTER SEVEN

ZOË had imagined that she would have to force herself to accept Justin's lovemaking, to tell herself it was for her son's life and just lie back and think of England!

But at the first touch of his lips on hers she knew that she had lied to herself for years. She was swamped with emotions—feelings so intense that they stole the breath from her body and moisture stung her eyes.

He'd never kissed her in quite that way before. She felt the soft touch of his mouth, the gentle nibble of his teeth against her lips, the lick of his tongue teasingly soothing the supposed bite, savouring the taste of her.

'So lush, so soft,' he breathed against her lips. 'Open your mouth for me, Zoë,' he husked, his lips rubbing sensually against hers, taunting her into sharing the pleasure, and she did...

Before, he had always been a silent lover, but now he had no such reservations, and his deep, throaty murmurings, interspersed with longer and deeper kisses, were her downfall—hot, damp heat filled her loins and she felt it burn through her whole body.

As she was held on his lap her arms, of their own volition, wound around his neck; her mouth followed where his led. The husky male scent of him surrounded and seduced her; she felt the rigid muscles of his thighs beneath her and she pressed into his hard body with hungry need.

'No,' he whispered roughly. 'Not here.' Rising to his feet, with Zoë held firmly in his arms, his breathing quick and unsteady, he strode through the apartment. He shouldered open the bedroom door, and kicked it shut with his foot, not stopping until he was standing next to the king-size bed.

She looked searchingly up into the dark eyes so close to her own. 'Justin, I...' She wanted some reassurance, perhaps, that it wasn't simply a physical thing.

'It's too late, Zoë. I'm too old for teasing games; I want you badly. Now!' he said harshly.

She trembled with fear or frustration—she didn't know which. 'Yes,' she murmured. It didn't really matter which! She had to go through with it for Val—but also, her own innate sense of honesty forced her to admit, for herself... She had had nearly four long years of celibacy and she had never stopped wanting Justin, however much she had tried to deny it.

She sighed, a deep, shuddering breath, as Justin stood her on her feet and quickly unbuttoned her dress, slipping it from her shoulders to pool in a heap on the floor.

'Nice,' he growled, his hungry eyes slanting over her near-naked form, the proud tilt of her full breasts, and the wisp of lace briefs cupping her feminine curls.

The urge to cover herself was compelling but juvenile. Justin had seen her naked countless times in the past, but it didn't stop her feeling helplessly exposed. Running her tongue nervously over dry lips, she forced herself to stand immobile, her arms at her sides; she couldn't afford to let him see her nervousness.

And he didn't. His dark eyes glittered as they followed the tip of her tongue, while the fingers of one hand hooked in her briefs and pulled them down. His gaze lowered lazily over her naked body and then, dropping to his knees, he slowly unfastened her suspenders and trailed her stockings down her legs, and finally he glanced up at her and undid her garter belt. His large hands curved around her waist and he brushed her stomach with his lips. Her body jerked in instant reaction, and she bit her lip to prevent herself crying out.

Justin rose to his feet and simply stared at her. 'I thought the first time I unwrapped my Valentine girl in this room that you were perfect.' He shook his dark head wonderingly.

She raised her eyes to his. And I thought you loved me, she wanted to cry, but didn't. In those days she had believed that love made the world go round. A brief, ironic smile flitted across her softly flushed face. With maturity had come realism. Now she accepted that it was simple thermodynamics...

They stared at each other, the air around them crackling with tension. He divested himself of his own clothes, never taking his eyes off her, drinking in the sight of her pale skin, the soft, full curve of her breasts, the secret, downy hair.

But Zoë was doing some observing of her own. 'Justin.' She breathed his name. Awed all over again by his superbly muscled form, which was naked and glowing golden in the dim light of one small lamp, she had forgotten how splendidly male, how powerful he was.

Then he lowered his head and pressed his mouth to the valley between her breasts. His hands curving around and down over her buttocks, he pulled her hard against him. His mouth trailed up her throat, and his dark eyes gleamed with a feral light in the semi-darkness.

'Remember that night, Zoë? The night you promised to be mine?' he demanded, a sharp edge to his deep voice. 'My own personal valentine.'

It was cruel of him to remind her—as if she could ever forget. She had imagined that it was a lucky omen, getting engaged on Valentine's day, but life had taught her differently. She slid her arms up around his neck and swayed against him.

'Forget the past and let's enjoy tonight,' she pleaded. For once she wanted to forget all her troubles, all the heartache, and surrender herself to the mindless pleasure that only he could give her. Tomorrow she would count the cost, but now now!

'Enjoy the sex; I take it you are protected?'

'Yes,' she lied.

'Of course, my wanton little wife.' His mouth covered hers again, but this time with passionate insistence.

She felt the need in him; her legs trembled against his, her stomach quivered against his hard, masculine life force, and she opened her mouth, her tongue twining with his. He pulled back sharply.

'Slowly, slowly, my darling.' Dazed by his kisses, she did not hear the sneer in his voice. 'It should be interesting discovering what you've learnt over the years,' he drawled with a cynicism that was lost on her as he swung her once more in his arms and deposited them both on the bed.

He looked down the length of her. 'You're as beautiful as ever.' His hand closed over her breasts. 'But before you were a girl; now you are a woman.' His thumb grazed the tip of her breast. 'A surprisingly voluptuous woman in some areas.' His head bent and as his mouth sucked the rosy peak she arched up towards him, fire shooting from her breast to her loins.

'You still like that?' He lifted his head to stare at her, his brown eyes glittering with sensual desire in the harsh contours of his handsome face. She met his eyes, her own wide and dazed with emotion.

'You know I do,' she whispered, her hands lifting to shape his wide shoulders, flow down his strong arms, and move to the broad expanse of his hairy chest. 'I like anything you do,' she confessed throatily, and, like a sculptor moulding a work of art, she traced his masculine form, her fingers delighting in remembering the satin-smooth feel of his skin. Her hands stretched to his waist and around over his firm buttocks.

'Zoë,' he growled, and leant down, his mouth lightly brushing her lips and then finding her breast once more. She lifted her hands and buried them in the thick, silky hair of his head, holding him against her as, arching, she offered him her aching breasts. She shuddered as his hot, moist mouth fed on one swollen nipple and then the other, until a strangled cry escaped her.

The touch of his tongue and the caress of his hand as it stroked seductively down her body, his long inquisitive fingers tangling in the bush of blonde curls at her thighs and pulling, gently teasing, before they slid deftly into the soft, feminine folds of her most secret flesh, were almost more than she could bear.

She was spinning out of control to a hot, healing place where nothing mattered but the pleasure he could give her and she could give him. His mouth followed the trail of his hands and she exulted in the hard rasp of his chin against her tender flesh, his seeking fingers that found every pleasure-point with unerring accuracy, the hard pressure of his mighty body.

She traced the length of his spine, her small hand curving around the firm male buttock, seeking the hard core of him, but suddenly he grasped her wrist and pushed her hand away, rolling on to his back.

'Not yet. Slow down,' he rasped urgently.

But Zoë ignored him; she was consumed by a burning urgency. Perhaps subconsciously she knew this was all she would have of him; tomorrow would bring grim reality, but tonight was hers.

She felt as though she had been in an emotional prison for years and had finally broken free. She followed him over, sprawling across his sweat-wet body, her long hair a tangled mass spread across his shoulders as her mouth found the male, pebble-like nipples buried deep in the soft, curling chest hair. She moved restlessly against him, her hands shaping his thighs as her teeth bit the tiny buds.

'God, Zoë, what are you doing to me?' Justin groaned and, grasping her around the waist, he lifted her slightly.

She raised her head and looked down into glittering black eyes, her own unfocused. She felt him shaking beneath her, then suddenly he lifted her higher and lowered her sharply down, impaling her with his male strength. She cried out as he filled her, her slender body clenching around him in convulsive need.

He raised his head and, catching the tip of her breast with his teeth, sucked the hard nipple into the dark cavern of his mouth with the same rhythm as he surged into her pulsating flesh. She heard his harsh moan as she recognised her own whimpering cries. Every nerve, every sinew in her body pulled tight with an excruciating tension. She battled to breathe, then her body convulsed in a rapturous fulfilment, the ecstasy prolonged as Justin increased the tempo to explode inside her.

'Zoë.' He rasped her name and held her hard down, his fingers digging into the flesh of her waist as his great body bucked uncontrollably beneath her in a shattering climax.

She fell against his chest; she felt his arms close around her; she heard the rapid pounding of his powerful heart beneath her ear, her own body twitching in the aftermath of love.

Some time later she didn't hear Justin's huskily voiced question, 'Are you OK?' She was asleep.

It was a long, dark tunnel. Water seeped from the arched roof and trickled down the rough stone walls to sink into the soil, turning the ground to mud. She was cold to the bone and terrified.

Then, in the distance, at the end of the tunnel, outlined in a silver glow, stood two figures. Zoë moved towards them, slowly, sluggishly, the mud holding her back. She saw them smile and her blue eyes widened to their fullest extent as she recognised them, her face radiant with joy. Justin and Val.

She tried to hurry, but as she stretched out her hand towards them the figures turned and she froze in horror as the boy vanished, disappearing into the man.

'No, no. Valentine!' she screamed.

'Zoë, Zoë, wake up.'

Her eyes flew open, the horror of the dream reflected in the blue depths. For a moment she was totally disorientated. But the large body looming over her and the hand on her head, smoothing her hair from her brow, were real.

'You were having a bad dream.'

'Justin,' she murmured, reality returning. She lifted her hand and outlined his square jaw, the slant of his cheekbones. He was warm and alive and in bed with her. But Val... God, no! She refused to see it as another omen. She was finished with superstition. It solved nothing.

He caught her hand and pressed it to his lips. 'I know I'm no oil-painting——' his dark eyes gleamed with ironic amusement '—but I can honestly say that you're the only woman I've driven into having a nightmare. I would never have mentioned our first night together if I had known it would cause such a violent reaction. Are you all right?'

She moved her hand around the back of his neck, her fingers tangling in his night-black hair. He hadn't guessed her secret, and she wasn't going to tell him. Not yet... She needed him tonight...

'More than all right,' she responded huskily, urging his head down and pressing her lips against his smiling mouth while her other hand found its way around his hard thigh.

Zoë leant up on one elbow. Careful not to disturb the sleeping man, she let her gaze wander over his rugged face, the softly curling hair. In sleep, Justin looked years younger and so like Val that it brought tears to her eyes. They had made love countless times—two healthy adults glorying in each other's body. She ached all over, but the biggest ache was in her heart. She could pretend to herself no longer. She loved Justin—always had and probably always would.

With the added maturity that the years and her worry over her son had given her she knew that if she had the last few years to live over again, she would never have left Justin. The only reality in life was the family. She had allowed stupid, girlish pride to wreck hers, and she had to bear the guilt for it.

She should never have let a drunken woman's ramblings, or the fact that her uncle had only been trying to do what he thought was best for her, break up her marriage. Nor should she have allowed Justin to think that Wayne was her lover because of childish tit-for-tat jealousy.

She should have stayed with him and fought for his love. It would not have changed the fact that their son was ill, but at least Val would have had the support of a father as well as herself over the past few terrifying months.

As the early morning sun splintered through the window, outshining the single lamp's gold glow, she made a momentous decision. She was going to swallow her pride and confess everything—tell Justin she loved him and beg his forgiveness for hiding his son from him, and, hopefully, they could go forward into the future, supporting each other and better able to face the trials to come.

She sighed contentedly, her decision made, and, wriggling down beneath the covers, put her arm around Justin's waist and snuggled up against his large, warm body. For the first time in ages she felt safe, protected and no longer alone with her worries, and, yawning widely, she fell into a deep, dreamless sleep.

Zoë stirred, opening her eyes lazily; the seductive scent of freshly ground coffee lingered in the air. She stretched out a hand but she was alone in the wide bed. Justin must be up making the coffee, she thought, a small smug smile lighting her eyes as the events of the previous night flickered through her mind. She hauled herself into a sitting position, and, flicking the tumbled mass of her blonde hair from her eyes, looked up.

'Good, you're awake.'

'Justin.' He was standing by the bed, naked except for a small towel carelessly tied around his hips, and the memory of the intimacies they had so recently shared made her blush scarlet. It was stupid, she knew, but she felt inexplicably shy.

He leant forward and he felt her heartbeat accelerate, sure that he was going to kiss her, but instead he placed a cup of coffee on the bedside table and straightened up.

'Thank you,' she murmured huskily, vitally aware of his imposing presence and the glitter in his eyes as they roamed over her flushed face. She felt her nipples harden as his gaze dropped lower. She was naked from the waist up and her first reaction was to pull the sheet up, but, with her decision of the early hours of the morning fresh in her mind, she didn't. She was an adult woman and this was her husband...

'Very nice,' he drawled mockingly, 'but I haven't time this morning; drink your coffee and get dressed. I'll drop you off at your hotel on the way to the gym.'

'There's no need. I'm quite happy to stay here until you get back,' she replied with a nonchalance she did not feel. She couldn't really blame him for suggesting the hotel. She had given him no reason to believe differently.

She pulled the cover up over her breasts and, bravely raising her eyes to his, added firmly, 'We need to talk, Justin.' She had been a coward once, but never again. 'I have a confession to make; it's important and after last night——' she had been going to say, I realise I love you, but she never got to finish the sentence.

'Last night was a one-off, Zoë,' he cut in ruthlessly. 'Good fun, but I'm not a fool. I know exactly why you were so willing to leap into bed with me.'

'But you can't...' This wasn't going at all as she had envisaged. She stared up at him, unable to fathom the brooding look in his dark eyes. 'I only realised myself...'

'I do read the gossip columns occasionally.'

'Gossip columns?' What on earth was he talking about?

'Cut out the innocent act, sweetheart,' he bit out. 'I've been expecting you for weeks—ever since lover-boy Wayne got himself engaged to a starlet. What happened? Get tired of you, did he?' he queried coldly. 'Or perhaps tired of waiting for you to be free?'

His black eyes narrowed angrily. 'My God, you have some nerve, I'll give you that. Did you really think you could walk back into my life when Wayne dropped you and expect me to take you back? Was that what your pathetic attempt at seducing me last night was all about?'

She flinched under his tirade, not really following his reasoning. 'No, it's not true,' she whispered, too stunned by his total misreading of the situation even to argue.

She grasped the sheet tighter around her suddenly cold body.

'"No, it's not true."' He viciously mimicked her feeble denial. 'That's your trouble, Zoë; you wouldn't know the truth if it got up and smacked you in the face. You never did, as you proved conclusively years ago when you ran out on me.'

'Please, Justin, you have to listen to me.' She swung her feet to the floor and stood up, the sheet draped haphazardly around her body. He caught her by the shoulders and held her away from him, but she swayed towards him, the urgency in her expression undeniable. 'I know I was wrong before, but I realised last night that I love you, and I——'

His fingers dug into her flesh for a second and then he flung her away from him with such force that she fell back across the bed, his fury hitting her like a blast from the devil's own fiery furnace.

'You bitch! You don't know the meaning of the word, and I've wasted enough time already this morning. I'm sick of your games. Get dressed and get out.' And, swinging on his heel, he flung out of the bedroom.

Zoë watched him leave, her eyes filling with tears. She brushed them away with the back of her hand and got up off the bed. She had done her crying over Justin years ago and nothing had changed. What had she expected?

Nothing, her common sense told her. A big fat zero… Wasn't that why she'd decided to get him into bed without telling him about Val? Because she knew, had always known, that he didn't give a damn for her? But he would be furious when he found out about Val.

Then she remembered Jess. The woman was probably due back any minute. Last night, in a sensuous haze, she had lost her wits completely. How could she have forgotten Justin's luscious girlfriend? But in the clear light of day the reality of her situation rushed in on her.

Quickly she washed and dressed and went looking for him. He had said that he was sick of games and that was good enough for her. She had no more time to waste. She found him in the kitchen; he was leaning casually against the kitchen bench, drinking a cup of coffee. He looked up as she entered, his dark eyes as cold and remote as a polar icecap.

'You took my advice, I see.' He glanced over her slight figure. She was dressed in her stylish clothes of last night but minus her make-up, and her hair was ruthlessly pulled back and fastened with an elastic band.

'Yes, but before I go I have something to show you.' Sitting down at the kitchen table, she opened her bag and, rummaging around, withdrew a snapshot and held it out to him. 'This is Val, our son—the reason I'm here.' She saw no point in softening the blow; Justin didn't deserve her consideration. When had he ever considered her?

He stepped towards her and took the proffered picture, glanced at it, and as she watched she saw him stiffen. 'I only have your word for that; this child could be any man's,' he said, cynicism icing his voice. 'I seem to remember you and I always took precautions. What kind of an idiot do you take me for, Zoë? Discovered how wealthy I am now, is that it?'

It was lucky that she was already sitting down because otherwise, at his denial of her child, she would certainly have collapsed. She had thought that she had covered every eventuality, but it had never crossed her mind that he would query his part in the parenting. She stared up at him through a mist of pain and rising anger which she did not attempt to hide.

'No, it's not your money I need, it's you. Val is three years old; he was conceived the night of Uncle Bertie's funeral. If you remember, it was the one time in our brief marriage you actually spent the night with me, and we did have unprotected sex.'

She caught a glimpse of shocked horror on his handsome face, but she didn't care if she hurt him. 'You're a lawyer.' Her mouth twisted in a bitter grimace. 'If you insist I'll agree to a DNA test to confirm the parenting, but it will have to be quick.'

He was caught and he knew it, but he was obviously not ecstatic at the thought of a child; his granite-hard features showed no flicker of emotion. She briefly closed her eyes, her head drooping on the slender column of her neck, her son, her ever present worry, swamping her mind.

'You knew you were pregnant when you left me,' Justin prompted stonily, and, pulling out a chair, sat down opposite her.

Zoë, her head bent, studying her clasped hands, either didn't hear or ignored his comment. 'He was born the following February—Valentine's day—hence his name.'

She was back in the past, a reminiscent smile softening her blue eyes. 'He was a beautiful baby, and it's stupid, I know, but I remember hearing this country and western singer on the radio. It was a song about a boy called Sue. He had given his son that name because he wasn't going to be around to look after him, and I thought, what with the day and all, Val was really very appropriate.'

Long fingers caught her chin, their pressure hard as Justin forced her head back until he could look into her face. She recoiled at the blistering fury leaping in his eyes.

'You knew—if not in England, in California.' The words came out harsh and clipped.

'Knew what?' She had not been listening to him.

His thumb and finger dug into her throat and she gasped at the pain. 'You knew you were pregnant the last time I saw you. Didn't you...? Didn't you?' he demanded harshly, his rugged face livid with rage. 'You could have told me, you cruel little bitch,' he snarled.

She forced herself to stay cool, though inside she was trembling in fear at the force of his rage. He got to his feet and she could sense the threat of violence in his hard body as he leant over the table, breathing down on her hapless head. 'You're hurting my neck.' She gulped.

His hand fell away and he was around the table in seconds. 'Tell me... I need to know.' His long fingers gripped her shoulders, digging into her flesh. 'What did I ever do to make you hate me?' he demanded tautly, his iron self-control slowly reasserting itself. 'Why? Why do you hate me so much you would deny me my own child?'

She was puzzled, not so much by his anger—she had expected that—but by the hesitation, the hint of pain in his usually authoritarian tone. 'I was going to tell you, but you said you never wanted to see me again. There didn't seem much point,' she said brittlely.

Justin briefly closed his eyes, and she could have sworn that she saw his wide shoulders shudder. His hands squeezed her shoulders; she glanced up at his face and their eyes met.

'God forgive you, Zoë, because I don't think I ever will,' he said with a finality that was chilling. But, worse, she recognised a look of such torment in the depth of his deep brown eyes that she was struck dumb.

'Where is he now? I want to see him. Does he know I'm his father? Thank God I didn't give you the divorce you wanted. He is legally my child, and you've cheated me out of three years of his life. Well, not any more, Zoë.'

He was making her head spin with his questions, his comments, and she couldn't think straight. But he never let up.

'I intend to fight you for him. I'll challenge you through every court both here and in the States. I want my son, Zoë. I will have him.' His lips twisted in a satanic smile. 'I will win, I promise you, and once I get him I intend to keep him...'

His words were cutting into her heart like a knife, and she couldn't stand any more. She had been battling to control her tumultuous emotions for far too long.

'Keep him? Keep him?' she cried. 'You fool, you don't understand. I would gladly give him to you this very second if only it would make him well.' Her eyes wild, she screamed, 'Val is ill—very, very ill. Why the hell do you think I'm here now? Do you think I enjoy leaving him with Margy while I trek halfway around the world seeking his father?' She was blinded by fury and fear, and, shrugging off his restraining hands, she leapt to her feet.

He was towering over her, large and intimidating, but she was beyond worrying about his threat. 'I would never have set foot in your home in a million years if it weren't for my son. But he needs you; you are almost his last chance, and I would sup with the devil if I had to, to save him.'

The tears filled her eyes but she dashed them away with the back of her hand. 'In this case, that happens to be you.'

She spun on her heel, not sure where she was going, but she was pulled back roughly into his arms and lifted completely off her feet.

'What the hell do you mean?' He looked down into her tempestuous little face. 'Ill?'

That was how Jess found them.

'My God! Justin, you didn't spend the night with her? How could you?'

Zoë felt his sudden tension as he slowly lowered her down the length of his hard body until her feet found the floor. She pushed herself out of his arms, red with embarrassment. His mistress was back... Her glance went to the tall, elegant woman and then to Justin's harsh face.

'You don't understand, Jess.'

The tender light in his eyes as he spoke to the other woman was enough for Zoë. She had to get out of there and fast.

'Understand? You're a fool, Justin.' She cast a disparaging glance at Zoë's tiny, dishevelled figure. 'You've always been a pushover for her. Will you never learn?'

'Not now, Jess,' he said tersely. 'Just leave. Please.'

Zoë picked up her bag from the table and began edging towards the door. She had done what she set out to do; it was up to Justin now. But she couldn't bear to be the third wheel in a lovers' quarrel; she hadn't the stomach for it.

'Zoë, where the hell do you think you're going?' Justin demanded, just as she was slipping out of the door and into the hall.

She stopped. 'I need to get back to my hotel; I need a bath, a change of clothes.'

She might have been tiny but she had an inner core of pure steel, and she had never needed it more than at this moment. She could not blame Jess for her fury; she felt dirty herself. But if the other woman's dagger looks were meant to unnerve her they would not succeed. Too much was at stake.

Zoë ploughed on bravely with her mission regardless. She firmly told Justin her room number. 'Call me when you're free. I'll be there until Monday.'

His black head tilted to one side and he studied her pale face with a chilling implacability. 'You're in no fit state to go anywhere by yourself, and I don't trust you not to disappear.'

'Disappear?' A glimmer of a smile twisted her lips, Margy's admonition ringing in her mind: 'Hog-tie him if you have to'. 'I can promise you there is no fear of that,' she said with a touch of irony. 'I'll be in all weekend waiting for your call——'

'Really, Justin, you're not going to fall for that?' Jess interrupted. 'You're far too intelligent.'

'Shut up, Jess.' Justin walked past her to Zoë, and, curling his fingers around the top of her arm, glanced back over his shoulder at his mistress. 'I'll call you later.' He looked down at Zoë. 'I'll give you a lift to your hotel.'

Zoë swallowed at the remote look on his darkly attractive face, and, with a brief nod of her fair head, she agreed.

She felt drained of all emotion as she walked with Justin through the underground car park to where a sleek black Jaguar was waiting. He handed her into the front seat and slid in beside her.

She watched him deftly manoeuvre the car out into the Saturday morning traffic with enviable ease. One hand rested lightly on the gear lever; the long fingers of his other hand curved delicately around the leather-bound steering-wheel.

She had a vivid image of those same fingers on her naked flesh last night and her pulse leapt with remembered pleasure.

He really was an incredibly sexy man, she thought, glancing sideways at his hard profile. Unfortunately he was completely lacking in morals where women were concerned. It was just as well, she acknowledged with dry irony, or she would never have ended up in his bed last night.

She sighed and stared out of the window. It was raining, the sky a dull, leaden grey and an accurate reflection of her state of mind. She sighed again.

'Valentine,' Justin drawled. 'What kind of name is that for my son?' He glanced at her, his face cold and expressionless. 'Though I shouldn't be surprised; you always were a fey, whimsical kind of child.'

She made no response, and they drove in a lengthening, tense silence that did not improve when they reached the Savoy.

'Get out,' Justin ordered curtly, and before she had gathered herself sufficiently to open the door and slide out he was around the car and taking her arm in a vice-like grip. He passed the car keys to the valet and hustled her into the foyer as if she were an errant child.

When he demanded her room key from Reception, she tried to object. 'There is——'

'Shut up.' He was in a furious temper beneath his controlled exterior, and he flung her into the lift as if she were a rag doll.

But it was no more than she had expected, she thought with stoical resignation.

CHAPTER EIGHT

ANY hope of her ordeal being over quickly was squashed as Justin, granite-faced, pushed her into her own suite and closed the door behind him.

He came towards her. 'Now talk,' he commanded arrogantly. 'And you'd better make it good. I want to know everything about my son, and what you've done with him.' His hands dropped to her narrow shoulders and he stood staring down at her, his black eyes burning on her. 'I've had it with you, Zoë; you've gone too far this time.'

For once the dynamic, powerful Justin had lost his poise; her revelations had clearly knocked him for six. But it gave her no joy. She had thought that after the night they had spent together... her realisation that she still loved him...

How naïve could one get? She shook her head in disbelief at her own folly. The arrival of Jess had shown Zoë just how degrading her position was. Justin wanted nothing from her but his son.

She drew on her last reserves of strength, determined to concentrate strictly on Val's welfare, and, wiping her own shame and humiliation from her mind, looked Justin straight in the eye and said flatly, 'Please let me go. I need the bathroom, and, in any case, what I have to tell you can't be discussed in a rage.'

She was a mother first and foremost and she refused to discuss her precious son in anger. Too much was at stake and it was vital that she win Justin's support.

A cruel smile smile curved his lips; he caught her face between his hands and pressed his mouth hard down on hers in a savage parody of a kiss, declaring his power and domination.

She swayed, her legs trembling, when he released her. 'Why?' Her tongue licked her swollen lips.

'A reminder!' he said tightly. 'I'll order coffee, but don't keep me waiting too long.'

Ten minutes later Zoë reluctantly walked back into the sitting-room. She had taken the time to have a quick shower and change into a pair of well-washed jeans and a baggy black sweatshirt. Barefoot, with her small face scrubbed clean and her pale, silky hair dragged back and fastened with a blue silk scarf, she had no idea how ridiculously young and vulnerable she looked.

A grim smile touched Justin's mouth when he saw her. His hand shook as he ran it through his thick hair. 'You look so damned innocent. How the hell do you do it?'

'Cursing me will solve nothing,' she said, her blue eyes flickering over him. He was perched on the edge of his chair, a coffee-jug and cups untouched on the table in front of him. She knew she had hurt him badly by denying him his son, but recriminations could come later. First, she needed to explain and get him back to the States with her.

She sat down on the chair opposite his and, leaning forward, filled two cups with the thick, dark brew. Automatically adding one spoonful of sugar to his, she handed it across to him.

'You remembered how I like my coffee; pity you couldn't have remembered to tell me I had a son as easily,' he said with biting sarcasm.

'Please, Justin. Let me tell you in my own way.'

'I can't wait.' His formidable, dark face looked grim. 'It should be interesting. It's not every day that a man is so spectacularly betrayed by his own wife.'

'I never wanted——'

'Cut the excuses, for God's sake! And give it to me straight.' His sensuous mouth curved contemptuously. 'That is, if your devious little mind can grasp the concept.'

She bowed her head, unable to face the banked-down rage in his dark eyes, and began to speak. 'Val is a beautiful little boy—a real live wire, full of curiosity for life, and he looks very like you.

'But last fall I noticed he was much quieter than usual; at first I put it down to the bad weather at the time.' A dry chuckle escaped her. 'My English half blaming everything on the weather, I expect.'

She glanced across at Justin and for a second she faltered, deterred by the unforgiving hardness of his expression.

She swallowed. 'He caught a cold. The doctor gave him antibiotics, and he seemed to recover, but not properly. After Christmas when he started pre-school he still wasn't a hundred per cent. The doctor took a blood test, and confirmed he was anaemic, but when, after vitamins and iron, he was still no better there were further tests.'

Her bottom lip trembled and she had to take a deep, steadying breath before she could go on. Reliving the past desperate weeks and exposing her pain to another person was one of the hardest things she had ever done.

'Go on,' Justin prompted implacably.

'We took a trip to the hospital in Portland; the consultant there recommended a transfer to New York University Hospital and a world-renowned consultant in the field, Professor Barnet. More transfusions, more tests, until a week ago they finally came up with the answer—Fanconi's anaemia, a very rare disease.'

She said the hated words by rote; it was the only way she could deal with the enormity of what had happened to her beloved boy.

'Cause not known. Treatment—a week on Monday Val starts a course of chemotherapy. Ideal solution—a bone-marrow transplant. The problem is that I've been screened and I'm not a match for him.'

Only then did she lift her head.

Justin had gone white about the mouth and his features had settled into a rigid, impenetrable mask, which made what she had to ask him a hundred times harder.

'I'm hoping you will be,' she said, her blue eyes huge and pleading in the unnatural pallor of her small face. 'It's not hard, Justin, believe me. A simple blood test, and, if you match, the transplant is a breeze—honestly,' she insisted urgently. 'A simple operation to extract the marrow from the base of your spine. Two nights in hospital—three at most; nothing worse than a backache.'

'Stop! Stop right there,' he commanded flatly. 'First, have you consulted the best medical opinion available?'

For the next half-hour Zoë was treated to a ruthless cross-examination, Justin's decisive yet politely impersonal questions beating down on her until she wanted to scream and finally did...

'But will you do it?' she cried. 'I have your seat booked on Concorde on Monday. Please simply say yes.'

'God! Need you ask?' Disgust made his lip curl and she squirmed at the contempt in his black gaze as he added, 'Yes, of course.'

Her head fell back against the soft cushion and she closed her eyes. 'Oh, thank God. Thank God!' The relief was tremendous. She had hoped that Justin would do the right thing, but she had never been sure. It was as if the weight of the world lifted from her shoulders. She opened her eyes and looked at him. 'You'll never know how much this means to me, Justin.'

'I think I can guess; he is my son as well,' he returned drily. Getting to his feet and turning on his heel, he strode across to the telephone. He dialled a number and, holding the receiver to his ear, turned and leant against the table, watching her with cold dark eyes, his long lashes flicking against his high cheekbones. 'There's no need to wait until Monday. We'll leave today.'

'But——'

He stopped her with a wave of his hand, and she listened in rising amazement as he instructed the unseen person at the other end of the telephone wire to have the jet standing by.

'How?' She seemed to be incapable of stringing two words together.'

His mouth curved sardonically. 'Easy, Zoë,' he said, coming towards her. 'I am a very powerful man in my own way.' He reached down and lifted her up out of the chair as if she weighed no more than a feather, his hands firmly around her tiny waist. 'But I certainly underestimated you, my dear wife,' he drawled harshly. 'Last night had nothing to do with Wayne Sutton, had it?'

She blushed fiery red as he set her on her feet, but kept a firm hold on her. 'No,' she mumbled; could he possibly have guessed? It was one thing to ask an estranged husband to donate bone marrow; it was quite another to try and get oneself pregnant by the same man, especially knowing he had a very lovely 'significant other' in his life.

'You have good reason to look ashamed,' he said with icy disdain, and, grasping her chin, he tilted her scarlet face back the better to see her. 'You deliberately let me do anything I wanted with your sexy little body last night in the hope of softening me up before telling me about my son.'

Now was the moment to tell him the truth—all of it. 'It...' She bit her lip.

'You're little better than a whore, but then I always knew that.'

She looked up sharply, meeting his contemptuous gaze with angry eyes. 'It wasn't like that,' she objected.

'Your reason was noble,' he admitted in a deadly quiet voice, 'But don't ever try to barter sex with me again. I will not be used that way. I prefer to do my own hunting.'

A dull foreboding made her shiver; if he ever discovered just how much she had tried to use him he would kill her... 'I wouldn't dream of it,' she said quickly, keeping a wary eye on him.

He smiled—a slow, wicked curve of his hard lips. 'Good,' he murmured, his arm tightening around her waist. His black head bent and his warm mouth fastened on hers in a long, sensuous kiss that made her heart thud in her breast.

She caught her breath as he pushed her away, staring up at him, bewildered and vaguely angry. 'Why did you do that?' she demanded shakily.

'You looked like you needed it, and I sure as hell did,' he grated. 'Now for the sixty-four-thousand-dollar question. What have you told our son about me?' The demand was curt, his dark face taut with resentment. 'If anything.'

Zoë had been expecting the question, but it still did not make answering him any easier. 'You have to understand—Val is very young, and, well, Margy my friend's daughter Tessa is his best friend. Margy's husband was a sailor and he was lost at sea in a round-the-world yacht race.'

'You told him I was dead...?' he rasped.

'No, no, I'm trying to explain. Val only asked once about his father. I told him you were a very important lawyer working thousands of miles away across the sea, but one day he would meet you. I thought...' Actually she hadn't thought very clearly at all; in the back of her mind she had simply thought, One day. But not yet...

'Don't bother, Zoë, I can read you like a book. After the five-year separation a quiet divorce and only then any mention of the child. I suppose I should be grateful he even knows I exist, but under the circumstances I don't feel particularly grateful. Call him. Now. I want to speak to him.'

Zoë glanced at her wristwatch. It would be early morning in Rowena Cove. Crossing to the telephone, she placed the call.

Within seconds she was speaking to Margy and, after exchanging the usual greetings, her friend demanded bluntly, 'Have you got him, Zoë?'

'Yes, yes, I have, and he would like to speak to Val. Can you put him on, please?'

'Hi, Mom. When are you coming back? Have you got me a present?' At the sound of her son's childish chatter Zoë's eyes misted with tears.

'Slow down, darling. I'll be home tomorrow and yes, I am bringing you a present.' Sensing Justin's presence behind her, she glanced over her shoulder. His dark eyes burnt implacably into hers as he mouthed the words Tell him, while Val's shout of joy and demands to know what it was rang in her ear. 'I'm bringing your daddy home with me; he's here now and would like to say hello!'

Numbly she handed the receiver to Justin, and watched silently as he spoke to his son for the first time. She choked back a sob, amazed to see his eyes luminous with tears. Only then did the full enormity of what she had done by denying him his son sink into her tired brain, and the feeling of guilt was crushing.

'Here. He wants to say goodbye.' The receiver was pushed back into her hand and she managed to pull herself together enough to finish the call.

She replaced the receiver, her hand shaking, the ecstatic delight in her son's voice ringing in her ears. Val sounded happier than she had heard him in months, and it only added to her own self-disgust.

'I suppose I should thank you, but I don't damn well feel like it! That was my son—my boy.' His angry words flayed her like a whip. 'And you only told me because you were desperate.'

He was right and she bowed her head in shame.

'Oh, for God's sake go! Go and have a rest and then pack. I'll be back in couple of hours. I have a few things to sort out—people to see—before we leave.' He was all brutal efficiency and she should have been glad. Instead she watched him walk out of the suite with a pounding heart and her thoughts in chaos.

They arrived in New York in the early evening, and before Zoë had time to catch her breath they were on another private flight out to Brunswick. Justin had done his homework well, and as he deftly swung the rental car off the interstate at her direction and along the small road that ran to Rowena Cove she could sense the tension mounting in his large body.

She glanced sideways at his grim profile, etched in the lights of a passing car, and her own fear seemed to lessen slightly when she thought of what he had to face.

'Is this it?' The car ground to a halt outside the front door of the cottage.

'Yes.'

'Nice, but hardly your style,' he murmured, following her up the porch steps, his travel bag in one hand, hers in the other. He glanced up at the comfortable-looking old house and then around the headland to the sea beyond.

She made no response as she fiddled in her bag for the door key; finding it, she opened the door, walked into the hall and switched on the light. She was bone-weary, jet-lagged and totally depressed. In a few hours' time Margy would be bringing Val home but until then all she wanted to do was collapse into bed. But good manners dictated that she take care of her guest first.

'Follow me; I'll show you to your room. If——'

'Correction.' Justin caught her arm and spun her round to face him; his hard black eyes clashed with hers, a derisory anger in their depths.

'Our room, Zoë. You sleep with me. I told you last night, I'm not into celibacy—especially when I have a perfectly good wife at hand.'

'My, you have changed your tune. I seem to remember you always preferred separate bedrooms,' she was goaded into replying.

'At the time I thought it was for the best, but after last night I realised what a mistake I had made. Your fragile exterior cloaks a strong, sexy woman and I have no intention of making the same mistake again.'

She looked up at him, puzzled. She didn't understand his comment, but she was too tired to worry about it. 'Right at this moment all you have is an exhausted woman,' she said flatly.

Until now she had not really thought about what bringing Justin into her life would entail; she had not thought of much at all beyond wanting to save her child. Seeing his harshly determined face, she knew it would be pointless to argue.

Turning on her heel, she proceeded up the spindle-railed staircase to the landing and along to the main bedroom. She dropped her bag on the bed and crossed to the adjoining bathroom. 'Make yourself at home, why don't you?' she flung facetiously over her shoulder as she closed the bathroom door behind her.

'Mom, Mom, I missed you.'

'Yes, darling, and I love you,' she murmured sleepily,

and felt the warm touch of lips on her brow. Reassured, she drifted back to sleep.

Zoë blinked; she could vaguely hear voices whispering and the sound of childish laughter. She blinked again and opened her eyes. The small face was peering over the edge of the bed, and she smiled sleepily.

'Hello, darling; you're up early,' she murmured, and then she noticed his small hand curved in a much larger one. She glanced sideways, and slowly up long, jean-clad thighs, a plaid shirt, to the smiling face of her husband. She blushed scarlet and scrambled up into a sitting position, pulling the bedclothes with her, the events of last night flashing through her mind. 'Good morning, Justin,' she mumbled.

'Is it?' he queried, with a conspiratorial grin at Val. 'What do you think son?' And as Zoë watched they both burst out laughing.

'Nearly afternoon, Mom. Dad and I've been waiting ages for you to wake up. I've promised to take Dad to my favourite picnic place. Mrs B has got everything ready.'

'What? Oh!' Her startled gaze flashed from father to son and back to the man again. 'Give me five minutes,' she said, flustered by the insolent gleam of masculine appreciation in his dark eyes as they lingered on her small figure, and inexplicably angry at the ease with which Val called Justin Dad as though he had known him all his life.

She glanced at their joined hands and a shaft of pained jealousy arrowed through her.

'Come on, son. Let's leave your Mum to drink her coffee and dress in peace.'

'Not until I've had a cuddle,' Zoë insisted, her gaze resting lovingly on Val's face. 'I've missed you, darling,' she murmured, leaning forward and wrapping her arms around his thin little body. She buried her face in his sweet-smelling hair. He clung for a moment and then began to wriggle free.

'I'm glad you're home, Mom, but hurry up.'

It was fifteen minutes later before, with hesitant steps, she descended the stairs and pushed open the door into the large family-room. Justin was sitting on the battered old hide sofa with Val curled up on his lap, his small face a picture of rapt concentration as Justin's deep voice was describing what the Tower of London looked like.

'When can I go, Dad?

'As soon as you're a hundred per cent——'

'Hey, what happened to our picnic?' Zoë cut in, and they both turned identical brown eyes up to hers and her heart squeezed with a hope and a longing so intense that she had to turn away. 'Race you to the car,' she said, and fled, with father and son a few steps behind her.

It was one of those perfect, early spring days; the sun shone with the first real warmth of the year, the trees were in bud, the grass, awakening from winter, was turning a richer green, and as Justin manoeuvred the Range Rover along the narrow, winding coast road, with Val strapped happily in the back, keeping up a constant flow of chatter, she felt a new sense of hope growing in her heart.

And the hope grew stronger and brighter with every hour that passed. They parked the car and, with Zoë leading the way, Justin swung Val up on his shoulders and followed her down the winding path through the pine forest to the sea.

'Isn't it great, Dad?' Val demanded, once more on his own two feet. 'I named it Pirates Cove and nobody else ever comes here.'

It was a lovely place; tall pine trees edged a narrow ribbon of sandy beach, caressed by the eternal touch of the mighty Atlantic Ocean. She breathed in the fresh, healthy air and glanced sideways at Justin. He looked magnificent, dressed in well-washed jeans and a heavy navy turtle-neck sweater that didn't quite cover the collar of his blue and red plaid shirt. But it was the expression on his tanned face that shook her.

His eyes gleamed with such tender love and care down on the excited, upturned face of his son that it bought tears to her eyes. Swallowing hard, she briskly set about unpacking the picnic basket. 'Run along, you two; I'll give you a call when it's ready,' she said brightly, spreading a blanket out over the short grass on the edge of the tree line.

'Do you want any help?' Justin asked, his hand resting lightly on her shoulder for a second.

The sensual warmth of his touch triggered an immediate response in her that flustered her completely, and she was reminded of the meek way she had crawled into bed with him last night and promptly fallen asleep in his arms.

She shrugged off his hand. 'No, no. You watch Val,' she said, and added curtly, 'Be careful. Don't let him tire himself out. He's not as strong as he looks.'

'I am capable of looking after my own son. I'm not the uncaring monster you obviously assume I am,' he responded cuttingly.

'Hey, are you cross with my mom?' a little voice piped up.

The two adults immediately turned to the small figure bundled up in a wool coat with a muffler round his neck, his little face serious.

'No, darling, of course not.' Zoë recovered first. 'It's just Daddy's funny English accent,' she placated the boy.

'When I'm grown might I talk funny like dad?'

'Not so much of the "funny".' Justin rumpled the small, dark head with an affectionate hand. 'Come on, son; it's time I taught you how to skim stones.'

It was like a day out of time for Zoë. With everything prepared she sat down on the blanket and watched the two most important men in her life. They were standing at the water's edge; every so often a husky male laugh mingled with childish chuckles floated back on the breeze. She clapped her hands in spontaneous applause when a stone actually did jump along the water, and when Val skipped back towards her she laughed out loud as an extra large wave splashed up Justin's back just as he turned to follow suit.

They feasted on chicken legs, peanut butter sandwiches—a favourite of Val's—and home-made chocolate cake, washed down with Coke and a flask of coffee for the adults.

'Here they come,' Val whispered, and dashed to where Justin was sitting, his legs splayed, and crawled between them, hugging one large knee. 'Watch dad.'

Zoë envied him his position and immediately blushed at the thought. Justin caught her eye and, reaching out, curled his fingers around her arm.

'Come on, you too, Mom,' he drawled huskily, and suddenly she was sitting pressed to his side, the three of them a perfect picture of a close family. They smiled in delight as another family—this time one of chipmunks—descended on the beach, cavorting in the fine sand. Val threw the nuts Mrs B always packed and soon the chipmunks were brave enough to come near and eat them.

'I don't believe it,' Justin murmured, his usually stern face softened into a boyish grin as he watched the cheeky animals.

All too soon it was time to leave. Zoë glanced at Val; he looked pale, his eyes heavy, and, with a few quick words to Justin, they were packed up and back at the car.

Carefully Justin lifted the little boy into the back seat and strapped him in while she slid into the front passenger seat. She glanced back over her shoulder worriedly. 'Are you feeling all right, my pet?'

Val's drowsy eyes opened wide. A beatific smile lighting his whole face, he said simply, 'That's gotta be the best day ever, Mom.'

Zoë swallowed the last of her wine and placed the glass down on the table beside her chair. She tucked her bare feet underneath her body, her eyes roaming around the room, looking anywhere except at Justin, lounging on the sofa opposite.

They had bathed and put Val to bed ages ago. Mrs B had gone after serving up a delicious dinner. Zoë had finished her coffee, drained the last of her wine, and was overwhelmingly aware of the fraught silence in the room.

'It's nice; I didn't think it was you, but after today I realise it is.'

She jerked up straighter in the comfortable armchair. 'What is?' she said, completely at a loss as to what he was talking about.

'The house—I like it. Mrs B showed me around this morning when you were still asleep.'

'Oh.' She looked around, seeing the place as a stranger would for the first time. The living-room was comfortable with softly cushioned chairs and one or two pieces of good Federal period furniture, actually made in nearby Portsmouth. She didn't buy a lot of antiques but when she did she liked the best.

'I imagined you living in something like Wayne's place at Malibu; obviously motherhood has changed you.'

'Not that much,' she said shortly, but she wasn't about to enlighten him about her relationship with Wayne, not with Jess in the background. Instead she flared defensively, 'The house was built in the eighteenth century and as soon as I saw it I fell in love with it.'

'So adamant,' he drawled. 'Hey, I approve.'

'Yes, well...' She trailed off. She was proud of her home. She had tastefully furnished the two main reception-rooms in Early American style. The family-room she kept minimally furnished for Val and herself to play in. The hall still retained the original panelling, with the added delight of some interesting carvings.

In the olden days the master mariners and craftsmen who had lived in the area had also turned their hand to interior design, and the same seaman who carved a figure-head on an old sailing boat had been just as likely to carve a staircase when on dry land.

Personally Zoë loved the fireplace in this room; it was a prime example of the work of a skilled carver, and, with the fire lit and the pretty Laura Ashley curtains and décor, the room was cosy and intimate.

Too intimate, she thought, her eyes sliding over Justin's long, lounging body. 'It's not that big—only four bedrooms,' she said quickly—anything to break the growing tension.

'We only need two,' he drawled mockingly. 'Though I think the smallest one will do as a study for me. I'll see about getting it set up tomorrow.'

'But will you be staying that long? I—I mean...' She stammered to a halt. How could she say, If you're not a match for Val you can go? It sounded so brutal.

'Let me make this perfectly clear, Zoë.' Justin straightened up, his deep brown eyes fastening on hers, anger in their depths. 'You came looking for me. You found me, and I'm back in your life to stay. You're my wife. Whatever the result of my screening—however long Val does or does not have—I will not divorce you, and after the other night when you couldn't wait to get into my bed...'

She felt the colour rush into her face at his reminder and flinched, tearing her gaze away from the sensual, knowing gleam in his eyes.

'You must have realised that in law it constitutes a reconciliation and we would have to be separated another few years before you could even think of divorcing me.'

'But what about your work, your career?' He couldn't really mean to give it all up and she certainly wasn't moving anywhere. She had a life, family, friends, a business.

Justin rose and strolled across to the fireplace, to lean one elbow casually against the mantelshelf. He turned slightly, his expression grimly serious as he started to speak.

'I can follow my career from virtually anywhere; to-morrow I will arrange for the installation of the right computers. I see no problem. As it happens I've just finished a particularly long case and I have a clear cal-ender for the next month. I had intended taking a holiday.' He studied her from beneath his lids, the tension rising.

'But that's not really the issue, is it, Zoë?' In two lithe strides he was beside her, his hip propped casually on the arm of her chair.

'No?' She swallowed nervously. He was looming over her, dark and dangerous. She wriggled uncomfortably in her seat and slipped her feet to the floor. But his hand slid under the heavy fall of her hair and curved around the back of her neck.

'The issue is Val and you and me.' He tilted her head back so that he was staring down into her wide blue eyes. 'Today Val thought for a second I was shouting at you. It mustn't happen again; the child has more than enough hardship ahead of him without our adding to it. Agreed?'

'Yes, yes, of course, but——'

'No buts, Zoë. You've done a great job with Val; he's a lovely boy, and he deserves the best. By that I mean two apparently loving parents. When he walks into the bedroom in the morning it will be to find his mother and father. Together. Understand...? No arguments, no fighting. A truce, if you will.'

So that was where he was leading. Why not? she asked herself. There was no surety that Justin would be a match for Val, and she had not given up hope of another pregnancy. In all honesty, she loved the idea of having another child irrespective of any health gains. She had been an only child and as a consequence had often felt lonely. In fact, she could have two or three...

She was beginning to feel quite euphoric; at least this time around he was prepared to share a bed with her, which was odd, when she thought about it.

She glanced up at him consideringly, through the veil of her thick eyelashes. He was so vitally male and yet before in their brief marriage he had rationed out their lovemaking and she still did not completely understand why. He obviously had no such hang-ups now if the other night was anything to go by.

Who knew? Propinquity might do what Zoë could not do before; he might actually fall in love with her. Then she remembered Jess.

'But what about your girlfriend?'

'Forget the girlfriend. I have.' His dark head bent, his kiss drawing all the air from her body.

CHAPTER NINE

'For Val,' Zoë murmured in brief defiance, against his mouth.

Justin's hands slid down and under her arms, their warmth penetrating the smooth cotton of her sweatshirt, burning into her as he swung her up and into his arms.

'For Val, yes. But don't kid yourself, Zoë,' he taunted, carrying her up the stairs. 'You want me just as much as I want you. You always have; the last four years haven't dampened the fire.' His lips moved sensuously over hers as he slowly slid her to the ground. 'Only banked it down for a while.'

She looked away from the passion burning in his eyes, the masculine confidence of his claim infuriating her. She tried to push him away and then she realised that they were in the bathroom. A sudden feeling of *déjà vu* engulfed her. The trouble was that Justin was right. She did want him. Years ago she had fantasised about sharing a shower with him.

She heard him sigh as he brought her up against the hard length of his body and any thought of resistance vanished. Her arms lifted to grasp his broad shoulders; she tipped back her head, offering her mouth, and the sensual, seeking warmth of his sent arrows of quivering delight soaring through her. His hand slipped beneath her sweatshirt and curved over her breast, and she groaned in agonised pleasure.

'Take your clothes off,' he said urgently. Pulling her sweatshirt over her head, he stepped back and swiftly pulled off his sweater and shirt and shed his jeans.

In a flurry, she shook off the rest of her clothes then hesitated, awed by the magnificent splendour of Justin's hard, aroused body. She felt the pounding of her blood in her veins, and as if from a great distance she heard his deep, husky voice.

'Ah, Zoë. I have waited years to do this,' he murmured, and then he took her into his arms, naked flesh to naked flesh.

She was burning, her senses swimming; she clung to him, her small hands curving around his broad back. She was sailing through the air! She was soaking!

'Ahhh,' she cried, her blue eyes widening to their fullest extent as she gazed bemusedly up into Justin's laughing face.

'I've fantasised for years about sharing a shower with you, little one,' he growled, his lips roaming over her eyes, her cheeks, and finally finding her mouth, while the water pounded down on them.

Wonderingly she gave herself up to his magic touch; she trembled when he picked up the soap and massaged the creamy lather all over her breasts and lower to her thighs, her legs, and back. She cried out, her fingers slipping on his wet skin. For a second their eyes met, his black, powerful, predatory, hers wild and wanting, and then he was inside her.

'Zoë, Zoë, are you all right?' She opened her eyes to gaze dazedly into his darkly flushed face.

'Better than all right,' she murmured. 'As fantasies go that surpassed them all.'

Justin scooped her hard against his shuddering body. 'God! I thought you'd fainted.'

'Silly.' She smiled bewitchingly up at him. 'It was ecstasy; the little death, I think the French call it.'

'Whatever. It's bed for you.'

Zoë sat on the dockside bench, an indulgent smile on her face as she watched the man and boy standing at the edge discussing the relative merits of the historic small boats riding at anchor. They had spent a wonderful couple of hours exploring the Maine Maritime Museum in Bath. Val had been intrigued by the shipyard, the joiner's shop, the rope-making, fascinated by the lobster exhibit, and completely entranced by the model boats.

It was only four days since Justin's arrival in her son's life, and yet, seeing them standing together hand in hand, one could believe they had been together always. A tinge of sadness dimmed her smile; this day out was a treat because very shortly Val was due in the hospital in New York to start the chemotherapy.

Justin had seen the doctor on Monday. She chuckled at the memory. She had gone with him to the surgery in Portland and to her surprise and amusement the arrogant, all-powerful Justin had gone pale at the sight of his own blood. Still, it was all the more courageous of him to have offered to be a donor, given his horror of everything medical, she realised generously.

His blood sample had been sent on to the lab in New York and tomorrow they were going to New York to talk to Professor Barnet and, she hoped, get the result. Because four days later Val was due back in hospital...

She closed her eyes briefly and sent up a silent prayer. Dear God, let it be a match.

'He'll be fine, Zoë. Stop worrying.' Justin joined her on the bench, his arm going comfortingly around her shoulder.

The past few days, living as man and wife, had been surprisingly easy for Zoë. No, not just easy. Locked in Justin's arms every night, for a while she forgot all her troubles and found comfort in his masculine strength.

But sometimes, like now, the worry for her son overwhelmed her.

She turned bleak eyes to his, but before she could comment Val was scrambling on to her knee. She looked into his beloved little face, which was so happy, and had an image of him a month from now, minus his gorgeous black curls, his face racked with pain and her heart clenched in anguish. She wanted to weep. But of course she didn't.

They ended the day with a very early dinner at a steak and seafood restaurant with a nautical atmosphere on Front Street in Bath. Justin, at Zoë's instigation, ordered the fresh lobster.

'You can't visit this part of the world without trying the fresh fish it's renowned for,' she insisted with a happy grin.

'Who's visiting?' Justin drawled sardonically, effectively dampening her mood.

She must never forget, she told herself sternly as Justin manoeuvred the car along the road home, he might be a tower of strength in her fight for her son's health, and he was a brilliant lover, as the past few days had proved, but however much she wished it otherwise he did not love her...

She remained silent for the rest of the journey home, and when Justin stopped the car in the drive she climbed out, but instead of going inside she hugged Val and gave him a quick kiss, saying, 'Daddy will look after you for an hour or two. I need to go and see Aunty Margy.'

Not looking at Justin, she set off walking down the hill. She had to get away for a while. She needed some space, some time to think, but Justin seemed to fill her every waking moment.

He had completely taken over; his computers were installed in one bedroom, he was installed in her bedroom, and everywhere he went in the house Val was with him.

She heard their voices, their laughter. She knew she was being stupidly jealous. Worse, not only was she jealous of Justin's rapport with Val, but she was jealous of her own son. Just once she would have liked Justin to look at her with the same fiercely tender love he lavished on Val.

Putting her red duffel coat tightly around her, she bent her head against the wind and walked into the village. A long talk to Margy might help, and in any case she was shamefully neglecting the business.

Half an hour and two cups of tea later, sitting in the studio at the back of Margy's cottage, Zoë felt relaxed enough to talk.

'He's an incredibly...not so much handsome as impressive-looking man,' Margy said, grinning. 'And certainly a three-timer. It's just a pity it wasn't you he was doing it with. But then the best are usually swine, because they know they can get away with it.'

Zoë had to laugh. 'It sounds awful when you say it out loud, but true none the less. I actually dragged him away from his latest girlfriend, you know.' The grin faded from her face. It wasn't amusing at all. It was tragic...

'What's wrong?' Margy asked.

'Nothing.' Zoë stood up. She hadn't told Margy her hidden agenda of getting Justin into bed—getting pregnant. So she could hardly tell her she was sleeping with him again, and totally humiliated by her inability to resist him. Idly she flicked through a pile of drawings for Thanksgiving. 'I should be helping you, Margy.'

'Don't worry, I can manage the business; you look after Val. And yourself. Don't let your ex bully you into anything you don't want to do.' Margy's concern was genuine but she spoilt it by adding, 'Mind you, good sex is hard to come by; you could send him down here.'

Zoë laughed. 'Down, girl.' Then she caught sight of the clock on the wall. 'Heavens! Is that the time?' It was almost seven, and, with a hasty goodnight, she left.

Margy was great at putting things in perspective, she mused as she walked briskly back up the hill, the few street-lamps casting an eerie glow in the twilight. Instead of resenting the sex she shared with Justin, she simply had to keep reminding herself that her priority was her son. She had to be hard and think of Justin and his sperm simply as possible donors. But with luck he might fall in love with her—an added bonus...

She stopped a few yards from the house; there was a strange car parked outside the front door. She wasn't expecting anyone. Her heart missed a beat. Val. No, she was panicking; she knew the doctor's car. It was probably one of the many electricians or computer men Justin had arranged, and, striding on up the steps, she pushed off her shoes on the porch and walked into the hall.

She slipped off her coat, and, brushing a few stray tendrils of hair from her eyes, she heard Val's laughter coming from the den. Silently she crossed the hall and pushed open the door. Val loved a surprise...

But it was Zoë who got the surprise; all the colour drained from her face as she took in the view before her. Justin was sprawled on the floor, Val balanced on his flat stomach, and draped over the old hide sofa, laughing down at him, was his girlfriend Jess.

Her immediate reaction was to storm into the room and throw the other woman out of her house, but as soon as the thought entered her mind she dismissed it. They had not seen her; they were too busy laughing. Quietly she stepped back into the hall and pulled the door to.

She had vowed to sacrifice anything to save her son, and the full enormity of what she had to do chilled her to the bone. She stood in the hall looking vacantly around her. She didn't cry. She couldn't; she had no more tears left.

Pride, self-respect meant nothing put against Val's life. Justin held all the cards; he might be Val's only chance, and if that meant she had to put up with his girlfriend in her home she had no choice.

A few moments earlier she had actually thought they had a chance as a family. Never in her worst nightmare had she envisaged Justin being so callous, so amoral as to invite his girlfriend to her home, especially as he had spent the last few nights in Zoë's bed.

She pushed open the door again and walked in. 'Hello, Val, darling.' She spoke to her son, and feigned surprise at seeing the woman on the sofa. 'Jess, isn't it? This is a surprise. What brings you here?' Justin had jumped to his feet and she flashed him a vitriolic glance. 'Or need I ask?'

'Zoë, I'm so sorry; I came as soon as Justin told me. If I can be of any help?'

'I'm sure Justin will be suitably grateful, but if you will excuse me it is well past Val's bedtime.'

Sweeping her son up into her arms, she glared at Jess over the top of his head. 'Justin can get you something to eat. We had an early dinner so I'm going to have an early night. It will give you and Justin time to catch up on everything, and he can show you out.' She spun on her heel...

'Zoë, wait,' Justin demanded, and, catching her arm, he said, 'You're not being very hospitable to Jess.'

'Sorry, but in case you've forgotten we have an early start in the morning.'

'No, I haven't forgotten and Jess has kindly offered to stay and look after Val for the day.'

'Stay here?' It was even worse than she had thought.

'Yes, where else?'

'Well, you know where the bedrooms are; you make her comfortable.' And, tearing herself away from his restraining hand, she quickly left the room with Val held sleepily in her arms.

She closed Val's bedroom door behind her, and carried him into his own little bathroom. He was too tired to be talkative; she washed him down, and pulled on his Bugs Bunny pyjamas, and carried him back into his room.

'Top or bottom?' She asked the same question she always asked and knew the answer.

'Top, Mom, and isn't Jess nice?'

'Yes, darling,' she agreed, lying through her teeth, as she lifted him up to the top bunk. Val had chosen the bunk beds himself last summer when he'd graduated from a cot. A local craftsman made them in pine, the ends lovingly decorated in small woodland animals. Zoë had thought at the time that although she was not going to have any more children they would be good when Val got older and had friends to stay.

Now she wasn't sure he would get much older, and in the past months had quite often slept in the bottom one herself. Tonight she intended to do just that.

'What story would you like, Val?' She rummaged through the dozens of story books on the matching pine desk. 'How about *Sinbad*?' She knew it was one of his favourites, but when she turned back to the bunk his eyes were closed and he was fast asleep. Leaning over him, she kissed his pale cheek, her heart full of love, and whispered the Lord's Prayer as she always did, adding a plea for his full recovery.

Tears hazing her eyes, she stripped off her own clothes and burrowed under the Daffy Duck coverlet on the bottom bunk. She closed her eyes. She did not want to think, but she could not close down her mind so easily. Last night she had slept in Justin's arms, and tonight he would be sleeping—no, not sleeping but something!—with the lovely Jess. In her, Zoë's, house.

Zoë had loved Justin once, and with his betrayal she had grown to hate him. Then, a few days ago, she had realised that she still loved him. But now she hated him yet again. The saying went that hate was the other side of love—one emotion but sometimes mistaken for the other. But as she lay curled up in the small bunk, her thoughts spinning like a windmill, she came to the conclusion that popular belief was wrong: it was possible to live with love and hate. Two opposite emotions could coexist in one person. Her hatred of Justin was real; she despised what he was. But she did love him.

She lay staring at the blank timber above her, wondering what the couple downstairs were doing now, and hating the images that her vivid imagination flashed in her mind. It didn't matter, she told herself. Nothing mattered but Val.

How long she lay there listening to the faint, reassuring sound of her son's breathing she had no idea, but suddenly the door opened and Justin walked in.

'So this is where you're hiding. I might have guessed.' He strolled across to the bunks, leant over and kissed Val, and then sat down on the edge of the lower bunk, bending his head to avoid banging it on the bar. 'Really, Zoë, you are being very childish. Jess was hoping to get to know you better.'

Her eyes, widening in horror, flew to his face. Incredibly he was deadly serious. She could not believe the sheer audacity, the barefaced cheek, the nerve... 'I—I——' She couldn't find the words. 'Oh, get out,' she finally said, defeated.

'Not without you, Zoë. Now be sensible.' His head bent lower and his lips sought hers.

'No,' she protested vehemently.

'Yes,' he drawled throatily, his hand sliding around her neck and lifting her face for his kiss.

'Let go of me and go. I want to stay here with Val tonight. Have you forgotten tomorrow is the day we...?'

Justin leant back, his hand falling from her neck. 'No, I haven't forgotten. How could I? It's my result we're talking about, Zoë, and I had thought we could comfort and support each other.'

'I need to stay here with Val.'

'And what of my needs?' he asked sardonically.

She could see the angry glitter in his dark eyes by the moonlight shining through the window, and for a second she thought she saw despair, but the moon drifted behind a cloud, plunging the room into darkness, and she dismissed the thought, saying bluntly, 'Go and see Jess; I'm sure she can help you.'

She watched him walk away, and suddenly she didn't want him to go. Surely it must have meant something that he had come to her first?

Leaping out of the bunk, she dashed to the door, in time to see him disappear into the one remaining spare room—Jess's. Well, what had she expected? she asked herself fatalistically, and with one last kiss for the sleeping child she crawled back in the bunk, pulling the cover up over her head.

The journey to New York the next morning was horrendous. Breakfast had been a silent affair. Stilted good mornings had been exchanged between the three adults. Zoë had given Val a quick kiss and a hug before getting into the car for the first leg of the journey.

She hated leaving Val with Jess. The only thing that had persuaded her had been the fact that she had arranged for Margy to pick Val up in a couple of hours, and she had finally found the spirit to tell the black-eyed witch to leave as soon as Margy arrived.

She glanced sideways at Justin as he drove the car through the early morning traffic. He was staring straight ahead, his expression dark and brooding, and he somehow looked so alone that she couldn't help it—she put her small hand on his muscular thigh. 'It will be all right, Justin; we have to think positive...' She needed to talk, perhaps to disguise her nerves, her own worst nightmare. 'I know you're frightened of blood, but don't worry, you'll be fine.'

'Me, worry?' He shot her an angry look. 'If anyone needs to worry it's you. You do realise that if I'm not a match you have, in the last few hours, completely alienated the only other person who can help?'

'What? What are you talking about?' she asked, completely lost.

'Stop playing the dumb innocent, Zoë. I cannot believe how nasty you were to Jess, and she is our last hope. You do realise that, don't you?' he demanded with icy sarcasm.

'Jess?' His girlfriend? A horrible black chasm opened in front of Zoë.

The car screeched into the airport car park, and Justin, without glancing at her, got out. 'Hurry; the plane is waiting.'

She had to run to keep up with him. 'Justin, wait.' But he chose not to hear and he did not even look at her until they were safely strapped into their seats on the plane.

'Some mother you turned out to be, allowing your personal prejudice to blight Val's chances.'

'Who exactly *is* Jess?' She ignored his biting comment and grabbed his hand, which was lying on the armrest between them. 'Tell me, Justin.'

'Don't be ridiculous; you know perfectly well she's my half-sister. She might have been unpleasant to you last weekend but she had her reasons, and as soon as I told her about Val she came over as quickly as she could to offer her help. Which for some perverse reason you refused.'

'Oh, my God!' Zoë clasped her hands to her head; she could not believe what she had done, what she had thought of Jess. 'But wait a minute.' She lifted her head, staring with haunted eyes up at Justin's dark, implacable face. 'You told me you only had a stepsister.'

'I did no such thing. Jess is my *half*-sister—we share the same father. Why else...?'

He stopped, his dark, piercing gaze scrutinising her white face. 'Wait a minute; you mean you thought Jess was my mistress? You actually thought I invited a girlfriend to share the house my wife and son call home?'

Hard fingers gripped her chin and turned her head to meet the searing fury of his glance. 'You actually believe I am so lacking in morality, so despicable that I would do something so low? My God! I knew you had a low opinion of me, but *that* low...'

'I—I...' She had no defence. He was right; it hadn't been Justin who had told her he had a stepsister.

A memory of the past flickered in her brain. She had been telling Uncle Bertie what a pity it was that Justin's sister could not come to the wedding, and Uncle Bertie had replied, 'Well, she's not really his sister. His mother died at birth and Justin's father married the girl's mother.' Zoë had automatically assumed that she was his stepsister.

'Enlighten me, Zoë. How do you suffer me to make love to you when it's quite obvious that you despise me?' His hand fell from her chin and he straightened in his seat. 'Stupid question. You love Val, I'll give you that. And if I were you I would start praying that the news today is good. Otherwise you'll be crawling on your belly to Jess.'

'Please, Justin, you have to believe me; I never realised Jess was your sister. If I had I would never have been so rude to her, and I don't despise you. It isn't like that.' It was pure jealousy she suffered from, she recognised, but before she could say so Justin stopped her.

'Cut the excuses, Zoë.' His mouth tightened into a grim line. 'We'll see Professor Barnet, and hopefully the news will be good. If not I will personally ask Jess to help. I'll do everything in my power for our son. But, as for the rest, I find it hard to accept a wife who will prostitute herself, however good the reason.'

She rushed into speech. 'But it wasn't—I meant it isn't... I never——'

'Forget it, Zoë.' Turning to the stewardess, he ordered coffee, adding, 'Anything for you, Zoë?'

'I'll have a cup of coffee,' she said impatiently. How could he be so cool and withdrawn when she was bursting with emotional questions? As soon as the stewardess took the order she began again. 'Justin, you don't understand...'

'Please, Zoë, we have a tense morning ahead of us. Leave it. And let's at least try to present a united front to Professor Barnet.'

She clutched Justin's hand as if it were a lifeline as they were ushered into the great man's room and sat side by side on two straight-backed chairs in front of the large oak desk.

'Well, Mr. Gifford, I must say I'm glad to see you.' Professor Barnet smiled from behind his desk. 'Zoë is a strong woman but she was badly in need of some support. And I'm happy to say all the signs are that you are going to be a perfect match for young Val.'

Zoë jumped up; she was laughing and crying at the same time, hugging Justin, hugging the Professor, hugging herself. Justin was a *match*.

'It's very gratifying, Mr Gifford, and your son is very lucky. There's no reason why he shouldn't eventually make a complete recovery.'

Recovery! The word was music to Zoë's soul as she collapsed back on the chair.

'I didn't want to distress Zoë unduly before, but his chances were extremely limited without the transplant. Oddly enough, statistically one is more likely to get a match from a male donor than a female.' Professor Barnet looked at Justin, a purely masculine smile lighting his keen blue eyes. 'We men are apparently still good for something in these feminist times.'

Zoë ignored the chauvinistic remark and turned back to Justin, her blue eyes swimming with tears of joy and gratitude. She naturally reached for his hand; he curved his own strong hand around hers and squeezed it gently.

'I told you it would be all right,' he said triumphantly, but the relief on his rugged features was plain to see.

'All thanks to you,' she murmured and, unable to contain her delight, their earlier argument on the way there forgotten, she leant forward and brushed her lips against his. For a second he tensed, and she thought he was going to push her away; instead he pulled her from her seat and into his arms, and kissed her—a kiss of fervent hope, a shattering release of tension, and, she prayed, the start of something new.

They were oblivious to the old man behind the desk, until a discreet cough brought them back to their senses.

Hastily Zoë slid back on to her seat, her face a rosy red. But Justin, with admirable self-control and efficiency, said, 'So where do we go from here, Professor Barnet?'

'At your age, after a kiss like that, I would have said bed.' He chuckled delightedly at his own joke and Zoë's rosy face turned scarlet but she could not help joining in the general laughter.

Half an hour later, when Professor Barnet escorted them out of his office, she felt like pinching herself. Val was going to be all right!

She clung to Justin's arm as they walked down the long hospital corridor, her eyes sparkling like jewels, her face more animated than it had been in months. 'I can't wait to tell Val. Do you think we should ring? Do you think we should celebrate?' She babbled on in a cloud of euphoria until suddenly Justin stopped dead.

'Zoë, calm down,' he commanded firmly, and, grasping her shoulders, he turned her around to face him. He stared down at her, his expression deadly serious. 'We will not ring Val and in any case he's far too young to understand. Apart from which there's still a long way to go before he's cured.'

His eyes held hers, and suddenly she realised that he was probably thinking of the operation he himself was going to have to have.

'Sorry.' As she said the word she realised exactly how much she owed this man, her husband. She lifted her hand to his square jaw. 'Justin, I really am sorry for everything.'

She should never have run out on him. With the worry over Val appeased she saw things clearly for the first time in ages. Janet Ord had married, according to Justin, after she had dried out. Had Zoë let gossip and the drunken rambling of a discarded girlfriend ruin her marriage?

Her fingers trembled on his chin, and for a moment she thought she glimpsed the familiar flicker of desire in his dark eyes, but it was gone as swiftly as his hands dropped from her shoulders.

'Forget it,' he said abruptly. 'Let's get home.'

Her hand fell to her side and quietly she walked along beside him, lost in thought. He had called the house at

Rowena Cove home. Surely that was a good sign? He must be coming to care for her.

But her relief at the good news for Val was overshadowed slightly by their argument over his sister and his enigmatic statement earlier—something about a wife who prostituted herself, however good the cause.

She shook her fair head slightly; she was seeing problems where there were none, she told herself firmly. All she needed to do was apologise to Jess and everything would be great.

With a new confidence in her step, she smiled broadly up at her husband. 'Home and bed,' she said cheekily.

'Certainly,' he grinned back, and her happiness was complete.

But five minutes later her confidence deflated like a burst balloon.

'Zoë Gifford. How are you? Happy now?'

Her head shot up and she was looking into the smiling eyes of Freda Lark. 'Yes, yes, I am.' She grinned and chanced a swift glance at Justin; he was standing smiling enquiringly down at the attractive doctor, and she had no choice but to introduce them.

'It's nice to meet you, Mr Gifford. I was quite worried about your wife for a while, but I heard your good news from Professor Barnet. I'm really happy for you both.' Still smiling, Dr. Lark turned to Zoë again.

'Mind you, after meeting your husband I can see my advice to get yourself pregnant as quickly as possible certainly wouldn't be any hardship for you.'

Zoë felt all the blood leave her face. What a disastrous coincidence, meeting Dr Lark. She felt Justin's eyes on her but she dared not look at him, sure that her face must have 'guilty' written all over it.

But Dr Lark had no such qualms, she realised with mounting anger as the other woman laughed flirtatiously up at Justin, and his answering grin was all male arrogance.

'I'll take that as a compliment,' he said suavely.

Zoë did not know how she got through the next few minutes; she cast a fearful, sidelong glance at him as he took her elbow and ushered her out of the hospital. The easy smile he had exhibited for Freda Lark had vanished and his handsome face was as black as thunder.

'Justin,' she said tentatively as they stood together at the roadside, 'I can explain.'

But with commendable ease he had flagged down a taxi. 'Get in and shut up,' he snarled.

What should have been the happiest journey of her life—she was going home with the best news in the world for her son—was fast becoming a nightmare. Justin didn't speak to her; his face was rigid; she could sense the anger coming off him in great waves, and it was only when they picked up her car at Brunswick that he deigned to look at her.

He swung round in the driving seat, his face murderous, his black eyes boring into her. 'At last we're alone.' He watched her for a long moment. 'My God, I was so wrong about you. I thought you were a fragile young woman in need of protecting, when in actual fact you're as tough as steel.'

Zoë bit her lip. 'I can explain,' she repeated quietly.

'"Explain"!' he roared. 'What kind of fool do you take me for? Last Friday night wasn't about softening me up to confess we had a son; it was all about getting yourself pregnant. Yet again without telling me.' He slammed his hand down on the wheel. 'Damn it, I asked if you were protected, you little liar.'

She had no excuse. 'I'm sorry,' she apologised miserably. She looked up at his angry face. 'But I was desperate; I thought...'

'You thought you would use me as a stud—that's what these last few nights were all about.' A harsh laugh escaped him. 'Tell me, Zoë, who did you imagine I was when you went wild in my arms? Wayne? Nigel? And God knows how many more.'

Turning back in his seat, he stared fixedly at his hands on the wheel of the car. 'A bloody sperm bank.' He swore violently. Then his gaze flashed back to hers, black and pitiless. 'Right time of the month, was it?' he demanded silkily.

Her face burned scarlet and she had nothing to say. She saw a muscle jerking wildly in the side of his face, but his lips curled cynically. 'Last night? Ovulation over, so back to the single bunk, hmm?'

She swallowed hard. 'It wasn't like that,' she whispered, but her response was lost in the roar of the engine. She glanced fearfully at Justin and without taking his eyes from the road he shook his black head.

'I'll stay long enough to see that Val is OK, and to discover if I'm to be a father unknowingly yet again. Obviously I'll want to keep in touch with my children, but I see no reason to delay any longer in giving you the divorce you requested.'

But she didn't want a divorce. She wanted Justin. But one look at the granite-hard countenance and and she knew now was not the time to tell him. Although she had started out determined to seduce him, and was guilty of what he had accused her of, as soon as he had touched her, kissed her, she had been lost to everything and had melted in his arms. She loved him...

Jess was waiting in the hall when they walked in. She took one look at their faces and said, 'Oh, no, I am sorry.'

'No need, Jess,' her brother responded, with a tight smile. 'I am a match. Val will be all right, and now, if you will excuse me, it has been a long day.'

CHAPTER TEN

ZOË watched his broad back as he walked up the stairs, tears in her eyes. Her son was almost saved but the euphoria she had felt in Professor Barnet's office had been replaced by a numbing certainty that Justin was lost to her forever.

'I don't believe this. What on earth have you done to my brother now?' Jess demanded harshly. 'He looks positively grim, when he should be celebrating.'

Zoë turned her tear-drenched eyes to the other woman and, mindful of who Jess was, said quietly, 'Can we talk? I owe you an apology, but if I don't sit down I think I might fall down.'

Five minutes later, seated on the sofa in front of the open fire, she glanced up at Jess, standing in the middle of the room, and she could not believe how blind she had been. Jess had the same eyes, the same hair—the resemblance to Justin had been there all the time if only she had not been blinded by jealousy and full of preconceived notions of Justin's penchant for large ladies.

'I never realised you were Justin's sister until today. I thought you were his girlfriend,' she confessed quietly.

'His girlfriend?' Jess exclaimed. 'You've got to be kidding; my brother has never looked at another woman in years. The day you ran off to the States with your lover you effectively emasculated the man. He was almost destroyed. Then you turned up in London again and crawled straight back into his bed. Now you're trying to tell me you slept with him thinking I was his girlfriend.

God! What kind of woman are you?' she asked derisively.

'A very mixed-up one,' Zoë muttered. 'I don't know where you got your information from but I never ran off with a lover. I loved Justin to distraction but I discovered he never loved me. That's why I left him.'

'You're mad!' Jess stared into her tear-stained face and something in the smaller woman's expression made her hesitate. 'You honestly believe what you're saying.'

'It's the truth.' Zoë closed her eyes briefly, reminded of the pain and disillusion of the past.

'Tell me,' Jess demanded, sitting down beside her on the couch. 'Give me your version.'

'Oh, all the signs were there.' Zoë sighed. 'I had hints that Justin's reason for marrying me wasn't love, but I dismissed them as idle gossip. Until the night of my twenty-first birthday.'

Once she started she could not stop; it was like a dam breaking, and for the next quarter of an hour she told Jess everything—the gossip of Mrs Blacket, Justin's withdrawal into work, the separate bedrooms, even his restraint in their intimacy, right up to the night of Janet Ord's revelations. Finally she described the fatal meeting with Justin in California where he had made it plain that he never wanted to see her again.

'Incredible as it seems, I believe you,' Jess said, with a shake of her dark head. 'How two intelligent people could make such a mess of their lives is mind-boggling.'

'Yes, well, I blame myself,' Zoë said, with a wry smile. 'I was young and easily hurt——'

'And my brother is a repressed fool,' Jess cut in. 'Listen, Zoë, I know Justin loves you. He told me all about you long before he married you. You were his one topic of conversation for years. He even joined your uncle's practice thinking it would enhance his prospects as a suitor.'

'But he always wanted to be a judge!'

'Rubbish, he thrived on international law, but he gave it up for you. He worshipped you, and being a closet romantic he worried himself witless about the age-gap between you.

'He told me about your eighteenth birthday, and how he had taken another woman to your party. He was being noble. He was convinced you had to have the chance of a career, to see something of the world, before tying you down.'

She wanted to believe Jess, but if it was true why had Justin been so restrained in the intimate side of their relationship? 'Why the separate bedrooms?' She did not realise she had voiced the question out loud.

'Perhaps I can guess,' Jess offered, casting a reflective glance at her pale, troubled face. 'What did Justin tell you about our parents?'

'Not much—simply that his mother died at his birth and his father married again. His stepmother died when he was in his teens, as did his father a few years later. He never talked about his family; that's why I had the idea he had a stepsister, nothing more. Until today,' she said drily.

'Typical!' Jess snorted, before continuing. 'Dad was a Spaniard who had settled in London as a young man. He met my mother in the restaurant he owned. She was a ballerina—tiny, exquisite, a bit like you but dark. Justin doted on her; she was the only mother he had ever known and when I came along five years later he was equally protective of me.

'We had a happy childhood. Our parents adored each other; they were always touching, loving. Every summer we went to our villa in Spain for the holidays. Justin was only fifteen when it happened—a scream in the night. He dashed to our parents' room to find my father standing naked by the bed, Mother dead of a heart attack. She died...' Jess hesitated '...during *the act...*'

'Oh, my God!' Zoë exclaimed.

'Exactly my reaction. But Justin was at a very impressionable age. Embarrassed by his parents' sexuality, he was horrified and disgusted, and blamed Father for Mother's death. I heard him raging at Dad that at his age he should have more control—he should be past such things.' The two women exchanged an ironic glance.

'The naïveté of youth,' Jess opined wryly, before continuing. 'Bertie Brown was Dad's lawyer and a family friend, and from then on Justin spent most of his free time with Bertie, supposedly because he was studying hard, but to me it was as if Justin deliberately squashed the Latin side of his temperament. When Dad died three years later Justin had never really forgiven him.'

'So what are you trying to say?' Zoë asked.

'I'm no psychiatrist, but I do know my brother. He had girlfriends over the years—not that many, but every one was an amazon of a woman until you.'

Zoë wriggled uncomfortably on the seat, a snatch of conversation coming back to her. Sara Blacket had insisted that Justin went for large ladies. Could there be anything in what Jess said?

'He wrote to me when he first met you when you were a child, and even then he was obsessed with you, convinced that you needed looking after—a tiny orphan with only an old man for company. When I finally arrived in London after the wedding, hoping to meet my new sister-in-law, I found Justin completely gutted because you had run away.

'He told me that he'd been ultra-careful not to frighten you, either in or out of bed. Until the night you said you were leaving him, and he lost control. At first he blamed himself, sure that he had terrified you the same way he did on your eighteenth birthday.'

'He told you about that?' Zoë asked incredulously, blushing at the memory. 'But I wasn't terrified—well, not of Justin, more of myself; the feelings he aroused in me were all too new,' she explained. 'How could he have thought he was at fault?'

'Quite easily,' Jess offered drily. 'You ran away to London and he barely saw you for two years. He thought he had made the same mistake again and that was why you ran out on the marriage.'

A comment from the terrible night of their argument slipped into Zoë's mind—Justin saying ironically, 'And I thought I was being considerate,' when she had taunted him with Janet's words about his sexual exploits. Could he have been telling the truth? Was Jess's almost too simple explanation the right one? If so she realised that she had made a mistake of mega, mega proportions.

Jess was still talking and she listened with mounting horror, and the growing conviction that Jess was right.

'Until, that is, he followed you to the airport the last day, saw you in the arms of your American friend and realised you had a lover, that you had betrayed him...'

'But I never...' Zoë cried.

'It's not much good telling *me* that. It's Justin you have to convince, though to be honest I was under the impression that the pair of you had sorted out your differences.

'He told me last Saturday in London all about the child. He was furious at your hiding Val from him, but I know my brother and I knew he had already forgiven you. You were sharing his bed again, and he was vibrant—fully alive for the first time in years. But if the look on his face tonight was anything to go by you've crushed him again.'

'No—deflated his ego maybe.' And in a few, succinct sentences Zoë explained her attempt to seduce Justin into making her pregnant and how he had discovered the truth. To her amazement Jess started to laugh.

'My God, what a pair.'

'Excuse me if I don't see the joke,' Zoë said sarcastically. 'The man I love is going to divorce me; that's not funny, it's tragic.'

'But don't you see? There is my beloved brother terrified of his own strength, determined to treat you gently, and there you are, a tiny woman, equally determined to get him into bed, never mind that you thought I was his live-in girlfriend.'

One dark brow arched elegantly. 'And look who won! It's hilarious; you're as strong as he is, if not more so. You make a great couple. Or you will if you ever get your act together.'

Jess's chuckle ended in a wide yawn. 'I'm going to bed. If you take my advice, Zoë, I suggest you set about seducing my brother yet again, simply for yourself.' And with that parting shot she got up and left the room.

For a long time Zoë stared sightlessly into the flames of the open fire, rehashing Jess's conversation in her mind. It made a lot of sense, and it explained a good deal of the past. If she believed her...

Standing up, she slowly walked upstairs. She hesitated outside Justin's door, then moved on to Val's room. She gazed down at the sleeping child, and said a silent prayer of thanks and hope for his well-being. She kissed his smooth brow, and headed for the bathroom.

Ten minutes later, showered, her only covering a fluffy white bathrobe belted loosely around her waist, and with her face scrubbed clean of make-up, her hair brushed to a silken silver sheen falling in soft waves down her back, she quietly closed her son's bedroom door, and tiptoed along the hall to her own room—the room she shared with Justin...

Her mind made up, she took a a deep breath and, squaring her slender shoulders, pushed open the door and walked in. A single lamp was burning on the bedside table, illuminating the figure reclining on the large bed.

'Justin?' she began unsteadily, her hands curled into fists to stop their trembling. He was propped up against the pillows, a book in his hand. He was bare-chested, the hand-crafted quilt draped across his thighs covering his essential maleness.

'Zoë.' She looked at his face and flinched at the look of cold anger in his dark eyes. 'Why are you here?' he demanded harshly, the hand holding the book lowering to the bed.

'This is my room,' she mumbled defensively.

'Possession is nine tenths of the law,' he drawled sarcastically, 'and last night you made it abundantly clear that you preferred to sleep with our son. If you imagine for a second that I will swap places with you and sleep in that bunk forget it.'

'No. I mean, I thought...' She was stumbling over her words, but he sounded so chillingly remote that she had no idea how to continue.

'Don't try to think. I've had quite enough of your machiavellian thoughts for one day,' he informed her hardly. 'Dr Lark saw to that.'

'That's what I wanted to talk about—I mean I didn't——' She could not find the words 'set out to seduce you'; after all, she had. How could she explain that within minutes of being in his arms again her only thought had been how much she'd missed and needed him?

'For heaven's sake! Get to bed; you look worn out.'

He lifted the book and resumed reading. She was dismissed... Her shoulders slumped and she half turned, and then she stopped. No, damn it! She would not meekly bow out. Justin had said, 'Get to bed,' and that was exactly what she was going to do.

Swinging on her heel, her blue eyes glittering with rising excitement, she ran across to the bed. A tug of the belt at her waist and a shrug saw her towelling robe fall to the floor, and, catching the corner of the coverlet in one hand, in a second she had jumped into the wide bed.

'What the hell...' he roared. The book went flying through the air and the quilt slid down to his lean hips as he raised himself up against the headboard and stared down at her with a look of incredulous amazement in his dark eyes. 'What do you think you're doing?'

'You did say, "Get to bed,"' she said innocently and, turning on her side, she deliberately placed her small hand on his hard, flat stomach; she felt his muscles tense and his hand dropped to grab her wrist.

'Don't be frightened, Justin,' she prompted sweetly, mischief dancing in her eyes. For once she had surprised him and she intended to make full use of the advantage. 'I won't hurt you.'

She felt him stiffen; his fingers on her wrist tightened like a manacle and suddenly she was no longer in control. She was flat on her back with Justin looming over her.

'I will never give you the chance again,' he said harshly, flinging one long leg across her thighs, pinning her to the bed, while his hands formed a cage at either side of her head. 'I've promised you I'll try and save our son. I've agreed to divorce you. Damn it, Zoë, what else do you want from me?'

She stared up at the ruthless, dark face and the breath caught at the back of her throat. His Latin temperament had certainly broken through now, she thought, a sliver of fear racing down her spine. But he looked tired as well as angry. Dark shadows under his eyes were accentuated by the tautness of the skin over his high cheekbones.

'Answer me, damn you.'

'Nothing else,' she whispered, and, dredging up her last vestige of courage, she added, 'In fact, I don't want a divorce either. I want to stay with you—in your bed, in your life.' She felt the blood pounding in her ears; the touch of his hard, hot naked body against hers was dangerously arousing.

He reared back and surveyed her through half-closed lids. 'Am I supposed to believe that?' he asked with dry cynicism, his narrowed gaze angling down over her breasts. She felt her nipples peak in instant response, and cursed her inability to remain calm around him.

'What exactly are you after now, I wonder?' he mused, and bent slowly towards her. Shockingly his tongue licked tantalisingly over one taut nipple, before he lifted his head and added silkily, 'Or shall I guess?'

'Only you,' she breathed.

'Funny, I seem to remember last night you couldn't get rid of me quick enough, and yet last Friday you couldn't crawl into my bed fast enough.' Taunting mockery glittered in his eyes. 'I was flattered until today, when I discovered you were simply using me as a stud.'

'I'm sorry, I should have told you the truth—trusted you to do the right thing,' she freely admitted, but he was not placated.

'Yes, damn it! Yes, you should.' He swore in another flash of anger, his dark eyes burning down into hers. But as she gazed helplessly up at him, expecting the worst, he took a deep, indrawn breath, his mouth tightened and he was once more in control.

'I've had time to think about it and in fairness I can't condemn you for using me; I don't like it, but you had the best reason in the world—Val.' He moved his leg slowly, tantalisingly up her thigh, still holding her gaze.

'But now, tonight, you say you want me. Odd, this, from a wife who ran off with another man. For a wife I haven't seen for years. For a wife who forced herself to sleep with me for the sake of a child.'

There was derision in his face as his hard eyes swept down over her, inspecting her nakedness as she lay beneath him, then back to her wide, luminous blue eyes. 'I'm not a complete idiot, Zoë. Come on, tell me. Why?'

His distrust was only to be expected, she thought. God knew, she had shown little enough trust in him during their brief marriage; a bit of bitchy gossip and the drunken ravings of an ex-girlfriend and she had taken flight. She had no intention of making the same mistake again. But where to start? The beginning, perhaps. It meant baring her soul, leaving herself open to his ridicule, but she was going to try.

'Because I love you; I've always loved you,' she said bravely, reaching up to lay her hand on his broad chest. He looked very big, very remote, but she felt the heavy thump of his heart beneath her fingertips, and noted a betraying flicker of his long eyelashes; it gave her hope and then he smiled, and a frisson of fear darted up her spine.

'And I am supposed to believe you, and clasp you to my manly chest? Is that why you're here?'

The mockery in his deep voice was evident, but she refused to be cowed by it. 'No, I don't expect you to believe me, but I fully intend to convince you eventually,' she said boldly, hiding her fear. 'You're a very large man, very strong—to some people your power might be intimidating, but it never was to me.'

Her face was sombre, her voice low. 'I remember the first time we met and you held me on your lap and dried my tears. You were my gentle giant, and I had a terrible crush on you. By my eighteenth birthday party, the crush had changed to love, and I wanted you so badly.'

He sent her a sharp glance, and smiled without humour. 'Not that badly—you were terrified when I kissed you, touched you.'

She chuckled softly, gaining confidence, 'Oh, no, Justin; I wasn't frightened of you.' She allowed her fingers to curl in his chest hair. 'You were so sexy, my dreamboat. But I simply panicked; I was terrified by my own reaction; the feelings were so overwhelming that I couldn't handle them. But later, alone in bed, I ached and wished you were with me.'

'You don't have to lie,' he growled, the wariness in his expression giving her more hope. 'I know I came on too strong and you were disgusted.'

'I wasn't disgusted then, and I'm not lying now. I've always wanted you,' she husked provocatively, her sapphire eyes fixed on his. 'I want you now.'

A cruel, sensuous smile twisted his hard mouth. 'Yes, I can believe that. Four years on, and a few lovers later, you're hardly the shy, young thing I married.'

She flinched at his harsh words, but could not really blame him for thinking so badly of her. 'There was no other man, ever,' she said bluntly, willing him to believe her. 'The only difference between the last few nights we have spent together and the brief duration of our marriage is that now you treat me as a mature woman.

'Before you saw me as a child bride needing protection. I never did; all I needed was you, in my bed at night—all night.'

She saw the glitter in his eyes, and for a moment thought she was winning—until he stopped her wandering hand on his chest with his own much larger one.

'Why should I believe you? The girl I married would never have dared to try and seduce a man into bed as you did with me last week.' He held her hand hard against his heart while his other hand laced through her long hair, lifting her face up to his. He studied her pale features through narrowed eyes; only a nerve twitching in his jaw betrayed his tension.

'The man I married would not have let me,' she said flatly. 'You were always in control, always restrained. Did you really think, young as I was, I wouldn't recognise the fact?'

'And that bothered you?' he asked quickly, a dark flush spreading across his high cheekbones. 'You wanted more?'

'Yes,' she said simply. 'But I was too young and too in awe of you to tell you, and then after Uncle died you became even more withdrawn; you worked all hours, and didn't seem to need me at all. Then tonight Jess told me that you thought you were too old for me; that you tried to be noble.'

She knew she had to discuss everything, get it all out into the open, but it was hard. Justin had given her very little reason to hope.

Nevertheless, taking her courage in both hands, she told him everything Jess had said and ended with, 'I know how your mother died, and I thought perhaps it wasn't simply that you didn't love me but maybe because you were trying to be considerate. I remembered you once said that.'

She was rambling on but did not seem able to stop; she was too frightened. What if she had made a mistake, and he didn't care for her?

'God damn you, Zoë! Why, oh, why did you not tell me this before?' His mouth ground down on hers and he kissed her as if he would devour her whole.

When she was finally allowed to breathe she gazed bemusedly up into his brilliant dark eyes.

'Have you any idea of the agony I went through, leaving you every night?' he groaned, easing her back into the bed, his large body hard over her. 'Too terrified to stay with you because I didn't trust myself to keep my hands off you, again and again and again.'

Happiness, sharp and sweet, surged through her. It was going to be all right. Justin slid his hand slowly down, over her breast, the indentation of her waist and lower, to linger on her slim thigh, and she moaned low in her throat. His hard mouth closed over hers in a ruthless, masterful kiss, and her hands helplessly sought his strong neck and tangled in his black hair.

He lifted his head, his mouth curving in a self-derisory smile. 'God, Zoë! You were my muse, my idol from the very first moment I saw you. You terrified me. I only had to look at you to want you, and I knew that if I touched you I'd be lost; you were, and are, everything I ever wanted. I loved you, but I was terrified of losing you. You were so young, so innocent, so tiny.'

'It wasn't because Uncle Bertie told you to marry me?' She sighed, closing her eyes and searching with parted lips for his mouth.

'No, Zoë.' He rolled off her and, propping himself up on one elbow, stared down at her flushed, bemused face. 'First it had little or nothing to do with my mother. In fact, some people might say it was a lovely way to go.' He chuckled. 'But Bertie was involved.'

'You don't need to tell me.' She wasn't sure that she wanted to know the whole truth.

'Hush, Zoë, I do. Jess was right in a way. I took Janet to your eighteenth out of a misguided sense of nobility, but one look at you in that mini nightgown and I was a goner.

'I was sure I had frightened you away for good, and I'm not proud of the fact but for the next few months I did have a brief affair with Janet. It meant nothing and was soon over. Eventually I confided in Bertie how I felt about you and the fact that I thought I had lost you forever. He told me not to be so negative.'

'So you did discuss me with Uncle Bertie,' she said warily.

'Exactly! And that was why, when you accused me of doing so, I couldn't deny it, but not for the reason you thought. Bertie was a shrewd old bird and advised me to wait a year or two, allow you to finish your studies and mature a little, and then try again with a little more restraint.'

'I see. I think.'

'He loved you deeply, Zoë—almost as much as I did—and I stupidly took his advice again later when we got engaged. It was his suggestion—the master suite. He thought if I took things slow and gentle, curbed my baser instincts...' He smiled wryly. 'Well, you know the rest. It backfired spectacularly.'

The refurbishment of the master suite had been her uncle's wedding present; she had forgotten that. 'And I thought you didn't care and you thought I was too young, too fragile...' She touched his strong face with one hand. 'And I allowed my insecurity and other idle gossip to chase me away from you,' she concluded sadly.

He stared, his face grim. 'Are you sure that was all that sent you running? Not the handsome Texan, your secret valentine?'

'I always thought you sent the cards. You pretended you had sent the last one,' she said, with a grin that quickly vanished under his scowling frown.

'I followed you the last day; I saw you at the airport.'

'I swear it was pure coincidence that I met Wayne in the departure lounge.'

He caught her hand in his, his fingers tightening painfully around hers. 'And was it coincidence that you shared his house?' he said, with an edge of cruelty.

'Necessity.' She stared up into his strong, attractive face and willed him to believe her. 'I had to wait until he'd arranged my finances, and I had nowhere else to go; I was a whimpering wreck without you. But Wayne and I were never more than friends.'

Slowly the pressure on her hand relaxed, and he said deeply, 'I believe you, Zoë.' He kissed her long and tenderly. Picking her up in his arms and rolling on to his back, he held her close against his strong body. 'I have to.' He groaned as he kissed her again with aching sweetness. 'I love you.'

She wanted him to make love to her, but she wanted him really to believe her, and, forcing herself to lift her head, she leant back, her hands splayed across his muscular chest.

'And I love you.' She gazed down, her eyes wide and pleading on his handsome face. 'And I only allowed you to think Wayne was my lover because when you arrived in California you were so cold.' She shuddered with remembered pain. 'So remote, and you never wanted to see me again.'

'I lied; I came to fetch you home, but when I saw you in that man's home, looking so sleek and content, I was so hurt, so angry that I could barely speak. I had to get away.'

'But you refused to divorce me.'

He tensed suddenly, and looked at her with hard eyes. 'I love you, I would do anything for you, but I'm not the kind of generous soul who would hand over the love of his life to another man.'

She studied him from beneath lowered lashes. 'Then why tonight did you say I could have a divorce?'

'Because the male ego is a fragile thing and you severely dented mine and I was furious.' He laughed and kissed her mouth. 'But by the time I got up here I'd calmed down.

'It wasn't so much the fact that you'd seduced me into bed to get yourself pregnant.' His black eyes lit up with amusement; he chuckled again. 'Actually I had the same idea that night, and I was as mad as hell when you told me you were protected.'

A wide smile curved Zoë's soft mouth, and, leaning forward, she bit his chin lightly. 'Devious devil; I did wonder who was seducing whom at the time.'

'Yes, well, what really hurt today was the realisation that even after the last few days when I thought we'd finally got it together——' his hand slid down over her buttocks, pressing her into his hard thighs '—certainly in bed,' he said thickly, capturing her mouth for a quick, hard kiss, 'you still didn't trust me enough to tell me the whole truth regarding Val.

'If you'd simply told me another child might be another chance for our son... Instead I had to hear it from a doctor—a total stranger. If there's no trust between us, we have nothing,' he said with blunt conviction.

'I'm sorry.' She sighed. She'd thought love was enough, but suddenly she saw that it would never be enough, not for her and certainly not for Justin. She glanced at his handsome face and shivered at his bleak expression.

'I do trust you,' she said urgently. 'I was too afraid—the last few months with Val, the worry, the uncertainty; I wasn't thinking straight.'

She swallowed the lump that had formed in her throat, and struggled to contain her tears. 'I was going to tell you I was pregnant in California until you dismissed me so coldly. But deep down I always knew you would do anything to help. Why else do you think I kept your name and made it Val's? Why else would I have told him about his father?'

She could do no more; she had told him everything. She waited, heart pounding. His body wanted her—she could feel the hard weight of him beneath her—and she wasn't above using sex if that was what it took. 'I do love you,' she whispered, moving sensuously against him, her slender limbs twining with his.

He gave a hoarse groan. 'I believe you. As I said before, I have to. It would kill me to lose you again.' And then his mouth closed over hers with ravishing sweetness, the kiss so poignant, so tender that her eyes swam with tears.

'Justin,' she said hoarsely as she felt his strong hands move over her, tracing her spine, curving her buttocks, and swiftly their positions were reversed.

His deep voice whispered husky words of love and need and explicit intent as he shaped her to his passion. Then his hard mouth found hers again, his hands cupped her breast, his fingers teasingly tormenting on the taut peaks, and his mouth slid slowly from her lips to her throat and lower until her body writhed in wild desire.

She gloried in his impassioned, guttural moan when her small hands explored his massive, hard, muscled body; she nipped his shoulder with small teeth in a paroxysm of delight when he finally slid between her trembling thighs, filling her with almost unbearable ecstasy.

Consumed by a wild, raw passion, he lifted her bodily from the bed and she clung to him with legs and hands and teeth, buffeted by the force of his possession. They rolled around the huge bed in a delirious frenzy of passion.

She saw his dark head rear back; his features were cast in stone, rigid with desire, then his muscular body moved with savage ferocity, his weight forcing her deeper into the bed. His dark eyes blazed with primeval need, and she revelled in his total loss of control until she cried his name, her body convulsing in endless, great, surging waves of earth-shattering pleasure.

Justin stiffened. Head thrown back, he grated her name, then his big body, finding its release, sank against her in a long, frenzied moment of soul-shaking oblivion.

Later, when she lay beneath him, aware of the weight of him and the hot dampness of their sweat-slicked bodies, she lifted her hand and swept a curl of black hair away from the beads of perspiration running down his proud forehead. 'I love you,' she whispered, exhausted but filled with a wondrous peace. She had her husband back, her marriage back.

'And I love you.' The truth was in his deep, dark eyes as he smiled down at her. 'I always will.'

'I know.' She smiled with sheer delight.

'Confident little seductress, aren't you?'

She laughed out loud. Then he kissed her gently and her blood began to pound all over gain.

Much, much later, entwined in each other's arms, they talked softly of their love, their son, their fears.

'Don't worry, Zoë, everything will be perfect. Take it easy,' Justin murmured, his mouth brushing tenderly against her ear.

'But will you? Take it easy, I mean.' She remembered the days after Bertie's death when he'd worked twelve to eighteen hours a day. 'When Bertie died you turned into a workaholic. Why?'

He gave her a twisted smile. 'Stubborn little thing, aren't you?' But she could see that he was hiding something.

'Are you going to tell me?'

'Darling.' He kissed the tip of her nose, his arms holding her closer. 'We've wasted so much time; let's forget the past, and go forward from here.'

Thinking clearly for the first time in hours, Zoë turned in his arms to look steadily into his beloved face. 'I know Jess said you joined Bertie's firm simply to enhance your prospects with me. Is that why you had to work so long? Because you didn't really like what you were doing?'

'I love my sister dearly.' Justin chuckled. 'But as an anthropologist she has a nasty habit of not simply examining cultures but also trying to analyse me.'

'Was she right?'

'Yes and no,' he drawled, amusement in his brown eyes. 'You see, when my father died——'

'Jess said you never forgave him.'

'Rubbish. Jess has obviously said far too much, and I can see that you're not going to rest and let my poor, worn-out old body get some sleep until you're satisfied.'

She curled sinuously against his naked flesh and felt his body stir. 'Not so old,' she teased.

'Stop that and listen,' he said, with a faint smile. 'I forgave my father long before he died. But after his death, when Bertie had sold the restaurant and wound up his estate, there wasn't a lot of cash. I was all for dropping out of university and getting a job. Jess was still at school and there was only enough money to finance her education.

'Bertie, bless him, insisted on helping out financially. He was very good to me all through law school; I paid him back every penny, but I still felt I owed him a debt of gratitude, and anyway I loved the old man. So later, when I was beginning to specialise in international law and he suggested I was wasting my talent and asked me to join his firm, I didn't like to disappoint him.'

'But...' Zoë's blue eyes showed her dismay.

Justin nuzzled her neck. 'And I might—I just might—have considered improving my chances with a certain stunning little blonde,' he teased, with a lazy smile. 'But to be serious. After Bertie died and the will was read——'

'You were upset he hadn't left you any money.'

'For God's sake, Zoë!' He tensed and looked at her with grim eyes. 'Let me finish. I never wanted his money, but I was surprised at how little he had actually left you.

I knew that tax would swallow up most of it, but it didn't matter to me in the least. I knew his dearest wish was that you and I should live at Black Gables and I earned more than enough for us to be able to continue doing so. But then you decided you wanted to sell the place.'

'Not really,' she said slowly, feeling slightly ashamed of her shallow younger self. 'I simply thought it would be an easy way to get to share your bedroom.'

Justin shot her a wicked, amused look. 'Rather a desperate measure, and I didn't realise that at the time.'

His expression grew serious. 'I could deny you nothing. But I could not bear to see you lose the house forever. So I worked all the hours I could—and then some—trying to make enough quick capital to buy the house, hoping that later in our marriage when the children arrived you might want to go back to the place.'

'You would have done that for me?' she said softly, shaking her head in disbelief at the depth of his generosity.

'I did.'

'What?'

Justin stared for a moment at her puzzled blue eyes, then laughed wryly, drawling, 'You never read the papers you signed that day at Malibu, did you? The same as you never touched the money I paid to your New York lawyer every month.'

'No,' she admitted.

His mouth curved. 'Don't ever change, darling.' He kissed her and said gruffly, 'I bought Black Gables and I've been waiting years for you to return. I had arranged for the month to be kept free so that I could come and look for you.'

Her heart stopped; she stared at him, her lips parted in an amazed O. 'You did that for...?'

'Yes,' he affirmed, with a long, lingering kiss, and once again only the muffled sighs and sounds of love enhanced the late night air.

Zoë was sitting strapped into a seat on Concorde, flying the Atlantic to England, almost a year to the day since she had last made the trip. To her disgust she was slightly plumper than last time, but the tiny bundle of white-haired, blue-eyed joy in her arms more than made up for it.

She glanced sideways, as did the man sitting beside her—her husband. He caught her glance and smiled, his dark eyes shining with love and contentment.

'Are you and Mary OK?'

'Of course.' She looked down into her daughter's chubby face, a secret smile dancing in her beautiful eyes.

Their daughter had been born on Christmas Day, and she had been all for calling her Holly. But Justin had flatly refused and insisted that the child have an ordinary name, so they had agreed on Mary. But only because Zoë had heard him, when he thought no one was around, telling 'Maria' in Spanish how much he loved her, and she knew from Jess that it had been their mother's name.

She leant back against the seat, a deep sigh of contentment escaping her.

'Tired, darling?' Justin asked in concern.

'No, simply happy,' she murmured, and he bent and brushed his lips across hers.

'Me too,' he said huskily.

She glanced past him to where her son sat straining at the belt around his waist in his excitement. The last year had been hard but the love they all shared had made life feel good.

The transplant had been a success; they were on their way to London with Professor Barnet's blessing. Val would still have to attend hospital every few months for a check-up, but, barring accidents, there was no longer any medical reason why he should not live a long and happy life.

Zoë smiled to herself. Always providing his father did not kill him first, she thought, as Justin answered Val's never-ending questions.

'How fast is it going, Dad? Do you know how much it weighs? How old is it? Will I see the Tower of London soon? You said I would...'

An hour later she sat in the back seat of the long, sleek Jaguar with Val beside her as Justin manoeuvred the car into the drive of Black Gables and pulled up at the entrance.

'Oh, boy!' Val exclaimed; he was out of the car before his father had properly opened the door. 'Is this the Tower of London, Dad?' he demanded, running around the car to stare up at the massive house.

Justin took the baby from Zoë's arms and held the small child steadily against his heart with one large hand, while with the other he helped her out of the car.

'Is it, Dad?'

The two adults smiled into each other's eyes. 'Welcome home, Zoë, darling,' Justin murmured, dropping a swift kiss on her softly parted lips.

'Dad, Dad, where is the rest of the city? Are you sure this is the Tower of London?'

Justin, with admirable restraint considering he had a baby in one arm and a four-year-old boy hanging on to the leg of his trousers, said feelingly, 'No, it is not, son; this is our home for the next few months. But if you're not very careful you could just find yourself spending Easter in the Bloody Tower.'

'Justin, really—you shouldn't swear in front of the children,' Zoë remonstrated.

'I am not swearing,' he averred, and, catching the amusement sparkling in her sapphire eyes, he added astutely, 'That is the popular name bestowed upon the place centuries ago by the unfortunate inmates who lost their heads.'

'Always the lawyer with the quick rebuttal,' Zoë mocked. Their eyes met and clung and together they laughed out loud...

Still laughing, they entered the old house that was full of memories, with the hope of generations more to be made...

Day Leclaire and her family live in the midst of a maritime forest on a small island off the coast of North Carolina. Despite the yearly storms that batter them and the frequent power outages, they find the beautiful climate, superb fishing and unbeatable seascape more than adequate compensation. One of their first acquisitions upon moving to Hatteras Island was a cat named Fuzzy. He has recently discovered that laps are wonderful places to curl up and nap—and that Day's son really was kidding when he named the hamster Cat Food.

Day is a much-loved romance author. Her first book to be published by Mills & Boon® was in 1993, and since then she has had more than six million copies of her books distributed around the world.

THE SECRET BABY

by

DAY LECLAIRE

To my mom, Hazen F. Totten, and my sister,
Diane H. Andre, for all their love and
encouragement and endless patience.
Thank you. You two are incredible!

PROLOGUE

HE'D done it. He had her. And soon...very soon...Sable Jameson Caldwell would know it.

Damien Hawke dropped into the over-stuffed white chair behind the huge, pretentious desk, a tight, grim smile playing about his mouth. The contract, signed and executed, lay before him on the white marble tabletop. He wouldn't have been human if he hadn't savored his moment of triumph. Savored the knowledge that after five long years he had Sable at his mercy. But it wasn't enough, he acknowledged. He didn't want her construction business—or, rather, her late husband's construction business. He wanted her.

And this time she wouldn't escape.

A small sound from the far side of the white and crimson office caught Damien's attention and he lifted his head. 'Have the arrangements been made, Lute?' he asked.

In response to the question, a huge man slipped silently from the shadows, his bald head gleaming in the subdued light. In years past, Lute's position would have been called many things. Valet, manservant, gentleman's gentleman. Damien simply called him friend.

'The movers will be here tonight to strip the room and deliver the furnishings to Miss Patricia.'

'Excellent.'

Damien stood and strode around the pedestaled desk, his shoes sinking into the blood-red carpeting. A large leopardskin floor covering blocked his path and with the toe of his shoe he kicked the pelt to one side. His gaze shifted over the exotic animal heads mounted on the harsh white walls and a flicker of distaste touched his stern features at the blatant obscenity. Every one of them was on the endangered species list.

'She will want her dead animals returned, yes?' Lute questioned.

'Knowing Patricia, I don't doubt it for a minute.'

Lute sighed. 'She dishonors her brother's memory and betrays her sister-in-law by selling her share of the family business but keeps her gaudy bits and pieces. Strange woman.'

Damien shrugged negligently. He couldn't care less about Patricia Caldwell. Not anymore. She'd served her purpose by giving him what he wanted most—forty percent of Caldwell's stock. It was the same percentage as Sable controlled. 'Money is Patricia's god. It always has been.'

Blackness settled on Lute's face. He smoothed his thumb and index finger across his white moustache and down to the narrow beard that framed his chin. It was a familiar gesture, a gesture that betrayed an inner turmoil. Damien folded his arms across his chest and waited for his friend to speak his piece.

'Money is a demanding god. A deadly god,' Lute said, before adding softly, 'But then, so is revenge.'

Damien's mouth tightened. He hadn't chosen the path he walked blindly. He'd taken every step with great deliberation. 'I want this room sanitized.' He spoke harshly, but Lute didn't flinch. Only one other person could confront Damien's anger with equanimity, with a soothing touch that calmed even the most savage beast. And he rarely spoke her name. 'I don't want one trace of cigarette smoke or that cloying perfume Patricia drenches herself in to remain.'

Lute inclined his head. 'It will be done. By Monday morning the office will be yours.' He turned to go.

'Have you seen her, Lute?' The question was torn from Damien, unexpected and unwelcome. They both knew of whom he spoke.

Sable.

'Yes.' The acknowledgement sounded hesitant, regretful. 'I have seen her.'

Damien tensed. 'And?'

'She looks much the same. Thinner, perhaps.'

'That's all?'

Lute turned around, his reluctance unmistakable. 'There were...shadows. Much sadness,' he admitted. His snowy brows drew together over soft blue eyes—eyes as old as time and as guileless as a baby's. 'And more sadness to come, yes?'

Again Damien shrugged. 'That's up to her. If she sells her shares of Caldwell's to me as Patricia did, she can walk away a wealthy woman. If she chooses to fight me...' his odd green eyes glittered with ruthless intent '...then I'll break her.'

'She will fight you,' Lute said, and without another word he left the room.

Damien stood motionless for a moment, his thoughtful gaze settling on the door that connected this office—*his* office—with the adjoining one. He didn't hesitate. He crossed to the door. The handle turned easily beneath his hand, the heavy oak panel swinging silently open. A single light, probably left on by the cleaning crew, shone from the desk by the windows. He walked into the room, leaving behind the hellish opulence that so suited Patricia for a soothing warmth guaranteed to assuage even the most tortured soul—stepping from harsh gold and crimson excess to the soft, mellow rose and yellow of Eden's garden.

Moonlight filtered through the tinted floor-to-ceiling windows, gilding the room with silver, and he shut the connecting door, shutting out the stink of stale tobacco and musk. The air here was sweet and smelled of Sable. He inhaled deeply, dragging the clean, fresh scent of her into his lungs.

And he remembered... Remembered their time together, their passion, their desperate need, their oneness. And her betrayal... He remembered that most of all.

For it wasn't a betrayal he'd easily forget...or forgive—a fact Sable would soon learn.

CHAPTER ONE

SABLE sensed him long before she saw him. She didn't need to turn around and search the crowd of faces behind her. The elevator was too packed to allow it, anyway. But she knew he was there. Somewhere.

She could feel the heavy touch of his gaze stroking along her spine as surely as if he'd reached out and put his hands on her. She closed her eyes, fighting her instinctive reaction. It had been so long since she'd felt the insidious yearning only he could arouse, felt the subtle clenching of inner muscles that signaled his presence. Her hand tightened on her briefcase and her breathing grew shallow. How could she still feel this way after five long, lonely years?

The elevator stopped and the doors parted, releasing a small wave of people, before drawing more in, pushing her deeper into the car and closer to... him. She shifted to one side and risked turning her head a fraction, allowing her gaze to drift casually over the occupants behind her. She stiffened. A man with distinctively streaked tawny hair stood with his shoulder braced against the back wall. Her heart pounded and acute fear momentarily robbed her of all thought, leaving behind blind panic—and a desperate, instinctive need to escape. Only the press of people held her in place.

Dear lord. It *was* him.

Her nails bit into her palm, the pain sharp and cruel. She barely noticed. All her attention was focused on him—and on what his return might mean. She drew in a shaky breath, forcing herself to suppress an almost overwhelming emotional response and to think. *Think*, damn it! she silently ordered. Why had he come? He'd only bring more misery. Misery and danger—danger should he discover all she'd kept hidden from him these past five years.

She faced forward. He didn't move—the distorted reflection from the copper-tinted doors told her that much. Instead he continued to lounge against the rear wall, waiting...waiting for what? For the car finally to be empty? For them finally to be alone? If she got off at an earlier floor, would he follow? She knew the answer to that. If she got off, he would too. And he'd know she'd panicked because of him. She didn't dare give him that much of an edge. Still... The pivotal question remained, scraping across sensitive nerve-endings like a serrated blade.

What did he want?

The next stop brought another influx of passengers and to her horror she found herself forced farther and farther back until she stood just in front of him.

'Sable,' he said in a husky undertone, the sound of his voice stirring fragments of bittersweet memories. When she didn't respond, he placed his hand on the small of her back. His fingers slipped over the soft rose silk of her skirt, closing on the narrow curve of her hip. He tugged her against him. 'Or should I say—Mrs Caldwell?'

She couldn't pull loose—they were packed in too tightly. 'Stop it!' she ordered, keeping her voice whisper-soft. She shot a quick glance to either side, relieved beyond measure to discover that the people nearest to them were caught up in their own quiet discussions. No one was paying the least attention to her.

Floor by floor the elevator progressed relentlessly upward. The moment a space opened in front of her, she tried to step forward, but he stopped her. He tightened his hold, pulling her deeper into his embrace, the warmth of his body cutting through the silk of her suit. His hand shifted to her waist, his fingers sliding beneath the bottom of her jacket and splaying across her abdomen, moving in an insidious caress. 'Not yet, my love. I'm enjoying this too much,' he murmured, his breath stirring the curls at her temple.

She stifled her cry of alarm, not daring to say anything, not daring to draw attention to her predicament. Instead she forced herself to be perfectly still and wait as the elevator dispersed passenger after passenger, moving ever upward toward her office on the executive floor. She felt like a mouse trapped in a cage with a ravenous tomcat—and nowhere to escape. Claustrophobia mounted with each stop they made, with every breath she drew. His soft laughter rumbled in her ear and she knew he found her helplessness amusing.

The car eased to a halt once more and the final occupant departed. It seemed to take an eternity before the doors slid closed, sequestering them in the small metal cubicle. Not waiting another moment, Sable ripped free of his hold. Then, gathering every bit of strength, feeling more vulnerable than she had in a long, long time, she turned and faced him.

Damien Hawke. Her former employer, former lover...and the father of her four-year-old son. Was that why he'd come? Had he somehow found out about Kyle? His expression gave nothing away. But then, it never did.

She forced herself to look up at him and instantly regretted it. She'd forgotten how intense his eyes could be. Or perhaps she'd chosen to forget. She could lose her very soul in those odd green eyes. They glowed with an inner light, hard and knowing and compelling, mesmerizing her in a way that was all to frighteningly familiar. They were the pale green of an arctic wasteland—fiery emotion encased in impenetrable ice. She'd never yet read an article about him that failed to mention the disconcerting power of those eyes.

'Hello, Damien,' she managed to say in an even voice. 'You always did have the most objectionable ways of making your presence known.'

He inclined his head, his gaze mocking. 'You're too kind.'

'Touching me like that... It was rude. It was...' She glared at him. 'It was unconscionable.'

He shrugged. 'It felt good. You know it did.'

She turned slightly, stung by the bitter truth, hoping she was managing to hide the intense, piercing desire, the gnawing hunger that being near him stirred. How could she have been so foolish as to believe those emotions had died? She took a deep, calming breath, drawing on all her professional reserves to see her through this unexpected confrontation.

'What are you doing here?' she asked with a composure that threatened to desert her at any moment. 'It can't be coincidental. It never is with you.'

He tilted his head to one side, watching her with open amusement. He possessed a disconcerting stillness, like a jungle cat—lazy, graceful and ready to pounce at the slightest provocation. 'You know me that well?'

'I know you all *too* well,' she responded tautly. 'I repeat, what are you doing here?'

He shrugged, a simple, careless movement. But she'd learned from long, hard experience that nothing Damien

did was simple. And his actions were never, ever careless.
'I warned you I'd be back,' he said.

'No,' she corrected him, daring to meet his gaze once more. 'You warned you'd have your revenge.'

His amusement died, leaving behind a wintry resolve she couldn't mistake. 'So I did. Thanks for the reminder.'

She fought to conceal her apprehension, knowing he'd be quick to take advantage if he sensed her vulnerability. When she'd worked with him, she'd admired his hunter's instinct, admired how that instinct had never once failed him. Now she feared it. 'Is that why you've returned? To take your revenge?'

'And if I have?'

The elevator eased to a stop and the doors opened. She hesitated, part of her desperate to leave the confines of the car and escape his presence. But another, more rational part warned that she'd be wise to find out what he wanted. He stepped forward, bracing open the doors, standing so close that she could once again feel the heat of his body, smell his spicy, distinctive cologne.

She searched his face, hoping for a clue to his thoughts. He wasn't a handsome man in the classic sense of the word; his features were far too strong, too potently masculine. But the high, arching cheekbones, the full, sensual mouth and knowing look in his eyes drew women with effortless ease. He was like a huge, lazy lion, powerful and secure in his domain. And he had no intention of revealing anything until he was good and ready.

He returned her gaze with an implacable reserve, forcing Sable to ask once again, 'Will you tell me why you're here?'

'Yes... In time.'

With a small exclamation of frustration, she started from the car. He reached out just as she passed, his fingers brushing her cheek. 'Still like silk,' he murmured.

She pulled back sharply, stepping into the hallway outside the elevator. 'Don't do that!' She hated the mocking humor that lit his eyes, the way he shook his head in mild reproof.

'That isn't what you used to say,' he murmured. 'You used to beg for my touch.'

She stared at him in disbelief, her black eyes huge and wounded. Cruelty had never been part of his nature. But then, she didn't know this Damien. Not anymore. Gathering the shreds of her dignity, she lifted her chin. Well, he didn't know her either. Five years had changed them both.

'Thank you for the reminder,' she said with gentle irony. 'I've made a point of learning from my past mistakes since we parted.'

'As have I.' His voice dropped, but she heard every harsh word as though he'd shouted. 'And you were a big mistake, weren't you, Sable? I'd have been better off embracing an adder. But the time's come to correct past errors.'

'Meaning?' she demanded.

'Meaning that you're going down. And I'm going to drag you there every hellish step of the way.'

That said, he stepped back into the car, leaving her to stare in shocked disbelief as the doors silently closed between them. How long she stood there she didn't know. It wasn't until her secretary touched her arm that she awoke to her surroundings.

'Mrs Caldwell? Are you all right?' Janine asked in concern.

Sable blinked. 'I'm sorry?'

'You're so pale. And look—you've dropped your briefcase.'

Glancing down in confusion, Sable saw that the black case had slipped from her numb fingers and lay drunkenly on its side. 'Thank you, Janine,' she murmured, stooping to pick up the briefcase. 'I'm fine.'

'Are you sure?' her secretary persisted. 'You don't look fine. You look rather... ill.'

Sable sighed. Janine had been her husband Leonard's secretary. After his death, she'd been offered a promotion, but insisted she'd be of more service working with Sable, helping in her struggle to gain control of the business and solve the problems of a company on the skids. And though Janine never unbent sufficiently to use Sable's first name she took a proprietorial interest in all aspects of Caldwell's, including her employer's well-being.

'Thank you, but I'm all right now,' Sable said, a hint of reserve coloring her tone. As much as she appreciated Janine's concern, she wasn't in the mood to field the older woman's questions. 'Do you have my notes prepared for the board meeting?' she asked, steering the conversation into safer channels.

Janine's mouth tightened, but she didn't press the issue. 'Yes, Mrs Caldwell. They're on your desk.'

Sable forced her mind to business matters, grateful for the need to concentrate, for the need to push every other consideration to the back of her mind. 'There should be a tape full of correspondence on the Dictaphone for you to transcribe. I'd like the letters to go out today. Is Patricia in yet?' At the lack of an immediate response, Sable raised an eyebrow in question. 'Janine?'

'Why, no, Mrs Caldwell. She isn't.'

That was a surprise. For all Patricia's faults, her sister-in-law always arrived early to work. 'Is it possible she's forgotten the board meeting is today?'

'I very much doubt it,' her secretary replied. 'I reminded her of it myself. Will there be anything else?'

'Nothing for now, thank you. Start on those letters if you will,' Sable replied, opening the door to her office. 'I'd like to review my notes before the meeting, so hold all my calls, please.'

'Even if it's Miss Trainer?'

Sable turned, a small frown creasing her brow. 'My request never includes her. You know that.' It was an inviolate rule that Kyle's nanny could interrupt any time, any place. Why would Janine think that had changed?

The secretary gave a small shrug. 'My mistake.'

'That's all right.' More than anything Sable wanted to escape into her office before the last vestiges of her strength ebbed completely away. Instead, she forced herself to stand patiently and offer an encouraging smile. After all, Janine was a valued employee. She shouldn't take the fallout for Damien's actions. 'I appreciate your checking. Is there anything else you need to discuss with me?'

'No. I'll get right to work on those letters.'

'I'd appreciate it.'

With a sigh of relief, Sable shut the door between her office and the reception area. Leaning against the sturdy oak panel, her head drooped like a flower on a broken stem. Here it was, only eight-thirty in the morning, and already exhaustion gripped her. Still ahead lay the board meeting—always a stressful occasion—not to mention discovering the purpose behind Damien's visit.

She glanced across the room toward Patricia's office. The door that separated them remained shut, not even the acrid stench of cigarette smoke seeping past the sturdy barrier. That in itself was unusual enough, a convincing testimony to Patricia's absence. Had she decided to boycott the meeting? It was a distinct possibility. Her sister-in-law hadn't taken kindly to being stripped of the chairmanship last month. If she could find a way to cause trouble, she'd do it.

With a sigh, Sable straightened and headed for the private bathroom that adjoined her office. Once there, she stared in the mirror over the sink for a long moment. Janine was right. She did look ill. All color had fled her face, leaving her cheeks ashen, her pallor intensified by the cloud of unruly black curls that had escaped the formal knot at the nape of her neck. Worst of all, her dark eyes were like two huge, bruised smudges, betraying all too clearly her vulnerability.

If Damien had seen her like this, he'd be after her like a shark on a blood trail. And he'd be just as brutal and merciless. Not wasting another minute, she opened a drawer in the built-in vanity and removed a cosmetics case. Applying blush and shadow with a practiced hand, she managed to conceal most of the outer traces of her distress. A final touch of rose-toned lipstick added the perfect amount of color to her face.

Turning her attention to her hair, she pulled out the pins that anchored it in place. Heavy curls fell in an unruly mass past her shoulders, effectively destroying the image of the super-competent executive. But not for long. A bit of water and a brisk brushing helped tame the more stubborn strands and she swiftly rolled her hair into a tight, formal knot.

Sparing a swift glance at her watch, she groaned in dismay. She had precisely twenty minutes to get organized. Hurrying to her desk, she sat down and flipped open the file Janine had prepared. But no matter how hard she tried to focus on her notes she couldn't stop her treacherous thoughts from centering on Damien and how his return would change her life.

Turning her chair to face the window, she stared out at the San Francisco skyline. Why had he come back? Why now, after all this time? She closed her eyes, rubbing a weary hand across her brow. She had a thousand questions—questions to which only Damien had the answers. And, knowing him, she wouldn't like those answers one little bit.

The moments before the start of the board meeting seemed like some horrible replay of her experience that morning in the elevator. Sable stood at the buffet with her back to the conference room, pouring a cup of coffee from a heavy silver carafe. The sudden thread of alarm that snaked along her spine caught her completely by surprise. Once again she felt the ominous clenching of her muscles, the swift, uncontrollable touch of desire bringing all her senses to full flower. And in that instant she knew *he* had returned.

Cornelius Becker, the board's oldest member, approached. 'Who is it that just walked in?' he demanded querulously. 'That man over there by the door. Doesn't he know executive sessions are closed to general members?'

Giving herself time to school her features into a composed mask, she returned the carafe to the table and added cream to her coffee. She turned slowly, certain of whom she'd see. Sure enough, standing in comfortable solitude, his mantle of authority absolute, was Damien. His gaze met hers from across the room, his brilliant green eyes alive with passionate secrets.

'That's Damien Hawke,' she said quietly, and took a quick, restorative sip of coffee.

'*The* Damien Hawke?' Cornelius sounded impressed. 'Do you know him?'

'Yes,' she admitted, her response sounding short to the point of rudeness. To her relief, Cornelius didn't appear to notice.

'I've wanted to meet him for quite some time now. Hawke is a brilliant businessman, positively brilliant.' He chuckled, his eyes inquisitive beneath his bushy brows. 'But then, if you know him, you're already aware of that, aren't you?'

'Yes,' she said, hoping the reluctance in her voice wasn't too apparent. 'I am.'

'Introduce me, my dear.' He rubbed his hands together in anticipation. 'I'm curious to know why he's here.'

A dozen excuses leapt to her lips, but she didn't voice a single one. Instead she returned her cup and saucer to the buffet table and walked with Cornelius across the room. He'd been her chief advocate when Patricia had fought to oust her from the board after Leonard's death a year ago. Without his backing, Sable would have lost everything. He'd also been the one to recommend her for the chairmanship in Patricia's stead when their business situation had worsened. His request was a small price to pay. Besides, she could handle a simple introduction, couldn't she?

She stopped directly in front of Damien, aware of the challenge in his eyes. Did he think he could cow her with one of his infamous looks of intimidation? He had a lot to learn. 'Cornelius, I'd like to introduce you to Damien Hawke. Damien, this is Cornelius Becker, one of our senior board members.'

The two men shook hands. 'I'm surprised to see Caldwell's biggest competitor at our board meeting,' Cornelius said. 'Do you own stock in Caldwell's?'

Damien folded his arms across his chest. 'Yes. I do.'

Sable couldn't conceal her shock. Her gaze flashed to Damien's. 'A recent acquisition?' she asked, amazed that her voice came out as steady as it did.

'Very recent,' he confirmed.

'You are aware that this is an executive session of the board?' Cornelius questioned. 'I'm afraid it's closed to common shareholders.'

'But then, I'm not a common shareholder,' Damien stated gently. 'And if there are no objections I'd like to address the board before the meeting.'

Cornelius frowned. 'Your request is highly unusual,' he observed. 'The decision will have to be Sable's.'

Damien's expression didn't change. He glanced at her. 'Do you have any objection?'

He wasn't surprised that the final decision would be hers, she realized. Which meant he'd known all along that she was the chairwoman. And in that instant true fear gripped her. Nothing that had happened so far today had been an accident. He had a purpose in coming. If she hadn't been so thrown by the shock of seeing him in the elevator, she'd have figured that out sooner. He'd wanted her off-balance because it gave him the advantage.

The question still remained, though... Her distraction gave him the advantage to do *what*?

'What are you up to, Damien?' she demanded. 'You never do anything without a game plan.' She'd learned that crucial lesson during the four years she'd worked for him. And, more often than not, by the time his competitor realized what that game plan might be, it was far too late. Apprehension gripped her. Could that be the case this time? Was she too late to alter his scheme?

A lazy smile tugged at his mouth. 'Finally catching on?' he asked. 'You never used to be so slow. Or perhaps you've just grown complacent. Not wise in today's business world.' His smile died. 'Not wise at all when you have competitors waiting to pounce on your most insignificant error.'

There was no mistaking the threat. It took every scrap of composure to turn to Cornelius and force out a light laugh. 'I've been rude to our guest. I've neglected to offer Mr Hawke some coffee. I don't suppose...?'

'Allow me, my dear,' Cornelius suggested with alacrity. 'How do you take it, Mr Hawke?'

'Make it Damien,' he replied. 'And I prefer my coffee like most things in life.' His gaze locked with Sable's, his words directed at her every bit as much as at Cornelius. 'Straight up and uncorrupted.'

'Black it is,' Cornelius said with a chuckle. 'And why don't I bring you another cup, Sable? Half coffee and half cream, right?'

'That's very kind of you,' she murmured.

'My pleasure,' he replied, and crossed the room to join the other board members milling around the buffet table.

'You're as charming as always,' Damien said the instant the older man had moved out of earshot. 'But then, that's your specialty, isn't it?'

'What is? Charm?' she asked, lifting an eyebrow in question.

'Charming old men, to be precise.'

She sucked in her breath, hot color blossoming across her cheekbones. 'How dare you?' she whispered.

He released a short, dry laugh. 'Why act so insulted? Your charm was a talent you used while working for me. A talent you used to hook a husband old enough to be your father. And a talent you continue to use, if Cornelius Becker's reaction is the norm.'

She refused to dignify his comment with a response. There wasn't any point. He'd think what he chose, no matter what she said. 'What's going on?' she questioned instead. 'What do you want, Damien?'

He tilted his head to one side. 'Wasn't my request clear enough for you? I want to address the board.'

Her hands balled into fists. 'That's not what I'm referring to and you know it. It's been five years. If you're here, it's to cause trouble. Why now, after all this time?'

He leaned closer, his voice low and intimate. 'Some things take time. Depending on what they are, it can even be worth the wait.' His eyes darkened, the intense green as cold and turbulent as a mountain stream. 'Especially when it comes to revenge.'

'You had your revenge, remember?' she responded tautly. 'You fired me and then blackballed me with every business in town. That's excessive even by your standards.'

'I didn't blackball you. I didn't have to. The other construction firms knew what you were without my saying a word, and they avoided you like the plague. My mistake was in not figuring out the truth sooner.' He grabbed her wrist, yanking her close. 'I allowed myself to be seduced by those big black eyes and your soft white skin. But that won't happen again. You can count on it.'

She drew in a panicked breath at his touch, helpless to prevent the sharp, uncontrollable desire that rocketed through her. Did he know? Did he sense her reaction?

She searched his face. Of course he did. The amused curve of his lips, the knowing gleam in his eyes all told her as much. Damn him! 'Let go of me, Damien,' she ordered in an icy voice, drawing back as far as he'd permit.

His grip tightened, and he forced her toward him again until their thighs met, his open suit coat brushing lightly across her breasts. 'Did you really think Leonard Caldwell could give you more than me?' He spoke softly, yet every word stung with biting sharpness. 'Is that why you sold yourself to him?'

She could feel the color drain from her face. 'You know nothing about my reasons for marrying Leonard.' Or did he? Don't let him know about Kyle, she prayed with frantic desperation. Please, don't let him know about our son.

'I know you decided he was the safer bet. I know that you leaked our bids to him. And I know that he married you. Was that the price you held out for? Marriage in exchange for theft?'

'I didn't steal from you!'

'The hell you didn't. I hope it was worth it. Because the time has come to pay for what you took.'

She stiffened, sudden fury overriding every other thought and consideration. 'I've had enough,' she announced. 'I want you out of here. And if you won't go quietly I'll call Security.'

To her consternation, he laughed. 'I don't think so. In fact, you're not moving until you've listened to every word I have to say.'

She attempted to twist from his hold, wincing as his unyielding grasp bruised her wrist. Short of creating a scene, she had little choice but to stand there and hear him out. She shot a swift glance over her shoulder. The other board members were busy availing themselves of the coffee and pastries spread across the buffet table. To her relief, they weren't paying the least attention to her conversation.

Resigned to the inevitable, she turned back to Damien. 'All right, I'm listening. But please let go first. You're hurting me.'

For a minute, she didn't think he'd do it. Then his grip eased and his thumb stroked across the narrow bones of her wrist. 'I'd forgotten how quick you are to bruise,' he said, a hint of regret flickering in his eyes.

'Forget it.' She dismissed his concern. 'I also heal fast.'

His jaw tightened. 'So you do. Thanks for the reminder.'

'What do you want, Damien?' she prompted softly.

His voice turned grim. 'Retribution. Oh, don't look so shocked, Sable. Even you must realize that no one steals from me and gets away with it. I don't take that sort of betrayal sitting down. I'm here to make that point crystal-clear.'

'I swear to you, Damien . . . it didn't happen that way. I didn't steal——'

'Stop it!' He didn't raise his voice. He didn't need to. The fierce expression on his face was more than enough to ensure her silence. 'We went through this five years ago. You can protest all you want, but it won't alter the facts. The leak came from you.'

Her gaze wavered, then fell. He was right. The leak had come from her. But it hadn't happened the way he claimed. It hadn't been deliberate. Not that that changed anything. He believed her guilty of stealing from him. And he didn't intend to listen to any excuses. All she could do was try and find out his intentions and mitigate the damage if possible.

'What do you plan to do?' she whispered.

'I told you. I plan to address your board.'

'About what?' She searched his face apprehensively. 'My marriage to Leonard? Our affair?'

He smiled without humor. 'That, sweet Sable, you'll find out along with the other board members.'

'Do you really think they'll care about our past relationship?' she questioned in disbelief.

He shrugged. 'Perhaps. Perhaps not.'

'What if I refuse your request?' she dared to threaten. 'If I don't permit you to address the board, what then?'

'I wouldn't recommend it,' he advised harshly. 'It will only make your situation worse.'

Worse than what? she wondered in dread. She bit down on her lip. If only she had a few minutes alone to think, to figure out what he might be after. 'I need more time.'

'You're out of time,' he informed her. 'What's your decision?'

She had no choice and they both knew it. She inclined her head. 'Address the board, if you must. But we'll have to wait for Patricia. She seems to be running late today.'

'That won't be necessary.'

'But——'

'Do it, Sable. We don't have time to discuss this further. Cornelius is coming over with our coffee. Now call the meeting to order and introduce me.'

'Don't give me orders. You're not running the show, Damien,' she retorted sharply. 'I am.'

'You are for the time being. That could change, so don't press your luck.'

She caught her breath and took a step away from him, something in his expression warning her not to push him any further. 'Gentlemen,' she announced in a carrying voice, 'if you'll take your seats, Mr Hawke would like to address the board before we begin.'

She took the coffee from Cornelius with a grateful smile and crossed to the head of the conference table. As she stood waiting for everyone to be seated, her gaze settled on a portrait of her late husband. He gazed down at her from the far wall, his smile as kind and gentle as the man had been. She struggled to draw strength from his memory. But it was a futile act.

Leonard had always been the one in need of strength, and she'd always been there to provide it. When he'd fallen ill, she'd assumed more and more of his responsibilities. Just before his death, he'd made his final request—that she protect Caldwell's from the vultures who'd try and steal it after his death, protect his business from corporate raiders . . . raiders like Damien Hawke.

Taking a deep breath, she turned to face the six board members. 'I've had a rather unusual request. One of our shareholders, Damien Hawke, has asked to address the board before we begin our meeting. I've agreed to his request.' She glanced at him as she took her seat. 'Damien?'

'Excuse the interruption, but what about Patricia?' Cornelius protested. 'I don't think it's appropriate to begin without her.'

'That won't be necessary,' Damien replied. He stood at the end of the rectangular conference table opposite Sable, one hand thrust in his trouser pocket. 'Effective today, Patricia Caldwell is off the board. I've arranged for copies of her letter of resignation to be delivered to each of you.'

No one said a word, identical looks of shock on every face. 'Resigned?' gasped one member. 'But . . . how?

Why?' His questions broke the silence. Others raised their voices in concern, decorum vanishing beneath sudden, noisy confusion.

'Please.' Sable cut through the babble. 'I believe that's what Mr Hawke intends to explain.'

'Quite right.' His smile of satisfaction said it all, told her all too clearly that her troubles had only just begun. 'Last week Patricia sold me her shares of Caldwell stock. With the public stock I've acquired these past five years, I now control forty-three percent——'

'*Forty-three*! That's more than——'

All eyes turned in Sable's direction. Throughout Damien's remarks, she'd kept carefully quiet, her hands clenched in her lap, struggling to keep from revealing any thought or emotion. Now she stared at Damien across the length of the table. 'What do you want?' she asked one final time. But the question was pointless. Now that it was far too late, she'd finally figured out his intentions.

'What do I want? Why, I want to replace Patricia on the board, of course.' A slow smile crept across his mouth and his eyes bored into hers. 'And I want to replace you as chairman.'

CHAPTER TWO

SABLE thrust back her chair and stood up. 'You can't be serious!'

'I'm dead serious,' came Damien's instant reply.

The others in the room might not have existed. Only the two of them were present, faced off across the room, locked in a not so private battle of wills. Their eyes met, his gaze harsh and relentless, and she knew without question that he wouldn't shift from his stance. He planned to take her down. His rigid posture, his squared jaw, the brilliant light of combat that sparked in his eyes all told her as much. No one could oppose Damien when he was in this mood and win. It wasn't possible. Never had she felt so vulnerable, so threatened.

He'd arranged all the moves beforehand. She'd lost the battle before it had ever begun, before she'd even realized there was a war. And though she'd never known Damien to allow his emotions to affect business decisions she didn't doubt for a minute that this was the exception to the rule. This wasn't just business.

It was personal.

'You can't just waltz in here and take over the board,' she informed him coldly.

'Can't I?' He looked at each board member in turn. 'The general voting public owns seventeen percent of this company. Sable and I, between us, own the rest. I only need eight percent of the outside shareholders voting with me to take over, whereas Sable needs eleven to retain control. If it came to a proxy fight, my name alone would generate the eight percent I require to take over Caldwell's.'

'He's right, Sable,' Cornelius muttered in dismay. 'He won't be able to remove us from the board until the next election, but——'

'But I'll put that six-month wait to good use, soliciting the votes I need,' Damien interrupted. 'By the time the next election comes around I'll have a whole new slate of board members ready and eager to run against you. And we'll win.'

'Our shareholders would never go along with that!' spluttered one of the more junior members.

Damien didn't bother to conceal his contempt. 'Won't they? After the profit statements you've posted for the past two quarters, I'm surprised they haven't already lynched the lot of you.'

'It was Patricia,' Cornelius spoke up. 'She——'

Damien cut him off. 'It doesn't matter who's at fault. The shareholders will blame you. If you fight me, you have my word, by the next election every last one of you will be gone.' He paused, giving them all time to digest his words. 'You'll be gone, unless...'

Sable sank into her chair, knowing that by doing so she'd tacitly relinquished the floor to him. Knowing, too, that her actions would speak far louder than any words. All through his comments she'd listened, trying to decide if there were other options available to them. So far, she couldn't see any. Damien had them over a barrel, and every person in the room had better realize it. Fast.

'Name your terms, Damien,' she said quietly.

'I want to be voted on to the board, effective immediately.'

Her hands clenched in her lap. 'And then?'

'I want the chairmanship.'

Everyone's attention shifted to focus on her reaction, the board members waiting with bated breath, for her response. She forced herself to relax against the upholstered back of her chair, crossing one leg over the other. She didn't dare allow them to see how badly Damien had shaken her. 'I'm out and you're in?' she asked, lifting an eyebrow in amused disbelief. 'Just like that? You know nothing about Caldwell's, nothing about the way it's run, the people who work here. And yet you want to head the company.'

He planted his hands on the table and leaned toward her. 'Are you questioning my abilities? You, of all people?'

Sable shook her head. 'I question neither your experience nor your abilities.' She spoke crisply, assuming her most businesslike demeanor. 'I do question your current knowledge of Caldwell's situation. And I question your ability to make appropriate decisions without the least familiarity with our employees or clients to back them up.'

'I know this business inside and out.' He dismissed her concerns with an arrogant shrug.

She inclined her head. 'I'm aware of that. As our chief competitor you would. But you don't know *Caldwell's* inside and out.' She fixed her dark eyes on him, meeting his fierce green gaze without flinching. 'I do.'

'You know my terms, Sable. Step down,' he growled.

She straightened. 'Hear me out first!'

For one frightening moment, she didn't think he would; she thought that he'd just walk away and make good on his threat. Then he nodded in agreement. He continued to stand at the far end of the conference desk like some warrior of old, his arms folded across his chest, his legs slightly spread and feet planted as though for action. She searched his closed expression for some sign of vulnerability, anxiously hoping to discover some betraying chink in his armor that she could use to her advantage.

She saw nothing.

'You have one minute,' he said. 'Convince me.'

'Very well.' She took a deep breath, marshaling her arguments with as much speed and logic as possible. 'I have no desire to get into a proxy fight with you, nor do I think it will benefit Caldwell's to have a new board, to lose the experience these gentlemen bring to their positions. I suggest a compromise.'

She almost choked offering even that much. But she didn't have any other option. Right now she had to find a way to salvage what she could from this disaster. She had to gain enough time to find a way to fight him...and win. Damn Patricia for creating this mess! She must be laughing her head off, hoping her actions would destroy Sable, perhaps even destroy Caldwell's. Leonard's sister had wanted revenge for having been forced to give up the chairmanship, and she'd taken it... Dear lord, how she'd taken it!

'What's your compromise?' Damien demanded.

'We'll agree to vote you onto the board...'

His mouth curled to one side. 'How kind of you.'

She gritted her teeth. More than anything she wanted to cut loose, to tell him what she really thought and felt. But she didn't dare. Not when he held all the winning cards. 'You own forty-three percent of the stock. It only makes sense that you should have a say in how the company is run,' she conceded.

'And the chairmanship?' The overhead lights picked out the streaks of gold gleaming in his thick tawny hair. He reminded her more than ever of a rogue lion. A rogue lion ready and able to take over her turf, to force his domination.

She took a deep breath. 'Leave the chairmanship in my hands for three months. That will give you time to familiarize yourself with Caldwell's and——'

'One month.'

'But——'

He shook his head, a quiet laugh rumbling deep in his chest. 'Did you think I'd grown soft in the past five years? That I'd stand back and allow you to call the shots? You should know me better than that.'

'I know you, Damien.' The words burst out before she could stop them. 'I certainly know better than to ever call you soft or to think you'd allow anyone to have authority over you. You lead the pack or no one does. Isn't that right?'

A smile touched his mouth and she suspected he found her loss of control humorous. When would she ever learn? she wondered in despair. She couldn't afford to make a single mistake with him. Not now. Not ever.

'That's right. I lead and you follow.' His smile died, his words hard and brutal. 'You're a fool, Sable, if you believe I'd give you three months to scramble for votes or to improve your performance record. If you don't step down at the next board meeting, everyone seated at this table will be gone as of the next election. You have my personal guarantee.'

'I could fight you,' she dared to threaten.

'And you'd lose.'

He was right and they both knew it. Slowly she nodded. Giving in to him had to be one of the most difficult tasks she'd ever undertaken. But she had to be sensible. She had to consider what was best for the board, for her employees, and for the business. Still... She couldn't just let him take it all, give up and walk away. She needed to buy some time.

Her hands tightened into fists and she forced the words past her lips. 'You'll have my decision about the chairmanship at the next meeting.'

His eyes narrowed. 'That's not an answer.'

She lifted her chin. 'It's all the answer you're going to get,' she bluffed, well aware that if he pressed for further concessions she'd be forced to give them to him.

'Hoping to find a loophole, Sable?' he mocked.

'Just covering all the possibilities,' she retorted. 'Wouldn't you, in my position?'

'Without question.' His voice dropped, the sound dark and intimate. 'But just so you know... I haven't left any loopholes. I never do. Whether you realize it yet or not, you're trapped with nowhere to escape. I have you, Sable.'

She couldn't mistake the threat, nor the intense animosity. It poured off him in waves. She stared in shock, fear creeping along her spine like icy fingers. He wasn't just talking about Caldwell's any more. Whether the others seated at the table were aware of it or not, Damien's remarks had turned personal again.

She bit down on her lip. Why was he still so furious, so hostile? Five years should have cooled the fire of his anger somewhat. Or had time merely banked the embers, allowing them to smolder until the perfect opportunity occurred to fan the flames? Still... All this passion over losing those accounts to Caldwell's. It seemed unreasonable. Her eyes widened as a sudden thought occurred to her. Or could it be more than that? Could it be... Kyle? Did he know about their son, after all?

She didn't have the time or energy to consider that possibility. Not now. Not when the entire board was waiting to see what she'd do next. She fought for strength, focusing her attention on the board meeting—and on the unpleasant, though necessary, task ahead.

'Gentlemen,' she announced in a brisk voice, flipping open the file in front of her. 'Let's cut through all the rhetoric and get down to business. I hereby call the board of directors for Caldwell's to order. According to our by-laws we need an immediate replacement for any board vacancies. We currently have such a vacancy. All in favor of Damien Hawke filling that seat, say aye.'

Not a single board member looked at her as they murmured their assent.

'Any nays?' she questioned drily.

No one spoke.

'The motion carries. Mr Hawke, welcome to the board. Please take a seat.' She didn't give anyone time to speak, but continued determinedly onward. 'If everyone will refer to their notes, we'll begin. Damien, feel free to use Patricia's copy. I'll have another set run off for you, if you wish. Cornelius, have we any old business to discuss?'

To her profound relief, he took over from there, leading the conversation and giving her time to recover. Through sheer force of will she kept an interested expression on her face, but the exact details of the ensuing exchange escaped her. All her attention remained fixed on Damien...on the angled sweep of his cheekbones, on the strength of his hands as he gestured, on the distinctive timbre of his voice.

It had been so long, so very long, since they'd parted. So long since she'd been this close to him. Until this morning, the last time she'd seen him he'd held her naked in his arms and kissed her with a depth and passion unmatched by anything she'd experienced before or since.

The memory alone left her shaken, had the power to make her tremble with a soul-crippling need.

She lowered her eyes in dismay. She should be paying attention to the board meeting, not fantasizing about Damien. But she couldn't concentrate. Especially not when she realized that he was watching her as intently as she watched him. He seemed to be biding his time, waiting for... What? Or was he simply absorbed in memories too? Were images of them as they'd once been flashing through his mind? Did he remember as clearly as she their first kiss, the first time they'd made love, that final, wrenching parting?

It wasn't until Cornelius reported on the status of their latest contracts that she awoke to the conversation, the abrupt transition between dreams and reality a brutal intrusion.

'Say that again,' she demanded, more sharply than she'd intended.

'We've lost another project, Sable,' Cornelius explained reluctantly. 'Luther has bailed out on us.'

'Luther! But he's been with us from the start. We built the first three phases of his Walnut Creek development. Why in the world would he walk?'

'We're looking into it, but Matheson is bewildered. They've gone with A.J. Construction and we haven't been able to find out why. At least, not yet.'

'Who is this Matheson?' Damien interrupted.

'He's our project director,' Sable explained tersely.

Damien's frown turned black. 'It must be something critical if Luther's gone over to the competition at the end of such a large development. And your project director has no explanation? None at all?' He spoke with quiet emphasis but from the way the board cringed he might as well have roared the question.

Actually, this wasn't the first client they'd lost, though Sable didn't dare admit as much. The gradual slump in business had begun during Patricia's tenure as chairwoman, a position she'd assumed a year ago, right after Leonard's death. She'd dismissed their concern, saying that it was undoubtedly a temporary condition, one that would correct itself given time. Clearly, she was wrong.

'We're looking into it,' Sable assured him, hoping to end the discussion before it turned acrimonious. She shot Cornelius a speaking look, willing him to pick up on her cues and change the subject.

With a quick nod of understanding, he cleared his throat, speaking hastily. 'Next we have——'

'Hold it. I'm not finished,' Damien cut in. 'And we're not moving on until I'm satisfied with your answers. What are you doing to correct this situation?'

'First we have to find the cause,' Sable explained. 'Once we know why the condition exists, we can take steps to correct it.'

'Thank you, Madam Chairman, but that's apparent even to me.' His sarcasm made her wince. 'What does this Matheson have to say?'

'Nothing,' she replied, her patience beginning to wear thin. 'Yet. As I explained, he's looking into it.'

'Not to my satisfaction, he isn't,' came Damien's immediate retort. 'Did we lose the account because of poor workmanship, inferior materials, cost overruns? What?'

His heated gaze passed over the other board members. To Sable's chagrin, none could meet his eyes, every last one of them becoming engrossed in reading his notes. Damien swore beneath his breath and for the first time that day she shared his feelings. It was hard to respect a board that couldn't answer such basic questions.

'I'll explain the urgency of the situation to Matheson,' she said, in the hopes of easing the situation. 'I'll speak to him today.'

'You do that.' His gaze clashed with hers, his eyes reflecting his contempt. 'I paid a hefty sum for my stock in Caldwell's. I'm not about to sit back and watch my investment go down the tubes due to your shoddy business practices. I want some answers and I want them now.'

'I told you. Matheson's working on it,' Sable tried again.

A muscle jerked in his cheek, a sure sign that he was struggling to keep his fury in check. 'Then he'll work harder. I want a preliminary report from him tomorrow and a comprehensive analysis on my desk by the end of the month. I also suggest that at our next board meeting each of the department heads attend and present reports on their projects and clients in person. I want them available to answer any questions we might have.'

What he really meant was any questions *he* might have, Sable realized. She didn't bother protesting. It would be pointless. He was like a river in full flood, sweeping any opposition aside with stunning force. While she'd been busy dwelling on the past, he'd waited for the perfect moment to take control of the meeting. And from long experience she knew that nothing she could say or do would wrest that control from his grasp.

The rest of the meeting proved as much. He directed the discussions, questioned everything and demanded exhaustive responses. And he cut through the pomposity, forcing the board members to focus on the facts. To Sable's secret amusement, the more recalcitrant of them soon learned that Damien didn't take opposition well. A few choice words tossed in their direction and they fell swiftly into line.

It reminded her of the old days—days when they'd worked side by side, days when observing him bending antagonistic boards to his will had filled her with an intense admiration and excitement. Days long gone.

Throughout the meeting, his challenging gaze came to rest on her with increasing frequency. Was he daring her to protest? Daring her to resist his blatant appropriation of her position? If so, he'd have quite a wait. This wasn't the time. She'd choose her own battlefield. And when the chance came to thwart him she'd seize it with both hands. In the meantime, she'd sit back and watch. Watch for the best opportunity and try and figure out his next move.

'That's the last of it,' Cornelius announced, relief palpable in his voice. 'Sable?'

'If there's nothing further, we're adjourned,' she announced.

Several of the board members thrust back their chairs and stood with alacrity. Sable took her time. Making a final notation, she straightened her papers and slipped the file folder into her briefcase. She sensed Damien's approach, though she refused to look his way. Her lack of response didn't deter him. He planted a hand on her shoulder, his long fingers sliding over her silk jacket and probing the delicate bones beneath.

'Let's go,' he stated without preamble.

She attempted to slip from beneath his hold, but he didn't release her and reluctantly she glanced up, her cheek grazing his hand. The accidental touch sparked an unexpected flash of heat, catching her by surprise. The reaction must have surprised him just as much, for his grip tightened reflexively, his fingers biting deep.

'You want to leave?' she asked, her voice low and husky.

'Yes.' His hold eased, his thumb pressing into the taut muscles along the nape of her neck, massaging the tiny kinks.

She relaxed despite herself, the slow, unrelenting caress provoking a response she'd thought long dead... hoped was long dead. She didn't want him touching her, didn't want to feel the heady rush of emotions that that touch inevitably wrought. She wanted to hate him, not—— Her eyes widened.

'We can't go.' She hurried into speech. 'There's a board luncheon after the meeting. We're expected to attend.'

He shook his head. 'Not today. I'm sure everyone will understand that you and I have important matters to discuss. Private matters.'

She tensed beneath his hand. 'I didn't think there was anything more for us to discuss. You've made your desires perfectly clear.'

'Have I?' An enigmatic smile played about his mouth. His fingers drifted upward to stroke the side of her neck and the sensitive area just beneath her jaw. Then his hand fell away, leaving her strangely bereft. 'You're so certain?'

Shc caught the thread of amusement running through his words and stirred uneasily. Was she wrong? Were the requests he'd made here today only the beginning? What more could he want? She thought of Kyle again, and fear, fierce and primitive, shot through her. Her heartbeat quickened, racing with the desperate, instinctive need to protect her child from harm.

'Damien?' she whispered through numb lips. 'What now? What more could you possibly want?'

'The only way you'll find out is to come with me.' He inclined his head toward the board members clustered in the far corner like a flock of broody hens. 'Make our excuses and let's go.'

She hesitated. 'Go where?'

'To my office.'

She longed to refuse his request. Unfortunately, however, it wasn't a request—it was an order. She debated arguing but, knowing Damien as well as she did, it would prove pointless. He was a man accustomed to getting his way, no matter what it took. Besides, if she wanted to discover what more he expected from her, she'd better take his orders for the time being.

'Give me a moment,' she capitulated with as much grace as she could muster. She joined Cornelius and made her excuses for her abrupt departure. His lack of surprise told her the change of schedule wasn't entirely unexpected.

'Be careful,' Cornelius muttered in an undertone. 'I don't know why, but he has it in for you.'

'You've noticed?' she retorted drily. 'You're right, of course. And I'll be very careful.' Not that it would do her any good. Gathering up her briefcase, she returned to Damien's side. 'I'm ready,' she announced, though it was a blatant lie. She doubted she'd ever be ready for what he had planned.

He didn't reply, simply opened the door and waited for her to walk out of the conference room. She turned automatically in the direction of her office and he fell in beside her. 'Will I need my briefcase?' she asked.

'No. I prefer to keep it casual.' He opened the door to her office and followed her in. 'We'll have lunch and see if we can't hash out the finer details between us.'

The finer details of what? she couldn't help but wonder. She dropped her briefcase on her desk and turned to leave, but he didn't seem in any hurry. Instead he wandered through her domain, examining the few personal pieces she kept at the office. He paused by her credenza and frowned, picking up a lopsided clay vase painted in brash primary colors—Kyle's last birthday present to her. He turned to face her and she stiffened, waiting for the inevitable questions, waiting for his keen intellect to reach what seemed to her such an obvious and logical conclusion.

He flicked the wilted zinnias that drooped over the lip with his fingertip. 'Either you've acquired a liking for primitive art or you're showing unusually poor taste.'

'I like it,' she said, fighting to sound normal. 'Isn't that the most important consideration when it comes to acquiring art?'

'Not according to the investors I know.' To her intense relief, he returned the vase to her credenza, his attention drawn to the simple gold-framed photo pushed to the back of the odd assortment of knickknacks. A bitter smile twisted his mouth. 'Ah. The dearly departed husband. What the hell did you ever see in him?' he questioned, picking up the photo.

'He... he was kind.'

'Kind?' Damien's mouth curled. 'He was an insipid fool who fell apart at the first sign of trouble.'

'He was a wonderful businessman,' she insisted, leaping to Leonard's defense.

Damien didn't bother to conceal his contempt. 'His father was a wonderful businessman. Leonard wouldn't have known a blueprint from a spreadsheet. In the few short years he managed the Caldwell empire, he lost everything his father had built up except the construction company. And if good old Lenny had lived he'd have lost that too.' His expression turned savage. 'Instead, his wife has that honor.'

She paled at the threat. 'Why, Damien? Why did you go after him? Was it...because of me?'

'What the hell do you think?'

So it was. She'd suspected as much, but she'd hoped against hope that she'd been mistaken. Guilt ripped through her. Hawke Enterprises and Caldwell's had always been rivals, each a huge conglomerate that spread into all phases of construction and development. At one time their rivalry had been a friendly one, but all that had changed shortly after her...betrayal and her marriage to Leonard. With methodical calculation Damien had stripped the Caldwell empire of every holding except the construction company, bringing the Caldwell family to the brink of ruin.

And it was largely her fault.

She'd met Patricia Caldwell at a trade show and they'd struck up a friendly conversation. Of course, she'd been Patricia Samson then. And Sable had never once connected Patricia Samson, older friend and mentor, with Patricia Caldwell, cut-throat rival. Well, Sable had paid for that small mistake. And if Damien's threat was anything to go by, she'd continue to pay.

She took a step back, staring at him as though she'd never seen him before. 'I can't believe your vindictiveness,' she whispered in an appalled voice. 'You'd cripple Caldwell's in order to get at me?'

He tossed the photo back on to her credenza, his amusement a vicious thing. 'You think I took Leonard down just because of you?'

'You didn't go after him until we married,' she retorted defensively. 'What else should I believe?'

He stalked closer, towering above her, his fury barely held in check. 'Correction. I didn't go after Leonard until you stole for him. He made the first move. All I did was finish the game.'

'That isn't how it happened! Why won't you believe me?'

'You try my temper,' he informed her through gritted teeth. 'Caldwell admitted everything, even if you won't. If he couldn't stomach a fight, he shouldn't have started one. And neither should you.'

'Stop it, Damien!' she said with sharp-edged impatience, her anger rising to match his. 'You keep insisting I stole from you and I keep telling you it wasn't deliberate. I'm guilty of trusting someone I shouldn't have, of exercising poor judgement, I admit it. But I'm not guilty of theft. Never that.'

He folded his arms across his chest, his expression carved into hard, taut lines. 'When did you start playing games, Sable? Or is lying one of your talents, now, too?'

'Patricia was a friend——'

He approached, crowding so close that she could scarcely breathe. 'Such a good friend that you handed her the Anderson account. Then you thought, What the hell? and gave her Vincent Zepher and his chain stores, too.'

She didn't know why she bothered, but she had to try to convince him one final time. 'I didn't know she was Leonard's sister. She was married at the time——'

'And let's not forget that little venture I'd planned for Martinique. They all went to Caldwell's thanks to you.'

'Samson. She said her name was Samson. How was I to know she was related to Caldwell's?'

Before she realized his intention, he snagged her arm, slamming her up against him. 'A year's work! I lost a full year's work. And you? You ended up married to the president of the competition. Now tell me firing you was unjust, that going after Caldwell was out of line.'

'I was indiscreet, I admit that,' she conceded, fighting his hold. 'But I swear to you, it wasn't deliberate.'

He encircled her waist, tugging her into the cradle of his hips. 'You saw a chance for a bigger prize. You put yourself on sale to the highest bidder. And Caldwell paid the price. Marriage in exchange for insider information, isn't that the deal you worked out?'

'No!' She strained away from him, desperate to convince him, more desperate to escape his touch, to escape the unbridled heat of his body. 'No, I swear I didn't betray you. Not like that.'

'Cut the bull, Sable!' One hand snaked up the length of her spine to the back of her head, his fingers thrusting deep into her hair. 'The other execs at the company told me you were the one, but I didn't believe them. It couldn't be you, I said, and I'd prove it.'

She shook her head, tears leaping to her eyes. 'I didn't know what she intended. I swear, I didn't know.'

'So we set a trap. Did you ever figure that out? I gave you false information. Imagine my surprise when Caldwell came in just below that bid—that fictitious bid. I guess Lenny was even more surprised when he lost the contract. Did he ever blame you? He couldn't have, since he married you anyway.' His voice dropped, his words harsh with fury. 'And now, my sweet, it's time to reap your reward for selling me out.'

She froze, the fight draining out of her. 'What do you want?' she whispered apprehensively, her hands splayed across his chest.

'I want you to sell me your shares of Caldwell's.' His smile terrified her. 'But, more than that, I want you back in my bed.' And with that he lowered his head and took her mouth in a fierce, plundering kiss.

CHAPTER THREE

DAMIEN'S kiss was merciless. His mouth crushed Sable's with a dominating force, filled with ruthless male aggression. Shocked to the core, she didn't even think to struggle. Not that she could have. He held her with one powerful arm wrapped around her waist, his fingers biting into her hip and clamping her against the taut, muscular length of him. His other hand was fisted in her hair, tilting her head back to give him complete access to her mouth. And he took full advantage of that access.

He parted her lips, invading the silky warmth within, ravaging with a skill she hadn't experienced in five long years. He knew her so well, knew how to drive her insane with light, teasing caresses, how to rouse her to a fever pitch with deep, passionate strokes, how to carry her so close to the edge that she could only cling to him, pleading desperately for more.

She moaned deep in her throat and in that instant the kiss changed. His embrace was no less forceful, but now he used his familiarity with her to wring a response that she was helpless to suppress. They'd always had an intuitive sense of each other's needs, had used that perception to turn their lovemaking into a joining of monumental proportions. The knowledge that that connection still existed finally shattered her control. She could no more resist him than the tide could resist the pull of the moon.

'Damien, why?' she murmured in a broken voice. Her hands slid up his muscled chest to his shoulders and she clung to him as though her life depended on it.

'I have no choice,' he muttered against her lips. 'And neither do you.'

He kissed her again and this time she opened to him. It was as though a thousand suns had joined together as one. A liquid heat burned through her with white-hot strength, flooding her with an avid hunger, an explosive desire. For too long she'd been forced to suppress her needs. She'd put herself second for years now, playing the various roles demanded of her. Mother. Nurse. Businesswoman. But Damien cut through to the heart of her, to the woman smoldering just beneath the surface, setting free the passions she'd kept so carefully in check.

After an eternity, he eased his mouth from hers. But he didn't release her. His breath fanned her face, hot and rapid. 'Did you respond like this to Caldwell? Tell me you married him for love and not money, Sable. Tell me you aren't a thief. Look at me so I can see the expression in your black eyes when you pervert the truth.'

She bowed her head, his words knifing through her with surgical precision. Their kiss, such a wondrous connection for her, was for him just a means of slipping beneath her guard. Why hadn't she realized? She should have known. 'You bastard,' she whispered. 'Haven't you done enough to me, without this?'

His hand cupped the back of her head, forcing her to meet his gaze. She'd always thought of him as a sophisticate—clever, polished, worldly. But in that instant all she saw was raw male savagery beneath a tailored suit. 'Did Caldwell even know what he was missing?' Damien taunted. 'Somehow I doubt it. But you knew. How was it, Sable? How did you feel when he touched you, kissed you, made love to you? How did it feel to sell yourself, body and soul?'

She fought him then, shoving against his chest. She ignored the wrenching pain as her hair snagged in his fingers, struggling to escape the bruising grip at her waist that held her snug against his loins. 'Let me go! You have no right to say those things to me. I didn't steal from you. I didn't!'

'You're lying.' He caught her wrist in his hands, forcing her arms down to her sides, holding her immobile. 'But right now I don't give a damn.'

'Damien, don't,' she begged, knowing what he intended. But her plea fell on deaf ears. Slowly he lowered his head and captured her mouth once more, drinking as though parched. And to her utter shame she didn't resist. Instead she responded with wild abandon, as though his touch alone gave her the sustenance she needed, gave her life itself.

The sound of the door being flung open behind them resounded through the room like a gunshot. 'Mrs Caldwell? I——' Janine broke off, her horrified gasp revealing the extent of her shock.

This time when Sable attempted to jerk free Damien allowed it. He turned to face the appalled secretary. 'Don't you know how to knock?' he demanded, his fury causing the color to drain from Janine's face.

'I'm sorry! I—I——' Janine's pale blue eyes glinted behind her glasses.

Sable struggled to catch her breath. 'What do you want, Janine?' she asked gently.

'The—the letters you asked me to transcribe. They're ready for your signature. Mrs Caldwell, I—you——'

'Leave them on your desk and go ahead to lunch. I'll sign them later.'

'And knock next time,' Damien practically growled.

'Yes, sir!' Janine murmured, and scurried from the office.

The minute the door closed, Sable faced the bank of windows and wrapped her arms about her waist. What a disaster. Janine had been fiercely loyal to Leonard, her devotion bordering on the obsessive. Without question she'd see the embrace as a defection on Sable's part. Would she understand? It shouldn't matter, but somehow it did.

'I didn't mean for there to be witnesses,' Damien said, his approach unnervingly silent.

Knowing him, it was as close to an apology as she'd get. Her mouth curved into an ironic smile. 'Interesting phrasing,' she murmured, turning to face him. 'You don't say, I didn't mean for that to happen. No. You say, "I didn't mean for there to be witnesses." Tell me, Damien, does that imply you planned our little embrace from the start?'

He shrugged, his expression giving no clue as to his thoughts. 'The kiss was inevitable. You know that as well as I.'

'Perhaps.' She didn't bother to argue the point. 'But it's not appropriate at the office.' Reconsidering her comment, she laughed, the sound empty of humor. 'Now that I think about it, it's not appropriate, period.'

'Isn't it?' He sounded indifferent, though his gaze told a different story. It swept over her, his dark green eyes smoldering with barely tamped desire. 'Your hair's come undone,' he told her softly. 'No, don't bother fixing it. I like it that way. It goes with the rest of you.'

Her hands froze halfway to her head. 'What does that mean?'

He smiled in satisfaction. 'No lipstick, mouth swollen from my kisses, cheeks still flushed with passion, blouse half-open. You look... alive, instead of like every other businesswoman in this city.'

Her hands flew to her buttons. When had that happened? Oh, lord. Was that how Janine had seen her? Sable swallowed the nervous knot in her throat and lifted her chin. 'Then you'll have to excuse me while I freshen up.'

Before she could move toward the bathroom, a light tap sounded at the door that separated her office from Patricia's and he shook his head. 'Sorry. You don't have time. Lunch is ready.' Ignoring her protests, he caught her hand in his and drew her across the room toward the door.

'But that leads to——'

'My office.'

Of course. She didn't know why she hadn't realized it sooner. Without a doubt, she could once again thank Patricia for this latest development. When he'd said they'd go to his office, she'd assumed he meant at his Embarcadero headquarters. It had never occurred to her that he meant right next door.

'We're eating in here?' she asked, and then caught her breath as she stepped into the room.

Gone were the hideous animal heads and pelts. Gone was the malodorous clash of perfume and tobacco. Gone was the heavy, pretentious furniture. Even the carpet had been changed from cardinal-red to a misty green. Splashes of taupe and rust and forest-green gave the room color and warmth. And huge ficus trees, palms and colorful birds-of-paradise plants filled each corner, a sure sign that Lute lurked somewhere in the background.

'Where is he?' she demanded, forgetting everything but her need to see Lute.

'Here, Miss Sable.'

She spun round with a cry of delight. Lute stepped from the balcony bearing an empty tray. Setting it on Damien's desk, he held his hands out to her. She didn't hesitate. She hurried to his side and gave him a hug and kiss, even though she knew such demonstrativeness embarrassed him.

'I've missed you,' she said, tears springing unexpectedly to her eyes.

'And I you,' his gruff voice rumbled in her ear. He pushed her gently away and examined her face with a critical eye. 'Shadows,' he murmured with a sad shake of his head. 'Still so many shadows.'

She frowned in bewilderment. 'What are you talking about? What shadows?'

He didn't answer her question. Instead he stroked his narrow beard and lifted a bushy white eyebrow. 'You are hungry, yes? Your lunch is waiting on the balcony.'

Damien stepped forward. 'Thank you, Lute.'

Lute's reserve returned, falling about him like a cloak, his manner once more formal and correct. 'Will there be anything else?'

'Perhaps later.'

Lute picked up the tray and inclined his head. 'Very good. Enjoy your lunch.'

'I'm glad he's still with you,' Sable said as they stepped out on to the balcony. She skirted the small linen-covered table set intimately for two and crossed to the stucco half-wall that overlooked California Street.

Damien lifted an eyebrow. 'Where else would he go?'

'I don't know,' she admitted, fingering the colorful impatiens blossoms filling the planters topping the wall.

Far below a trolley bell rang out, attempting to clear a path as it fought its way through the heavy summer foot traffic. 'From what little he's said, I gather he doesn't have any family. Except you, of course.' She looked over her shoulder at him. 'He's been with you for a long time, hasn't he?'

'Since I was nineteen.' He joined her, resting a hip against the wall, his back to the view. Bright sunshine streaked through his hair, glinting in the browns and golds, dancing off the occasional russet strands. 'Why the sudden curiosity?'

'I've always been curious about Lute. But...' she shrugged '...I never wanted to offend him by asking questions about his past.' She shot Damien a mischievous glance. 'So I'll offend you instead. How did you meet?'

She didn't think he'd answer—during the years she'd known him it had been a taboo subject. But, almost pensively, he said, 'Lute saved my life.'

Sable suppressed a tiny gasp. 'Saved your life? How?'

'In a barroom fight. I was...wild. Crazy. And very drunk. I started an argument in some dive over in West Oakland. Not a smart move.'

'You went to a bar in West Oakland?' She couldn't picture it. He'd never talked much about his background. But she'd always imagined he'd come from a wealthy family—a degree from Stanford didn't come cheaply. 'And they served you liquor when you were only nineteen? That's illegal.'

'So's using a fake ID.'

She tilted her head to one side, a teasing smile playing about her lips. 'What were you doing, slumming?'

It was the wrong question. She realized it the minute she spoke. His face closed over, sudden irritation slashing deep lines from his cheekbones to the taut corners of his mouth. His eyes narrowed, the green like chips of ice. 'What would you know about slumming?' he bit out. 'You've always had everything handed to you.'

'That's not true!' she denied, stunned by the sudden attack. 'I've worked for what I have.'

'Is that what marriage to Lenny was? Work?' She flinched from the bitter cynicism in his gaze. He reached out then, snagging the silk lapel of her jacket with his index finger. 'Let me guess what sort of work.'

She jerked free, outrage bringing a hot rush of color to her cheeks. 'You know nothing of my life with Leonard. Nothing!'

'And you know nothing of my background,' he retorted pointedly.

She caught the implication and frowned in concern, her anger fading as she reconsidered her assumptions. From his reaction to her comment, she must be very wrong about his background. Which suggested he hadn't been slumming. And if that was the case, then . . . 'What in the world were you doing in that bar, Damien?' she asked softly.

He didn't avoid the question as she suspected he would. 'I suppose I was trying to kill myself,' he answered, and straightened. 'You ready to eat?'

'Eat?' She stared at him, stunned. 'No, I'm not ready to eat. What do you mean you were trying to kill yourself? Why? How?'

He wasn't going to answer, she could tell. 'I think that's a story for another time,' he said, confirming her suspicion.

As fruitless as she knew it would prove to be, she couldn't let the subject drop. 'What about Lute?' she asked. 'Will you tell me that much of the story?'

She could see the tension tightening the muscles across his shoulders and chest. His hands closed into fists, though his voice remained amazingly dispassionate. 'One of my attackers had a tire iron. Lute took the blow meant for me. If it had landed, I'd be dead. Instead Lute had his forearm shattered and his skull cracked open. He spent three months in a coma. When he woke up he'd lost his memory.'

'He didn't remember the attack?'

A strange smile played about his mouth. 'Oddly enough, that was the one thing he did recall. At least, he remembered me. Except for that brief moment in time, his past was a blank. Who he was, where he'd come from, even his name, had all been wiped clean.'

'But he has a name...'

'Lute was the first word that passed his lips after he woke. We never have found out what it means or its importance, if any. But it...stuck.'

Her brows drew together. 'And he's been with you ever since? You've never been able to find out anything more about his past?'

'He's happy with the life he has.'

It didn't quite answer her question, but she didn't see any point in pressing. 'Why didn't you tell me about this before?' she asked.

'Lute likes his privacy.'

She gazed at him in bewilderment. 'But you've told me now. Why, after all these years?'

He crossed to the table and removed the covers from the platters. 'I only tell his story if he wants it told.'

It took a few seconds for the full significance of that to sink in. Though once it had it left Sable more confused than ever. For some reason, Lute had allowed

Damien to reveal his story. But why now, after all this time?

'Let it go, Sable,' Damien insisted, an impatient edge to his words. 'It's getting late and I still have a lot of work to accomplish this afternoon. Let's have lunch and get down to business. That's why we're here, remember?'

'I remember,' she retorted, stung. 'But it's not like we're complete strangers. We have a past——'

'That's unfortunate, I agree,' he cut her off with cool precision. 'But I have neither the time nor the inclination to dwell on that past. And I wouldn't think you'd want to, either.'

Heartless bastard! How could he say that, as though all their memories were painful ones? 'You're right,' she managed to say, holding her head high. 'I don't.'

Without another word, she took the seat he held out for her, determined to keep all further conversation strictly business. Despite the awning that shaded them, the warmth of the midday July sun made it too hot for a jacket and she removed it. Damien followed suit, shedding his own jacket and loosening his tie. Next he unbuttoned the cuffs of his shirt and rolled them up his forearms to expose the Rolex she'd given him for his thirty-fifth birthday.

She lowered her eyes to hide her reaction, stunned that he still wore it. They'd been in Hawaii at the time, celebrating the finalization of the Simpson deal. He'd been astonished when she'd handed him the gift box and she'd found it highly amusing that he'd forgotten it was his birthday. What had followed had been one of the most treasured nights of her life. He'd carried her out to the rock pool behind the house they'd rented and made love to her beneath the stars, made love to her as though they were the only two people left on earth and that moment the only moment that mattered.

She bit down on her lip. Would she ever forget their years together? Would she at least come to view them with dispassion? Somehow she doubted it. No matter how Damien regarded the past, no matter how much he wanted to dismiss its importance, it linked them with bands as unbreakable as time itself.

'Wine?'

Her gaze jerked up to meet his. 'What?'

'Here.' He poured her a glass of Riesling. 'You look like you could use this. Where were you, Sable?'

'Hawaii,' she admitted, seeing no point in lying. She accepted the glass, her fingers gripping the stem so tightly that she feared it would snap off in her hand. 'Your watch,' she added as an explanation. 'It reminded me of Hawaii.'

His eyes narrowed, but, 'Drink the wine,' was all he said.

She didn't normally indulge during the day, but something in his expression demanded compliance and she took a hasty sip. It was delicious, light and tangy with a fruity aftertaste. 'Why do you still wear it?' she questioned, aware that she was treading on dangerous ground, but not caring. So much for sticking to business.

'It works.'

Well, she'd asked for it. What had she expected? For him to declare his undying devotion? She picked up her silverware and fixed her attention on the plate in front of her, infuriated by the sudden tears that blurred her vision. He must have sensed her loss of control for his wine glass slammed on to the table.

'Stop it, Sable! Stop the games. I gave you everything. Everything! And you chose to betray me. You left my arms and ran straight into Caldwell's. What I offered wasn't enough for you, was it? Lenny had more and so you gambled on him. Gambled and lost.'

'That's not true.' She looked up, heedless of the tears glittering in her eyes. 'I didn't turn to him until much later. He offered me a job when no one else would. I was desperate. I couldn't get work. The bills were mounting.'

'Don't hand me that. You couldn't have been all that desperate. I know for a fact you had a ring on your finger withins weeks of leaving me.'

'Six weeks,' she said in a hopeless voice. The day after she'd discovered she was pregnant, to be precise. Leonard had insisted they marry when she'd informed him of her condition and she'd been in such a state of shock, so emotionally distraught, that she hadn't the energy to put up much of an argument. In truth, she just hadn't cared.

'You never did go back to work,' he continued. 'Not until Lenny was on the verge of bankruptcy and you had no other choice.'

There was a reason why she hadn't continued working. She'd been obviously pregnant by then, and, afraid that someone would suspect the baby was Damien's, she'd spent the months after her marriage secluded in Leonard's house awaiting Kyle's birth... and missing Damien with an intensity that had wiped every other thought and consideration from her head. Afterward, she'd remained home caring for Kyle because Leonard had preferred it that way, and she hadn't been in much of a position to argue. In fact, it wasn't until his business had been in a shambles and he'd fallen too ill to continue on his own that she'd convinced him to let her help.

'Marrying Leonard was a last resort.' She despised the hint of entreaty that crept into her voice, but she couldn't seem to help it. 'I phoned you countless times, but you wouldn't take my calls, wouldn't see me.'

'What was the point?' he demanded. With a sharp expletive, he thrust back his chair and crossed to the stucco wall. He stood with his back to her, his shoulders stiff and straight beneath his crisp white shirt. 'I didn't trust myself to see you. I was rather...angry at the time.'

He stared down at the street corner far below, his jaw set in an uncompromising line, but she knew he didn't see the jugglers and pantomimists performing for the summertime crowds. He'd turned inward where she couldn't follow, revisiting some long-ago memory. She sensed he fought to keep his control, to maintain his distance emotionally. It was a distance he'd successfully held on to all through the years they were together, a distance that had threatened to destroy their relationship. It very well might have, if Patricia hadn't succeeded first.

'You didn't trust me, Damien. In all the years we were together, you never let me in, never once let down your guard.' She left the table and crossed to his side, daring to rest a hand on his arm. He shoved his fist into his pocket, his biceps bunching beneath her fingers. 'If you'd truly loved me, you'd have known I could never have betrayed you. And you would have moved heaven and earth to help prove my innocence.'

He didn't look at her as she'd hoped. His face remained a stony mask, revealing none of his thoughts. A sudden breeze whipped his hair from his brow, drawing her attention to his profile, to the arrogant sweep of his cheekbones, and to the full, sensuous mouth and squared, determined chin. A muscle jerked in his jaw.

'You married Caldwell. That told me everything I needed to know.'

'There was a reason!' she protested urgently. 'I——'

'Enough!' His control finally snapped, anger consuming him, the anger an even more persuasive deterrent than his icy reserve. He faced her then, his hands closing on her upper arms. 'You made your choice. You chose Caldwell. Now you have another choice to make. Let's hope you show more sense with this one.'

She refused to shrink from his fury, to allow him to intimidate her. 'What are you talking about?'

His eyes glittered with ruthless intent. 'Caldwell's. I want it and you're going to give it to me.'

'I'm supposed to simply hand my shares over to you and walk away?' she demanded in disbelief. 'Just like that?'

His thumbs began a relentless circling, smoothing the ivory silk of her shirt over her arms. 'No, not just like that. I'll pay you for your stock.'

'But at well below market price,' she guessed, struggling not to shiver beneath his touch.

He inclined his head. 'Very astute, Sable. There's also one other condition.'

Something in his tone warned her that she wouldn't like this latest stipulation and she stiffened. 'What is it?'

'I want you in my bed again.'

Her eyes widened and she fought her breath, unable to believe what she'd just heard. 'You can't be serious!'

'I'm dead serious.'

She shook her head, struggling to slip from his grasp. But he held her close, forcing her to face him. 'No, I won't! What makes you think I'd agree to something like that?'

His smile was cold...heartless. 'You'll agree. I promise you, you'll agree. Because if you don't I'll make your life a living hell. And after all the years we worked together you know I'm capable of it.'

'I know all too well,' she shot back.

He laughed in genuine amusement. 'Then you also know I'll do it.'

'But why?' The cry broke from her, filled with anger and hurt. 'Why are you doing this?'

His laughter died, replaced by grim intent. 'Have you any idea how much you cost my firm when you sold out to Caldwell's? It wasn't just a year's work you stole. People lost their jobs. Worse, it became common knowledge that there was a leak, which meant that I lost people's trust. And that, my love, is going to cost you.'

She didn't bother arguing, explaining her error in judgement yet again. If he hadn't listened earlier, he certainly wouldn't listen now. Besides, Caldwell's wasn't her only concern. She had Kyle's welfare to think of. If he ever found out they'd had a son together, he'd have the perfect weapon to use against her—a much more potent and damaging weapon than Caldwell's. And, considering how badly he wanted retribution for past wrongs, it was a weapon he wouldn't hesitate to use. Still... To sleep with him...

'I won't do it,' she whispered. It would kill her to be held in his arms again, to give in to his passion, knowing all the while that he took her for revenge instead of for love. 'I won't sell myself to you.'

He lifted an eyebrow. 'Why not? You sold yourself to Caldwell.'

She flinched, every scrap of color draining from her face. In a sudden twisting move, she jerked free of his arms and stepped back, wrapping her arms around her waist. It was as though he'd shattered something precious deep inside of her. Something irreplaceable. A treasure beyond price.

'Sable——'

She shook her head, raising her hand to hold him at bay. 'Don't say any more, Damien. Don't say another word. Just stay away from me.' To her relief, he made no attempt to touch her, but he watched her as though concerned. Concerned? She closed her eyes. Not a chance. He'd just proved how little he cared.

His cruelty actually had a salutary effect, she discovered. It killed all emotion, laying bare her choices. Choices she needed to weigh carefully. Damien didn't know about Kyle. He couldn't, not when she logically analyzed all he'd done and said so far. Which meant that he'd only come after her to get his hands on Caldwell's and exact some petty revenge. Well, he could have his revenge. If it would protect her son, then she'd give it to him without hesitation. For the longer Damien remained in her life, the greater the chances that he'd find out about Kyle. And that was one risk she couldn't afford to take—no matter what the personal cost.

She opened her eyes and looked at him with unwavering resolve. 'If I sell, and I stress the word "if", will that end things between us?'

'What do you mean?'

'If I agree to your..."conditions", will you leave me alone?' Her voice trembled, but she couldn't seem to control it. Not when it took every ounce of her willpower just to stand here and make such a heartrending offer. 'Will you get out of my life and stay out, permanently. Never contact me again, never phone or...or see me?'

He stilled, eyeing her with a predatory watchfulness that terrified her. She could practically see him analyzing her request, seeing the hidden meaning beneath the surface words. 'What are you up to, Sable?' he murmured.

'Having you appear in my life so unexpectedly is . . . is distracting,' she invented with a swiftness born of desperation. 'I want to make sure it doesn't happen again. I want to get on with my life without having to look over my shoulder to see what you're up to. Is that such an unreasonable request?'

'And in exchange for my leaving you alone you'll sell me Caldwell's at a cut rate? You'll sleep with me?'

She shrugged, the movement stiff and unnatural . . . revealing. 'Even at a cut rate I'll have more money than I can ever spend. Of course, I'd need time to consider the rest of your offer, but I think we can come to terms.' She shot him a warning glance. '*If* you consent to my stipulation.'

'So agreeable. I wonder why . . .?' He caught her chin in his hand, tilting her head so that she couldn't avoid his gaze. 'What are you hiding?'

'N-nothing! I'm not hiding anything.'

'Liar,' he accused softly. 'You should be fighting me tooth and nail. Instead you're rolling over in defeat.'

'Is that what you want? A fight?' She turned her head to the side and his fingers slid along her jaw with tantalizing gentleness before dropping away. 'Sorry to be so uncooperative. But, as you've already pointed out, I know you, Damien. And I know what you're capable of. Why should I put myself through that? It doesn't make sense.'

'All very logical,' he conceded. 'But somehow I don't quite buy it. I can see the panic in your eyes, Sable. In your face. Tell me what you're hiding.'

'I'm not hiding anything,' she lied frantically. 'Do you want Caldwell's or don't you? I'd think you'd be pleased that I'm giving in, giving you what you want.'

He glanced away, effectively concealing his thoughts from her. 'You're right, of course,' he said after an endless minute. 'We'll finalize the details tomorrow.'

'And if I sell you'll stay out of my life from then on?' She wanted that point crystal-clear.

'I'll see to it that our paths never cross again . . . if you sell.' He looked at her then, his eyes alive with both threat and promise. '*And* if you sleep with me.'

Dear lord, what had she just agreed to? She might as well have signed her own death warrant. 'Fine.' She took a hasty step back, then another and another. If she didn't escape soon, she'd crack wide open, ruining everything. 'If you'll excuse me, I have work to do.'

'You haven't eaten,' he pointed out.

She glanced at the table and quickly away, her stomach churning. She couldn't face eating with him, couldn't handle exchanging polite, meaningless conversation. Not after all he'd done. 'Please make my excuses to Lute. It would seem I've lost my appetite.' And with that she turned and bolted, aware of his intent green eyes boring into her back every inch of the way.

By the time Sable arrived home, she could barely put one foot in front of the other. She tossed her briefcase on to the living-room couch, her shoulders drooping from a combination of exhaustion and stress.

'Mommy!' an excited voice called from the stairway—a voice that brought her more joy and happiness than she'd ever thought possible.

She turned, weak tears trembling on the ends of her lashes. 'Kyle,' she called, dropping to her knees as he raced into the room. An instant later she held an armful of heaven to her breast. She closed her eyes, resting a cheek on the top of his head. His thick dark hair tickled her nose and she smiled, relaxing for the first time that day. She could face any adversity, overcome any obstacle, so long as she had him to come home to each day.

'You're late,' he accused, wriggling free of her embrace and tugging at the pajama bottoms that threatened to slide down his narrow hips.

'I'm sorry, sweetheart. But I'm home now. Have you had dessert?' She held out a hand. 'Why don't we scrounge some milk and cookies from the kitchen and you can tell me all about your day?'

He hesitated, his teeth worrying at his bottom lip. 'Nanna said no more,' he confessed with a reluctant sigh, clearly torn between being honest and receiving the unexpected treat.

'I'll tell Nanna it's OK,' she assured him solemnly.

'OK,' he agreed, and grinned, reminding her with heartbreaking suddenness of Damien.

For the first time she blessed the fact that he'd inherited her coloring. During the pregnancy she'd prayed for a child with tawny hair and vivid green eyes, and though his features were the image of Damien's they were hidden beneath a mop of ebony curls and flashing black eyes. Only under close scrutiny could she see the familiar squared jaw and high, sweeping cheekbones. Even the wide, sculpted mouth was identical to his father's.

He slipped his fingers into hers and tugged at her hand. 'Come on!' he urged, and she allowed herself to be towed in the direction of the kitchen.

Maybe it was listening to Kyle's childish chatter or her intense exhaustion. Perhaps it was the pain of seeing Damien again and realizing how thoroughly he despised her. She never quite knew what decided her, but halfway through her second chocolate-chip cookie she reached a decision.

Tomorrow she'd go in and talk to Damien. She'd insist that they come to terms. She'd agree to sell him her interest in Caldwell's at whatever price he offered—she'd even consent to sleeping with him. She'd do anything he asked, if only he promised to stay out of her life. She gazed down at the top of her son's head and caught her breath. To protect Kyle... That was worth far more than her Caldwell stock. She closed her eyes, fighting to hold her tears at bay.

It was even worth more than her pride and self-respect.

CHAPTER FOUR

KNOWING she wouldn't get a wink of sleep, Sable spent the entire night planning her speech, marshaling her arguments, and considering all possible alternatives. The next morning she wasted no time, but went directly to Damien's office, prepared to negotiate her release. Pushing open the connecting door, she stared in frustration at the empty room.

He wasn't there.

A small sound caught her attention and she turned to discover an attractive blonde standing by Damien's credenza, her arms loaded with files. 'May I help you?' the woman asked.

Sable nodded. 'Perhaps you can. I'm Sable Caldwell. I'd hoped to speak to Damien.'

'It's a pleasure to meet you, Mrs Caldwell.' The woman put down the files and offered her hand. 'I'm Lisa, Mr Hawke's secretary. I'm afraid he won't be in today.'

'He won't...?' Sable could only stare. 'But I'm supposed to meet with him.'

Lisa stirred uncomfortably. 'Yes, Mrs Caldwell. He mentioned you might stop by. He said that you could call him if it was urgent, but he'd prefer to put your meeting on hold until tomorrow.'

'Tomorrow...?' Sable's mouth snapped closed. She refused to reveal the extent of her outrage, refused to utter the words trembling on the tip of her tongue. He'd done this deliberately. He knew they were supposed to get together, to discuss terms. And he had to guess, even if he didn't know for certain, how anxious she'd be about this meeting. Undoubtedly this was one more way to torture her, to keep her off-balance. 'Thank you, Lisa,' she managed to say in gracious tones. 'It's not in the least urgent. I'll speak to him tomorrow.'

'Yes, Mrs Caldwell,' Lisa murmured, and, with a final uncertain glance over her shoulder, went back to sorting the files.

Stifling a sigh, Sable returned to her office and shut the door. How thoroughly deflating. She crossed to her desk and collapsed into her chair. Swiveling to face the windows, she stared blindly at the San Francisco skyline. Had he known she would have a speech all prepared, would be determined to battle for better terms? Probably. He had an unerring instinct for reading people and had used it to stunning effect during the years she'd worked for him. Now he was using that instinct in his dealings with her. It was incredibly unsettling.

A light tap sounded at her outer door and Ryan Matheson, Caldwell's project director, stuck his head in. 'Excuse me, Sable,' he said. 'Do you have a minute?'

She swung around and smiled. 'Of course. Come in and have a seat. What can I do for you?'

'This is rather awkward,' he began, clearly ill at ease.

If Damien was involved—and she didn't doubt for a minute that he was—she suspected it would prove to be very awkward indeed. 'Sit down, Ryan. I assume this is about the report Damien requested.'

He sank into the chair in front of her desk. 'Yes, it is. Mr Hawke spoke to me at length about Caldwell's having lost the final phases of Luther's condo development and asked that I prepare a report accounting for his defection.'

Reading between the lines, Sable imagined Damien had done a lot more than just speak to Ryan. Chewed him out was more likely. 'He's very concerned about the situation,' she said in classic understatement.

Ryan ran a distracted hand through his rumpled brown hair. 'As am I. The problem is, Luther isn't the only job we've lost in the last year. Though until recently I seemed alone in my concern——' He broke off, shooting her a nervous glance. 'Miss Caldwell said... well...'

Patricia had told him not to press the matter, she guessed, hoping perhaps that ignoring the situation would make it go away. 'That's no longer the case,' Sable explained gently. 'The entire board supports Damien's request.'

'I'm relieved to hear it.' He cleared his throat. 'Which is why I came directly to you.'

She frowned in bewilderment. 'I'm not sure I understand, Ryan. What's the problem?'

He fidgeted, clutching a sheaf of papers between sweaty hands. 'Well... I've spoken to Luther a number of times, trying to pin down the real reason for his jumping ship, asking if there was anything we might have done that could be responsible for his switching to A.J. Construction. I mean, I've looked at everything—costs, workmanship, materials, union problems. The works. And there's nothing there. Except...'

'Except?' she prompted, completely mystified by his nervousness.

'Yes... Well...' He fingered his collar, then broke into speech. 'Except that they turned down our bid. It was sorta peculiar. Very last-minute. One day we had it in the bag and the next day we were out.'

'I don't suppose you could be more specific?' she asked, struggling to conceal her exasperation. 'What do you suspect happened?'

He looked at her, then quickly away. 'I think we were underbid.'

She didn't understand his nervousness. 'That happens all the time in this business, doesn't it? I mean, it's unfortunate, but——'

'It doesn't happen. At least, not like this,' Ryan cut in abruptly. 'We built the first three phases for Luther. That alone should practically guarantee our getting the final contract. Plus, they're not admitting to any problems with the actual construction. In fact, we've met all our deadlines and come in under budget. So why dump us? It doesn't make sense. Our site manager is still in shock. He can't explain the sudden switch. I mean, we were caught flat-footed. And... and there have been rumors.'

'What sort of rumors?' she asked uneasily.

'Rumors of a leak.'

'A *leak*?' She jackknifed upright in her chair, staring in disbelief. 'There must be some mistake.'

He cleared his throat. 'There's no mistake. From what I hear A.J. Construction didn't just underbid us, they walked in with our package in one hand and a list of bargains and perks in the other. They offered a better deal on every aspect of the project, using our prospectus as a guideline.' His gaze flitted about the room, never once settling on her. 'As you know, that information is supposed to be highly confidential. I can't explain how they got hold of it, but I thought you should be made aware of the problem since my report to Mr Hawke... I hope you understand... I really have no choice, given the situation.'

Icy tendrils of dread snaked through her, settling like a lead weight in the pit of her stomach. 'You're telling me that the possibility of a leak will figure prominently in your report?'

He finally looked at her, the hint of pity in his expression impressing on her the seriousness of the situation more clearly than anything he'd said to date. 'That's precisely what I'm telling you.'

'I appreciate the warning.' She fought to think, to scramble for a plan of action. How was this possible? If Ryan was right, who could be responsible? A sudden thought occurred to her. 'I'd like a list of all personnel who had access to this bid information.'

'Everyone?' he asked.

She didn't hesitate for a minute. 'Every last person, including you and me.' She leaned forward, leveling her gaze on the project director. 'Assuming there has been a leak, I want to find out who is responsible, and fast—if possible, before that report hits Damien's desk.'

He eyed her suspiciously for several long minutes, as though assessing her sincerity. Slowly he relaxed. 'I'll draw up the list,' he said, but then a note of apprehension crept into his voice. 'Sable, you'd better know. The facts won't be easy to refute. And suspicion is going to fall on the most obvious target. And I don't have to tell you who that would be.'

Her eyes widened. No, he didn't. His expression said it all. If she didn't find out who had leaked the information, she'd hang for it based on past history alone. And Damien would be first in line with the lynching rope. Panic threatened to overwhelm her. Her hands curled into fists, her nails biting into her palms. She had to calm down and think. First things first. 'When will you complete your final report?' she questioned tautly.

'Mr Hawke said to have it on his desk by the end of the month. That gives you three weeks.' He lowered his voice. 'Three weeks, assuming we don't lose any more contracts the way we lost this one. If we do... Sable, when this comes out, the board's going to ask some tough questions——' He broke off, staring miserably at the floor. 'And you'd better have the right answers.'

'I understand.' It was a lie. She didn't understand at all. 'And Ryan?'

He looked up. 'Yes.'

'Thank you.'

'I'm...I'm sorry.' He stood up. 'If there's anything else I can do...'

She inclined her head. 'You'll be the first to know.'

The minute the door closed behind him, she reached for the phone and put a call through to Alex Johnson, president of A.J. Construction. To her frustration, he was out until late that afternoon, but his assistant promised to relay the urgency of her message. The rest of the day she spent liaising with Ryan Matheson in an attempt to draw up a list of possible suspects.

The very act made her physically ill.

By six that night Sable had reached the end of her rope. She closed her eyes and leaned back in her chair, forced to concede temporary defeat. She'd gone over and over the list that she and Ryan had formulated. Every last name on it was someone she trusted and respected. What in heaven's name was she supposed to do next? How could she uncover the truth? The phone rang at her elbow and she snatched it up, praying it would be Alex.

'Johnson here,' the caller announced abruptly. 'You phoned, Mrs Caldwell?'

'You can't be surprised to hear for me,' she commented, deciding to get right down to business. Why waste time on pleasantries when not one aspect of this whole situation was in the least pleasant? 'Not once news of the leak . . . leaked.'

He laughed, a great booming sound of genuine amusement. 'I guess not. Certain individuals at Caldwell's must be major league ticked about that. Snatched Luther right from under your noses, didn't we?'

'With a little help,' she said drily.

'Is that what you're calling about?'

'Of course.'

'You want me to keep my—er—source confidential, is that it?'

Her brows drew together. 'No! I want you to tell me where you got your information. Who gave you the copy of our prospectus?'

A long moment of silence greeted her response. 'This is some sort of joke, right?'

'No, it's not a joke,' she snapped. 'You have the Luther project and nothing's going to change that. But, as a businessman, you can appreciate our predicament, I'm sure. We need to find the source of your information. Are you willing to help us?'

'Are you taping this call?'

'No, of course not.'

'Are we on speakerphone or something?'

'Our conversation is completely confidential. No one even knows I've called you.'

'Then you're wasting your breath.'

'You won't tell me who's responsible for giving you a copy of our bid?'

'You already know who give us the information.' He spoke sharply, impatiently.

She sighed in frustration. 'Mr Johnson, if I already knew, I wouldn't be calling you, now would I?'

'I'd say that depended.'

'Depended on what?'

'On whether you were hoping this call would cover your backside. Why the game, Mrs Caldwell? *You* gave us Caldwell's prospectus. Did you think I hadn't been told? Use your head, woman! I'm the one who authorized that hefty little sum we paid you. So quit wasting my time with pointless phone calls. And don't bother me again unless you have more information you want to sell.'

'No, wait! Please!'

It was too late; he'd already hung up. The receiver fell from her hand, clattering into the cradle. He thought she'd sold him the information, she realized in disbelief. But...how? She didn't understand any of this. How could he think she was to blame? Could someone be using her name? If so, who? And why? A sob caught in her throat and she pressed trembling fingers to her mouth, fighting the urge to break down and weep. What in heaven's name was she to do now?

'Sable?'

Shc jumped, a soft cry escaping before she could prevent it. Damien stepped from the shadows and she stared at him with huge, panicked eyes. 'You startled me,' she managed to say.

He removed his suit coat and loosened his tie, his green eyes watchful. 'What's wrong, Sable?'

'Nothing. Why...why do you ask?'

'Your phone call. From what little I overheard you sounded rather desperate. And you look...' He tilted his head to one side, his brows drawing together. 'You look frightened. What is it? What's wrong?'

For an insane moment, she considered telling him everything, throwing herself on his mercy and begging for help. She stopped herself just in time. How could she have forgotten, for even one tiny minute, that Damien had no mercy? To hand him the information about A.J. Construction would be as good as insuring her own destruction. It would be just the weapon he'd need to ruin her completely. And she didn't doubt for one minute that he'd take full advantage of it.

'It's just a small problem,' she murmured, keeping her response deliberately vague. 'Nothing I can't handle.'

'You sure?'

She stood up, praying her legs would hold her. 'Positive.' He didn't believe her, she could tell. She wished he weren't so observant, or that she was better at dissembling. 'What are you doing here? Lisa said you wouldn't be in until tomorrow.'

'I had some files I needed to pick up. I also hoped to find you here.'

'Why?'

'So I could invite you to dinner.'

'Why?' she repeated, this time with a suspicious edge.

His eyes narrowed. 'Interesting answer. Most people respond to a dinner invitation with a polite yes or no.'

'We're not most people,' she pointed out. 'And after yesterday I'm sure you can understand my hesitation.'

He tossed his suit coat and briefcase on the chair in front of her desk. 'If you'd rather, we can wait until tomorrow and have our discussion here, at the office. Or we can go out, have a relaxing dinner and negotiate in private.' He folded his arms across his chest. 'Which would you prefer?'

With all that had happened today, she'd completely forgotten about Damien's ultimatum. A hysterical laugh bubbled up inside her. Such wonderful choices. She could sell her shares in Caldwell's and end up as the scapegoat for the leaks plaguing the company, or she could stay, try and find the real villain and suffer the consequences Damien threatened for not selling.

'Dinner would be fine, thanks.' To her horror, her voice broke. He took a quick step toward her, but she snatched up the phone, holding it to her chest like a shield. 'Let me make a quick phone call and I'll be ready.' To her relief, the betraying wobble vanished and she sounded almost normal.

'Sable, what——?'

'Not now!' She took a quick gulping breath. 'Please, Damien. Not now.'

She sensed that he wanted to argue, to force her to confide in him. But to her relief he didn't press her. With a reluctant nod, he returned to his office, presumably to get his files. She didn't waste any time in placing a call to Millie Trainer, Kyle's 'Nanna', to warn her of the change in plans. She also had a swift, one-sided conversation with Kyle. 'I'll see you when I get home.' Noisy smacking sounds blasted her through the earpiece and a smile broke free for the first time that day. 'I love you too, sweetheart. Bye.'

Just as she hung up, Damien returned. He crossed the room and dropped a handful of files into his leather case. 'I didn't realize I'd be ruining your plans for the evening when I invited you to dinner,' he commented.

How much of her conversation had he overheard? she wondered. Too much, judging from the black expression darkening his face. 'You aren't ruining my plans,' she said with amazing calm. 'You've just postponed them.'

His mouth tightened. 'I see.' He picked up his briefcase and slung his suit coat over his shoulder. 'Shall we go? I have a car waiting.'

She nodded in acknowledgement and led the way to the elevators. Standing at his side within the confining cubicle as they rode to the underground garage, she couldn't help but remember yesterday morning—remember how it had felt to have her back pressed tight against his broad chest, his warm breath stirring the curls at her temple, the slow, possessive stroke of his hand stealing up her hip as his fingers fanned intimately across her abdomen. She shivered. It seemed as if an eternity had passed since then.

A moment later the doors parted and he motioned her toward the sleek limousine idling a few steps away. 'When did you start using a driver?' she inquired with a saccharine-sweet smile, praying he wouldn't sense how disturbing she'd found those brief, intrusive memories.

He didn't take offense, as she expected. Instead he shot her an impatient glance. 'Can the wisecracks, Sable. You know I only use the car when I'm entertaining clients.' He opened the door before the chauffeur had a chance. 'Get in.'

She obeyed, sliding across the plush leather seats. 'Is that why you canceled our meeting today?' she asked, more abruptly than she'd intended. 'Because you were busy entertaining clients?'

He joined her, sitting far too close for comfort. He shot her a sharp glance and sudden understanding dawned in his eyes. 'It wasn't deliberate, Sable,' he said in a surprisingly gentle voice. 'This appointment came up without warning and I couldn't postpone it. Didn't Lisa tell you to call if you needed to speak to me?'

Sable stared out the window as they left the garage, his unexpected kindness more difficult to deal with than his animosity. 'She told me.' They turned onto Montgomery Street, working their way toward the bay. Rush-hour traffic had only eased slightly, making it slow going.

'Besides, I thought an extra day would give you time to think, to consider all your options.'

She rounded on him. 'You didn't leave me any options, in case you've forgotten.'

'I gave you two: to sell——'

'Or to suffer the consequences,' she cut in harshly.

His searching gaze settled on her face once again. 'What's wrong, Sable?' he murmured.

She stiffened. She didn't want his understanding, his consideration. She could stand up to his fury; she'd fall apart beneath his tenderness. 'You know what's wrong. You've put me in an untenable position. What do you expect? For me to act as though nothing's happened, that dinner tonight is a pleasant diversion?'

'No. But I do expect a certain level of professional behavior.'

That tore it! Her gaze flashed upward to lock with his. 'If this were a business predicament, I'd be thoroughly professional. But this isn't business. This is personal and you damned well know it. So I'm afraid you're stuck with a less than professional response.'

She regretted losing her temper the moment she saw Damien's reaction. He looked like a tiger that had just sprung from its cage.

'You want to drop the pretense, is that it? Fine,' he practically snarled. 'I'm happy to play hardball. But don't complain if it gets rough. Remember you asked for it.'

'I didn't ask for a thing!' The words burst from her. 'This whole situation is your idea, your decision. You want to hurt me and this is the means you've chosen to do it.'

'Hurt you?' A small, enigmatic smile touched his mouth. 'How is that possible? You have to care in order to be hurt.'

Before she could rally sufficiently to respond, the limousine eased to a stop and the driver opened the door. Stepping from the vehicle, Sable stiffened, realizing they'd arrived at a pier where a familiar-looking launch rocked against its mooring. She spun around. 'Where are we going?' she demanded.

'You know where.'

She paled. There were only two possibilities, neither one acceptable. 'Damien, no. Don't do this to me.'

He caught her arm and urged her toward the boat. 'I'm offering dinner, Sable, not torture. This will give us the privacy we need.'

'So will my office.' She stopped at the bottom of the ramp leading to the launch and turned to face him. 'Why don't we have this conversation tomorrow?'

He stood square in the center of the gangway, blocking her line of retreat. 'I explained that to you. I don't want anyone from Caldwell's overhearing our conversation.' He spoke in quiet, implacable terms. 'That means it's either Nikolai's or my place. Now, which will it be?'

The alternatives went from bad to worse. She glanced longingly at the limo. 'Once again, you leave me no choice.'

He didn't move. 'Which will it be?' he repeated.

She sighed. 'Nikolai's.'

'I thought as much.' He assisted her aboard. 'Inside the cabin or out?'

'Outside,' she decided. 'I don't often get the chance to enjoy the sun and sea air.'

She settled in the padded seat close to the bow. A moment later, they cast off. A stiff breeze caught at her hair, teasing the curls about her face into total disarray. But she didn't care. Despite the tension of the coming evening, she slowly unwound beneath the waning rays of the sinking sun. Off toward the entrance of the bay, ghostly tendrils of fog crept steadily across the water toward them, enshrouding most of the Golden Gate Bridge so that only the bright red peaks of the uppermost spans rose above the roiling mist.

'That's better.' Damien spoke from behind her.

She brushed a stray curl from her eyes and glanced back at him. 'What's better?'

'You're beginning to relax.'

'It's been a stressful day,' she confessed.

'I could tell. You looked like you'd shatter into a thousand pieces at the first wrong word.' Without warning, he removed his suit coat and dropped it around her shoulders.

It was such an intimate gesture, possessive, protective, strangely arousing. The warmth from his body still clung to the encompassing folds of the jacket and his cologne teased her senses. She shut her eyes to conceal the sudden rush of tears. 'I still might shatter,' she surprised herself by admitting. 'I'm feeling a bit delicate.' But how much of that feeling could be attributed to the events of that day and how much to Damien's presence she couldn't say.

'You want to talk about it?'

She shook her head, emotion closing her throat. 'It's nothing you can help with,' she told him in a husky voice. 'I have to take care of it on my own.' She sensed his withdrawal, but it couldn't be helped. How could she trust him to help when he'd made his desire for revenge so clear?

They didn't converse after that. Sable didn't mind. She enjoyed being on the sea again even if it was in the confines of the bay. She tipped her head back and watched the gulls dip and wheel overhead, relishing the rock and sway of the boat as it motored through the choppy waters. All too soon they approached the lights and bustle of the village of Sausalito. She adored the winding streets and specialty shops of the small, Mediterranean-style community. She and Damien had whiled away many an hour at some of the sidewalk cafés. The launch bypassed the center of town and continued further north, coming alongside the narrow pier by Nikolai's.

Nikolai himself came out to greet them, shaking hands with Damien and kissing Sable effusively on both cheeks. 'It is good to see you together again,' he declared in his deep, booming voice. He wrapped a beefy arm around her waist and guided her up the ramp to the restaurant. 'Come. Your table is ready. And dinner tonight... well, let me just say it will be a surprise and a delight.'

'It always is with you,' Damien commented.

'This is true. So tell me, Mr Hotshot Businessman, what have you done to my Sable?' Nikolai glanced over his shoulder and glared, while Sable watched on in amusement. It never ceased to amaze her, the latitude Damien allowed his friend. 'She looks like she carries the weight of the world on her shoulders. This is your fault, yes?'

'Some of it,' Damien conceded, with a humorous glint in his eyes. 'But I believe today's weight is all her own doing.'

'This is not good. I won't stand for it on your first time back to my restaurant in so long. Wait one minute.' Nikolai snapped his fingers. 'I have just the thing. Something that will make her forget all problems for the night.'

'*Her* is still here, in case you've forgotten,' Sable remarked drily. 'And I'm fine, thank you very much.'

'Fine? Hah! You make a good joke.' Nikolai threw open a side door that led into a private parlor overlooking the bay. 'Sit and relax. I will return with a small treat in a few minutes.'

The room he showed them to was one of two on the premises and might have graced any fine home. It was small and intimate, with a table set up in an alcove affording a gorgeous view of Richardson Bay and Angel Island. And further in the distance glittered the lights of San Francisco. Off to one side of the room, chairs and a love seat were grouped in a secluded semicircle around a fireplace. Instead of a fire, a huge dried-flower arrangement filled the grate, the refreshing aroma of eucalyptus teasing the senses.

Determined to postpone the discussion that she knew Damien was impatient to begin, Sable excused herself to go and freshen up. In the bathroom, she splashed cold water on her face and retouched her makeup, using a heavy hand with the blush. For reasons she couldn't explain, she also unpinned her hair, leaving the dark curls loose about her shoulders. Stepping back from the mirror, she nodded. It helped. She didn't appear nearly as drawn.

Returning to the private dining room, she found that Nikolai had brought two huge goblets filled with a green iced drink. Sections of tropical fruit, a paper umbrella and half a dozen tiny plastic monkeys festooned the rim in crazed abandon.

'What is it?' she questioned, eyeing the concoction suspiciously.

'It's called Nikolai's Nectar and he warned that he won't bring our dinner until you'd drained the glass.'

'Uh-oh. Have you tried it?'

He shook his head, his expression amused. 'I thought I'd wait for you.'

'Coward.' It took two hands just to lift the goblet. She took a quick sip from the straw and nearly choked. 'If I drain what's in this glass, I won't be able to eat any dinner because I'll have passed out,' she observed.

'I suspected as much. But a little won't hurt you.' He picked up his own glass and crossed to the love seat. 'Come and sit down and enjoy the view. Our discussion can wait a while.'

Until she'd consumed more of Nikolai's Nectar? she wondered in a rare moment of cynicism. Not likely. As soon as she figured out a safe place to dump it, half this drink would be plant fertilizer. Or would that kill the poor plant? She nibbled at her lower lip. She'd just have to risk it.

Instead of joining Damien on the love seat, she kicked off her pumps and curled up on the padded window seat near by. If she was to keep her head, she needed to stay as far from him as possible. She took another sip of her drink. And she needed to slow down her consumption of this green stuff. A huge potted philodendron stood within reach and she snuck out a finger to see if it was real.

'Don't bother,' Damien said. 'It's fake. You'll just have to drink it.'

'Is there anything that escapes your notice?' she complained, jerking her hand back.

'No, nothing.' He stood and walked toward her. His voice lowered, deepened. 'Your hair is on fire.'

She stared up at him, her breath catching in her throat. 'What?'

'The lights outside the window are red.' He reached out, his fingers brushing back the curls framing her face. 'They're caught in your hair, like hot embers licking at a nugget of coal.' He towered over her—large, indomitable and more attractive than any man had the right to be.

She closed her eyes to shut out the potent sight. 'Damien, don't,' she whispered, gripping the icy glass between her fingers. 'Not tonight. I can't bear it.'

'Look at me.' His thumb brushed her cheekbone and she trembled helplessly. 'Look at me,' he repeated. Slowly she lifted her gaze to his. He stared down at her, his green eyes darkening with unwavering resolve. 'It's too late to stop. We play this game to the bitter end. Fight me and you'll only make it more difficult for yourself.'

'Don't do this,' she pleaded. 'You'll regret it. I swear you will. Just let me go.'

He shook his head before she'd even finished speaking. 'I can't. I won't.'

She really hadn't expected any other response. She struggled to recover her composure. 'You...you said we didn't have to discuss business now,' she reminded him. 'Have you changed your mind?'

'No. We'll wait until after dinner as agreed,' he said. 'There's something else I'd rather discuss, anyway.'

She gazed at him apprehensively. 'What is it?'

A final glimmer of daylight caught the steely glitter of his eyes before dusk overtook the room, plunging his face into shadow. 'Who the hell is Kyle?' he demanded.

CHAPTER FIVE

PANIC set in and Sable shrank into the deepening shadows, hoping her expression wouldn't betray her. Thank heavens no one had bothered to switch on the lights. 'How do you know about Kyle?' Even to her own ears her voice sounded thready and nervous.

'Your phone conversation.'

'You listened?' She couldn't believe his nerve.

'Your voice carried,' he corrected her. 'Close the door next time you want privacy. Now, who is he?'

Sable lifted the glass to her lips and took a long, desperate swallow, stalling for time. 'That's none of your business,' she said at last.

'You're right. It's not. Is he your lover?'

'No!'

'He lives with you, doesn't he?'

'Yes!' She took a quick, steadying breath. 'I repeat, it's none of your business.'

'Who is he, Sable? You might as well tell me. Because if you don't I'll find someone who will.'

She stiffened. It wouldn't be too difficult to find that someone, either. Quite a few people at Caldwell's knew about Kyle. Eventually, Damien would find a chatty employee willing to talk about the son she'd given birth to a mere seven months after her marriage to Leonard. It was a small wonder he hadn't found out already. And once he did discover the truth it wouldn't take him long to put two and two together and figure out why she'd been so anxious to keep Kyle's existence a secret. After all, if he were Leonard's son, why the big mystery?

No, she didn't dare risk telling Damien anything. His anger at learning about the leaks five years ago would be nothing compared to his anger should he learn about Kyle. She licked her lips, tasting the fruity tang of her iced drink. With luck it would give her a bit of courage, because she needed every scrap she could muster—even the temporary kind courtesy of Nikolai's Nectar.

She lifted her glass, meeting his fierce gaze over the rim with a calm she was far from feeling. 'Kyle's a relative.'

His eyes narrowed. 'I thought you didn't have any relatives.'

'Well, you thought wrong.' Her voice sharpened. 'And I won't answer any more of your questions about him, so don't bother asking.'

A mocking smile tugged at the corner of his mouth. 'Good try...but wrong. You'll answer my questions. It's just a matter of when. Is he related to Caldwell?'

She glared at him, furious that he insisted on pursuing the conversation. 'This is ridiculous. Why do you care who he is? What if he is my lover? What is it to you?'

'Is he?' The question came, swift and clipped. 'Is that why you're being so secretive?'

'No! I just don't understand why you're persisting with this. You've been out of my life for five years now. Why the sudden interest in my personal affairs?'

'Affairs?'

She made an impatient gesture. 'You know what I mean. Why pursue this particular issue?'

He tilted his head to one side, watching her with a nerve-shredding intentness. 'Because something doesn't add up and I'm beginning to suspect that Kyle is part of it. Care to explain him to me now?'

'Not really.' She lost it then, unable to stand another minute of his probing. 'Stay out of it, Damien! I'm warning you, this is none of your business.'

He lifted an eyebrow. 'Are you threatening me?'

'No,' she quickly denied. 'As I said, I'm warning you.'

'Strange how your warnings sound so much like threats. I think... Yes.' He nodded in satisfaction. 'I think it was a threat. I must be getting close for you to try something so pointless, not to mention desperate.' His eyes narrowed. 'But I'm not quite as close as I intend to get, my sweet Sable. Not by a long shot.'

'Damien...' she whispered in distress. The air seemed thick and heavy, and she struggled to breathe, struggled to think of a way to call him off the chase, to quell his hunter's instinct. But nothing came to mind, and she sat without moving, mesmerized, held like a frightened deer by the predatory gleam in his bold green eyes.

To her intense relief, the door opened behind him and a waiter bearing a huge tray entered, followed by Nikolai. 'What? No lights?' He flicked a switch by the door and a soft, muted glow filled the room. 'This is better, yes?'

Damien ignored him, leaning closer to Sable. 'And just so you know,' he murmured. 'This discussion isn't over, just postponed.'

She fought her panic and anger, and summoned a tight smile. 'Don't count on it.'

He straightened and stepped back from the window seat. 'Oh, but I am counting on it. Your challenge has been met. Let the games begin.'

Nikolai approached, curtailing any further conversation. 'Ah, good,' he said, beaming in delight. 'You have finished your drink. You like?'

Sable stared down at her empty glass in dismay. Sure enough, only a cherry remained, swimming at the bottom in a puddle of melted ice. 'It was delicious,' she confessed.

'Yes. I agree,' Nikolai said without a trace of modesty. 'And dinner, it is even better. Come and sit. Joey! What do you wait for? The candles, you young fool. Light them. Our guests are hungry.'

Sable crossed to the table. Dinner at Nikolai's always came as a surprise. They were never permitted to order. Their meal consisted of whatever Nikolai felt like preparing that day. Never once had she found cause to complain and she suspected that tonight would prove no different. Damien held her chair while Joey lit the candles.

'And now, my most popular creation.' With a flourish Nikolai presented their appetizer. 'Oysters Alcatraz.'

Sable inhaled sharply, shooting a startled glance toward Damien. From the humor lightening his expression, the significance of being served the fabled aphrodisiac hadn't escaped him either. 'My favorite,' she claimed, practically choking on the words.

'The favorite of all lovers,' Nikolai boasted with brash aplomb. 'And, to celebrate your return to my establishment, I wish to treat you to a bottle of my finest champagne. The favored drink of lovers to go with the favored food. What could be better, huh?'

He positioned an ice bucket and stand at Damien's elbow and made short shrift of removing the wire and foil from the bottle. A moment later he poured the foaming champagne into flutes. Scrutinizing the table one final time, he gave a nod of satisfaction. '*Na zdorov'e*!' he saluted them, and then he and Joey disappeared out the door.

'All the trappings of a romantic evening,' Sable murmured, attempting a smile. 'Little does he know.'

Damien speared an oyster, consuming it with obvious relish. 'Nikolai knows far more than you might think.'

That gave her pause. 'Such as?' she questioned, raising an eyebrow.

'That we're here to discuss business. Try an oyster. They're quite good.'

She picked up her fork and scooped a morsel from the shell, slipping it into her mouth. The meat was smooth and tender, and the asparagus young and crisp, with just the proper hint of anisette and a sinful amount of butter. He was right. They were perfectly delicious. 'If Nikolai knows it's a business dinner, then why...?' She gestured toward the oysters and champagne.

'He hopes we'll end up discussing more than just business.'

Oh, he did, did he? Well, not if she could help it. She lowered her gaze and applied herself to the oysters. The mere thought of renewing their conversation about Kyle caused her muscles to clench in dread.

To her relief, Damien kept the conversation casual, and Sable found herself relaxing. She even laughed at some of his stories. He had so many wonderful qualities and she'd fallen in love with each and every one of them—his strength, his passion, his brilliance. But most of all she loved those rare moments when he let down his guard, when he revealed the compassion and kindness that only a very strong man felt comfortable exposing.

They finished the last of the oysters and a companionable silence settled between them. 'How did this summer's picnic go?' she asked impulsively.

Hawke Enterprises sponsored a yearly picnic for handicapped and underprivileged children that kicked off the opening of their summer camp. Located in the mountains, far from the city, the camp was run by trained professionals and gave the children an opportunity to experience many of the activities they wouldn't otherwise be able to enjoy—horseback riding, canoeing, water sports... The list was endless. But most of all the counselors stressed teamwork and fought to instill self-respect and self-confidence in the children.

It was a charity that was dear to Sable's heart, one she'd continued to donate to even after she'd been fired, though she'd been careful to keep her contributions anonymous.

'The picnic went very well. We received a lot of media attention this year, which helped with donations. Enough came in to purchase the land for a second camp.'

'Really? That's wonderful! I... saw the segment they did on the news.' She peeked up at him, her dark eyes gleaming with barely suppressed laughter. 'Did you get ribbed about it?'

'For weeks.' He frowned, though she knew he wasn't really annoyed. 'Damned kid. Jerome. That was his name. He did it on purpose—waited until the camera focused on me before letting fly with that water balloon.'

Sable bit down on her lip to keep from laughing. 'Your expression was priceless. I think the newscaster really believed you were going to kill that poor boy.' She wrinkled her brow, struggling to remember. 'What did she say?'

'She didn't say anything—at first. She shrieked loud enough to be heard in three counties,' he said in disgust. 'Then she yelled, "Save the poor boy before that beast murders him!"'

'It only made her look foolish,' Sable said consolingly. 'I'm surprised they didn't dub it out.'

He shook his head in satisfaction. 'They couldn't. It was a live broadcast. And when it played so well with their viewers they repeated it intact.'

She chuckled. 'Much to the newswoman's chagrin, I'm sure.'

It had been an electric moment. The aloof businessman, water dripping from his hair and shoulders, faced off against a pint-sized devil bent on mischief. When Damien had snatched the youngster into the air, Sable had thought the newswoman would have a conniption. And then he'd pretended to slip, tumbling with Jerome into the shallow wading pool behind them, and the tension had been broken with hysterical laughter.

But the most poignant moment of all had been when Damien and the boy had surfaced, totally drenched and grinning with unmistakable male camaraderie. Jerome had thrown his arms around Damien's neck, clinging to him with such a look of adoration that it had brought tears to Sable's eyes. And Damien... He'd ruffled the boy's short, wiry hair, the most incredible look of tenderness creeping across his stern features.

Was that how he'd be with Kyle? she wondered wistfully. Would he show that same caring, allow his guard to drop sufficiently to let love, in the shape of a small, impish boy, wriggle in? A picture formed in her mind, a picture as precious as it was impossible and her breath caught in an audible gasp.

He instantly keyed in on her reaction. 'What's wrong?'

She dropped her gaze to hide her pain. 'A passing thought. A foolish thought.' And that was precisely what it was—foolish.

'Something you can share?'

She shook her head. 'I don't think so.'

'More secrets?' He leaned across the table, clasping her hand in his. 'One of these days they're going to catch up with you. What will you do then, Sable?'

She shrugged uneasily. 'I'll cross that bridge when I get to it, I guess. What else can I do?'

'You might try honesty for a change.'

She tilted her head to one side. 'That from a man bent on revenge?' She tugged her fingers from his grasp. 'I don't think so. But thanks for the suggestion.'

'I hope you don't regret it.'

'I hope not too,' she whispered.

But she already did. Unfortunately, regretting the choices she'd made five years ago could prove dangerous in the extreme, picturing Damien with Kyle even more so. Still, she couldn't help wondering if she'd made a horrible mistake, if she shouldn't have somehow forced a confrontation with Damien, told him about her pregnancy. But he'd been out of the country—beyond her reach. And she'd been afraid—afraid of what he might do to her and their child, afraid that he'd use her vulnerability to exact an unconscionable revenge. She'd also discovered in the past days that that fear, reasonable or not, hadn't diminished with time.

She glanced at him. He sipped his champagne, the candlelight highlighting the sweeping curve of his cheekbones and catching in the green of his eyes and the streaks of gold in his hair. She'd explored every inch of that face, knew it as intimately as her own. It was only his thoughts and emotions he kept so closely protected. Her mouth compressed. If she'd told him about her pregnancy, more than likely he wouldn't even have believed the baby was his. He'd as good as accused her of sleeping with Leonard at the same time she'd been with him. No, she'd made the right choice in keeping Kyle's existence a secret.

Their main course arrived then. To her delight Nikolai had prepared lobster thermador, her very favorite dish. 'Seems he's pulled out all the stops,' she murmured once the waiter had departed.

'Nikolai is a romantic,' Damien said. 'He wants everything perfect, hoping this will be the start of a second chance for us.'

'If that's what he's hoping, he's going to be sadly disappointed,' she said lightly. 'Though I'm surprised he knows so much about our private life.'

'Private? Hardly. Your defection was quite public,' he stated coolly.

'And you've never forgiven me for that, have you?' She selected a rosy cube of lobster dripping with sauce and Swiss cheese. It practically melted in her mouth.

'Forgiven?' he questioned harshly. 'No. Nor have I ever understood it.'

Her fork crashed to the table. 'You never understood because you wouldn't accept any of my explanations!'

'You mean your lies?' he bit out.

'They weren't lies. Oh, this is ridiculous!' She clenched her hands, her voice tight with fury. 'You preferred to believe that I'd lie and cheat, that I'd actually steal from you, rather than see the truth. You even dared to suggest that I could conduct an ardent affair with you while taking another man to bed on the side. Have you any idea what that did to me, knowing how little you trusted me, Damien?'

His expression frosted over, his eyes flashing a warning. 'The proof was incontrovertible.'

'Only to a closed mind,' she insisted. 'You were looking for an excuse to doubt me and I want to know why.'

He picked up his champagne flute, swirling the contents so that tiny bubbles shimmered in the depths of the pale gold wine. 'You're imagining things.'

'Am I?' Suddenly it seemed quite clear. The fact that he'd never completely let down his guard with her, but had always kept a small part of himself aloof and distant, became oddly significant. 'Am I imagining it, Damien?' she asked intently.

He returned her gaze and she'd never seen him more remote, more withdrawn. 'Don't try and dump this in my lap. Right after I fired you, you accepted a job from Caldwell. What else was I to believe?'

'I had no choice!' she insisted sharply. 'I had bills to pay!'

A muscle leapt in his jaw. 'That's a load of crock and you know it. Selling those bids to Caldwell's should have made you a wealthy woman.' His mouth twisted. 'Of course, marrying Caldwell made you even wealthier.'

Every scrap of color drained from her face. 'I won't discuss my marriage with you. It's absolutely none of your business. But I will say this.' She leaned forward to emphasize her point, her voice trembling with the strength of her passion. 'If I'd sold information to Caldwell's as you claimed, I wouldn't have had to work—money wouldn't have been an issue. But what about if I didn't sell you out? What if I didn't lie? Did you ever consider that?'

He didn't relent. 'I considered it. Until you proved me wrong.'

'I keep telling you—it was all a horrible mistake!'

'Then why work for the man?' he demanded, animosity breaking through his rigid control. 'It damned you in everyone's eyes. Even you must realize that.'

'I realize it. Dear lord, I've *lived* with that knowledge hanging over my head every day of the past five years,' she cried. 'But I had bills to meet, a rent to pay, food to buy. And no one would hire me...except Caldwell. I turned him down the first two times he asked, insulted that he'd think I'd work for a company capable of such duplicity. But as the weeks passed my pride wasn't as important as earning a living, putting food on the table. So I accepted his third offer and thanked heaven for his persistence.'

'Why was he willing to hire you?'

'Maybe because I'm good at my job.' Her gaze, angry and defiant, locked with his, condemning him for his relentless suspicion. 'Or maybe he hired me because he knew the truth—knew exactly how his company got hold of that bid information, knew that I never deliberately betrayed you. Perhaps he even felt guilty.'

Damien grew still, his head cocked to one side, and for the first time Sable thought she might have struck a chord with him. 'So why marry him?'

His question dashed all hope. 'He asked.' The answer was flippant and did nothing to redeem her. But she didn't care, couldn't care. What else could she possibly say? That she'd married Leonard because she was pregnant and adrift, and more frightened than she'd ever been in her life?

His eyes narrowed, cynicism tainting his expression. 'Interesting how thorough your explanations have been. Until now, that is. Until you have to try and justify why you married a man old enough to be your father.'

The fight drained from her. She couldn't win this battle; she'd been foolish even to think it possible. Dropping her gaze, she applied herself to the lobster. 'You forgot to mention,' she murmured drily, 'that Leonard was old enough to be my father *and* stinking rich.'

He released an exasperated sigh. 'Your humor is out of place.'

She could either laugh or she could cry. But she sensed that once the tears came she'd be unable to stop them. She forced a shaky smile to her lips. 'Right now,' she admitted with devastating candor, 'a sense of humor is all I have left.'

Annoyance flashed in his eyes for a fleeting moment, but whether it was directed at her or himself she couldn't tell. 'Then eat,' he directed briskly. 'Just let me know when you're ready to do battle again.'

She did as he suggested, enjoying the rare treat of a dinner out. It wasn't until they were sipping the last of the champagne that he resumed their discussion. 'Have you reached a decision about selling your Caldwell shares?'

'Back to business?' she asked with notable reluctance.

'Afraid so.'

'I...I'm willing to sell,' she confessed. 'But I'd like time.'

He inclined his head. 'How much time?'

'I'm not sure.' Replete, she pushed her plate aside. 'The end of the month should be sufficient, I guess.' That gave her until Ryan submitted his final report to complete her inquiries. If she hadn't found out who'd leaked the information to A.J. Construction by then, it wouldn't matter how much time Damien allowed. She'd be cast in the role of head scapegoat and that would be the end of it.

'Why do you need time? What are you hoping to accomplish in the next three weeks that could change anything?'

How could she possibly answer that without revealing what she'd learned from Alex Johnson? What excuse could she use? She bit down on her lip. 'I——'

'Does your hesitation have something to do with what happened at Caldwell's today?' he cut in abruptly.

'Excuse me?'

'You heard me. That phone call I walked in on before we left the office. Did it have anything to do with losing Luther's development project?'

'Why would you think that?'

'You're dancing around your answers again. Talk to me straight for once,' he ordered, irritation clear in his voice. 'You were upset—more than upset—by that call.'

'That's none——'

He tossed his linen napkin on to the table. 'Don't say it. Not again. Because unless that call was personal it's very much my business. I won't have you keeping secrets from me, not ones that affect Caldwell's.'

She hated deceiving him, hated the role she was forced to play. 'It was personal,' she claimed.

'You're lying,' he snapped. 'You're lying and I know it.'

She stiffened. 'How?'

He laughed, the sound incredibly weary. 'Sometimes your face is so open and clear, it reflects your every thought. Your eyes grow soft, like a rich black mist. And other times the light fades from your eyes and there's nothing there, no thought, no emotion, just this...murky emptiness. And that's when I know you're lying.'

She lowered her gaze, appalled that her most intimate thoughts and feelings were so easily read by him. 'Please, Damien. I'd rather not discuss that particular phone call.'

'Then let's discuss Luther. This entire situation reeks of a conspiracy. Why not admit it?'

He was taunting her deliberately, she could tell. He wanted to assess her reaction. She looked at him, suppressing her fear, forcing herself to deal with the problem with calm resourcefulness. 'You suspect there's been a leak, don't you?' she asked, cutting to the bottom line.

'You're damned right I do. I've spent the past twenty-four hours looking into it. And I've discovered that this isn't the only account we've lost. There have been four others in the past year. An interesting pattern, wouldn't you say?'

That did take her by surprise. 'So many? I had no idea. Do you really think those others had information leaked too?'

'Too?' he questioned sharply, her comment clearly condemning her. 'So you *do* think A.J. Construction had inside information on the Luther project.'

She sighed in defeat. She shouldn't have had quite so much of Nikolai's Nectar. She certainly shouldn't have followed it with several glasses of champagne, not when she needed to keep her wits about her in order to deal with Damien. 'Ryan's looking into the possibility. At least, he is with Luther.' Her brows drew together. 'It worries me, though, that you think they're all connected.'

'It should worry you more that I think you might be responsible,' he retorted.

Her mouth tightened. 'Is that what you plan? To blame me like last time?'

'Ah, but you were guilty last time.'

She pushed back her chair and stood up, crossing to the window. Lights from numerous boats twinkled out on the bay, though fog concealed most of the view. 'I'd like to leave,' she stated quietly, wrapping her arms around her waist.

His reflection appeared just behind her. 'Running away, Sable?'

'I prefer to call it a temporary retreat. I'm tired and need time to regroup.' She swung around. 'I want you to think about something, though. If I leaked that information, what possible motivation could I have?'

'I don't know,' he conceded slowly. 'But then, it took me a while to figure out your motivation before.' He dropped his hands on her shoulders, drawing her close. 'You'd better not be responsible for the leak. Because this time I won't hesitate to press charges. And then you won't have to worry about selling me your shares: you'll lose them to me.'

She didn't fight him as she should. Exhaustion gripped her and she relaxed against him, resting her head in the crook of his shoulder. Just for a minute she'd close her eyes and pretend that his hold was an embrace, his intent to comfort rather than accuse.

'You'd better not be responsible for the leak.' His words rang in her ears. She had so little time left to uncover the actual villain and vindicate herself. Unfortunately, she couldn't expect any help from Damien. Tears pricked her eyes. 'Maybe I should just sell out now.'

'You can. But I'll put a clause in the sales agreement. If you're guilty, the deal's off.'

She glanced up at him. 'Then I'll have to find the real culprit, won't I?'

He cupped her cheek, his thumb brushing her jaw. 'Are you sure she isn't right here?'

'Positive,' she said without hesitation.

He didn't argue, though she suspected he didn't quite believe her. 'Time will tell,' was all he said. 'Are you ready to go?'

She nodded. 'There's just one last thing I'd like to ask before we leave.' She licked her lips, steeling herself for this final battle. 'I...I have a request.'

Laughter lightened his eyes, the green as bright and vivid as newly unfurled leaves. 'Why doesn't that surprise me?'

'It's about your other...condition.'

He didn't pretend to misunderstand. 'About our sleeping together?'

She nodded. 'Were you serious about that?'

'Very.'

'Why?' The question burst from her before she could stop it. 'How could you insist on such a thing?'

His expression darkened, desire slipping across his face, heating his eyes and hardening his body. 'Because you're a temptation I can't resist. You're like a pool of water in the midst of a scorching desert. And I've been lost in that desert for five long years. I have to taste you, slip inside you, see if you feel as good as I remember or if it's all an empty mirage.'

'But not this way,' she argued desperately. 'Not with threats and coercion. Not with such cold-blooded deliberation.'

His laugh had a wry, husky quality to it. 'There's nothing cold-blooded about the way I feel.'

'You'll regret it, I swear you will,' she tried again.

He shrugged. 'Then I'll regret it.' His fingers slipped beneath the heavy fall of her hair, thrusting into the thick curls at the base of her neck. 'What's your request?'

Nervous dread balled in the pit of her stomach. 'If you insist on holding me to this . . . this *stipulation*, then I want to be the one to decide when and where.'

He inclined his head. 'Agreed.'

'No!' she cried recklessly. 'There is no agreement. There's only your demand and my submission. That certainly doesn't constitute an agreement.'

'It doesn't matter what you call it.' His arms tightened around her, fitting them together like two interlocking pieces, neither one complete without the other. 'This is what it's all about. The warmth of my hand against your breast, the stirring of our bodies when they touch. Our lips meeting, tasting.' His voice deepened. 'The feel of your body beneath mine, open and eager.'

Heat flashed through her, burning with an unmistakable urgency. 'But it's not love!' she protested, battling against the primitive hunger sweeping through her like wildfire.

Amusement flickered in his eyes. 'I never said it was. Call it love or concede it's lust. Whichever it is, I intend to enjoy it. And so will you, no matter how much you try and deny it.'

'No!' She shook her head, wishing she could refute his words, struggling to resist what was fast becoming more and more irresistible.

He didn't permit any further opposition, his method of silencing her immediate and effective. He lowered his head and kissed her. She murmured in dissent, but his mouth absorbed the distressed sound. He didn't force her; he didn't need to. Instead he reminded her of the intense delight to be found within his arms, seducing her with slow, deep kisses, teasing kisses, soul-wrenching kisses.

Reality deserted her, leaving her careening out of control. He was the sun, coaxing her toward his brilliant fire. She surrendered to his pull, spinning where he willed, bathed in his golden heat. Her heart had never truly belonged to her, she realized then. It had always rested within his care, his to cherish or destroy.

His mouth slid from hers and she gasped for breath, fought for sanity. 'You can't do this to me again. I won't let you!'

'You can't stop it. You're mine, body and soul. You've always been mine.' His hand caressed her hip and her response came as surely and naturally as a wave to the shore. 'You see? Deny it all you want; it doesn't alter a thing.'

She bowed her head. 'You won't change your mind?' she whispered.

'I can't. I won't.'

She lifted her head, tears trembling on the end of her lashes. 'Then heaven forgive you, because I never will.' And with that she ripped free of his arms and ran for the door. She had to get away, she had to leave *now* before she lost all control. Flinging it open, she threw an anguished glance over her shoulder, her expression filled with accusation and hopeless desire. And then she plunged into the fog-filled night.

CHAPTER SIX

'SABLE! Sable, stop!'

She heard Damien's footsteps pounding on the deck outside the restaurant, giving chase—and gaining on her. She ran recklessly onward, intent on escape, the breath sobbing in her throat, tears blinding her path. She'd always known that it would come to this, both of them reverting to their baser instincts—she the prey, fleeing before the predator, Damien giving chase, moving with cat-like speed, running her down to earth. Her heel caught on an uneven plank and just as she pitched forward his hands closed on her shoulders, saving her from a nasty fall.

'What the *hell* do you think you're doing?' he demanded, spinning her round to face him.

She tore free of his hold. 'Take your hands off me! I'm going home. Alone.' She swept her hair back from her eyes and glared at him with all the defiance she could muster, refusing to shrink from his wrath. To her confusion, he didn't look angry as much as concerned.

'You want to go home? Fine. I'll take you there.'

She shook her head stubbornly, trembling with emotion, struggling to catch her breath. 'I said alone. I'll... I'll catch a cab. Or take the ferry.'

He stepped between her and the walkway toward Sausalito. 'Not a chance. You came with me, you leave with me.'

'No! I'll——'

'Forget it, Sable.' His tone brooked no opposition and he shifted closer, as though in anticipation of her bolting again. 'You're not going home alone. I'll escort you to the launch. You can wait for me there while I settle up inside.'

She drew in a deep, shaky breath. She'd overreacted, she realized, allowed him to get to her, to break through her defenses. She'd panicked when she most needed to keep a level head. But it was all too much. Every time she turned around she faced a new battle—a battle she had no chance of winning.

Slowly she nodded, her rebellion draining away, to be replaced by an oppressive weariness. 'All right,' she said in a cool, remote voice. 'You may take me home.'

'Thank you.' Irony colored his words.

'No more, Damien,' she said, with a tiny sigh. 'Please. I've had enough.'

He apparently concurred. Wrapping a protective arm around her waist, he guided her down the ramp to the dock. 'Wait here,' he ordered, then stilled. Tucking a lock of hair behind her ear, he tilted her face toward the lights ringing the restaurant, his brows drawing together in a fierce frown. His thumb feathered across her cheek, tracing the path of her tears. 'You're exhausted.' He sounded almost apologetic. 'I should have realized.'

She didn't trust his compassion. It was just one more weapon in his arsenal, the latest attempt to slip beneath her guard. 'I'll be fine again tomorrow.' She had to be. There wasn't any other choice, not with the clock ticking steadily toward her doom. She had to act, not rest.

He helped her aboard. 'I'll be right back. Don't disappear on me.'

'I won't,' she murmured, and collapsed on the padded seat in the bow. She didn't have the energy to find her own way home, anyway. She certainly didn't have the energy to indulge in another chase. And that was precisely what would happen should she run. Damien would come after her again, and what might happen should he be forced to catch her a second time didn't bear consideration.

She stared out at the boats moored at a nearby yacht club. Sounds drifted across the water to her—the slap of waves against fiberglass hulls, the groan of wood dipping and swaying atop the choppy crests, the distant clang of a buoy marker. She found it oddly soothing and she relaxed against the seat cushions, taking a deep breath of rich, salty air.

Dinner with Damien had been a bad idea. A very bad idea. It had brought back too many memories, left her far too vulnerable. From now on she had to keep their relationship strictly professional. She couldn't allow herself to fall into the trap of thinking there could be anything more than Caldwell's between them—certainly not the love affair they'd once experienced. That path led to disaster. And she had too much at risk even to consider anything so insane.

Damien returned to the launch then, her purse beneath his arm. She couldn't believe she'd left it behind. She really must be losing her grip. He joined her in the bow, sitting much too close. But since she could hardly shift her position without subjecting herself to more of his caustic remarks she stayed put.

'You sure you don't want to go inside the cabin?' he asked. 'There's quite a breeze.'

She shook her head and he didn't attempt to change her mind. Instead he draped his jacket about her shoulders, just as he had on their trip over. A few minutes later they cast off, motoring out into the bay. Fog cocooned them, ebbing and flowing about the boat and dusting Sable's hair with diamond-like droplets of dew. It was as though they existed in their own little world, just the two of them. In the distance a fog horn broke the silence, the sound muffled, its mournful cry an accurate reflection of her own despondency. She closed her eyes, totally drained, the rocking of the boat, the throb of the engines lulling her toward a peaceful oblivion.

She stirred just as they docked, the launch bumping gently against the pier startling her awake. Good heavens, how could she have fallen asleep? It seemed incredible. She stiffened, realizing then that Damien held her. She must have turned into his embrace as she slept for he supported her securely, her head cushioned against his shoulder, his arms wrapped firmly about her waist. How many times during their years together had she drifted off in this very position? And how many times in the past five years had she awakened in the middle of the night, her arms empty and aching, her pillow damp with tears? Too many. She drew away, murmuring a flustered apology.

He made no comment, simply helped her to her feet, his hand beneath her elbow as she fought for balance on the lurching deck. 'I had the captain call ahead. The car should be waiting.'

'What time is it?' she asked, slipping his jacket from around her shoulders and handing it to him.

'Around midnight.'

'So late?'

He shrugged, not in the least concerned. 'We were at Nikolai's for quite some time. We had a lot to discuss, if you remember, a lot to settle.'

Not that they had managed to settle their differences, she realized uneasily. If anything, their positions were more adversarial than ever. She walked with Damien to the limo, giving the driver her Pacific Heights address before getting in.

'I thought Caldwell had an estate in St Francis Woods,' Damien said as the car pulled away from the pier. 'What was it called? Rat's Nest?'

'Fox's Lair. And you don't need to sound so sarcastic. Your place in Sausalito isn't exactly shabby.'

'So, what happened to the Lair?' he questioned.

'Leonard sold it,' she replied, hoping the brevity of her response would put an end to his questions.

It didn't.

'Why?' he persisted.

She glanced at him, something in his tone arousing her suspicions. Why the questions? What did he want now? But the shadows that cut across his face defeated her attempts to decipher his expression. 'He sold it trying to save the design firm.'

'A pointless gesture.'

She laughed shortly. 'You should know. You're the reason the firm went bankrupt.'

'Wrong,' came the biting retort. 'Lenny was the reason the firm went bankrupt. I merely took advantage of his bad business decisions. If it hadn't been me cleaning up after him, it would have been someone else.'

She turned to look out the window. 'My mistake.'

'You don't believe me, do you?'

She faced him again, holding on to her temper through sheer grit and determination. 'I believe you did everything within your power to break Leonard. And you succeeded. I also think there's no point in discussing this further.' For once luck was with her and they pulled to a stop on the steep slope outside her house, putting an end to the discussion. 'Thank you for dinner. Goodnight.'

He caught her hand before she could open the door. 'Let me tell you something. It didn't take much effort to bring Leonard down. I could have sat back and done nothing and he'd still have ended up losing everything. All I did was expedite the inevitable.'

'Why, how charitable of you, Damien. I'm sure my husband appreciated that,' she said with undisguised contempt. 'Now let me go!'

He actually had the audacity to laugh. 'Not a chance.'

Anger barbed her voice, her words coming fast and furious. 'Oh, but you will. Once your conditions are met, you'll be out of my life. And this time it'll be for good. I'm not Leonard. You may take Caldwell's from me, but you won't destroy me like you did him. I won't let you.'

'No, you won't, will you? You'll fight me every step of the way, bending when necessary, but never breaking.' His hand cupped her cheek. 'Well, fight all you want, my love, but it won't make any difference. You belong to me. You always have. It's time you faced that fact.'

The breath hissed from her lungs. 'That changed five years ago, Damien. What we had is gone.'

'I wish it were,' he told her roughly. 'Otherwise I wouldn't want to do this every time you come near.'

Not giving her time to react, he lowered his head and took her mouth, took without mercy or hesitation. He drove his hands deep into her hair, holding her close. It was exquisite, a rapture that swept away all knowledge of right or wrong, all awareness of propriety. It was raw and elemental and powerful and she clutched at his shirt, opening to him, the need to respond an instinct she found impossible to withstand.

'You see?' he muttered against her lips. 'It's still there, in every word you utter, every look you give, every touch we exchange. We're connected. You're mine, Sable. Deny it all you want, but it won't change the truth.'

'No! No, you're wrong.' With a tiny cry of distress she grabbed the door handle and scrambled from the limousine, intent on escaping to the safety of her house. Before she could, however, Damien stepped from the car.

'Sable...'

Reluctantly, she turned around. 'What is it now?' she demanded.

He held out her purse. 'I thought you might want this.' He paused, a hint of a smile playing about his mouth. 'Otherwise I might be forced to come in and return it to you. And I suspect you'd rather that didn't happen. Or am I mistaken?'

He wasn't mistaken and they both knew it. Without a word, she snatched the purse from his hand and hurried up the stairs to her door. She was running away again—an act guaranteed to catch the interest of a hungry predator. Once she'd reached the relative security of her porch, she risked a quick glance over her shoulder. Damien stood, leaning negligently against the door of the limo. But it was the expression on his face that followed her inside, followed her to the privacy of her bed and into the depths of her dreams....

It was the intent, savage expression of a lion about to pounce.

* * *

Damien appeared at the connecting door to Sable's office first thing the next morning. 'Got a minute?' he asked, his demeanor thoroughly businesslike.

'Sure,' she replied a trifle warily, tucking Ryan's latest missive out of sight. Not that it revealed anything vital—just more possible names. More *impossible* names.

Meeting Damien's aloof gaze, she realized that last night might never have been. Not a hint of emotion disturbed the calm tenor of his voice, or touched the cool green of his eyes. She shouldn't allow his remoteness to throw her; certainly it hadn't all the years she'd worked for him. Separating business from their personal life had been as easy as slipping on and off a pair of shoes. Back then she'd bathed in the warmth of his love, secure that nothing could ever harm their relationship.

Or so she'd thought.

'I want you to clear your schedule in the mornings for the rest of the week,' he informed her.

She lifted her brows in surprise. 'Why?'

He tapped the papers in his hands. 'We have two vital contracts coming up for bid and I want us to work together on them—make sure we have all our bases covered.'

In other words, he wanted her working with him where he could keep an eye on her. She didn't air her suspicions, but nodded agreeably. 'Which contracts are these?'

'A shopping mall in Concord and a state-of-the-art computer complex for Dreyfus Industry.'

She sat back in her chair, impressed. 'Those are huge. Can we handle them?'

'Not alone. I'm going to pull my construction company in on this too.'

She titled her head to one side, her eyes narrowing in thought. 'What are you up to, Damien? Are you thinking about a merger, by any chance? Hawke absorbing Caldwell's?'

A strange smile crept across his mouth, further arousing her suspicions. 'Not at all,' he claimed. 'There's no advantage in consolidating the two firms. But there's a big advantage to pooling our resources on occasion.'

'And this is one of those occasions?'

'I think so.' He crossed to her desk, edging a hip on the corner closest to her. 'As long as we're discussing this, there's something else we'd better address.'

What now? she couldn't help but wonder. 'Yes?'

'I want to throw a reception the end of next week and hold it here. Doesn't the twentieth floor have facilities for occasions like that? A ballroom or something?' At her nod, he continued. 'Since the top management at Caldwell's has changed, I think it's important to have a friendly get-together with our key employees and principal clientele.'

'I see.' She tapped her blotter with the end of her pencil, the only outward sign of her annoyance. 'And you want me to make the arrangements, is that it?'

His smile was devastating. 'You were always good at it, Sable.'

'I still am,' she informed him coldly. 'But there's no point in playing games. Why not admit your plan right up front? You want me to throw the reception and introduce you around in order to make it clear to Caldwell staff—as well as to our clients—that you're in charge.'

His smile faded. 'Very astute. But don't look so offended. You've already agreed to sell your shares of Caldwell's to me. It's not like I'm taking anything away from you. Consider throwing this party a small statement of intent on your part—a guarantee, if you will. Our employees aren't stupid; nor are our clients. They'll read between the lines.'

'Read that I'm out and you're in?' He inclined his head in agreement and she asked, 'So, what's the rush? Why not wait a few weeks?'

His expression grew cold and hard. 'Someone is leaking information. You know it and I know it. You say you're innocent. If that's true, then someone else out there is responsible. I want to make it clear that they aren't dealing with an easy mark any more. They're dealing with me. And I don't take this sort of thing lying down.'

'An easy mark!' She straightened in her chair as she absorbed the insult. 'You must be joking.'

He didn't back down. 'Assuming you're innocent, that's precisely what you've been. This situation should have been caught and stopped months ago. And you damned well know it.'

'I wasn't in a position to stop it,' she protested. Not while Patricia ran the company.

'You still aren't.' He covered her hand with his, stopping the agitated rapping of her pencil. 'Now, will you organize the reception, or shall I handle it?'

She yanked her fingers from beneath his and tossed the pencil on to her blotter. 'I'll take care of it.'

'Fine. Lute has coffee ready. Shall we get started on those bids?'

Her mouth compressed. 'Of course,' she said, and stood, sweeping her papers together. 'Give me a minute to speak to Janine. I'll have her begin the preliminary arrangements for your reception and be right with you.' But she didn't like the idea of this party. Not one little bit. Unfortunately, however, she didn't have much choice in the matter.

The next week flew by. Between working with Damien, pulling together the information necessary to submit the bids, and going over preparations for the reception with Janine, she scarcely had time to catch her breath.

'Wait a minute,' Sable called to her secretary one afternoon, releasing an exasperated sigh. 'I've given you the wrong stack. These are the menus; you have the reports for Dreyfus. If I let that data out of my sight, Damien will have my head on a platter.'

With an understanding smile, her secretary traded papers. 'I thought those figures looked a little high for stuffed artichoke hearts.'

'Hmm. I'm not so sure. They seem darned close to me. How many refusals have you gotten for the reception?'

'Only one,' Janine admitted in surprise. 'Seems everyone's at a loose end this Friday.'

'More likely they've arranged to be at a loose end,' she said with a dry laugh. 'I think they find the whole situation too intriguing to pass up.' Janine hesitated, clutching the papers to her chest, and Sable lifted an eyebrow in question. 'Is there something else?'

'I was just wondering... Are you planning to leave the company, Mrs Caldwell?'

The question wasn't entirely unexpected, not considering the secretary's familiarity with her past—and Damien's. 'I'm thinking about it,' Sable admitted.

Unflattering color mottled Janine's cheeks. 'But what about Mr Caldwell?' she questioned tightly. 'It's an insult to his memory, turning his company over to that man.'

Sable trained her dark gaze on the older woman. 'I assume by "that man" you're referring to Mr Hawke,' she said gently. 'In case you've forgotten, he owns the majority of shares in this company, something he acquired without any help from me. If it makes you feel any better, Damien has no intention of dismantling the company or changing the name—at least, not as far as I know. With luck, the name will live on, even if there are no Caldwells actively running the business.'

Janine lowered her eyes. 'Yes, Mrs Caldwell. You're right, of course.'

Deliberately changing the subject, Sable said, 'If you'd call the caterers with those final changes, I'd appreciate it. And check with the florists about the centerpieces. They seemed rather iffy about the delivery time.'

'I'll get right on it,' Janine promised, making a final notation on her pad. 'Is there anything else?'

Sable sighed. 'A thousand things, I'm sure. But none you have to worry about right now. Thanks for your help on this one. I couldn't have done it without you.'

Janine nodded abruptly. 'It's my job.'

The door shut behind the secretary and Sable leaned back in her chair, closing her eyes. How many other employees felt as Janine did? she wondered with regret. Did they all believe she and Patricia had betrayed Leonard's memory? Though she agreed that it was a shame there weren't any Caldwells left to run the company, she didn't entirely blame Damien for that. Leonard and Patricia had to accept their fair share of the responsibility, too. Damien couldn't have bought his way into the company if Patricia hadn't sold out. Nor could he have driven them to the brink of bankruptcy if Leonard hadn't been such a poor businessman. Still... Caldwell's without a Caldwell. It was sad.

The next two days slid by as rapidly as the previous week. Sable stayed in constant touch with Ryan

Matheson, hoping against hope that they'd find something of significance before his report was due. But with only ten days remaining neither of them had been able to uncover how the bid information had been obtained or who might be responsible. Though after her discussion with Alex Johnson Sable had her suspicions. Now all she had to do was figure out a way to prove those suspicions.

To her relief there were also no further leaks, but she felt as though she stood on the edge of a towering cliff waiting...waiting for a storm hanging just offshore to break, waiting for the gale-force winds to sweep down from the heavens and hurl her over the edge into the abyss below. Her fate seemed inevitable, the only question...*when*.

Friday dawned bright and clear and Sable packed a garment bag to take to work. She doubted she'd have time to go home and get ready before the reception. Between double-checking the final arrangements for that night and tying up loose ends with Dreyfus before the weekend, it seemed the wisest course to bring a suitable dress with her and change at work.

Promptly at five that afternoon, the door between her office and Damien's opened, and he glanced in. 'I'm heading down to the gym for a quick workout and shower. I'll stop by in an hour so we can go to the reception together.'

'That's fine,' Sable said with a nod. 'I have a few odds and ends to finish up and then I'll change.'

'OK. One hour.' And with that he disappeared.

Twenty minutes later she threw down her pen and stretched. Lord, she was exhausted. She couldn't wait until tonight was behind her. She wasn't looking forward to the knowing glances and derisive comments hidden behind artificial smiles. Though, after five years, she should be used to it.

Shoving her papers to one side, she crossed to the bathroom. She took her time, brushing out her hair and piling it on top of her head in a formal knot. Next came makeup, just a bit more dramatic than she normally wore. Thank goodness women could hide behind such a colorful and distracting facade. She needed every advantage she could get. Tilting her head to one side, she nodded, satisfied with the results. Her dark eyes were bright and clear, her coloring healthy and, though her smile might be a bit fixed, with luck, no one would notice.

Next she stripped off her suit and, unzipping the garment bag, removed fresh underclothes and the cocktail dress she'd decided to wear. She'd bought it before Leonard's death and had never had the opportunity to wear it. A brilliant red, it made the perfect statement—bold, undaunted and elegant.

She slipped on the dress, pleased with the fit. It molded her figure, cupping her breasts and hugging her waist. Circling the dress at the hips, layers of filmy scarves had been cleverly and unobtrusively attached. As light as air, they fell like the petals of a flower to just below her knees. When she stood perfectly still they lay flat, a soft and supple skirt. But the moment she stirred, the bright red scarves shifted with a life of their own, billowing and swaying as though to some secret music.

Slipping on heels the same flame-red color as her dress, she dabbed a touch of perfume at her pulse-points, and checked the mirror one final time. She hesitated, lifting a hand to the base of her throat, and then reluctantly crossed to the garment bag, removing a velvet box.

Flipping it open, she stared down at the ruby-and diamond-studded choker and earrings—Damien's last present to her. Aside from her wedding rings, it was the only expensive jewelry she'd kept. When Leonard's businesses had started to go downhill, she'd insisted that he sell the few pieces he'd given her.

Well, if Damien could wear her Rolex, she could wear his necklace and earrings. Not giving herself time to reconsider, she removed the jewelry from the satin bed and put them on. The gemstones flashed against her skin like bright red danger beacons. Trouble ahead, they seemed to warn. It was a warning she was forced to ignore.

Returning to the office, she discovered Janine delivering a final stack of mail. 'Anything urgent?' Sable asked, glancing at the pile.

'No, nothing.' Shoving gray-streaked bangs from her face, Janine frowned down at the desk. 'Now how did that get mixed in with your mail? This isn't addressed to you.' She reached into the pile and plucked out a large manila envelope. Across the upper left-hand corner, in huge block letters, was written 'A.J. Construction'. 'This goes to Mr Hawke. I'll just drop it on his desk on my way out.'

Sable licked her lips, staring at the envelope in her secretary's hand. Oh, no. This couldn't be good. Why in the world would Alex be contacting Damien? It could only mean one thing. She bit down on her lip. That storm swept ever closer to her precarious stance on the cliff. 'You're going down to the reception, Janine?' she managed to ask, praying her voice wouldn't reveal her agitation.

'Yes, Mrs Caldwell. I want to make sure the caterers are ready to go and give everything a final check.'

'Fine.' Sable forced her gaze away from the envelope. 'Thank you.'

Janine smiled. 'My pleasure.' She crossed to the connecting door that led to Damien's office and rapped lightly. Not receiving an answer, she walked in. A minute later she reappeared, empty-handed. 'Is there anything you need before I go?'

Sable shook her head, not daring to trust her voice again. She waited a full five seconds after Janine left before crossing to Damien's office. She hesitated in the doorway, debating the ethics of what she intended. But she had to get a look at that envelope. She had to get a look *in* that envelope. Slowly, she pushed the door wide and crossed the threshold. Her heart pounded and her breath came in quick, shallow gasps. She'd never done anything remotely like this before. If she was caught...

She glanced quickly over her shoulder as though expecting to find Damien lurking in the shadows, ready to leap out at her from behind the potted palms. This was ridiculous. The longer she delayed, the greater the likelihood she'd be caught. Boldly, she stepped forward, traversing the room, her heels sinking into the soft green carpet.

Janine had left the envelope square in the center of Damien's desk. Nothing else marred the surface and sunlight poured from the window, drawing immediate attention to the missive. It didn't have a mailing label—at a guess, it had been hand-delivered. A slashing masculine script had scrawled Damien's name across the front, and at the bottom 'private' had been printed, the word underlined twice. It had to be from Alex—there was no other reasonable explanation. But what had he written to Damien? She had to know.

Taking a deep breath, she reached out a trembling hand to pick it up.

'What do you think you're doing?' came Damien's voice from just behind her.

CHAPTER SEVEN

WITH a gasp, Sable whirled around, the petal-like scarves of her skirt flaring out around her. She lifted a trembling hand to her throat. 'You frightened me!'

'Did I?' Damien cocked an eyebrow, closing the distance between them. 'I wonder why? Doing something you shouldn't, sweetheart?'

She stared at him, her eyes huge and fearful. She didn't dare answer his question—not if she wanted to live. 'You could have given me some warning you were there,' she protested weakly, 'instead of sneaking up on me like that.'

'I could have. But since it's my office I didn't see the need.' He stopped inches from her, his height and breadth emphasized by his black silk suit, his wintry gaze more of a threat than she'd ever thought possible. If it was his intent to intimidate, he'd succeeded. Admirably. 'I repeat, what are you doing in here?'

'Just...just delivering some mail.' She gestured toward his desk. 'It got mixed in with mine.'

'The president of Caldwell's delivering mail.' His mouth tightened. 'What's wrong with that picture?'

He didn't believe her. She could see it in his face, in the clenched fists he held rigidly at his sides. She licked her lips and saw his eyes darken, saw the smoldering desire he couldn't quite suppress. And she knew what had to be done—no matter how much it went against the grain. Deliberately, she stepped away from the desk, hoping to draw his gaze from the incriminating envelope.

'You're right, of course,' she said with mocking lightness, throwing a provocative glance over her shoulder. 'I should have handed your mail over to Janine. That way you would have received it sometime Monday, instead of tonight.'

To her relief, he turned from the desk to watch the enticing sway of her hips and the seductive dance of the scarves as one moment they shifted to reveal an outrageous expanse of leg, and the next swirled closed.

He ran a hand through his damp hair, rumpling the tawny waves. 'What the hell are you wearing?' he demanded, his voice rough with emotion. He ripped his tie loose from his collar, flicking open the top two buttons of his dress shirt. The sophisticated businessman vanished, to be replaced by a man as tough and dangerous as he was irresistible. A man who watched her every move with savage intensity.

'Do you like it?' She paused in the doorway between their offices, leaning against the jam. The skirt parted again to flash a length of creamy white thigh.

He came after her then, moving with unmistakable purpose. She froze, her heart pounding wildly in her breast. Perhaps she'd played the role of the seductress a little too well. Clearly she'd started something he had every intention of finishing, even if she didn't. Color streaked across his cheekboncs and a muscle jerked in his jaw. But it was the look in his eyes that held her immobile, her spine pressed rigidly to the wooden doorframe. He stared down at her with such passionate craving that his green eyes burned hot and iridescent. The next instant his hands closed around her shoulders and, with a muttered expletive, he dragged her into his arms.

'Damien, no! The reception!' she reminded him with a startled cry.

'Right now I don't give a damn about the reception. You asked for this. Hell, you practically begged for it. And I'm not about to refuse your invitation.'

His mouth closed over hers and white heat consumed her, desire kicking in harder and faster than ever before. With each renewed touch, each devastating kiss, her need for him grew, grew to monumental proportions. This had to stop, before she lost all control, before... Oh, God. Before she lost her heart to him all over again. Five years ago, he'd nearly destroyed her, his defection a shattering blow. She couldn't repeat the experience. She'd never survive it.

She wrenched her mouth from his, dragging air into her lungs in great, heaving gasps. 'We can't do this. Not here. Not now.' Not ever.

'Then when? You said you'd name the time and place. So name it.' His hand followed the line of her hip, slipping between the petals of her skirt until he found the smooth curve of her thigh. His fingers glided across her skin in slow, sensuous circles and her knees buckled, forcing her to cling to his shoulders. 'Tonight,' he urged. 'Come home with me tonight.'

She shook her head. 'I can't,' she murmured. His hand shifted slowly upward and her voice broke. 'Don't. Please, Damien.'

'Why the delay?' he demanded. 'You want me. Do you think I can't tell, that I don't see the desire in your eyes, feel you tremble every time I touch you?' He pressed closer, trapping her against the doorway. 'I know what you're feeling because I feel it too. I can't come near you without wanting to rip off your clothes.'

She turned her head to one side, her eyes squeezed shut. 'You don't just want me—you want revenge,' she protested, fighting to retain her sanity. 'Sometimes I think you want it more than anything else. You intend to use me and once you do, once you've had your satisfaction, you'll toss me out of your life again. Well, I can't let you treat me with such contempt. I don't deserve it.'

'Contempt?' His hand shifted from her shoulder, dropping to play across the upper swells of her breasts. 'Does this feel like contempt to you?'

No. It felt like heaven. She turned her head to look at him, her gaze direct and unflinching. 'Where will it lead, Damien? Once you have what you want, what then?'

She sensed his withdrawal and braced herself against the anguish sure to follow. His hand slid from her breast and she had her answer, without his ever having to say a word. He didn't want her—not on a permanent basis. Once he'd had his fill, he'd walk away. And no matter how much she tried to tell herself she didn't care, that he'd never kept the truth of his intentions from her, his silent acknowledgement was a torment beyond calculation. Oh, Damien, whatever happened to us? Who'd have believed it could ever come to this?

His gaze fastened on the ruby choker circling her neck and he reached out, running his thumb over the glittering stones 'Caldwell let you keep this and the earrings?' he asked, his change of subject a welcome relief. 'I'm surprised.'

She shrugged, hoping the gesture looked casual, indifferent, that she successfully hid the desolation he'd wrought. 'Leonard didn't know I owned them,' she admitted.

He gave a short, harsh laugh. 'Let me guess. If he had known, he'd have suspected I'd given them to you. And once he'd realized they came from me he'd have sold them to help bail him out of his financial mess.'

'He'd probably have considered it poetic justice,' she admitted.

'And damn your feelings on the matter?'

'Possibly,' she conceded. Unquestionably. 'But they belonged to me, not him.' And she couldn't bear to part with them.

Damien's mouth curved. 'Yeah, well, Lenny liked taking things that didn't belong to him. I'm glad you kept them. They suit you. So does the dress for that matter.'

'Thank you,' she said lightly. 'And now, if you'll give me a minute to freshen up, I think it's time we went down to the party. We're already five minutes late.' And heaven only knew what their employees and guests would make of that. Whatever they thought, it wouldn't be far from the truth.

His hand gripped her elbow, preventing her from moving. 'You still haven't told me where or when.'

'No, I haven't, have I?' He wasn't slow on the uptake; nor did he bother to hide his displeasure. She pulled from his grasp and stepped away from the door, turning her back on him. She could feel his eyes boring into her spine.

'Sable.' He waited until he'd captured her attention, his expression stern and ruthless. 'Just so you know... I keep all the bid information locked in a safe.'

Fierce color heated her cheeks and in that moment she almost hated him. The irony of it made her want to weep. She hadn't been after the bids, but the whole purpose of her venture into his office had been equally damning—

to steal Alex's envelope. She couldn't very well protest her innocence when she had so much to feel guilty about.

'I'll keep that in mind for future reference,' she said coolly, and disappeared into her bathroom, using the precious moments afforded her to recover her poise.

Five minutes later they entered the party and it proved every bit as bad as Sable had feared. All eyes turned in their direction, a momentary hush descending on the gathering. She faltered just enough for Damien to notice.

'What's wrong?'

'Sorry,' she murmured, making a swift recovery. 'All the attention threw me for just a moment.'

His brows drew together. 'You're chairman of the board, president of Caldwell's. You must be used to this sort of attention by now.'

'Perhaps I should have said infamy rather than attention,' she said in a dry undertone.

'If you're infamous, you have only yourself to blame,' he retorted with a noteworthy lack of sympathy.

'So you keep telling me.'

Her spine ramrod-stiff and her head held high, she swept down the stairs to the ballroom as she'd done innumerable times before. She wouldn't allow them to defeat her, to intimidate her.

To her utter astonishment, Damien gained her side before she'd gone more than two steps. His arm slipped around her, his hand planted square in the middle of her back. The gesture was duly noted. He might as well have put a sign around her neck, proclaiming that she had his protection. It meant more to her than she could possibly express, but it provided a false sense of security. She couldn't trust that he'd protect her. After all... he hadn't before.

The next two hours proved the most difficult of Sable's life. She greeted Caldwell's clients, introduced Damien, and then forced herself to stand passively at his side while he seized the conversational ball. It didn't take anyone long to figure out that the winds of change were sweeping through the company, and that Damien was the force behind those winds.

She met the speculative looks with a false calm, deflected the barbed comments with pleasant smiles, and cloaked herself behind a facade that even the most objectional remark couldn't penetrate. But all the while she retreated emotionally, withdrawing further and further, determined to keep a small, innermost part of herself safe from harm.

The worse moment of the evening occurred when they crossed paths with Patricia, who'd come as the guest of one of their clients. Sable stared at her former sister-in-law in disbelief, stunned by the sheer audacity of the woman. She'd sold Caldwell's down the river, yet joined in the discussion as though nothing had changed.

'So,' Patricia said during a lull in the conversation, 'how did you enjoy your moment of power heading Caldwell's? Or didn't it last long enough to enjoy?'

Sable didn't bother to dignify the question with a response. 'I'm surprised you have the nerve to show up here,' she said instead.

'Why? I've done nothing to be ashamed of.' Patricia lifted an eyebrow. 'Have you?'

A worried-looking Janine joined the small group at that point, forestalling Sable's reply. 'Excuse me, Mrs Caldwell. With all the confusion earlier I forgot to deliver a message—from Kyle.'

Sable stiffened, not daring to look in Damien's direction. But she didn't doubt for a minute that she had his undivided attention. 'Was it urgent?'

'I don't believe so. He did ask that you phone home.'

'Thank you, Janine. I'll return his call in a few minutes.'

'And how is Kyle?' Patricia questioned, slanting a knowing smile in Damien's direction.

Sable struggled to remain calm. If she revealed even the slightest hint of panic, her former sister-in-law would take malicious delight in disclosing precisely who Kyle was. 'He's fine,' she replied steadily.

Patricia turned to Damien. 'Have you met him?' she asked with mock-innocence.

'Not yet.'

The brevity of his response spoke volumes and amusement gleamed in Patricia's eyes. 'Yes, Sable does like to keep him all to herself. You'll have to get her to introduce you some time. I think you'd find it well worth your while.'

It was the last straw, and Sable's composure shattered. 'That's enough, Patricia!' she snapped, instantly regretting her loss of control. All eyes focused on her and she fought to regain her equilibrium, offering a remote smile. 'If you'll excuse me, I have a phone call to make.' And with that she turned on her heel and hastened from the room. She had to get away, had to escape before she betrayed herself any further.

Returning to her office, she placed a quick call home. Millie picked up the phone, her calm greeting going a long way toward soothing Sable's agitation. 'He called you?' the nanny questioned in astonishment. 'The little rascal! I had no idea he knew your work number.'

'But everything's all right?'

'Just fine. I put him to bed over an hour ago and haven't heard a peep out of him.'

'Thank you, Millie. I should be home soon.'

Ringing off, Sable rubbed her temples, the beginnings of a headache setting in. She hesitated, glancing in the direction of Damien's office. If she intended to get a look at Alex's communiqué, it was now or never. Taking a deep breath, she crossed the room and pushed open the door. This time she didn't hesitate, but hurried directly to Damien's desk and picked up the envelope.

She wanted to rip it open. She wanted to destroy it before Damien had a chance to read the contents. But at the last moment she knew she couldn't do it. No matter what anyone believed, she hadn't leaked the bids. To do so would have gone against ever tenet she'd ever held dear. And so did this. That decided, she opened her hand, allowing the envelope to flutter back to the desk.

'So it wasn't the bids you were after earlier.'

Swearing beneath her breath, she slowly swiveled to face Damien. He stood, leaning against the doorjamb, his arms folded across his chest. She looked at him and shuddered. His face was dark and forbidding, his eyes the only thing revealing any expression—and those glittered with a white-hot rage. She'd made a serious error in judgement and soon she'd pay for that error.

'No, I wasn't interested in the bids,' she replied with amazing composure.

'What's in the envelope?'

'I don't know. I couldn't bring myself to open it.'

'Give it to me.' He held out his hand and, with no other alternative, she picked up the envelope and relinquished it to him. 'Shall we go?'

She didn't dare argue, not when his fury simmered just below the surface, ready to explode with volcanic force at the first sign of opposition. 'Go where?'

'Back to the party,' he informed her tautly. 'It's on the verge of breaking up. We'll stand there—together—until the last person has left and then we'll leave.'

'We'. The two of them. Her hands curled into fists. 'And then?'

'I'll take you home.' His expression flayed her. '*Then* we'll open the envelope and see what you're so desperate to keep from me.'

It was as though all her emotions had iced over. She couldn't think, couldn't feel, couldn't comprehend the fact that total disaster awaited around the next bend. She might as well have been an automaton. Without protest, she returned with him to the party and stood at his side until the room had cleared. She smiled. She shook hands. She even managed to string words together into complete sentences. She must have made sense, since no one seemed to notice anything amiss.

And all the while Damien stood at her side. He kept the incriminating envelope rolled in his fist, slapping it relentlessly against his thigh. If his intention was to drive her to the brink of insanity, he was unquestionably succeeding. By the time he decided to leave, her nerves were shredded. It wasn't until he'd assisted her into his black Jaguar that she came to life.

'I don't want you coming home with me,' she began.

'Tough.'

'I'm serious, Damien. You can't come in.'

He stopped at a stop sign and glanced at her, the lights from the dash playing across his taut, unforgiving features. 'I'm coming in.'

She shook her head. 'Not a chance.'

He accelerated through the intersection, and started up a hill, shifting gears with the ease of long practice. 'You either agree or I continue on to Sausalito. And if we do that, count on it that you won't need to worry any more about where or when we make love. The decision will be out of your hands.'

She inhaled sharply. 'You can't do that!' she protested. 'You promised.'

'I can and I will. And you won't fight me about it, either. At least, not for long. Not if your response earlier is any indication.'

'That's a foul thing to say!'

'It's honest and it's accurate.' He shot her an impatient look. 'Now which will it be? My place or yours? Decide before this light changes or I'll make the decision for you.'

It didn't take any thought. There was only one choice. She sent up a small prayer that Millie had made Kyle pick up before going to bed. Otherwise they'd be discussing far more than just the contents of that envelope. 'Take me home,' she finally said.

His laugh held a sardonic edge. 'Now why doesn't that surprise me?'

She didn't speak for the rest of the drive. He parked outside her house, curbing the wheels and setting the emergency brake. She didn't wait for him to open her door. All things considered, the small courtesy would be painfully out of place. Damien followed her up the steps to the porch, waiting impatiently at her side while she unlocked the front door. Walking in behind her, his footsteps echoed on the inlaid oak flooring. Sable glanced up the steps leading to the bedrooms. Millie had apparently retired for the evening; all was quiet.

'Lenny had good taste,' Damien commented. 'A bit of a comedown from Gopher's Hole, of course——'

'Fox's Lair!'

He shrugged. 'Whatever. When was this place built? 1906? 1907?'

'1907. Right after the earthquake. And Leonard didn't choose the house, I did—a month after he died.' She tossed her purse on to the hall table. 'Now, are we through with the pleasant chit-chat or shall we debate whether the leaded windows are originals? Or, if you'd prefer, we could marvel over the fact that the framework and upstairs flooring are made from redwood.' She lifted her chin. 'Well?'

His gaze settled on her face and she wondered if he could see the tension in her expression, sense her exhaustion. 'What I'd like is a cup of coffee,' he finally said.

'Excuse me?'

'Coffee. That amazing bean they grow in South America and ship here. You know. Grind it. Brew it. Drink it.'

'I know what coffee is! I just don't understand. I thought you'd want...' She gestured toward the envelope fisted in his hand.

His mouth tightened. 'Oh, we'll get to that soon enough. But first...coffee.'

There was no point in arguing. But she wondered if this wasn't a delaying tactic. Did he hope the mysterious Kyle would choose to join them? Heavens, he'd better not. She shot a surreptitious glance toward the living room. It appeared tidy enough, none of her son's toys readily apparent. She'd just have to risk it.

'Have a seat, I'll be right back,' she said, and headed for the kitchen. Moving as swiftly as possible, she scooped a blend of her favorite coffee into the coffee maker. Next, she removed two mugs form the cupboard and set them on the counter.

'Anything I can do to help?' Damien asked, appearing in the doorway.

She froze, shooting a sudden, panicked glance toward the refrigerator—a refrigerator plastered with Kyle's artwork. 'Not a thing. I'll join you in a minute.' Take the hint! she willed silently. And get out of my kitchen. The coffee maker burbled and a final drop of coffee plopped into the glass carafe. Snatching up the mugs, she filled them to the brim. 'Let's go,' she urged.

His brows drew together. 'I thought you preferred half coffee, half cream.'

'I decided to take a leaf from your book and try it straight up and uncorrupted,' she said as calmly as she could manage.

A smile edged across his mouth. 'Black?'

'Black,' she confirmed, moving toward the living room. 'Shall we?' He didn't protest, nor did he look in the direction of the refrigerator. She could have cried with relief.

'I wouldn't think you'd be so eager to open this envelope. Nor hear what I have to say about your efforts to steal it.'

A thousand possible comebacks flashed through her mind, not one of any use. After all, she *had* planned to steal the envelope. She couldn't very well deny it. Even explaining that she'd changed her mind would be pointless, merely underlining her initial guilt. 'I'd rather get this over with,' she said with a frustrated sigh. 'Besides, I'd like to find out what's in there, too.'

'You don't know?'

'I have my suspicions.' She sat down on the couch, cradling the mug between her hands. And that was when she saw it.

On the carpet at her feet lay one of Kyle's shoes.

She choked.

'Something wrong?' Damien questioned.

'Coasters! Could you...could you hand me a coaster, please? They're on the end table beside you.' The minute he turned, she scooped up the telltale evidence and thrust it between the cushion and the arm of the couch. Frantically, she looked around for the shoe's mate. Knowing Kyle, it could be anywhere.

He handed her the wooden coaster. 'Lose something?'

'Yes. *No*!' To her abject horror, tears of desperation flooded her eyes. Terrified that he'd notice her loss of control, she lowered her head and took a hasty sip of coffee. Without the cream to cool it, it scalded her tongue, and she gasped at the pain, the breath sobbing beneath her lips. She blinked rapidly. At least now she'd have an excuse for her tears.

Damien reached out and took the mug from her trembling hands, setting it on the coaster. 'Calm down,' he told her quietly. 'Getting upset isn't going to change anything. Now let's get this over with.' And in one swift move he ripped open the envelope.

She flinched at the sound. 'Well? What does Alex say?'

'He confirms that someone at Caldwell's is leaking information, and as proof has sent a copy of the prospectus we prepared for Luther.' He studied the papers. 'This is our bid, there's no question about that. It came from our office.'

'Why would he send it to you?' she asked with a frown. 'It doesn't make sense. Couldn't you pursue legal action against him?'

Damien shook his head. 'He knows I won't, that all I want is the person at Caldwell's who's stealing the information. As to why he'd help me...' His mouth twisted. 'I imagine that as long as you and Patricia headed the company he didn't have many qualms about helping himself to this information.'

'But once you came on board all that changed?' The sheer audacity of it took her breath away. 'It's all right to steal from women, but not from men?' she questioned incredulously.

'If you and Patricia had acted the first time this had happened, he wouldn't have thought that,' Damien retorted sharply. 'Instead you let it be known that Caldwell's was an easy mark. But Alex knows me. He knows I won't stand still for theft, that I'll uncover the truth, no matter who I have to take down to do it. He's just throwing me a bone and moving out of the way, hoping I won't come after him.'

It made sense. Unfortunately. 'Did he...did he add anything else?'

'Yes.' Damien's gaze locked with hers. 'He suggests I watch my back.'

She licked her lips. 'But what about the person who leaked the information? Does...does he say who it is?'

'Not in so many words. But he doesn't have to.' He tossed Alex's papers on to the coffee table in front of them. 'Tell me, Sable, why did you think he'd pin it on you? What proof does he have?'

'I...I don't understand.'

'Yes, you do. You tried to get hold of Alex's letter, not once but twice. You're terrified. I see it in your eyes. I can hear it in your voice. He must have some sort of evidence of your involvement or you wouldn't have been so desperate to get your hands on this envelope.'

'He doesn't have any proof!' she cried. 'He can't.'

'Then why are you so frightened? What's going on?'

She bowed her head. 'I don't know,' she confessed. 'I wish I did.'

He thrust a hand through his hair and got to his feet, crossing to stand by the fireplace grate. Stripping off his suit coat, he slung it over the arm of a nearby chair. Next, he loosened the dark red tie at his throat. He couldn't have stated his intentions more clearly. He planned to stay as long as it took in order to get to the bottom of this situation.

He faced her, the snowy-white dress shirt clinging to the full, muscular expanse of his shoulders. His jaw was clenched, and he thrust his hands into his trouser pockets, the black silk pulled taut across his thighs. His movements were filled with a volatile impatience, as though he barely held himself in check.

'Let's begin again,' he bit out. 'You don't seem to realize how close you are to disaster. I suggest you be frank with me, while you still have the chance.'

Her gaze jerked upward. 'Is that a threat?'

'It's a promise. Now what does Alex Johnson have on you? How are you involved?'

Perhaps he was right. Perhaps the time had come to level with him. Damien wasn't joking. Without question he planned to seek legal action against the person responsible. She had to find a way to convince him of her innocence or she'd take the fall.

'All right, Damien. I'll tell you what I know.' She struggled to gather her thoughts, trying to determine the best place to start. At the beginning seemed sensible. 'After Leonard's death last year, Patricia took over as chairwoman, and we started losing the occasional contract. None of us thought much of it. I mean, you can't win them all. Ryan Matheson expressed concern, but Patricia refused to listen. And since she was in control...' Sable sighed. 'The rest of us fell into line.'

'So the problem was ignored?'

'Yes,' she confessed. Looking back, the decision seemed foolish in the extreme. But at the time... 'After this last board meeting, Ryan approached me, warning that there were rumors of a leak.'

'And warning that that fact would figure in his report?'

'Figure predominately.' She met his eyes without flinching. 'I swear to you, Damien, it never occurred to me there might be a leak. It seems so obvious now. But then...' She shrugged helplessly. 'Right after my meeting with Ryan, I decided to try and find out who was to blame. I hoped to uncover the guilty party before Ryan completed his report to you.'

She couldn't tell if her confession angered him. He stood quietly, listening intently, his face expressionless. 'So, what did you do?'

'I asked Ryan to prepare a list of all possible suspects—anyone who'd had access to the information. And then I called Alex Johnson and asked him to name his source.'

Damien released a bark of laughter. 'Did you really think he'd tell you?' he asked in disbelief.

Warm color swept into her cheeks. 'No. But I hoped he'd say something that might clue me in.'

'And did he?'

'Alex was very generous,' she admitted huskily. 'He told me precisely who had leaked the information.'

Damien straightened, his gaze sharpening. 'And?'

She plucked at the filmy scarves of her skirt. It was all so hopeless. 'He said I had leaked the information.'

'He *what*?'

'He said I had leaked the information,' she repeated stoically.

His eyes flamed and his hands clenched into fists. 'And did you?'

'*No!*' She bit down on her lip, quickly lowering her voice. If Kyle heard her, he'd be downstairs like a shot. 'Of course I didn't. But what's so frightening is... I believed him, Damien. Alex isn't lying when he says it's me. I mean, I'm not guilty, but he's convinced I'm responsible.'

Damien turned slightly, staring into the empty fireplace grate, his brows drawn together in a fierce frown. 'Have you any idea why he might think that?' he questioned.

'I have an idea.' She hesitated, not certain that she wanted to discuss it. 'But I have no proof. It's just a suspicion.'

'Tell me,' he ordered.

'Patricia's last name is also Caldwell. Perhaps he confused us.' Spoken aloud it seemed totally inane.

Apparently Damien thought so too. He shook his head. 'Alex isn't stupid. Sorry, Sable. It's too convenient. Wasn't she the one you pointed the finger at last time?'

Her mouth tightened. 'You asked and I've told you. She kept the board from investigating the problem sooner. She had access to the Luther bid. Maybe Alex just heard the name Caldwell and assumed it was me.'

'Why would he think that?'

'For the same reason everyone else assumes it,' she retorted. 'My reputation precedes me.'

'But why would Patricia leak the information? What's her motivation?'

Sable shrugged. 'To get even? She sold her shares of Caldwell's to you because the board removed her as chairwoman. Once she'd sold out, I suspect she'd think it served us right if the company lost business. And there's one other reason. She's always held us responsible for destroying both her brother and her family's business. Not that I entirely blame her for feeling that way.'

He turned then, his face set in hard, implacable lines. 'There's one way of knowing for sure whether or not she's guilty.'

'Which is?'

'She no longer has access to company files. Therefore, if she's responsible, the Luther development should be the last bid that's leaked.'

She couldn't fault his logic. But for some reason her fear didn't ease. 'Assuming she's the one who did it,' Sable murmured.

Damien's smile made her very, very nervous. 'You've sworn you're innocent. So, who else could it possibly be?'

A tiny sound distracted her, a sound only a mother would notice—the stealthy turning of a doorknob. She hastened to her feet, the petals of her skirt fluttering about her knees in an agitated swirl. 'Is there anything else?' she asked, struggling to conceal her panic. 'I'd like to call it a night, if you don't mind.'

He tilted his head to one side, his eyes narrowing. 'And if I do mind?'

She gripped her hands together, desperate to get rid of him. 'I've answered your questions to the best of my knowledge. I think we should sleep on it.'

'What a good idea.' He started across the room and she saw desire flare to life in his eyes. She knew that look—and knew where it would lead.

'No,' she whispered in dismay. 'Oh, no! I meant sleep on it and...and discuss it further in the morning.' She darted across the room and snatched up his coat. Keeping him at arm's length, she hurried toward the foyer.

Damien followed. Just as they reached the entranceway, he dropped a hand on her shoulder and spun her around. 'What's going on, Sable? What's your hurry?'

A floorboard creaked, the sort of sound a house made when it settled for the night...or the sound a small boy made when he was sneaking down the hallway. If Damien heard, he gave no indication. 'I'm exhausted.' She faked a yawn. 'See? It's time for you to go.' She grabbed at the doorknob, jerking desperately at it until it finally opened.

He leaned a shoulder against the oak door and it crashed closed again. 'I'm not leaving. Not without this.' Before she could react, he pulled her into his arms and kissed her.

Even knowing that Kyle was slipping ever closer to the stairway behind them, even knowing that at any moment disaster would strike and her worse nightmare would be realized, she couldn't help but respond. Her hands crept up his chest, circling his shoulders, and she clung to him, opened to him, returned his kiss with a passion she couldn't deny. When he finally released her, every thought in her head had vanished. She could only stare up at him, her eyes huge and wonder-struck.

Thunk.

Her brow wrinkled, reality slowly returning. She knew that sound. Kyle made it when he slid, step by step, down the stairs. *Kyle*! She didn't waste another moment. With a gasp, she ripped free of Damien's arms and attacked the door again. Finally, *finally* it opened. 'We'll talk in the morning,' she cried. She thrust Damien's coat into his hands and shoved at his chest with all her might.

Thunk.

To her astonished relief, he took a step backward over the threshold. She didn't think twice. She slammed the door in his face. Turning, she saw how close she'd been to total calamity. Kyle slid into view, his face wreathed in an ear-to-ear grin.

'Mommy!' he shouted.

She hastened to the steps, scooping him up into her arms. 'I missed you,' she whispered, hugging him close. Thank heavens. Oh, thank heavens she'd been in time.

Or so she thought.

The door squeaked open behind her.

'I assume this is Kyle,' came Damien's dry voice.

CHAPTER EIGHT

DAMIEN leaned against the front door, his cool, watchful gaze sweeping over Sable, before settling on Kyle. 'It would seem we have more to discuss than just that envelope. No wonder you were in such a hurry to get rid of me.'

Sable's grip tightened around her son. 'How did you know?' she whispered. 'How did you know to come back in?'

Damien reached into the pocket of his suit coat and he tugged out Kyle's shoe. The sneaker rested on his palm, looking absurdly small compared with his hand. 'I believe this matches the one you shoved under the couch cushion.'

So he'd seen, had known all along. She closed her eyes, her distress increasing by the minute. 'I have to put Kyle to bed.'

He couldn't seem to stop staring at the boy. Not that Kyle minded. He returned the scrutiny with equal intensity. 'He's your son.' It wasn't a question.

There was no point in denying it. The truth was self-evident. 'Yes, he's my son,' she confirmed.

Her agitation grew to an unbearable level and she stood, lifting Kyle into her arms. He'd gotten too old and heavy to carry like this, but she dreaded what Damien might do... might say. She was terrified that he would ask that all-important question. And she didn't want her son—their son—present when it happened.

Kyle wrapped his arms around her neck and his legs about her waist, content to watch and listen. He showed no fear, no shyness. She knew he was busy weighing up the situation—and the man. As soon as he'd formed an opinion, he wouldn't hesitate to express it, for good or bad. Just like his father.

'He looks like you.' Damien broke the prolonged silence. He glanced at the sneaker, seeming surprised to discover he still held it. Crossing to the hall table, he set it gently beside her purse. 'As soon as I found the shoe, I realized Kyle had to be a child. But I couldn't be certain he was yours. You'd told me he was a relative. That covers a lot of ground.'

'So, now you know.'

'Yes. Now I know.' He stood—tense, wary. He'd wandered into uncharted territory and wouldn't begin his attack until he'd completed his analysis of the situation.

She didn't dare afford him the time for that analysis. 'I need to go upstairs now,' she informed him, not caring if she sounded abrupt. 'I'll see you on Monday.'

'Wait.' He held out a hand, as though to detain her physically. Then he pulled back, thrusting his fist into his trouser pocket, his eyes darkening with some turbulent emotion. 'Wait for just a minute, if you would.'

For a crazy instant she thought his expression showed a momentary regret, a flash of longing. But she knew she must be mistaken. Damien experiencing regret? Damien needing something or someone? Not a chance. He didn't need anyone. Not her. And not her son. 'What do you want?' she asked. 'It's late and I'm tired. I'd rather we continue this another time.'

'I'm sure you would. But I wouldn't. Tell me, Sable—why the big secret?' he demanded. 'Why go to such extreme lengths to keep me from finding out?'

His momentary hesitation had vanished, replaced by unmistakable strength and authority. This was the Damien she knew so well. He watched her keenly and she couldn't get an image out of her mind—an image of a jungle cat catching wind of his prey. She had to flee. Now. Before it was too late, before he'd made up his mind whether or not to give chase. 'This isn't the appropriate time for questions, Damien. I...I have to put Kyle to bed.'

'May I join you?'

That he'd ask permission instead of demand the right revealed just how moved he was by Kyle. But she couldn't allow compassion to influence her judgement. 'I don't think that would be a good idea,' she began.

Kyle turned his head, his mouth close to her ear, and whispered, 'He can come. Day-man can come.'

She bit down on her lip, his mispronunciation of Damien's name as deeply affecting as his request. She wished she could refuse, wished she could race up the stairs and escape the coming discussion. 'It would seem that I've been overruled,' she said, darting a swift, reluctant look at Damien. 'Kyle would like it if you'd tuck him in for the night.'

Man and boy exchanged a long look, a look that excluded her, a look of complete understanding. Damien inclined his head. 'Thank you. I'd like that.' He glanced at her. 'He's too heavy for you to carry. Let me take him.'

Without a moment's hesitation, Kyle held out his arms, and, with no other choice, she relinquished her son. *Their* son, she reminded herself yet again. It was time she faced facts. Damien and Kyle belonged together. She'd always known it, always resisted that knowledge because she was afraid. Afraid that Damien would want her son—but wouldn't want her. They ascended the stairs together, almost like a family. It was a treacherous thought, an unrealistic thought.

'Which way?' he asked at the top of the steps.

'The first room.' She gestured to the right and moved ahead of them, pushing open the door to Kyle's bedroom. 'In here.'

Damien looked around. 'Nice,' he approved. 'Why the bunk beds?'

'For friends,' Kyle answered the question for her. 'And 'cuz I like it. The top is my fort.' He pointed at the ceiling. 'See the stars?'

Damien tilted back his head. A whole galaxy of glittering stars and planets, applied with glow-in-the-dark paint, spread across the ceiling. 'Clever.'

'And the bottom is my cave.' He wiggled free of Damien's arms and clambered on to the lower bunk. 'See? I put blankets all around so it's dark. And Mommy lets me draw on the wall like a real caveman.'

'She does, does she?' He shot her an amused look.

'It's only the one wall,' she murmured. 'And it saved the rest of the walls in the house from any further artistic endeavors.' She turned her attention to her son. 'It's time for bed, sweetheart. Where are you sleeping tonight? You need to choose.'

Kyle settled cross-legged on the mattress, his brows drawn together in thought. Sable caught her breath. He looked so much like his father, it was frightening. She glanced nervously at Damien. Did he suspect the truth? Did he see himself mirrored in those miniature features? If so, he gave no sign.

'Here. In the cave,' Kyle decided, and burrowed beneath the sheet. 'But I wants Day-man to tuck me in.'

Damien didn't wait for a second invitation. He dropped to one knee beside the bed. With a giggle, Kyle kicked off the sheet and for the next few minutes a wrestling match ensued. Damien made a big production of pulling up the covers and tucking them beneath the squirming little boy. The instant he finished, Kyle churned his arms and legs until the bedcovers were strewn half on and half off the bed. With a growl of mock-fury, Damien would then start the process all over again. Inevitably, Kyle tired and finally gave in to Damien's persistence, allowing the sheet and blanket to stay put.

Damien ruffled the boy's dark curls, the gesture tender beyond belief. 'How old are you, Kyle?' he questioned unexpectedly.

Alarm streaked through Sable and she stepped forward. 'Please, don't——' she began.

'Six,' came the sleepy retort, though with his lisp it sounded more like 'thix'.

'Six?' Damien repeated, lifting an eyebrow.

Velvety eyes opened, the ebony depths twinkling with laughter. His smile widened into a grin. 'I'm gonna be six. I'm gonna be six t'morrow. Right, Mommy?'

Sable smiled, relaxing ever so slightly. 'If you want to be.'

His freckled nose wrinkled. 'Maybe I'll be ten. Or a lion.' He bared his tiny teeth and curled his fingers into claws. 'I can growl real good.'

'I'm sure you can,' Damien agreed with a husky laugh. 'Goodnight.'

'You gonna come tomorrow?' Kyle asked. 'You can if you wants to.'

'Thanks. I'd like that. But if I don't see you tomorrow, I'll see you again soon. OK?' It was the perfect response. Kyle readily agreed, and, with a huge yawn, curled into a tight ball, his lids drifting closed.

Without a sound, Damien and Sable crept from the room. Neither spoke as they returned to the living room. She glanced at him, considering what she'd say, how she'd explain the truth so that he'd understand, so that he wouldn't hate her. He wasn't going to take this well, and she couldn't blame him. They should have had this little talk years ago.

He took up his stance by the fireplace again, his profile turned to her, one hand planted on the mantel as he stared down at the slate hearth. She knew he was gathering his thoughts for the coming discussion, and she stared at him, drinking in the strong sweep of his brow, the taut, angled curve of his cheekbones, the firm, determined chin and passionate mouth.

She caught her breath in dismay. She loved him, she realized then, the knowledge as stunning as it was undeniable. She'd never stopped loving him. Even when he'd hurt her, when he'd withdrawn his support, her feelings had never truly died, only been buried. All these years. All these long, lonely years she'd kept her emotions on ice, refusing to allow anyone close—except Kyle.

And now she knew why. Because throughout that time she'd held on to the secret hope that she and Damien would have another opportunity, that there would come a time when they'd find each other again. She closed her eyes. And now that they finally had, any chance of them working out their problems was doomed to fail. He wouldn't forgive her for keeping Kyle a secret, any more than he'd forgiven her for betraying him. The knowledge came as a devastating blow.

She glanced at him, exhaustion slipping over her, and she struggled to conceal her regret... and her yearning. 'Is it really necessary to go into this tonight?' she questioned. She could predict his answer, but hoped that he might relent and let her off the hook.

He turned his head, an unexpected smile touching his mouth. 'You've been ducking this conversation since I bought into Caldwell's,' he told her drily. His amusement died, his eyes darkening with emotion. 'He's a beautiful child, Sable. But he's not six. How old is he?'

She sank to the couch, burying her hands in the filmy layers of her skirt. So now it began. 'Four,' she told him, without delay or evasion.

'Four...?' He stilled, a sudden, savage light growing in his eyes. 'Four...or four and a few months?'

She knew the point of the question. If Kyle was just four, he would be Leonard's son. If he was more than that... 'Four and a few months,' she whispered.

He didn't react, didn't show any emotion. But a vein throbbed in his temple and the muscles in his jaw clenched, warning that he wasn't as calm as he appeared. 'Kyle's the reason you married, isn't he?'

She nodded, her heart pounding. 'Yes,' she admitted, waiting for the other shoe to drop, for him to draw the ultimate conclusion.

'You were already pregnant when you married Caldwell, weren't you?'

'Yes,' she repeated.

Fury erupted, sweeping across his face like a dark tide. She could see him fight it, struggling to keep his temper in check. He didn't succeed. 'Six weeks after leaving me you were pregnant and married to that son of a bitch? Six *weeks*!'

She stared in bewilderment, confused by what he'd said. He couldn't believe.... He didn't think that Kyle was *Leonard's*, did he? 'Damien, wait a minute. You have it all wrong. I can explain——'

'Explain! Explain what?' He straightened, stepping away from the mantel, and she stiffened, the unadulterated rage in his expression causing her to shrink back against the cushions. 'I won't bother asking if there's any chance Kyle's mine.'

'*What*?'

'Oh, don't look so insulted.' He thrust a hand through his hair, the movement filled with barely suppressed violence. 'Hell, it must have been a close thing, a matter of weeks between the time you left my bed and crawled into Caldwell's. There had to have been a momentary doubt over who fathered your child. I'm surprised it didn't occur to Lenny. Considering his lack of principles, I'm amazed he was willing to marry you at all. He had to have been damned certain the kid was his. How did you convince him? Or didn't he know about us?'

He couldn't have shocked her more if he'd slapped her. 'You bastard!' she whispered.

'That's why you were so anxious to keep Kyle a secret, wasn't it? Once I knew about him, you had to realize I'd suspect the rest—that you were in cahoots with Caldwell from the start, sleeping with him, supplying him with bid information.'

'No!'

He came closer. 'No, you weren't conspiring with Lenny, supplying him with bid information?' he ripped into her. 'Or no, you weren't sleeping with him?'

She leapt to her feet, determined not to cower on the couch, refusing to show any weakness or vulnerability that he could twist to his advantage. 'I never told Leonard anything about your contracts or your clients. I let certain facts slip to Patricia, I've never denied that. But I never, ever discussed Hawke Enterprises with Leonard. Nor was I sleeping with him.'

'Well, if you weren't sleeping with Lenny before the leaks, you sure as hell had to be sleeping with him right afterward. Your son's proof enough of that.' His sarcasm cut her to the quick.

'You've got it all wrong!' she protested.

'Then why did you keep Kyle's existence a secret these past two weeks?'

'Why in the world would I want to tell you about him?' she shot back. 'Why would I tell you when it would give you one more weapon to use against me in this little vendetta of yours?'

'You think I'd use a child? That I'd ever do anything to harm your son?' His affront would have been laughable if matters weren't so heartbreaking.

'That's precisely what I think. You'd do anything and everything in your power to hurt me; that's the whole reason you bought into Caldwell's. Why would I think you'd make an exception for Kyle?' she demanded. 'What have you done that could possibly lead me to believe that?'

'Don't you dare dump this on me,' he bit out. 'What the hell was I supposed to believe? You've lied to me from the beginning. About the bids. About Caldwell. About your own son.'

'I haven't! I've been trying to tell you——'

He snatched her into his arms then, his body taut and hard, his anger a tangible force. 'Have you any idea what it does to me, knowing you allowed that piece of slime to touch you? Knowing he fathered a child with you?'

Tears clogged her throat, making it a struggle to speak, but she had to explain, had to make him understand what she'd gone through, how she'd felt. 'He was good to me at a time I had nowhere to turn. You had deserted me. I was unemployed and alone. If it hadn't been for Leonard...' Her voice broke, distress heavy in her voice.

'All I know is that you betrayed me. Of all the things you could have done, you chose the one I could never forgive.' His hands slid across her bared shoulders, slipping upward to cup her face. 'Kyle could have been our son. Has that ever occurred to you?'

The truth trembled on her lips, and almost—almost—she confessed everything. 'Damien, I have to tell you——'

He shook his head. 'You don't have to say another word.' His expression might have been carved from granite. 'The facts speak for themselves. If you hadn't been so greedy, so treacherous, Kyle could have been mine.'

Tears threatened to overwhelm her. Was that what he really thought of her? 'And what if he had been?' she asked. 'What then?'

His passion, his fury, broke free. 'Then I could have watched you ripen with my child. I could have been there when you gave birth to him, seen him suckle at your breast, been a father to him. Instead you took all that from me and gave the privilege to another man.'

She inhaled sharply. 'You hate the idea that he could be Leonard's, don't you? You hate Kyle because of who his father might be.'

'I want to hate you both,' came the furious response. He closed his eyes, fighting some inner demon, the anger slowly draining away. 'But I can't. Not after seeing Kyle, touching him, hearing his laugh. Dear God, Sable.' The pain in his voice was nearly her undoing. 'He could have been ours.'

'No, he couldn't have been,' she told him raggedly. 'Because you don't want a real son, let alone a real wife. You want someone without failings, someone perfect, without flaw or human foibles. Well, we can never be like that. For Kyle to be your son would mean letting down your guard and trusting, risking your heart. And for me to be your wife would mean believing in me despite all evidence to the contrary. And you've never been willing or able to do that, have you?'

He didn't deny it. 'And Caldwell was?' he asked instead.

'Yes,' she retorted without hesitation. 'For all his faults, Leonard loved Kyle unconditionally, without a moment's reservation. And he defended me, believed in me when no one else would. And I'll always be grateful to him for that.'

'Grateful?' He instantly honed in on the word. 'Is that what you felt for Leonard? What about love? Or wasn't that important to you?'

She didn't pretend to misunderstand. 'I love Kyle. That's more than enough.'

'Is it?' His voice dropped, grew husky and seductive, and his hands slipped deep into her hair. 'Are you sure?'

She licked her lips, her gaze slipping from his. 'Positive.'

'Let's see if I can't change your mind about that.'

His thumb drifted across her mouth, teasing her lips apart. And then he took them with his, delving within, tasting with a deftness and delicacy that stole her heart yet again. She couldn't help capitulating, offering up her mouth in sweet surrender. He held her with a tenderness that made resistance impossible, exploring with barely restrained passion, his gentle seduction doing far more to sweep aside any lingering doubts than a more determined assault.

'Tell me what you want,' he murmured, his mouth drifting to the sensitive juncture between her neck and shoulder. 'Tell me you want me—want me here and now. There's no point in waiting any longer. You know Caldwell never made you feel like this, that you never came close to sharing with him what we once had. Let me prove it to you.'

She stiffened, pulling back, sanity slowly returning. 'Is that the point of all this? To prove you're a better lover than Leonard?'

He shook his head. 'I don't need to prove it. You already know what we shared was unique. It's not something we'll find again. You just don't want to admit it because of Kyle, because it might hurt him to know that Caldwell didn't measure up. So you've made your husband into a saint, someone Kyle can be proud of. But he wasn't. There's a lot you don't know about the man.'

Anger stirred. 'And you intend to tell me, is that it?'

'No. It won't change anything for you to know.' He released her. 'You're not in the mood to continue this, so I'll leave. But I want you to think about something.'

'What's that?' she whispered.

'Is Caldwell the man you want your son to emulate? Is he who you intend to hold up to Kyle as a role model?'

Long after he'd left, she stood in the middle of the room, unmoving, his words ringing in her ears. He was right. Leonard wasn't the proper role model for Kyle. Only one man could properly handle that responsibility. And that was Damien.

* * *

At the crack of dawn the next morning, Kyle crept into Sable's bedroom. Climbing on to her bed, he bounced on the mattress until, with a groan, she rolled over and fixed him with a fierce glare. 'What do you think you're doing, young man?' she demanded.

'Bouncin',' came the unconcerned retort.

She sighed. Clearly, her son was no easier to intimidate than his father. '*Why* are you bouncing on my bed at...' she fumbled for the clock '...six in the morning? Kyle!'

'Time to get up. Where's Day-man? I wants to play with him.'

She collapsed back against the pillows. Uh-oh. 'Stop bouncing. You're making me dizzy.'

He grinned, bouncing harder. 'Day-man! Day-man! Day-man!'

'He's not here.' But she wished he were, wished it with every fiber of her being. She released a soft groan, ruthlessly clamping down on the stray thought. She couldn't keep yearning for the impossible. She'd been down that road before and knew it led straight to disaster.

'When's he comin' back?'

'I'm not sure.' Hoping to end the inquisition, she grabbed him about the waist and tickled his ribs until he collapsed laughing. 'Come on, munchkin. Let's get breakfast.'

'Day-man comin'?' he asked, gazing expectantly up at her.

She sighed. 'No, Kyle. He's not coming for breakfast.'

To her disgust, the questions about Damien set the pattern for all of Saturday. Since business demands had taken up so much of her time these past two weeks and it was Millie's day off, Sable decided that a trip to the zoo would be a welcome treat.

'Can Day-man come?' Kyle instantly questioned.

'Not this time.' He didn't protest, but she could tell by the frown creasing his brow that her answer didn't please him. 'We'll invite him next time,' she offered, hoping it would suffice. To her relief, he accepted her suggestion without further complaint.

It was a perfect day, the weather warm and sunny, a light breeze alleviating the heat. She snapped a thousand pictures of Kyle imitating the various animals. And the whole time she thought about the situation with Damien. She'd been wrong not to tell him the truth last night. He wanted Kyle to be his son, she realized with a guilty pang. She'd seen the truth in his eyes, heard it in his voice. And, no matter what she'd said, he'd be a good father.

As for her accusation that he'd be unable to let down his guard enough, that he wouldn't risk his heart...Kyle would take care of that. Before Damien even knew what hit him, his son would slip in and take hold. It saddened her to think of all the years the two had already lost. She couldn't allow them to lose any more, not when it was within her power to prevent it. She couldn't be that selfish, couldn't allow her fears to stop her from doing what she knew to be right.

'Mommy,' Kyle shouted. 'I see Day-man!'

Before she could stop him, he took off, racing toward a man standing by the lion pit. His height and streaky brown hair resembled Damien's, but Sable realized instantly that Kyle had made a mistake. By the time she'd reached her son, he'd realized it too, and darted back to her side.

'I'm sorry,' she panted, breathless from her run. 'He thought you were someone else.'

'Hey, no harm done,' the man replied, offering an engaging grin.

Kyle clung to her legs, glaring at the stranger, furious that he wasn't Damien. 'Where's Day-man?' he demanded. 'I wants him here.'

She gathered him close, giving him a consoling hug and kiss. He returned her embrace with childish enthusiasm. How much longer would that last? she couldn't help but wonder. Soon he'd be too big, too embarrassed for such open affection. 'Damien promised he'd see you soon. And he will. You'll have to be patient.'

Kyle set his chin. 'T'morrow,' he insisted.

'We'll see. No promises, though.'

She handed him the camera and showed him how to snap a picture. The distraction worked...this time. But, knowing her son, it wouldn't last. He wouldn't be satisfied with anything less than Damien's presence. She closed her eyes, facing the inescapable facts. Kyle should have a strong male role model. Someone to share those special father-son activities. Someone to look up to and imitate. The time had come to surrender to the inevitable.

The time had come to tell Damien the truth about Kyle.

CHAPTER NINE

WITH her mind made up, Sable didn't dare wait until Monday to confront Damien with the truth. Instead she decided to track him down Sunday evening after dinner, her best chance of catching him at home. By delaying until then, she'd also have another day to spend with Kyle, and wouldn't have to leave him with Millie until after he'd been put down for the night.

She took full advantage of the few hours allotted her, the brief time she had with her son both precious and fleeting. And with every passing moment she realized how many special occasions Damien had missed... and how much he would resent her for that loss. Immediately after she'd tucked Kyle into bed, she left for Damien's. It had been years since she'd been this way—crossing the Golden Gate Bridge and driving into the hills above Sausalito.

It was like coming home.

She pulled into the driveway, parking at the side of the house as she'd done countless times before. A string of low-wattage outdoor lights marked the pathway to the house, and she climbed the steps along the terraced bank to the front door, dreading the moment she'd see Damien, dreading the conversation to come.

Lute answered her knock, greeting her with a smile of satisfaction. 'Ah. Miss Sable. I've been expecting you.'

She hesitated, gazing up in bewilderment. 'You have?'

'Most definitely.' He stepped back. 'Please come in. Damien is out right now, but you may wait for him, if you wish.'

'Thank you, I would.' She followed him into a huge common room that overlooked the water. 'How did you know I'd drop by?'

A slight smile touched his face. 'Your conscience would force you to. You would want to correct Mr Damien's assumption that your son was fathered by Leonard Caldwell.'

She stared at him, stunned. 'You *know*? How?'

'It was not an unreasonable conclusion, once I heard of young Kyle's existence.' He turned to face her. 'There were many mistakes made five years ago. Neglecting to tell Mr Damien you were pregnant was but one, am I right?'

'Yes,' she conceded. 'Though somehow I doubt Damien will be as tolerant as you over this particular mistake.'

He stroked his beard, his pale blue eyes filled with sympathy. 'Time is often needed to rectify these errors. And time is often essential to bring the situation full circle and allow for healing...for understanding. I think that is true in this case.'

He was right, of course. How he was able to see it so clearly escaped her, but he'd focused on the most critical elements. Five years ago Damien hadn't been ready to trust, hadn't been ready to hear the truth, let alone accept it. An apprehensive frown creased her brow. 'I just hope I haven't waited too long,' she murmured.

'Perhaps you have. Perhaps not.' He gave a small shrug. 'We shall see. I will bring you something to drink, and then I must leave you. Damien will return soon. Until he does, please make yourself comfortable.'

For a long time she stood by the window, darkness stealing into the room like a soft, protective blanket. She stared down at the lights of the town and harbor, and out across the wide, majestic sweep of the bay, with a calm she hadn't experienced in ages. A quarter moon slipped into the sky, its benevolent radiance a balm to her soul.

For the first time since Damién's return, she felt at peace. No matter what happened now, she'd finally confront a fear that had haunted her for five long years, face it and deal with it. She'd also correct a cruel wrong. Kyle would have a father and Damien would have a son. Nothing could be more important than that.

After what seemed an eternity, Damien's key scraped in the lock at the front door and she turned, waiting for him. Her heart pounded in her breast and her mouth grew dry. She gripped her hands together, praying for the strength to get through the coming discussion. He strode into the room, not bothering to switch on the lights, the moonlight apparently providing him with all the illumination he needed.

He unbuttoned his shirt and crossed to the small wet bar at the opposite end of the room to her. She heard the chink of glass as he poured a finger of whiskey, heard his almost inaudible sigh as he sipped the liquor. Moving toward her, he placed his glass on a side table and stripped off his shirt. He tossed it carelessly over the back of a chair and picked up his drink again, running a hand through the mat of hairs covering his chest.

He still hadn't seen her. She swallowed against the thickness in her throat. She should say something. But she didn't want to. She wanted to watch him—watch the animal grace of his movements, watch the ripple of muscles when he lifted the glass to his mouth, watch the play of light and shadow as moonlight danced across his bronzed chest and arms.

She knew the instant he sensed her presence. His entire body tensed and he pivoted with a swiftness that took her by surprise. 'Sable?' He spoke softly, his voice deep and husky, laced with irresistible demand.

'I should have said something when you first came in,' she hastened to tell him. 'I'm sorry, I——'

His glass hit the table beside him with a crash and words deserted her. She stared as he approached, her eyes huge and dark, and filled with a helpless vulnerability. He stopped inches from her. Silently, he reached for her, sliding his hand along the curve of her hip, drawing her close. She inhaled sharply, every sense keenly attuned to the bare expanse of his chest, the sultry warmth of his body, the unique, musky scent of him.

'I was just thinking about you... about us,' he said in a quiet undertone. 'You wanted to choose the time and place we made love.' He cupped her chin, tilting her head until the moonlight splashed across her face, revealing every fleeting nuance. 'Has the time come? Is this where and when, Sable? Is that why you're here?'

She shook her head. 'No. This has nothing to do with our agreement.'

His smile glimmered in the darkness. 'Good. Then it can be for the two of us. No conditions, no bargains, no deals. Just you and me. Together. The way it should be.'

'I haven't come to make love,' she started to tell him.

He lifted an eyebrow. 'Are you sure?' His hold tightened, and he tucked her into the cradle of his thighs, his eyes darkening at her small cry of distress. 'Are you positive?'

She fought the desire streaking through her, fought for sanity, fought for words and the breath to speak them. And all the while her hands crept up the ridged expanse of his abdomen, slipping into the thatch of crisp brown hair covering his chest. 'I came to talk.'

'No!' He objected with a vehemence that astonished her. 'No more talk. I'm sick of the arguments, of the suspicion. I want you, Sable. I want you without conditions, without questions, without doubts. Just you and me, a man and a woman, together the way nature meant us to be.'

'You make it sound so poetic,' she whispered sadly. 'But it's just lust, just sex... not love.'

He brushed her mouth with his thumb, the touch so gentle and tender that it made her want to weep. 'It was never just sex between us and it never will be.' But she noticed he didn't call it love either.

He didn't give her time to think, let alone argue. Without waiting for a response, he bent slightly and lifted her into his arms. She buried her face in the crook of his neck, pressing her lips to the warm juncture there, aware that her very silence committed her. She'd steal these few cherished moments for herself, give herself one last night to look back upon when all else had been irretrievably lost. It wasn't right and it wasn't fair, but it was as essential right now as the very air she breathed.

Once in the bedroom, he removed his arm from beneath her knees, allowing her to slip down the length of him. Her breasts grazed his chest and his breath quickened in response. The buttons of her blouse were a barrier swiftly dispensed with, the silk blouse stripped from her and sent floating to the floor. The thin, lacy bra provoked a more leisurely exploration. He traced the line between French silk and creamy skin, dipping into the cups to palm the softness within.

Sable moaned, the sound whispering between them. 'Damien, please.'

'Please what?' he demanded. 'Tell me what you want, my love.'

'I want you,' she confessed. 'I want you to make love to me—not out of revenge, but because you need me as much as I need you.'

He unclasped the tiny hooks at her back, the straps of her bra dropping from her shoulders, the silk falling away. 'This isn't revenge,' he told her, his eyes burning with a fierce heat. 'This is inevitable.'

She knew he was right, knew she belonged with him and only him, that they had been building toward this moment since he'd first reappeared in her life. He dropped to one knee, his hand cupping the back of her calf, before drifting upward beneath her skirt to the garters anchoring her stockings. With a flick of his thumb he released them one by one. She trembled within his hold, her fingers sinking into his hair as she fought for balance. Like the brush of a feather, the nylons glided down her legs. He lifted one foot, then the other, removing them.

And then he rose, his hand tugging at the zipper of her skirt, stripping away her remaining garments in one easy move. She stood before him, motionless, vulnerable and afraid, yet wanting his possession with a desperation she couldn't deny. Moonlight etched a path across the room, caressing her nudity, the silvery glow turning her skin to alabaster and sparkling in her hair like stars glittering in a midnight sky.

'So beautiful,' he murmured, molding her breast with his hand. 'So perfect.'

Tears gathered in her eyes and she bowed her head, pressing her lips to his chest. He groaned, the sound ripped from his throat, savage and raw. She felt the intensity of his desire and nervous dread feathered along her spine. 'It's been a long time,' she told him softly. 'I'm not sure I'm ready for this.'

'It's all right. There's no hurry,' came his gentle assurance. 'I won't hurt you.'

But he already had hurt her. And she knew, as surely as the sun would rise in the morning, that he would hurt her again. Worse, she would let him.

Once again he swept her into his arms. He was all strength, tough sinew and taut muscle and she reveled in his maleness. He carried her to the bed and placed her tenderly on the sheets. When at last he joined her, there was nothing between them—nothing but moist heat and sweet surrender. She reached for him, opening to him, soaring on wings of endless passion. And he took her, affording her that wondrous deliverance that she could find only in his arms, taking her body as completely as he had taken her heart. And as the night passed she fell in love all over again, helplessly, hopelessly, endlessly.

Forever.

Morning slipped silently into the room. For Sable, it came all too early. Sitting on the edge of the bed, Damien woke her, brushing the curls from her face, his fingers drifting across her cheek in a fleeting caress. She stirred, opening her eyes and blinking sleepily up at him.

'Good morning,' he said simply.

'Good morning, yourself,' she replied with a yawn, then looked at him in surprise. 'You're dressed for work.'

'I decided to go in early.' She started to throw back the sheet, but he stopped her, pressing her back against the pillows. 'You have plenty of time to get ready.'

She studied his expression nervously. Not a hint of passion marked his face. He returned her regard with a steady gaze, his green eyes cool and detached. This didn't look good. 'We need to discuss something before you leave,' she said, plucking at the bedcovers.

'Yes, I know.'

She didn't care for his tone and sat up, sweeping her hair from her eyes. 'I'm at a bit of a disadvantage here,' she murmured, tugging the sheet more fully across her breasts. 'Or was that the idea?'

He didn't answer her question, instead asking one of his own. 'Why did you come here last night? You said to talk. Talk about what?'

She took a deep breath. 'About Kyle,' she admitted.

He nodded, as though he'd known all along. 'I woke up in the middle of the night and couldn't get back to sleep because something was bothering me, teasing at the back of my mind. I started thinking about why you'd come, what could be so urgent. And then I thought about Kyle. All of a sudden the answer was there.' He looked at her, his eyes dark and turbulent. 'Kyle's my son, isn't he?'

The words hung between them, stark and divisive. 'Yes,' she whispered, and waited apprehensively for his response. It wasn't long in coming.

'My son.' Rage stirred, deep and powerful, sweeping across his face like a river in full flood. '*My son*! And you allowed Caldwell to get his hands on him. You gave that bastard my child! How could you do that?'

'I didn't *give* him anything,' she was swift to deny. 'I married him. He was Kyle's stepfather. There's a difference.'

He stood, moving away from her as though he couldn't bear to be too close. 'Don't split hairs with me. You allowed him to raise Kyle. You kept our child's existence a secret from me. Tell me why you did it,' he ordered. 'Explain it to me so I can understand.'

'You know how it ended between us.' She clutched the sheet in a white-knuckled grip. 'You refused my phone calls, wouldn't see me. You've never denied that——'

'That's an excuse!' His hands clenched, his chest rising and falling as though he'd run a marathon. 'You could have found a way to get in touch if it was that important. Hell, you knew where I lived, where I worked. It wouldn't have been that difficult to force a confrontation.'

She knelt on the bed, pulling at the sheet and wrapping it around her like a sarong. Lord, she'd give just about anything for some clothes. But she didn't dare take the time, didn't dare postpone this conversation for another second. 'You were out of the country by the time I realized I was pregnant. What was I supposed to do? Tramp through the jungles of South America until I found you? I had to put the welfare of my child first.'

'*Our* child,' he flashed back, his eyes dark with condemnation. 'And marrying Caldwell was not putting Kyle's welfare first. He was an easy way out. You couldn't have managed on your own, or gotten in touch with me when I returned? You had to sell yourself to that man?'

'I didn't sell myself to him!' She fought the urge to weep, refusing to betray any sign of weakness. Logic was all Damien would understand—cold, hard logic. She lifted her chin. 'What if I had gotten through to you? How would you have responded if I'd come to you claiming to be pregnant?'

He didn't answer immediately. At last he admitted, 'I'd have suspected you either made it up or——' He broke off, thrusting a hand through his hair.

'Or asked whose baby it was,' she finished for him. 'By the time I realized I was pregnant, I worked for Leonard. You'd already accused me of having an affair with him. Remember?'

'I remember.'

'This would have been all the proof you needed. You would never have believed you were the father. And even if you had, in your anger, you might have been tempted to use Kyle against me. I couldn't let you do that.' She bowed her head. 'It would have destroyed me.'

A muscle jerked in his cheek. 'So, why didn't you tell me about Kyle sooner?'

'When? After his birth?' She bit down on her lip, regret touching her features. 'I couldn't do that to Leonard. Not after all he'd done for me.'

Damien's mouth tightened. 'How about a year ago, when Leonard died? How about over two weeks ago, when I joined Caldwell's? Why the *hell* didn't you tell me then?'

She shook her head. 'I couldn't risk telling you the truth. Not when you were so intent on revenge.'

'And last night?' Cynicism edged his words. 'Tell me, Sable, what was that all about?'

She gazed at him in alarm. 'I don't understand.'

'Yes, you do. What was the point of last night? Did you hope going to bed with me would temper my reaction?'

'No! Don't you dare even suggest such a thing.'

He took a step closer. 'Or perhaps you were fulfilling our agreement, after all.'

She refused to back down, to show the slightest sign of intimidation. 'I keep telling you, there was no agreement. You demanded I sleep with you the same way you demanded I sell out to you. But in the end I would have refused. I won't go to bed with you just to satisfy your lust for revenge.'

'Then what was last night?' he repeated.

She looked at him, her heart breaking. 'I thought last night we made love,' she whispered. 'I guess I was wrong.'

He didn't contradict her. His eyes narrowed, his face growing taut and remote. 'I have to get to work,' was all he said, and turned from her. But he paused at the doorway, his back to her, throwing over his shoulder the words, 'You should have told me, Sable. I deserved that much.'

In another moment he'd leave, and she might never have another chance to explain her actions. 'I was afraid!' she cried, in her desperation admitting her deepest terror. 'I was afraid you might try and take Kyle away from me.'

'I still might,' he replied harshly, and walked away.

'You don't mean that! You can't mean that!' But it was too late. He was gone.

Sable didn't waste any time after that. She hurried to dress, desperate to get home, to get away. The house was silent and empty as she left, Lute nowhere to be seen. Climbing into her car, she headed back toward the city, the morning rush-hour traffic making the trip intermi-nable. Once home, she showered and changed, painfully aware that her arrival at work would be delayed still another hour. Sure enough, by the time she walked through the front door at Caldwell's, it was well past nine.

'Good morning, Janine,' she greeted her secretary with a calm she didn't come close to feeling. 'How was your weekend?'

'Just fine, thank you.'

'Anything I should know about before we get started?' Sable asked, pausing by the door to her office.

Janine hesitated, her gaze slipping away. 'I... I'm not sure.'

Sable frowned. 'You're not sure?' What in the world did that mean? And then it hit her. Damien! She didn't know how, she didn't know why, but without a doubt he was behind that odd look on her secretary's face. 'What's going on?'

'It's just...' Janine shoved her glasses higher on the bridge of her nose, her pale blue eyes glinting behind the huge lenses. 'The board is meeting in the conference room, but they didn't say anything about you joining them. I——'

Sable didn't wait to hear more. Without another word, she hastened down the hallway toward the boardroom. Already she could hear muffled voices coming from behind the sturdy oak panel, voices raised in argument. She didn't bother to knock. She thrust open the door and walked right in.

Silence descended on the room with a stunning immediacy. They were all there, seated around the conference table, every one of them wearing identical expressions of outrage mingled with guilt. All except Damien. He sat at the end of the table, in her seat, clearly in charge, and as cool and commanding as she'd ever seen him.

She closed the door behind her with a decisive click. 'Am I interrupting something?' she asked in a deceptively calm voice.

'Sable! We... I... Damien...' Cornelius stuttered to a stop, ducking his head like a schoolboy caught cheating in an exam.

She folded her arms across her chest, eyeing the board members one by one. Only Damien could return her look. She fixed her attention on him. 'What's this about?' she demanded.

He leaned back in her chair. 'We're having a little talk about information leaked to Dreyfus Industry.'

'Leaked!' For a minute, Sable thought her legs would fold beneath her. 'You're joking.'

'I assure you, it's no joke.'

'But I thought Patricia——'

He shook his head. 'It would seem your guess about Patricia was wrong. She's not involved.'

She stared at the board members in bewilderment. 'Why wasn't I told about this? Why didn't you wait until I came in before starting?'

A wintry smile touched Damien's mouth. 'Because you're the prime suspect.'

Pain ripped through her, pain and anger and disbelief. So this was how he'd decided to take his revenge, to get even for Kyle. How could he? She closed her eyes, grief stealing over her. *How could he*? 'I won't let you do this,' she whispered. 'I didn't leak any information. It's not possible.'

'It came from you, my dear,' Cornelius spoke up at long last, his tone weary. 'Damien has incontrovertible proof.'

She opened her eyes. This wasn't the time to show weakness. She had to be strong, uncover the facts so that she could straighten this out. She stepped further into the room, her gaze never once leaving Damien. 'And what is this proof?'

He picked up the file in front of him and flipped it open. Removing a set of papers, he tossed them down the length of the table. They were the bid sheets she and Damien had worked on together for Dreyfus. 'The figures I gave you... they were false. I would have thought you'd have learned your lesson five years ago.'

She left the papers scattered across the table and lifted her chin. 'Oh, that's right. That's how you caught me last time, isn't it?'

'And you fell for it again.'

She gave a careless shrug. 'Just out of curiosity, how did you manage it?'

'I called the president of Dreyfus and warned him that a competitor may come calling with a copy of our bid—but that the figures would be wrong and to discredit it. He phoned and—surprise, surprise—a competitor had our prospectus in hand.'

'How did you know it came from me?' she questioned. 'Any number of people could have leaked it.'

'Each copy of our prospectus was coded.'

'Very clever, Damien,' she said, impressed. 'I assume my code showed up.'

He inclined his head in agreement. 'Yes. Your code showed up.'

'So, what do you intend to do?'

'What? No denials? Aren't you going to tell us you're innocent, that you've been set up again?'

'Would it do any good?'

'Sable! For heaven's sake,' Cornelius cried. 'Tell him you didn't do it. Explain to us what happened.'

She shook her head. 'There's no point,' she said gently. 'Damien would never believe me. Because that would mean he'd have to trust me, trust me despite all the evidence to the contrary. And he could never do that.'

To her astonishment, Damien smiled, genuine humor glittering in his eyes. 'No, I couldn't, could I?' Then his expression closed over and he turned his attention to the other board members. 'Gentlemen, it's time for a vote. All those in favor of removing Sable Caldwell as president and chairman of the board, say aye.'

There was a long moment of silence. Then, one by one, every last member murmured his assent.

'Any nays?'

No one said a word.

'Then the motion carries.'

For a split second, Sable didn't move, couldn't move. Then she stiffened her spine, glaring at each one of them in turn, her contempt plain to see. 'It would appear you've won after all, Damien. I'll tender my resignation, effective immediately.' Then, without another word, she left the room.

CHAPTER TEN

SABLE hastened back to her office, thrusting open the door and dragging air into her lungs in great, heaving gulps. How could he? How could Damien do that to her? Did he really believe in her guilt? Or was this part of a larger scheme—a more merciless form of revenge now that he knew about Kyle? What in heaven's name was she going to do?

'Mrs Caldwell?' Janine stepped from the shadows by the window. 'Are you all right?'

Sable started, lifting a hand to her throat. 'Janine! I...I didn't see you. I...' She closed her eyes, struggling for control. 'I'm fine, thank you.'

'Is there something I can do?'

'No,' she said, then changed her mind. 'Wait. Yes, there is. I wonder if you'd mind getting me a box from the mailroom?' she asked quietly.

'Is there something wrong?' Janine stepped closer. 'What's happened?'

Sable fought to keep her voice level, to keep from expressing the emotions that threatened to rip her apart. More than anything she wanted some privacy in which to break down and weep. 'I suppose you should know,' she said with a weary sigh. 'I've resigned. Effective immediately. If you could get a box for me, I can——'

'Resigned!' the secretary interrupted. 'Whatever for?'

'Janine, please.' Sable's voice broke and she covered her face with hands that trembled, struggling to pull herself together. 'There's been a leak within the company.

It's been traced to me, so I've been forced to resign,' she confessed.

'A leak?' Janine adjusted her glasses, her brows drawn together in a frown. 'You mean the information on one of our bids was given out to another construction company?'

'Yes.'

'But...why in the world would they think you did it?'

'I'd rather not go into that right now, if you don't mind,' Sable said, fast approaching the end of her rope. 'A box. I really need a box so I can pack my things.'

To her eternal relief, Janine obeyed without further comment. Sable glanced around the room, tears glittering in her eyes. So, it finally ended. First Leonard, then Patricia, and now, at last, she'd be gone too. And Damien would have won. He'd have exacted his revenge. Or would he have?

What about Kyle? she wondered uneasily.

'Mrs Caldwell?' Janine reentered the room. 'I have a box for you and some newspaper to wrap any breakables. Shall I help you pack your things?'

Sable nodded. 'Thank you. I'd appreciate that.'

It didn't take long. They removed the knickknacks from the credenza and from the top of her desk, and all the while Janine talked—talked endlessly, offering soothing little homilies interspersed with denigrating comments about Damien. Sable listened with only half an ear, tempted to defend him, but knowing she'd be wasting her time. Janine wouldn't change her mind about Damien—any more than Damien would change his about Sable's guilt.

She picked up Kyle's vase, running a finger over the bright primary colors. She'd known all along that

Damien was incapable of trusting. He hadn't believed her before, hadn't supported her; why would she expect him to this time? But what she hadn't anticipated was how badly that defection would hurt. She wrapped the vase in paper, facing one inescapable fact. She loved him. Loved him with all her heart. And somehow she couldn't quite accept that he could hold her in his arms, share such a passionately magical moment as last night, without feeling something in return. It just wasn't possible.

'I don't care what anyone says.' Janine continued her non-stop chatter. 'I'm sure if you leaked that information you had a good reason.'

'If I...' Sable looked at her secretary in shock, yanked from her thoughts with brutal suddenness. Where had that come from? 'Janine, I had nothing to do with that leak. How could you even think such a thing? Surely *you* know me better than that?'

Janine stirred uncomfortably. 'Of course I do, Mrs Caldwell. If you say you didn't do it, I believe you. It's just...'

Sable gazed at her secretary in despair. Would she be branded a thief forever, tainted in everyone's eyes by accusations that didn't have one iota of truth to them? 'It's just what?'

The secretary shrugged. 'I wanted you to know that I wouldn't blame you if you had leaked the information.'

'But I——' Sable broke off. What was the use? 'Thank you. I appreciate your support.'

If Janine noticed the irony in the comment, she gave no sign. She picked up the photo of Leonard, staring at it for a long moment. 'Losing that account to A.J. Construction would put Mr Hawke in a very bad light,' she said, almost contemplatively. 'After what he did to

Leonard, to Miss Patricia... it would be the perfect revenge—a well-deserved revenge. I just thought you should know...I don't blame you.' She placed the photo gently into the box and closed the flaps.

'Am I interrupting?' Damien stood at the door, his gaze sweeping over them with nerve-racking intensity.

'What is it, Damien?' Sable asked with a weary sigh. She gestured toward the box. 'As you can see, we're almost done here. What more could you possibly want?'

He looked at Janine and jerked his head toward the door. She didn't need any further urging. She slipped from the room, leaving Sable to face Damien alone. He slammed the door closed. 'We have to talk.'

'Talk about what?' she demanded. She didn't want to talk. She wanted to be held by him, kissed by him, told that he loved her and believed in her. Clearly, she wanted the impossible. 'Shall we discuss how you stole my company out from under me? Or how you framed me for something I didn't do? Or shall we examine your quest for revenge—revenge because I married Leonard, because I didn't tell you about Kyle?'

'I'm not here to debate our personal life.'

She folded her arms across her chest. 'Oh, that's right, this is strictly business, isn't it? I shouldn't take it personally. Well, how about this...? Now that I'm gone there won't be anyone left to blame when we lose another big account. You're so busy pointing the finger at me that you're neglecting to put your energies where they're truly needed—into finding the guilty party.'

A grim smile tugged at his mouth. 'I think by removing you from the scene the leaks will stop.'

'Well, you're wrong.' Hopelessness glimmered in her dark eyes. 'Why didn't you come to me? Why didn't you discuss the Dreyfus situation with me so we could work together to find whoever leaked the information?'

He shrugged. 'Since the prospectus was yours, it seemed . . . ill-advised to discuss it with you.'

'So instead you just oust me from the board based on the evidence from the prospectus alone?' It didn't make sense. She didn't know why, but she suspected he was being evasive. 'How long have you known about our bid being leaked to Dreyfus?'

He hesitated, then admitted, 'Their CEO called me on Saturday.'

She turned white. '*Saturday*!'

'We met Sunday afternoon to hammer out a private agreement. That's why I was so late returning home.'

'Which means...' She stared at him in despair. 'When I came to see you last night, you knew it was my prospectus that had been used. *You knew*! And yet you still made love to me, led me to believe . . .' It was a struggle to speak, to say the words without breaking down. 'When I came to you last night, you'd already planned to remove me from the board, hadn't you?'

'Yes.' The word hung between them, bald and cold and inescapable.

'How could you?' she whispered. 'How could you do such a thing?'

His eyes narrowed, turning hard and distant. 'You're always talking about trust. I should trust you, support you, believe in you despite all evidence to the contrary. Where's your trust, Sable?' He approached, catching her arm and yanking her close. She tried to fight, to pull away, but he wouldn't release her. He cupped her face, his thumb feathering across her cheek. 'It's different when the shoe's on the other foot, isn't it? Blind trust. You expect it, but you're unwilling to give it. The moment there's so much as a whisper of a doubt, you suspect the worst.'

'And why not?' she cried, catching his shirt in her fists. She glared up at him, wishing she could look into those cool, remote features without wanting him. Wishing she didn't care so very, very much. Wishing something as simple as his touching her cheek wouldn't stir such a passionate response. 'What have you ever done to make me believe in you, trust in you? You've come into my life again, demanding I sell out to you, demanding I sleep with you——'

'What about Kyle?' he came right back at her. 'What about Leonard? What about all the secrets you've kept from me? It's a two-way street, Sable. You want trust, but you aren't willing to give it any more than I am.'

'It's never been a two-way street with you,' she instantly denied. Her hands slipped from his chest and she took a small step away from him. 'You've never been willing to let me in, not completely. Isn't it time you told me why?'

His hand fell from her face and he let her go, his mouth tightening. For a minute, she didn't think he'd answer. Then he said, 'It's an old story. Over long ago.'

'But it changed you,' she replied. 'It has to do with that night in the bar, doesn't it? When you were nineteen and Lute saved your life.'

He nodded. 'I was a fool. I thought my world had ended.'

'Why?' she whispered. 'Tell me why.'

He ran a hand across the back of his neck, staring at the carpet, lost in thought. Finally, he spoke. 'I came from a wealthy background. Big house, fancy cars, top schools. And then one day I woke up and it was all gone. My father's business went under and he declared bankruptcy. It was...difficult, but we knew we'd work it out, that we'd recover.'

'Then why...?'

'I had a girlfriend. We were both in our second year at Stanford University. It was serious—we talked about a future, marriage. In my youthful arrogance I was certain she'd stand by me, that my family's financial reversal wouldn't matter.'

Compassion touched her. 'But it did.'

He inclined his head. 'Once knowledge of the bankruptcy became public, I wasn't even allowed in the door. I got it into my head that it was her parents keeping us apart, that we were some sort of modern-day Romeo and Juliet. So I slipped into her room that night only to discover that Jennifer felt the same way her parents did. I was welcome to come in the back door, she graciously offered; she'd even be happy to let me in her bed again. But marriage? An open relationship? Not a chance.'

Her heart went out to him. 'And so you learned that women were only after one thing.'

He didn't deny it. 'Money is a great motivator,' he said in a dry voice.

'It can be.' She approached, laying her hand on his arm. 'But love is an ever greater one. Jennifer didn't love you or she would have stood by you. She betrayed you.' Sable waited for that to sink it, before adding, 'I never did.'

'Didn't you?' Weary cynicism tainted the question. 'Why should I believe that? Because you once claimed to love me?'

She didn't hesitate for a moment, didn't dare hesitate or evade the truth. 'Yes, Damien. I loved you five years ago and I love you now. I've always loved you. Do you really think last night would ever have happened if I didn't?'

His expression closed over. 'Why not? Or are you trying to tell me you also loved Caldwell?'

She refused to back down. Instead she looked him straight in the eye. 'I never made love to Leonard. Not once. Our marriage was strictly platonic. You're the only man I've ever made love to, the only man I've ever wanted to make love to.'

A muscle jerked in his jaw. 'Is this another lie?' He rasped out the question.

She shook her head. 'I've never lied to you—except about Kyle. And that was by omission only.'

'It was one hell of an omission!' His anger died as quickly as it had flared and he shot her a searching look. 'You're serious about your relationship with Caldwell?' At her nod, he asked, 'That last night we were together. Do you remember it?'

How could she forget? It had been the last time she'd seen him. They'd held each other through the night, making love with an ardor and desperation that she had never forgotten, knowing that their world was slowly being ripped apart by lies and suspicions. In the morning, he'd walked out her door and out of her life, refusing ever to see or speak to her again. 'I remember all too well.'

'I went to see Caldwell that day, to demand an explanation for the business we'd lost to them. He confirmed what you said—that you'd let certain information slip to Patricia without realizing who she was. He also said that once you did know, once the truth came out, you'd gone in with them, deciding to take your chances with Caldwell's. He claimed you'd leaked that last project on purpose and showed me a copy of our bid as proof.' He looked at her, his hands clenched, his body tensed as though for a blow. 'He also implied that you two were having an affair.'

'And you believed him,' she stated sadly. Oh, Leonard! Why did you do it? she lamented silently. Had she misjudged him all these years, seen him as her savior when in fact he'd been anything but?

Damien nodded. 'The evidence weighed heavily against you.' He released his breath in a long sigh. 'I don't know. It was...easier to buy his version.'

'I can only guess that Patricia managed to obtain that bid through ulterior means. I never knowingly gave the information to Caldwell's. But I was their unwitting conduit. I've never denied that.' She bit down on her lip. 'Do you still believe he told you the truth about me...about our relationship?'

'No.' Not a shred of doubt shaded his voice, and for the first time hope crept into her heart. 'There's something else you should know. I didn't blackball you with the other construction companies.'

She caught her breath. 'Leonard?'

'Leonard,' he confirmed. 'I suspect he did it so you'd have no other choice but to work for him. Your pregnancy must have played right into his hands.'

Had it happened that way? Was it possible? Later, when she had the time and privacy to consider what she'd learned, she could regret all that had happened five years ago. But more important matters concerned her now, more pressing problems. 'What about now, Damien?' she asked anxiously. 'What about the Dreyfus leak? What's going to happen?'

It was as though a door slammed in her face. His expression closed over and he shrugged. 'I'm looking into it,' he claimed.

'That's not what I mean.' She looked at him, confronting her worst fear. 'Are you going to prosecute?'

His gaze flashed to hers, an odd expression sweeping across his face. 'That's up to the board.'

She made an impatient gesture. 'You know the board will do whatever you recommend.'

'A decision hasn't been reached yet,' he insisted, refusing to give her the reassurance she so desperately needed.

So that was it. Despite all the grand words, despite all attempts to clear up their differences, nothing had changed. The tiny spark of hope she'd so carefully nurtured died. She cleared her throat. 'In that case, I want you to do something for me.'

'What is it?'

'If the board chooses to prosecute, I want you to take care of Kyle for me.'

He couldn't conceal his exasperation. 'What the hell are you talking about?'

'I'm talking about Kyle and what would be best for him,' she said carefully. 'I...I put it in my will years ago. If something happens to me, Kyle is to go to you. But I hadn't anticipated an eventuality like this. I hadn't thought about the possibility of...' She lifted her chin. 'You're to take him if things get nasty.'

She turned, unable to bear another minute. Snatching up her box of personal possessions, she fled from the room, hurrying down the hallway toward the elevators. Balancing the carton on her knee, she stabbed at the button. Finally the doors opened and she stepped into the car along with half a dozen others. Damien appeared then, sprinting between the doors at the last possible instant.

'We need to talk,' he announced, taking the box forcibly from her arms.

She refused to look at him, afraid he'd see the tears she was struggling to hold at bay. 'About what?' she asked softly, darting a quick glance at the other occupants. Why here? Why now? She couldn't take much more of this.

Damien didn't seem to care whether they had an audience or not. 'You'd trust me to take care of him?' he demanded. 'You'd trust me with Kyle?'

'I'd trust you with my life,' she declared passionately. 'Haven't you realized that yet? I'd trust you with my greatest possession—and that's Kyle. And if you say you don't believe me, or ask for proof, I'll never, ever forgive you.'

A youthful-looking executive turned to Damien. 'I believe her,' he offered. He glanced at Sable. 'I believe you.'

A shaky smile trembled on her lips. 'Thank you,' she murmured, blinking rapidly to clear the sudden tears. 'I appreciate that.'

Damien swore beneath his breath. 'Sable... I know you didn't do it.'

It took a full minute for his comment to sink in. The elevator stopped and a few of the passengers got off. The young executive started to, then changed his mind, staying put. The door closed again. 'What did you say?' she demanded.

'He said——'

She rounded on the eavesdropper. 'I heard what he said!' She peeked up at Damien, that tiny kernel of hope bursting to life once more. 'Say it again.'

A reluctant smile touched his mouth. 'I said, I know you didn't give our prospectus to Dreyfus.'

The elevator arrived at the ground floor and neither of them moved. 'Come back upstairs,' Damien said—softly, gently, tenderly. He glanced at the avidly watching executive and pointed at the open door. 'You. Off.'

An instant later they were alone and the elevator doors closed. It was like that first day when he'd approached her, only this time Damien hadn't come to destroy...but to heal. It wasn't until they were moving upward again that Sable gathered the nerve to ask the question uppermost in her mind. 'How do you know I'm not responsible? Do you have proof?'

'No. Yes.' He ran a hand through his hair. 'I don't have anything concrete, but...' He seemed to grapple with his response, searching for the right words. 'I've watched you, Sable. All the years we were together, you never demanded anything of me, and you gave everything. Then it went bad, and you fell in with Caldwell. But you stuck by him, too. As he lost one company after another, as his wealth diminished, you didn't walk away. Instead you rolled up your sleeves and pitched in to help. That shocked the hell out of me.'

'He was my husband.' There was no getting around that fact.

Damien shook his head. 'No, he wasn't. Not in any way that counted.'

'You still haven't explained why you decided I was innocent.'

'You said something to me once. You said that I should have known you could never betray me. That I should have moved heaven and earth to help prove your innocence.'

'What I said was that if you *loved* me you'd know I could never betray you. If you *loved* me, you'd move heaven and earth to prove my innocence,' she corrected him softly. 'So...do you? Do you love me?'

His eyes gleamed like polished jade. 'Why else would I have had you thrown off the board?'

The doors opened then, and the moment was lost before she could grab hold of it. He stepped from the car, and she followed, struggling to hide her disappointment. 'Why *did* you have me removed from the board?' she questioned as they headed back down the hallway.

He waited until they were in her office, with the door shut against all possible intruders. 'It's obvious someone hopes to pin this on you. I wanted you clear of the line of fire while I figured out who it was.'

'And have you?'

He shook his head, his frustration evident in the tense set of his shoulders and taut line of his mouth. 'No. Not yet.'

'Won't Alex Johnson tell you?' A small line formed between her eyebrows. 'I must admit, I don't understand it. I thought he wanted to avoid antagonizing you. So why in the world would he risk your anger again by——?'

'What did you say?' He tossed the box on her desk, heedless of any damage he might cause the contents. Turning to face her, he grabbed her by the shoulders. 'How did you know that?'

She stared at him in bewilderment. 'Know what?'

'How did you know it was Alex who approached Dreyfus? I never released that information. The only other person who could know is the thief.'

She stared at him, her eyes huge with anguish. No! It couldn't be happening. He'd just started to trust her again. He couldn't be accusing her of this. Not again.

She swayed, clutching at the lapels of his jacket. She couldn't continue living like this, spending a lifetime on the edge, constantly being doubted by him. She couldn't! If that was what he intended, there was no hope, no possibility of a future together.

'What are you asking me?' she whispered.

'Who told you it was Alex?' Damien demanded impatiently, sweeping a lock of hair from her face. 'Come on, Sable. Don't hold back now. Because whoever told you is the one we're looking for.'

For a long moment she couldn't speak, she was so overcome with emotion. He didn't doubt her. Dear God, he didn't doubt her! To her disgust, she burst into helpless tears. Throwing her arms around his neck, she lifted her tear-stained face to his. 'Please kiss me,' she begged. 'Quickly.'

He didn't need a second prompting. His mouth found hers, tasting, teasing, seducing with hot, desperate kisses. The rapture was instantaneous, raw and primitive, touching a primal chord deep in her soul. She couldn't seem to get enough, his touch healing the pain, driving away the suffering of the past few weeks... of the past few years. How long it was before the embrace ended she never knew.

He gazed down at her, brushing the dampness from her cheeks, his eyes dark with passion. 'Now will you tell me? Or do I need to use force?' he asked, his voice filled with tenderness. 'I can torture you with kisses, tie you to my bed for a month until you confess who told you about Alex.'

'As tempting as that sounds, I'll tell you.' She sighed. 'It was Janine.'

He nodded, not particularly surprised. 'Janine. I should have known.' A cold, ruthless light entered his eyes. 'Ask your secretary to step in here, will you?'

The next half hour was the most painful of Sable's life. It didn't take long for Damien to goad the truth from Janine. And, once the virulent outpour began, it flowed swift and deadly.

'Leonard never loved you,' she informed Sable venomously. 'He was using you. It was me he should have married...would have married. But Patricia convinced him not to. She told him the only way they could defeat Hawke Enterprises was if Leonard married you. It was the biggest mistake he ever made. Because of you he lost everything—his company, his health, even his life. But I wasn't about to let him die in vain. I got even.' She glared in triumph. 'No one suspected me or limited my access. After all, I've been with the company forever. So, I took you all on. First Patricia and then the two of you.'

Overwhelmed by Janine's malice, Sable slipped closer to Damien, burying her face against his shoulder. He didn't wait to hear any more. Calling for Security, he had Janine removed from the premises.

'What are you going to do to her?' Sable murmured, safe within the circle of his arms and determined not to leave his protective embrace anytime soon.

'I'm not sure. I'm reluctant to prosecute, but I also can't stomach the idea of her getting away with it. I expect we'll settle out of court.'

'She must have loved Leonard very much.'

Damien shook his head. 'That wasn't love, at least not the kind I'm familiar with.'

Sable licked her lips, staring up at him with her heart in her eyes. 'And what sort are you familiar with?' she whispered.

'The sort that withstands all adversity. The sort that never dies,' he responded promptly. His hand slid up her spine, molding her against his heat, stoking the fires that raged between them with such spontaneous abandon. His voice deepened. 'All I have to do is look at you, touch you, hear you speak and I realize how very much I love you.'

'But you came back for revenge,' she dared to remind him.

'That's what I told myself.' His fingers slipped into her hair and he brushed his mouth over hers, an infinitely gentle touch. 'But the truth is...I couldn't stay away. Why did you think I was so desperate to have you back in my bed? I knew once I had you there you'd be there to stay.'

And she would. 'What about the board? What are you going to tell them?'

A slow smile crept across his mouth. 'I'm going to demand to know why they had my wife removed as president and chairman of the board. And I'm going to tell them that if they ever do it again I'll get rid of every last one of them.'

She stilled. 'Your wife?'

The laughter died from his expression and he gazed down at her with stark intensity. 'If you'll have me. And if Kyle will have me.'

The tears came again, tears of sheer joy. 'I think I can convince him.'

'And you? Will you have me, Sable? Will you marry me?'

'Oh, yes. I love you, Damien. I can't imagine life without you. I don't want to imagine a life without you.'

There was no further need for words. His mouth came down to meet hers and she melted against him. It was finally over. The secrets of the past were laid to rest, and the future lay ahead, bright and beautiful and infinitely precious.

A future she intended to grasp with both hands and never let slip through her fingers again.